THE SEVEN EXALTED ORDERS

Deby Fredericks

WolfSinger Publications ⸙ Brackettville, Texas

Chapter One

"In the name of King Sedlin, let this council come to order." Sea Lord Chrysen silenced the chamber with a tap of her gavel. "Who has business for the Collegium of Mage Lords?"

Stone Lord Senorith rose from his high seat. "I do."

Chrysen nodded graciously. "Come forward, brother magus."

As Senorith made his way to the podium, faint whispers echoed upward into the shadowy dome of Arkanost's Grand Collegium. Lamps mounted on the curving wall spread a thin layer of smoke through the air. Sitting in the front row, Ryamon blinked against the sting.

"They will listen," he said to himself. *"They have to understand."*

He glanced around, seeking to calm his nerves. The dais of white limestone loomed at the center of the chamber. Though polished to a fine sheen, it was shaped in a severe, plain style. The rigid lines were softened only slightly by drapes of silken fabric dyed in the colors of the Seven Exalted Orders. Senorith stood behind a similar podium facing the dais.

"My brother and sister magi," the Stone Lord began, "I come to speak for my novice, Ryamon of Dalgest."

Below their banners, the Mage Lords sat in their robes of office. Each held a lacquered staff. One or two of them glanced at Ryamon. He tried to look back steadily. Though he was dressed in gray robes, like any Stone magus, his blood jumped as restlessly as the flames in the lamps. This was what he had been waiting for.

The rest of the chamber held rows of hard benches, where Ryamon squirmed along with the other petitioners. A little farther down the front row, three nobles sat on embroidered pads. A prim-looking older woman was accompanied by a younger man and woman. These were observers from the court of King Sedlin. Their names had been announced when they entered, but Ryamon hadn't been paying attention. The younger lady fanned herself idly.

Then the Stone Lord's voice brought his attention back to the dais. "Through no error of his own, this novice has been incorrectly placed within the Order of Stone. It is Fire that calls to his spirit. I ask Akayel, as my brother magus, to accept this novice into the Order of Fire."

"*Say yes,*" Ryamon begged silently.

Akayel's eyes narrowed with displeasure. "Is this some sort of joke?" he hissed.

Ryamon's hands clenched in his lap. He might look like a Stone magus, but it wasn't his nature to endure in silence. That was exactly the problem.

"Indeed not," Senorith replied. "This novice has great potential. He has worked hard. Through study of the strictures, through fasting and vigil, and even by smoking the sacred *sibban*, he has done all a student could do. Such determination would be a credit to my order, if Stone was his natural Element."

"Enough!" The Fire Lord's voice sizzled with irritation. "You could waste all day telling me how wonderful your novice is. I still wouldn't want him."

Fury and despair exploded within Ryamon. It was all he could do to keep his place, to not cry out in shock. Stone was not his true element—Fire was! He had known it since he was a boy feeding twigs to his mother's cook fire. The Order of Stone had been only a temporary stop, a chance to learn the most basic techniques. He hadn't thought the different element would matter. His mentor, Cerdych, had seemed sure of it.

After all his struggles, Ryamon could barely shape bricks. He couldn't wait to be free from the Order of Stone. How could the Fire Lord reject him?

Up on the dais, Chrysen asked, "Why not? You know he has power."

Ryamon felt a flicker of hope as she set the gavel on the desk before her. Even the other mage lords thought Akayel was being unfair. Maybe they could talk some sense into him.

"He's taken no vows." Klaive, the Storm Lord, glanced a question at Senorith.

"Correct," Senorith affirmed.

"Doesn't every order welcome new novices?" Minarik, the Blood Lord, asked mildly.

Being questioned seemed to infuriate Akayel. "Do you think me desperate for followers?" he retorted. "Are my standards so low?"

"I have a different concern." Salovik, the white-bearded Ice Lord, spoke for the first time. He was calm, like the Stone Lord, but spoke with a cold edge of spite. "If you knew the young man's power was not right for your Order, why did you take him? You should have sent him on to Akayel. Someone might get the wrong idea, Senorith."

A murmur started among the watchers as they realized what Salovik was implying. The Seven Exalted Orders were rigidly separated. Each had its Mysteries, ways of power it kept from the others. Salovik was suggesting Ryamon's transfer was a scheme to steal secrets from the Order of Fire and pass them back to Senorith.

Despite himself, Ryamon leapt to his feet. "Not so!"

Some of the audience tittered at his reaction. Up on the dais, Murcrys the Shadow Lord, turned to share a sly smile with Klaive.

"He certainly sounds like one of yours, Akayel," she remarked-ed. The Fire Lord scowled.

"Ice Lord, you go too far!" Chrysen scolded. "There is no reason to question Senorith's intentions."

"There never is, until it's too late," Salovik answered with a chilly smile.

Meantime, the Stone Lord turned. A somber glance warned Ryamon clearly to sit down and be quiet. His face burned and bitterness flooded his throat, but Ryamon obeyed. He was only a novice. Soon he might not even be that. His only hope was to let his mage lord handle this.

Senorith turned back to his peers. "It saddens me to hear you say this, brother."

He didn't sound angry, but his voice reverberated through the walls of the Grand Collegium. Some in the audience glanced around, as if suddenly remembering the building they sat in was made completely of stone.

"I'm sure Salovik meant nothing by it," Murcrys said softly. Her voice held a hint of steel. Salovik didn't bother to reply.

"My brother, if your concern is that he's already touched the element of Stone," Minarik said, "it shouldn't be a barrier. Senorith says the Stone does not answer him. And there is precedent from long ago…"

"That time has passed," Klaive quickly interrupted.

Again tension flared through the audience. Ryamon found himself glancing warily at the three noblemen who represented the king. Each of the Exalted Orders tapped only one element.

Nobody was going to offend the throne by suggesting a change.

"We cannot go back to that," Chrysen agreed.

"Precisely my point." Akayel's raised his hand with the appearance of piety, but his lingering irritation showed through. "His spirit is already tainted. It would be a step back to the evils of olden times."

Ryamon stiffened, swallowing fresh rage at being dismissed as tainted.

"None of us want that," Murcrys soothed. "I believe Minarik meant to say that just attempting to touch the spirit of Stone shouldn't interfere if he truly joins with Fire."

"It doesn't matter," Akayel insisted. "I have no need for a novice who's failed at another Mystery."

Ryamon couldn't stand to look at the pack of them, sitting up there and deciding his fate as if he was an animal they could buy and sell.

Senorith seemed to accept defeat, for he patently asked, "Then what should become of a novice who cannot serve my Order?"

"Send him home, if he does not love his element. Or let him work in the kitchens. I don't care," Akayel sniffed.

Senorith answered with a curt bow, then walked back to take his place on the dais. Ryamon glared up at the mage lords, his head pounding with rage and despair. They looked like a row of wax puppets, he thought. Not one of them had a living heart.

Murcrys turned her head slightly, a gleam in her dark eyes. With her psychic powers, she might have heard his angry thoughts. Compared to the magnitude of his loss, it hardly seemed to matter. He stared at the fists in his lap.

"If I may," someone interrupted.

"Of course, Countess," Salovik said at once.

Ryamon spared a sullen glance to see the older noblewoman had risen. Guilberta, that was her name. Full skirts rustled as she swept over to the lower dais. She wore a stylish gown of black brocade, close fitted in the sleeves and buttoned tightly up the back with a froth of lace at the wrists and neck. Silver hair was pinned up under a dainty black hat. Feathers bobbed as she inclined her head toward the seven magi.

"I am sure his majesty would prefer the novice remain with his order, even if his training has ended," Guilberta said in a clear, precise tone. "We cannot have half-trained magi wandering the realm. Too many unfortunate accidents might result."

"Of course, the king's wishes are of great importance," Klaive replied. All the mage lords seemed strained, Ryamon thought. They didn't like the king's authority any more than he liked their powers.

After an exacting curtsey, Guilberta returned to her companions. The young nobleman rose to greet her. He was also garbed in a fine black suit and gazed up at Guilberta with open admiration. The younger lady hadn't even stopped fanning herself. Once again, Ryamon swallowed against the sour taste of defeat.

An uncomfortable silence had fallen. After a moment, Sea Lord Chrysen cleared her throat. "Do any of us have other business to bring forward?"

"I do." Minarik, the Blood Lord, rose to make his way toward the lower dais. He was a slight figure in the crimson robes of his order. Ryamon could hardly see him through the haze of despair over his eyes.

"It grieves me to speak of this shame upon my house," Minarik said. A sheaf of parchment rustled nervously in his hands. "In the district of Selkest, a novice of Blood has abandoned our order."

Ryamon listened without caring as the audience started to whisper again. To be a Fire magus had been his life's dream. How could he give it up and work at menial chores? It was utterly unfair. Ryamon couldn't succeed as a stone magus, but he wasn't allowed to leave, either? And the collegium wouldn't do anything about it. They were sadists, all of them!

"The initiate who was training her reports the novice, Valdira, had always displayed unusual talents. Naturally, she was forbidden to use them." Minarik raised his voice slightly as the murmuring grew louder. "Initiate Silma directed her to use only the approved techniques—"

"What do you mean, unusual?" Chrysen interrupted.

Again parchment rustled as the Blood Lord turned to a thin volume among his stack. After glancing through it, he said, "Novice Valdira can communicate with animals and plants."

"Plants?" Klaive repeated. A breeze of humor seemed to blow through the collegium. Even Senorith looked amused.

"Do they have a lot to say?" Murcrys added with a sarcastic smile.

"Regardless," Salovik said with chilly severity, "such unlawful activity cannot be tolerated. Why did your initiate not report this sooner, Blood Lord?"

"Self-defense, of course," Murcrys answered before Minarik could. "She would been seen as derelict in her duty. No one would want to admit that."

"Even though it was true?" Akayel snapped.

Chrysen tapped her gavel lightly. When the chamber was quiet, she asked, "Where do matters stand now?"

"Novice Valdira has run away from Silma's home in Lornest," Minarik answered. "For those who have never been there, Selkest is in the southwest of Arkanost, along our border with Costera. It's an area of mountains and heavy forest. One who knows the area well could hide there for a long time."

A rogue magus? Ryamon felt his disappointment and frustration coalesce into a searing hatred. He played by the rules, even when it hurt. Look where it got him. But this novice, Valdira, didn't care about rules. She just did what she wanted. Oh, if he had five minutes with her...!

"She's gone renegade?" Klaive asked. All humor vanished as the mage lords united in their concern.

"Since we know how his majesty feels about this sort of thing," Senorith said, with a stoic nod toward Countess Guilberta, "there can be no question of what we must do."

"Send an inquisitor," Chrysen said.

"Bring her back to face charges!" Akayel flared.

"If she won't obey her mage lord, she must be imprisoned," Salovik said.

"Someone should invite her to speak with us," Klaive agreed. "I would like to ask her a few questions."

His gentle, ironic tone made it clear he didn't mean a polite request. Still, Ryamon seethed. If only he had the power of Fire, he would go to Selkest himself. He would make sure the upstart was punished.

"Then I will direct one of my Blood Masters—" Minarik began, but the Shadow Lord interrupted.

"I have a better idea." For some reason, Murcrys was looking at Ryamon. The sly look in her eyes cooled his fury by several degrees. "Wasn't there a young man in the audience who wished to prove his mettle? Let him take up the task. If he succeeds, it should prove his worth. Come, Akayel, what do you say?"

"I have no objection," Senorith said.

In an instant, Ryamon was on his feet again. "I'll do it!"

No one tittered this time. Murcrys and the others stared hard at the Fire Lord. Akayel's shoulders sank slightly with exasperation. Finally he flicked the air in a weary gesture.

"Oh, very well. Let him try. I suppose I might reconsider."

Relief flooded Ryamon, turning his stiff knees soft enough to wobble. He bowed with a jerk and sat down. The seven mage lords fell to discussing how to phrase their message, but Ryamon stopped listening. Looking up at the Fire Lord's thin face, it was impossible to tell if he meant what he'd said, but a new purpose burned within Ryamon. He had to go to Selkest. It was a chance —his last chance—to enter the Order of Fire. No matter what, he had to try.

~ * ~

Phareth, initiate of Shadow, sat cross-legged, trying to concentrate on his strictures instead of his empty belly. Unfortunately, there was little to distract him. The cramped chamber held only the chair he sat on and a narrow wooden bed.

It was late afternoon. A small slot of window admitted enough light to read by, but it was too high to see through. Phareth could faintly smell the damp earth of the garden outside the brick walls. He imagined the tidy rows of lettuce, carrots, cabbage, and onions.

He longed for that quiet haven. Phareth loved the green plants because they didn't think. There was no need to guard his mind from them. Nor had they any secrets to pry loose—just the occasional insect. But, alas, he could have no solace until he had fasted and done penance.

Phareth blinked and forced his eyes to focus on the translucent parchment of his lesson book. He read, *A shadow sees, but is not seen. It hears, but is not heard. A shadow deceives, but is not deceived. It knows, but is unknown.*

He turned his head, closed his eyes, let the book slip from his fingers. Pages fluttered; it struck the floor with a soft thud.

These were the most important rules in the Order of Shadow. He had known them since childhood. Yet, somehow, he had broken them all.

Phareth still didn't understand what had happened. Logoll

hadn't been his first mission. He knew how to be careful. His stomach churned with frustration. By the midnight moon, he *had* been careful! It wasn't enough. Now the Order of Shadow was fouled by scandal, the most spectacular failure of an assignment in decades. And it was all his fault.

Phareth leaned back for a moment, not seeing the brick wall opposite him. He had to accept it somehow, subdue his pride and acknowledge his part in the fiasco. In all likelihood, he would be spending more time than he wished in the garden, once his penance was done. No one was likely to trust him with sensitive information again.

He sighed and leaned forward, reaching for the book. As his fingers brushed the cover, another presence inserted itself into his mind.

"What is it you think you're doing?" Murcrys asked. The Shadow Lord's thoughts were like leather, supple and yet tough enough to resist any attack. *"Is all this fasting supposed to impress me?"*

Phareth paused, uncertain how to respond. Penance was the usual way to atone for one's errors. The Tower of Shadows held several cells just like this one, for exactly that purpose.

He sensed the Shadow Lord's impatience and answered meekly, *"No."* Although, now that she mentioned it, perhaps he had been making a bid for her attention.

"There's no sense hiding," Murcrys told Phareth. *"Yes, everyone knows. Yes, they're all talking. Just show your face and be done with it."*

Her very thoughts prickled with irritation. Phareth listened, knowing better than to argue when Murcrys was in this mood. If he strained, maybe he would pick up some echo of sympathy for his misery.

"I understand," he replied.

"Then take off the hair shirt and come to supper," the Shadow Lord instructed.

"Yes, Mother."

Her presence withdrew. Phareth didn't see much point in telling her he wasn't wearing a hair shirt, nor whipping himself to prove his resolve. It was the Stone magi who did those things, showing their power by hardening their skin to turn away pain.

At least Murcrys still acknowledged their relationship. With her support, it might be possible to rebuild his shattered career. Somehow.

Slowly he retrieved the book and dropped it onto the bed. He felt dizzy for a moment when he stood, no doubt due to the two days' fast he was about to break. He paused at the door to straighten his plain black robe. The door handle turned with a sound like a whip-crack.

Barefoot as any penitent, Phareth walked along the cold tile floor, turned sharp corners, and descended the main stair toward the refectory. Other magi were going the same way, but none walked with Phareth. Some wore white novice robes, and others the black of full initiates. All had the same expression, tranquil and yet with shuttered eyes, reflecting the mental discipline of the Shadow Magi.

Phareth kept his own guard up, yet he struggled with his emotions. No one openly laughed at him, and he was glad of that, but he discovered he didn't like to be ignored, either. As the son of the sitting Shadow Lord, and a rising star in his own right, he was accustomed to a certain amount of attention, even deference. Now no one even looked at him. Phareth felt strange and insubstantial, as if he wasn't completely there.

His feet were real enough to get him to the refectory, at least. The long tables stood in their ranks, lined with initiates on the left, novices on the right. A handful of masters occupied a shorter table across the head of the room, together with the Shadow Lord. Phareth hadn't seen his mother since the formal debriefing on his return, yet she gave no sign she saw him enter.

He moved toward his accustomed place, then faltered as his gaze caught on an unexpected gap. Kylethia had always been a welcoming presence among the shadow magi, an eager student, capable beyond her years. Even before she passed her initiation, they had been much together. Phareth had trusted Kylethia as he did no other, not even his own mother—trusted her enough to take her with him to Logoll, whence she would never return.

Or perhaps it wasn't really trust. Once she became an initiate, Kylethia was no longer required to keep chaste. The mission had seemed an ideal opportunity to work together more closely. Certainly Kylethia had been eager. Her presence may have been the fatal distraction that led to disaster. Still, Phareth couldn't bring himself to blame his lover. Her irrevocable absence haunted him.

A low chime sounded, signaling the beginning of the meal.

Phareth sat, not caring where he was. He ate what was passed to him, scarcely tasting the ham and steamed cabbage. Sweet bread with raisins no longer held any charm. Afterward he stared into his empty plate and wondered what to do with himself. He had no clear duties here.

Murcrys might have been watching Phareth after all, for he felt a mental tug. He left his dish and approached the head table with a trepidation he didn't let show. Murcrys had dark hair and eyes, like Phareth. With her black robe, she seemed to have been cut from the shadows as one piece. Beside her sat Master Gallitaw, pink-cheeked and bald. Thick spectacles gave his eyes a strange, swollen look but he watched Phareth approach with a piercing gaze.

Murcrys kept her expression neutral, a warning that Phareth must not presume on their relationship. He bowed to her and added a polite nod to Gallitaw.

"You are between assignments, Initiate." Murcrys spoke aloud, not troubling to raise or lower her voice. Though no others glanced their way, Phareth was aware of nearby diners straining to hear her words. He was sure his mother felt their interest, too, but she did not react. "Master Gallitaw can always use assistants. You will join him in the classroom tomorrow morning."

Gallitaw? Phareth schooled his expression, though he was once again aware of the master's probing stare. Gallitaw worked with novices at the most basic level. This was clearly a demotion, perhaps even a broad hint that Phareth should work on his own basic skills. But, really, what else could he expect?

Phareth bowed again, making sure to include Gallitaw this time. "I will be there."

Chapter Two

"Must you go?" Cerdych asked.

"Yes," Ryamon snapped. "I have to go. The Mage Lords command it."

"I'm sorry," Cerdych sighed.

Ryamon didn't answer. He scowled as the morning sunlight blazed in his eyes. Cerdych hurried after Ryamon.

Since he was Ryamon's mentor, he should have been in the lead, but Ryamon couldn't help stalking ahead. Cerdych was a true stone magus, slow and steady even when he was late. Well, Ryamon wasn't. If he missed his barge, he thought his heart would burst. Also, he suspected Cerdych wanted him to say this wasn't his fault, and he couldn't do that. In large part, Ryamon's situation was Cerdych's fault. He wasn't going to lie about it.

The Polvest docks were a frantic moil of ships' crews, hand carts, porters and passengers. The river laid its wet stench thick in the air. Ryamon side-stepped to avoid the swinging weights of a boom crane. Once clear, he paused to look for the passenger barge that was to take him upriver.

Spotting the faded crimson letters, MEKTILD, he set off through the press with new energy. Cerdych, middle aged and stout, had a hard time keeping up until the dock workers stepped aside to let them through.

The common folk respected magi, though they didn't like or trust them. All who saw Cerdych and Ryamon knew what they were. Full-length gray robes identified them as Stone magi, and symbols down the front showed their ranks as initiate and novice. Their hair hung long over their shoulders, because magi never had to worry about getting it tangled by manual labor.

Yet, in truth, Ryamon's person was at odds with his attire. He was barely 19, with the lanky frame of a youth grown into a man's height but lacking manly muscle. His hair was coppery, his eyes blue as a low-burning fire. A wide-brimmed straw hat would keep the weather out of his face. From his wide belt a tiny volume dangled, ivory leaves engraved with the strictures of his order. He also wore a leather waypack and walked with a sturdy staff which could also serve as a weapon if needed.

There was a short line at the boarding plank. Ryamon joined it. Catching up, Cerdych reached out as if to clasp Ryamon's shoulder, then let his hand fall to his side.

"My boy, I wish you well," he said. "Your task will not be easy." Ryamon frowned, hoping he wasn't about to tell everyone on the docks about the renegade magus. The Collegium wouldn't want those kind of rumors starting. Cerdych merely added, "Be cautious."

Ryamon should have known regret at leaving his mentor, but he felt only simmering anger. He bowed stiffly, rejecting the older man's concern.

"I'll be careful."

A crewman offered him a wooden token carved with a crown, the mark of Polvest. Ryamon stowed it in his belt pouch as he strode up the ramp. When he got off the barge, he would give it back along with his payment.

A longhouse ran down the center of the deck. Glancing inside, Ryamon saw rows of wooden bunks with identical blankets folded in identical stacks. He looked them over but didn't choose one yet. It might not be smart to leave his waypack unattended.

Returning to the deck, he saw the ramp being pulled up behind a sea magus in blue robes. The man spoke briefly with the ship's master, then climbed a ladder and emerged on the longhouse roof. Ryamon sensed the tingle of magic in the air. A moment later, the barge started to move. His burning impatience eased a little. At last, he was on his way!

From his vantage point, the sea magus piloted the barge through the crowded harbor, shaping the currents to guide it. Ryamon watched with vague envy. It must feel good to be so sure of his skills. Once across the harbor, the magus got off at a stone jetty. A team of greater monti waited there. Soon the giant mammals were hitched to the barge. They labored along the bank, towing it upriver.

The streets of Polvest were too narrow for monti, so Ryamon hadn't seen them often. At first it was interesting to watch the great beasts. Each was twice a man's height, with tree-trunk legs, saggy brown skin and a curling sweep of nose. Their famous tusks had been capped with iron balls. Another greater montus passed on a barge headed downstream. They trumpeted shrill greetings to each other. The noise made Ryamon's ears ring.

Then he realized the monti were walking along a path so smooth that it must have been shaped by stone magi. It was a mocking reminder of his mission. He went back to his cramped bunk to brood.

Ryamon understood why magic had to be controlled the way it was. Long ago, Arkanost had been ruled by wizards who were so cruel that the people rose up in revolt. Afterward, the Seven Exalted Orders had been created. Each had access to only one element, so no magus could accumulate too much power.

Under the king's authority, the Seven Exalted Orders were carefully balanced against each other. Indeed, the seven Mage Lords were far more strict with each other than non-magi could ever be. Unfortunately for Ryamon, the constant rivalry meant he was stuck in the wrong order with no way out. Unless he brought Valdira to her senses, of course. Given his inability to command the sole element allowed him, it would take a miracle.

With bitter honesty, Ryamon asked himself what he would do if he failed. If he could never have the power of Fire, would he be willing to settle for Stone after all? Could that be enough for him? His pride said no.

Yet the alternative was to give up all magic. He would never feel the power flow through his hands again. Could he really stand to be a mere scribe or kitchen worker? Again, his deepest heart said no.

Ryamon didn't know what to do. Akayel had told him to find something in Stone to love. Yet if he learned to master stone, he would surrender the purity that Akayel prized. He would lose everything.

He hadn't reached any conclusion ten days later when, the barge stopped at the riverside town of Elvest in the County of Hinost. Ryamon paid his fare and stood on the quay. The boards seemed to heave under his feet even though his eyes knew he was standing still. Slowly, controlling his vertigo, he crossed the street and dropped onto a stone bench.

Ryamon sat for a moment, watching the flow of dock workers and townsfolk around his position. Everyone seemed busy, intent on their work. They all had a purpose. What did Ryamon have?

A young woman in a pretty linen dress descended the same plank he had just come down. She stopped and looked around.

The wind gusted, making the ribbons on her straw-hat flutter. A voice cut through the commotion of the busy dock; a smile lit the girl's face as her young man ran to greet her. Ryamon watched, faintly embarrassed, as they embraced. Then the man stepped back and picked up her baggage. Talking animatedly, the couple strolled past Ryamon. He looked down, feeling like an intruder on their happiness.

Until he saw the pair, Ryamon hadn't realized how isolated he was among the Stone magi. How lonely. Before he left Dalgest, he had spent a lot of time courting various girls, seeking the one who was perfect for him. Of course, all that had to end once he knew he would be leaving for Polvest. It would have been unfair to woo a girl and leave her behind.

Still, Ryamon had hoped to find someone who followed her heart as passionately as he did his. But who could there be for him in the drab halls of the Stone Tower?

A fresh wave of vertigo swirled over Ryamon. This was a waste of time. He couldn't cling to dreams. He had to work with what he had. Breathing deeply, he let the rock's solidity flow into him. It wasn't exactly love, he thought as the dizziness faded, but it was something he could appreciate.

When he had his land legs back, he collected a new token and got aboard a dray bound southward. Two wooden carriages were hitched behind a lesser montus. Though smaller than its huge relatives, the animal was still far taller than a man. Shaggy reddish fur covered its hide. Its tusks were short and straight.

The carriages were divided into compartments. There weren't many travelers, so Ryamon got one to himself. Even as he settled on a hard seat beside the small window, a whip cracked outside. The carriage lurched into motion.

Clearly this road had never felt a magus's touch. It was muddy in some places, rocky in others. No part of it was smooth going. Ryamon looked out the window, watching the whitewashed cottages of Elvest give way to rolling plains. Hinost was famous for its grain fields. The wheat was brilliant with the green of late spring.

Before long, the peaceful vista became boring. Somewhere on that rutted road, Ryamon made the decision he had been trying to avoid. He had to get serious about Stone. It was the only power he had to overcome Valdira.

He lifted the tiny book that dangled at his waist and propped his feet on his waypack as the dray bumped along. The strictures were the guiding principles of his Order. One by one he turned the pages, trying to meditate on their teachings.

Stone is patient. It knows neither anger nor fear. Ryamon read the words several times, feeling both fear and anger churn within him. The lesson had no meaning at all for him.

Stone is strength. It does not bend to whim or chance. This Ryamon understood. Stone magi were builders. They gave the kingdom roads and bridges, buildings great and small—things that had to last.

Stone does not hurry. In its own time it takes its form. That was Cerdych, all right, making Ryamon repeat exercises over and over. Remembering made him shut the book with a groan. He hadn't ever understood most of those lessons.

Ryamon had read through the strictures so many times before. Every time, they bored him. How could dull Stone ever compare to the warmth and energy of Fire?

The montus didn't move at any great speed, but the beast never seemed to tire, either. Some nights the carriages stopped along the road and Ryamon slept on the wooden bench in his compartment. Whenever they came to a town, he walked around to stretch his legs and looked for objects built of stone. When he found one, even if it was just the wall beside the road, he ran his hands over the coarse material or leaned up against it, searching for something he could admire or connect to.

Sometimes he was able to sense how some other stone magus had formed the rock. Other times, the stones were natural and had never been shaped at all. If he sensed cracks deep enough to weaken the structure, he shaped the stone to erase them. It was easier than he remembered. Maybe because no one was looking over his shoulder, demanding that he succeed.

Finally, Ryamon was doing what he was supposed to do all along. He hated it. In fact, the better he got at shaping stone, the worse he felt. As a boy, he had heard stories about a wizard king who punished his enemies by forcing them to don iron boots. Wearing these, they couldn't walk any faster than a slow hobble. If the victim tried to take the enchanted boots off, they shrank and squeezed their feet until they begged for mercy. Eventually they would be crippled, no longer a threat to his regime.

Being in the Order of Stone was a curse that clung to Ryamon in just the same way. The more he struggled to escape, the more it ensnared him.

The villages got smaller and smaller as the montus carriage lurched and rumbled on. Ryamon was the only passenger left when it reached the end of its route five days later. He would be on foot from here, so he paid off his token and went to the local market. There he got dry bread, hard cheese, strips of jerky, and directions to the village of Lornest, Valdira's former home. With dull determination, he set his hat on his head and started walking.

Gone were the rolling plains of central Arkanost. Rugged hills now loomed over him, deep folds of land covered with a dense pelt of trees. The tang of pine floated on the breeze. When he crested the first ridge, rocky spires rose in the distance. Ryamon tried to remember the map Cerdych had shown him back in Polvest. Travel and frustration blurred his memory, but he didn't think he would go as far as the mountains.

How close was he to the border? Ryamon knew little of the kingdom across the mountains except that it was called Costera. There was no commerce between the two domains, only partly because of those mountains. Costera still had a wizard king, and Sedlin of Arkanost didn't want his subjects getting any ideas. No doubt Terlith of Costera felt the same way.

Ryamon fell back to brooding as he followed the narrow road. He could feel stone all around him, sometimes lying deep and sometimes just below the surface. At dusk, he ate a cold meal and formed a shallow trench in the rocky ground for his bed. The night air was harsh, but he didn't build a fire. It would hurt too much to feel its power so close by and know it was forbidden.

Pine needles did little to soften his bed, and they left his robes sticky the next day. Ryamon slept poorly. *Stone is patient,* he reminded himself grimly as he chewed and chewed on smoked meat. After coming all this way, he wouldn't let little things stop him.

Three more days passed, and three more nights of rough camps. He heard plenty of noise in the woods, from screeching birds to chattering squirrels, but saw no larger animals. Ryamon kept his staff close anyway. There might be packs of eridow or a shorbak, even herds of wild monti.

Through it all, doubts clung to him like the dust of the road. It felt like much longer than three days when he crested a final ridge and looked down on a patch of farm fields and whitewashed cottages. Ryamon couldn't keep back a surge of bitter humor. How could any trouble come from a little scratch like that?

Grim anger settled upon him as he started down the road toward Lornest. Ironic, that he was finally gaining some control of his element, and it made him angrier than ever. Now that he was joining with Stone he could never be a Fire magus, so what was the point of this whole trek?

Yet he couldn't stop after coming so far. *Stone does not bend to whim or chance.* Ryamon had said he would do this. He would do his work as quickly as he could, and then go home.

If he still had a home anywhere.

~ * ~

"He looks like a fat old frog."

A young woman's voice tickled Phareth's inner ear like a gentle breeze, except that the wind didn't usually sneer with bored contempt. Phareth had been walking between the tables where the novices were seated. Now he stopped. Dark eyes searched the lecture hall.

At the head of the room, a wooden tripod supported a large slate, on which were written the words, *Silence is the Essence of Shadow.*

Gallitaw stood beside the slate, intoning, "…but how can nothing be something? To the common person it seems absurd, even mad, but we who dwell in Shadow understand that substance itself is no more than illusion…"

Phareth didn't envy Gallitaw having to teach arcane theory. The truth was simple, but trying to explain it in words was practically impossible. Still, it didn't help if the novices weren't paying attention. He stood quietly, alert for another jeer. He didn't like doing it, but this was his job.

"Ribbet, ribbet," the young woman croaked to herself. No doubt she thought it clever.

Phareth strolled to the front of the room, where he stood facing the class. He waited for Gallitaw to finish his sentence before raising a hand. The novices tensed. After three weeks of Phareth's prowling the lecture hall, they had an idea what was coming.

"Initiate?" Gallitaw asked courteously.

"Selydra," Phareth said in a calm, neutral tone. "Tell the class what animal you were just comparing Master Gallitaw to."

Novice Selydra paled. Her horrified gaze darted first to Gallitaw and then around the chamber, where she found no help, and finally back to Phareth. He would know if she lied—and he would announce that, too.

"A…" Selydra's voice squeaked high. She pressed her fingertips to her mouth. In a barely audible murmur, she finished, "A frog."

The classroom rustled with titters as the novices reveled in Selydra's blunder. Phareth merely nodded, indicating her truthful reply.

"Anything else?" Gallitaw asked, as calmly as if the insult had never been spoken.

Phareth was about to shake his head, but then he heard it: *What an idiot. Can't she keep her shields up?* It was a young man's voice this time. Phareth turned his cool regard to the back of the classroom.

"Raistlyn," he called. "Tell the class what you just said about Selydra."

Raistlyn turned red instead of pale. His adam's apple bobbed as he swallowed. Then he answered with loud defiance, "I said she's an idiot!"

More snickers. Selydra stiffened in her seat, a telepathic squeal of embarrassment radiating around her. Another girl at the table leaned over, rubbing Selydra's shoulder.

Phareth's eyes had not left Raistlyn. "And what else? You were saying she can't…" he prompted.

"Keep her shields up," Raistlyn muttered, shamed now because he obviously hadn't kept his shields up, either.

"We must all keep our shields up," Phareth said with stern impartiality. "Everyone here is a Shadow magus. Talking to yourself is just like talking out loud. We can all hear you. It's a nuisance to the rest of us when you don't conceal your thoughts. Remember, a Shadow hears and is not heard."

There was a brief pause, and Gallitaw asked, "Is that all, Initiate?"

"Apparently…" Phareth began. Then, to his disgust, he heard another illicit whisper and corrected himself. "…not. Meaga. I am wearing baggy robes. How can you possibly know how tight my ass is?"

Another girl sank in her seat. Gales of embarrassed laughter echoed in the small chamber. Even Gallitaw raised his eyebrows in surprise. Phareth stood straight-faced and let them all laugh. These were very new novices, just learning to shield their thoughts. Humiliating them was harsh, but effective as a motivation for learning to guard their thoughts at all times.

Not so long ago, Phareth had been one of them, struggling to keep his defenses up and suffering mortal agony when some initiate caught a stray thought and made him announce it to everyone. It had taken Phareth two months to master shielding, but he had had the advantage of his mother's early teachings. Some of his fellows had suffered as long as six months before they caught on.

As the laughter began to die back, Phareth extended a mental probe toward Gallitaw. The master turned slightly toward Phareth, giving his permission.

Phareth sent, in a confidential tone, *"I never understood, when I was your student, why you always seemed so angry."*

Gallitaw smiled briefly. *"You were no better than these brats. Called me a sour apple, I believe?"*

"Something like that."

"Now then! That is quite enough," Gallitaw called in a whip-crack voice that brought swift silence to the lecture hall. "If we all have our shields securely in place, let us return to the topic. 'Silence is the Essence of Shadow…'"

~ * ~

Lornest was even smaller than Ryamon had thought, a mere cluster of huts on the banks of a wide stream. It was hard to believe these were the headwaters of the magnificent Silver River. There was no hint of the glory in Polvest, far downstream. The whole place was dusty. It stank like a farm. But under that, it felt as rigid as the rocks that crowned the hills of Selkest. Ryamon sensed the weight within himself, a pressure on his lungs that never seemed to ease.

As he entered the town, Ryamon was aware of eyes upon him. Men working in the fields stopped to watch him. Behind low walls, women paused in hanging out their laundry. For all the watchfulness, no one called a greeting. Ryamon was a stranger—always suspect—and worse, a magus.

Besides, he didn't need help. He had grown up in a town just like this. Even the central square, with its fountain and well, was laid out in a similar way. There wouldn't be an inn in a place this small, but Ryamon knew there was a Blood Magus here, Initiate Silma of Beglost. As a sister magus, she ought to offer hospitality.

Besides, it was Silma who had been training the novice, Valdira, and reported her defection to Blood Lord Minarik. She should be willing to help find the runaway.

It wasn't hard to locate Silma's house. With her healing magic, she was an important local figure, so her cottage was one of the largest ones. Its stone walls were white-washed, the roof of neatly trimmed thatch. A blood red banner hung from the edge of the broad porch, proclaiming Silma's order.

Around the house, a garden of fragrant herbs grew—for medicines, he supposed. A small fountain played on one side of the brick path. An olive tree grew on the other side. A brass bell hung beneath the crimson banner, but Ryamon did not pull the chain to make it sing. The Blood Magus stood waiting. She leaned on a staff and watched him approach.

"You are an inquisitor?" Silma's soft voice held a trace of doubt. She looked Ryamon over, taking in his youth and the fire in his hair.

"That's right." Ryamon sketched a bow, as novice to initiate. "Will you let me rest here for the night?"

"I will," answered Silma.

The Blood magus was not old, though silver streaked her dark hair and her deep red robe covered an ample form. Still, she had that dignity about her. Her staff was red, but not lacquered as the mage lords' were. It seemed to have been stained, then carved so that the pale inner wood showed through. The design held many spirals and suns. Perhaps it was the gift of some grateful patient she had healed.

As she led him inside, Ryamon saw the interior of Silma's home was as comfortable as her person. There was a wide hearth and wooden furniture with padded cushions. They were embroidered, no two alike. Shelves on one wall held scrolls of parchment and jars of herbs in neat order.

Silma showed Ryamon the ladder to a small loft above the main room. When he climbed back down, without his waypack and hat, she was pouring hot water into a teapot. She set out two cups, a plain red stoneware, and lifted the cloth cover from a basket of spice cakes.

"You must understand," Silma began as she settled in the chair opposite Ryamon. "I did not send for an inquisitor."

"No?" Ryamon helped himself to one of the cakes.

Silma shook her head. "I am worried about Valdira. I don't want her to be punished."

"Is that an option?" Familiar anger smoldered in Ryamon's breast. "There are but seven Exalted Orders. No one may step outside those bounds."

"She still could be brought back to us." Silma leaned forward with urgency. "It's simply that she must be helped to see her place. If she remains in the hills too long, I fear she will go mad."

"There may be room for compromise," Ryamon admitted reluctantly, "if she presents herself as the Collegium demands."

But Ryamon doubted it. Indeed, he hoped they would make her suffer. If he couldn't have a reprieve, why should some peasant girl receive one?

Silma said nothing else, merely poured from her teapot into his cup.

"You must be tired from such a long journey," she said. "This will help restore your strength."

"Thank you," Ryamon spoke from habit rather than gratitude. The steaming brew had an odd, yellowish color. It tasted sharp and sweet at once. He couldn't decide if he liked it.

"Tell me about Valdira," Ryamon said, putting the cup aside. "Did you know her well before she became a novice?"

"Know her?" Silma chuckled. "I was there to birth her!"

Ryamon felt his cheeks burn. He buried his annoyance with stony patience and asked, "What led her to break faith with you?"

"Her father," Silma replied with a brisk, unsentimental snap. "Marton. Always drinking, that man. And when he's drunk he wants to hit something. His beasts, his wife, his child, it makes no difference. Do you wonder that Valdira looked outside herself for strength?"

Perhaps Silma wanted to provoke sympathy for her protegee. Ryamon saw something else. He frowned.

"Knowing her family's instability, you chose to train her?" he asked. "Didn't you consider that she might have a temper, too?"

"Of course I did." Silma waved curtly, dismissing Ryamon's argument. "What else could I do? I often sheltered her mother, and Valdira spoke freely to me. That girl has a great talent. Do you know, she was just seven when she first told me she could hear the trees. She was in and out of the woods all day, hiding from her father. I knew of no such power in any of the Exalted Orders. Neither did the Blood Lord, when I reported it to him."

That was a surprise. Ryamon didn't remember Blood Lord Minarik saying Silma had reported Valdira's deviant powers before she ran away. He was as shallow as the others, it seemed.

"Valdira heard the trees of the wild," Silma went on, unaware of his thoughts. "She understood them and they obeyed her. I knew then that she must be my pupil. Out of deference to custom I waited until she was thirteen, and prayed all the while Marton would not kill her in one of his rages."

"There can be no magic outside the hierarchy," Ryamon insisted. "It's forbidden! And you encouraged her?"

"I know, I know." Silma nodded impatiently. "Her way is something new, an unexpected event. Such a gift should be nurtured, as I would have done within the House of Blood. True magic cannot be denied or it will rot, like a carrot left too long in the ground. To waste such a gift would be wickedness indeed."

"Is this the teaching of Blood?" Ryamon challenged.

Silma opened her mouth, but before she could speak a silvery chime interrupted them.

"Pardon me." She seemed as glad to escape the conversation as Ryamon was. She crossed the room slowly, leaning on her cane.

Through the open door, Ryamon heard a man's voice: "Dama Silma? Partren's been kicked by the montus. Right in the head. Can you come?"

"Yes, of course. Wait a moment, Torwerd." Silma was all business as she hobbled back into the cottage. "Forgive me, but I must go."

"You must follow the code of your Order," Ryamon said with some irony. He rose, leaving his tea to grow cold on the table. "I will wait for you."

And he did, sitting on the porch as the afternoon light grew longer. Ryamon was amazed Silma didn't lock her door. He could have taken this opportunity to go through her work room, spying out the ways of Blood.

But that wasn't the mystery he craved. To avoid any hint of impropriety, Ryamon read over his strictures without really seeing them. Again he felt the heaviness within him, the elemental power he didn't want pressing on his heart. A light wind rifled the olive tree. After Silma's tale of talking trees, Ryamon eyed it suspiciously.

Near dusk, Silma returned. She seemed tired, and there was little talk between them that night. Ryamon wondered if her Blood magic had been enough to help the unlucky farmer, but he didn't pry. After supper, he retired to the loft.

Though his legs ached with long walking, Ryamon did not rest easily. The rebellious novice, Valdira, must have stayed in this same quiet loft. It bothered him to think she had slept in the very bed he was borrowing. He felt as if she was there somehow, spying on him.

Chapter Three

Phareth woke with a wild shout. He sat up, fumbling toward wakefulness. His heart thumped in his chest and his night shirt was damp with sweat. The dim light of a low-burning lamp showed the outlines of his small private chamber. The bedclothes were twisted, clinging to his legs. Why was he awake?

He had been asleep, too deeply even for dreaming, but there had been voices in the night. One he didn't recognize, the other he could never forget. The sound of that voice had sparked his panic and sent him churning awake.

Phareth breathed deeply, trying to control the chaos within him. Images jumbled together in his memory: a secret meeting, soldiers bursting in. Stunning them with his Shadow magic. Then the eruption of Kylethia's panic in his mind. Fleeing through twisted alleys, searching the dark city. The horror and helpless anguish as his lover's life faded from his mind.

He rubbed a chill hand over his sweaty face. All that had been over weeks ago. He was in Polvest, safe. Why should the trauma revisit him now?

As Phareth calmed himself, he felt half a dozen mental probes. Magi in neighboring chambers must have heard his cry.

"It was a nightmare," Phareth apologized. One by one, the concerned presences withdrew.

Shamed, he disentangled his feet from the bedclothes and composed himself to meditate, patching his frayed shields. He would be forgiven the lapse. Such things could happen while one was sleeping. He still didn't like making such a foolish novice mistake. He hoped no one would mention it to his mother.

After a moment, Phareth got up and poured water from the urn on the bedside table. He sipped it, straightened the sheets and lay back down. Embarrassment gave way to alarm. He wasn't the kind who imagined things. Some part of it must have been real.

He vaguely remembered hearing voices, a conversation. And Darmosh, his nemesis, had been part of it. Darmosh was a wizard lord, one of Costera's elite. Could his magic reach all the way from Logoll? Phareth didn't know that it couldn't. If Darmosh was communicating with someone in Polvest, that was a very bad sign.

Yet he couldn't go to Murcrys with vague accusations. He needed more information. Phareth lay in the dark, alert for any more nighttime discussions. All he heard now was the stubborn hiss of silence.

~ * ~

Eager to be away, Ryamon broke his fast and replenished his supplies. He thanked Silma and shouldered his waypack. The Blood magus came with him to the door.

"Let me tell you, young man," she said briskly. "You will get nowhere quoting dogma at Valdira. You must think farther, wider, deeper if you hope to touch her heart and bring her back to us."

"I'll remember," Ryamon said. In his mind, he brushed the sentimentality away. He didn't want to touch the runaway's heart or any other part of her. She meant nothing except for duty.

The world outside Silma's door was vague and gray. Mist rose from the river, veiling the rocky hills and turning the sun to a watery disc. Noises of farm and craft came muffled through the haze. Ryamon saw but a few ghostly figures through the fog. Or perhaps he was the ghost, an unquiet spirit passing through their stolid world.

He followed the narrow road into the hills. Thick fog gave the air a curious, granular quality. As he trudged along, he had too much time to think. It grated on him that Silma asked mercy for her wayward novice. No one was trying to help him, after all.

Ryamon remembered Silma saying Valdira listened more to the trees than she did to people. Even a doting teacher could get annoyed with a student who ignored lessons to focus on something else. Like a novice of Stone who was fascinated by candle flames.

He tried to push that thought away. Still, he thought he understood Valdira's situation. He could remember exactly the first time he heard the voice of a fire. He had been ten. His mother's cooking fire complained it was hungry and he ran to bring it wood. The hissing and snapping as it fed on dry twigs kindled a fire of its own in his heart. From that moment Ryamon had been hungry himself, craving the power of Fire.

He had always tried to do the right thing, to play by the rules. His curse was to be born into a family of quarrymen who worked the white limestone of Dalgest. Dalgest had no Fire magi, but many Stone magi. One of these was Cyrdich, an initiate who often worked with his father. Ryamon jabbed at the ground with his staff. It had been Cyrdich's idea to offer the basic training which, he said, would serve Ryamon in any of the Exalted Orders. Cyrdich had assured the family he could enter into the Order of Fire when he was ready.

Ryamon had been so eager he believed Cyrdich, trusted him. Looking back, he had to wonder if his mentor had ever intended to keep his promise. Cyrdich must have known what would happen. Perhaps, like Silma, he simply wanted to claim a likely student for his own Order.

The road was climbing, but Ryamon kept on at a punishing pace. *Stone does not tire,* as the strictures said. At a shallow brook, he paused to drink and relieve his aching lungs. The water cooled his throat, but it didn't quench the fury in his heart. He had been trying to live in the wrong world for so long. It just couldn't go on anymore.

As the road wound higher into the hills, it dwindled to a narrow path bordered by sword-grass and thistles. When it led him above the level of the fog, he saw the magnitude of his task for the first time.

Hills rolled away on every side, numberless as the waves of the sea. Green trees covered them like a montus's thick pelt. Weathered granite crowned the hills, yet even that did little to distinguish one from another. The fog was like an ashen quilt hiding the village below. There was no sign of man's presence except the track beneath his feet.

Somewhere in this wilderness was the one he sought. How would he ever find her?

With magic, of course. For a magus of any order, the answer was always magic. Silma said Valdira was living among the trees of the wild, so the pulse of her forbidden magic would run through the forest. Even a novice like Ryamon could sense its echoes and track them to their source.

And then what? He didn't know.

The place where he stood was a low knoll barely above the level of the mist. A little higher up, granite pillars leaned against each other. He stood in their shadows and meditated for a time. When he was ready, Ryamon reached out to place his palm against the nearest boulder.

The stones answered more quickly now. A familiar stiffness came into his chest. For a moment he struggled with the feeling that he couldn't breathe. Irritated with himself, he shook his head and settled his shoulders to try again. Stony strength and patience flowed into him. In turn, Ryamon sent his spirit into the rocks. His thoughts flowed from hill to hill, under forest and stream, seeking, seeking.

He quickly discovered a strange element. It shifted and flowed, not at all like Stone. He couldn't get a firm grasp on it. Returning to himself, Ryamon focused on the source. He fixed it in his mind, so he could find it as easily as he did Stone, and tried to gauge the distance between them.

For the moment, the trail seemed to lead where he needed to go, so Ryamon followed it onward. It was almost noon, yet the woods remained gloomy. The trees were mostly oak and birch, with conifers like gaunt giants towering over them. Here and there a snag scratched at the sky. The branches moved constantly, though Ryamon felt no wind. Their leaves rustled and hissed, like gossips in the streets of a town. He found himself straining to hear words among the whispers.

The farther he went, the more those trees disturbed him. He kept thinking he glimpsed faces among the branches, only to find them gone when he turned. Sweat tickled at the back of his neck, and not only from exertion.

After a time the hills curved north and the path went with them. Ryamon sensed that his goal lay farther west. He left the road, moving among the rocks where they broke the crest of a ridge. Even with his staff, it was hard going. Fir and spruce trees hung massive boughs in his way. Blackberry canes clawed at his robe and sometimes pierced the skin beneath.

Ryamon came to a tangle of deadfall lying directly across his path. As he raised a foot to climb over, a flock of grouse burst from the branches. They seemed to be right in his face, beating him with frantic wings. Ryamon gave a startled cry. He sat down, suddenly and awkwardly. It hurt.

For a moment he rested, absorbing the impact. As he did, his stomach growled at him to eat. Ryamon took out a dry roll and his waterskin. He leaned against a boulder and stared at the thicket while he ate. His chest felt tight again, this time with pent-up frustration.

It seemed impossible that the trees were intentionally interfering with his progress. They were just plants. How could they feel or react like this? Of course, the same could be said of rocks, and they responded to Ryamon's magic. This had to be Valdira's power at work. It was a lot more effective than it had sounded, back in the Grand Collegium.

Regardless, he had to get through. It wouldn't be by reason, so he had to use force. What power could make the trees give way? Fire, of course—but that element was denied him. What else? Maybe a woodman's axe. He didn't have one. Yet, perhaps, his small skills could still be enough.

Ryamon stuffed the last bit of bread into his mouth and sent his thoughts into the rocks around him, looking for just the right piece. Soon he kicked aside a matt of pungent needles to reveal a chunk of granite half-buried in the coarse soil. He knelt to pry it loose, ignoring the tiny crawling things whose roof he had just stolen.

Crouching on his heels, he concentrated on the rock between his hands. He smoothed away cracks and flaws. Then he laid his staff against the broader end. Granite flowed to enclose the wood for a handle. Ryamon willed the other side thin and flat, forming the familiar blade of an axe. The staff didn't make a perfect handle, but he thought it would serve.

Now he looked up at the trees, with their shifting faces and hissing tongues. He smiled and strode to the jumble of deadfall across his trail. A fallen tree lay at the center of it. Ryamon spread his feet for balance on the tilted ground. He let the makeshift axe swing to measure its weight. Then he raised the axe, letting his left hand slide up the smooth shaft. Over and down, with all the strength in his shoulders. The blade bit deep into dry wood. It made a very satisfying smack. Some years had passed since Ryamon last cut wood for his mother's cookfire, but some things, once learned, you do not forget.

He made a few more practice chops. From the restless sighing all around, he guessed the trees perceived what he was doing. Then Ryamon turned and swung his waypack on. He strode down the hill, right into the face of the forest.

This time, he found a gap he could push through. It took hard work, though. The woods resisted his every step and the gloom beneath the trees hid many snares. Pine needles, Ryamon learned, were as sharp as their name. The air was cold and damp, heavy with the bitter scent of rotted leaves. He stumbled over hidden branches or stepped into holes. Soft soil and leaf-mold shifted beneath him, sucking at his boots. The branches were like a thick blanket, smothering him. He longed for fire enough to burn them all.

As he got farther from the rocks on the hilltop, his borrowed strength faded. Still he kept moving toward his goal, one step after the last. When his irritation built to a peak, Ryamon pictured Akayel's haughty face in the trees and swung his axe freely. It was little enough for revenge, but it gave him new strength when his legs ached.

At last he came to a sluggish stream in a clearing. The water's gurgling sounded morbid in his ears. The only other sound was his own ragged breathing. Ryamon stopped, facing a rank of slim young birch trees on the opposite side. They looked like the bones of some enormous dead creature. He paced the clearing and found no way to get out. In fact, he couldn't even find where he had entered.

Valdira's power again. As if this could stop him.

The trickling brook and creaking trees sounded like muffled laughter. Ryamon's heart clenched with frustration. He sighted on the tantalizing thread of Valdira's magic, then set his feet in the soft bank and raised his axe with grim joy. The blade bit deeply into pale bark. Its voice broke the silence with a sharp report. Trees shuddered as Ryamon struck them. He could feel their hate reflecting his own.

After several sound blows, Ryamon felt his feet slipping. He pulled his right foot free of the sticky mud to adjust his stance. To do that, he leaned on his left side. His foot suddenly sank into mud up to the knee.

With a cry of disgust, Ryamon struggled against the cold, slimy stuff. He felt for Stone to support him, but it was far below, too distant to reach. The muck held him as tightly as iron bars. He planted his right foot higher on the bank and pulled, but his left foot wouldn't move. Ryamon could feel a band of pressure across it. His toes were hooked on something under the mud, perhaps a tree root. And now his right foot was sinking, too. He braced his axe on the bank, pulling against the mud. His left leg begin to slip free. Slowly, slowly.

Too slowly. He heard a sudden snapping, saw motion in front of him. Ryamon looked up to see the tree he had been cutting fall straight at him. With a shout, he thrust his axe upward. The trunk was heavier than its slender girth implied. The best he could do was push it over to his right.

Ryamon couldn't keep back a cry as the tree pounded his shoulder. It sent his hat flying and knocked him face-down in the mud. Branches battered his head, tore at his robes and hair as they raked down his back. He kicked, trying to crawl out from under it. Sharp pains lanced up his left leg from the ankle. Then something popped in his knee.

Ryamon screamed. He cursed the pain. He spat cold mud. Filthy ropes of hair plastered his face. He could hardly see. By the time he calmed down, he was in it up to his waist. The tree lay across Ryamon's back, pinning him. It was all he could do to keep his face out of the suffocating mud. He spread his arms, mud-slick fingers catching at a tangle of exposed roots. Ryamon's knee throbbed fiercely. When he tried to pull himself forward, the pain was unbearable.

He lay still for a moment and just breathed. That last block with the axe had probably saved him from being impaled by a branch, but the end result wasn't much better.

The clearing was a trap, Ryamon now realized. The trees had observed his methods and found a way to turn his axe against him. He hadn't thought he cut the trunk so deeply, but it seemed a tree could fall if it wanted to. Now he was up to his chest in mud. The stuff felt cold as ice, draining his warmth and strength. That and the pain already made him shiver. When he got tired, he might drown after all.

If only he commanded the power of Fire! Ryamon's thought was fierce with rage and pain. He would burn those trees, burn them all!

But Stone was all he had. Useless Stone. What could he do with that? In desperation his thoughts reached out, seeking Stone. He found something else. The power he had been tracking was very near. Suddenly it didn't matter that he had been following the runaway to bring her back in line.

"Help," Ryamon croaked. "Help me!"

Even as he called out, he heard the squish of light steps over damp ground. Trees creaked excitedly all about his prison. Then leaves rustled vigorously. Branches twisted aside, pushed by a firm hand.

Valdira was not at all what Ryamon expected. From Silma's warnings, he had thought she would be a wild child with tangled hair, garbed in animal skins. Instead he saw a peasant girl in sturdy boots and a homespun dress. A plaid scarf covered gold-brown hair done in a circlet of braids. Her features were coarse and common, but not dirty, and her eyes were some color he could not name.

The rogue magus looked down at him calmly. Ryamon looked back, all too aware of his helpless position. She put her hands on her hips and smiled mockingly.

"So you're what they've been going on about." Ryamon's axe lay near her foot. She prodded it with the toe of her boot.

Fear gripped him, cold as the mud that leached his life away. Would she help him or leave him to die? Ryamon summoned all his courage not to lie to her.

"I suppose I must be," he said.

She laughed then, short and sharp as the branches pressing into his back. "If you've gone to this much trouble, I may as well hear what you have to tell me."

"Now?" Ryamon asked, addled.

"Are you in that much of a hurry?"

"No."

Valdira knelt, gathering her skirts with one hand and laying the other flat on the ground. The simple movement created a vibration Ryamon could feel through the clinging mud. Nothing else seemed to happen. As the echoes faded, the whispering trees fell silent, attentive. Valdira straightened and crossed out of Ryamon's sight.

"Now what did you do that for?" she scolded. Ryamon didn't think she was talking to him. She must have gone to the other side of the birch tree, for it began to jerk. A few determined tugs had it off him. He relaxed a little without the heavy branches trying to push his face into the mud.

"Thank you," he began.

She cut him off with another short laugh. "Don't thank me yet. I've called for a friend to help dig you out."

Who could be her friend, out in this wilderness? The stabbing pain in Ryamon's leg told him it didn't matter. Help was help. He held his tongue and shivered.

In a haze of hurt and cold, Ryamon lost track of time. Soon he heard something moving in the brush behind him. It sounded big, and the deep panting sounds did not reassure him. He twisted, raising a new ache in his shoulders, and got a blurred glimpse of thick black fur, massive paws with gleaming claws, little eyes behind a wet black nose.

Ryamon gave a choked cry. "That's a shorbak!"

"I know." Valdira snorted at his reaction. Despite the beast's massive shoulders overtopping her head, she wasn't afraid at all. "She'll dig you out like a squirrel from its hole."

"Dig me out and eat me?" Ryamon squeaked despite himself.

"No," Valdira drawled scornfully. "Just lie still, if you're scared. That's what you do if a shorbak attacks. Don't you know anything?"

"How would I know that?" Ryamon snapped.

"Huh. City boy."

Ryamon swallowed another retort. He had little choice, anyway. He could feel the warmth of a huge body behind him, and the snort of hot air as the animal snuffled down his neck. Mud and water sloshed around him as great claws began to scoop it away. Ryamon let his head rest on his forearms and tried not to look appetizing.

No one had warned him about Valdira's powers. They said she could talk to trees. But she did so much more—she had summoned a wild animal and seemed to be controlling it. This didn't fit within any of the Exalted Orders. He should have been indignant at this fresh evidence of her rebellion. Instead, he felt terrified. How powerful was she?

Much as he questioned Valdira's methods, he had to give her credit for results. It wasn't long before the mud's weight eased. Pushing with his elbows, he could almost begin to wriggle free, except for the overwhelming pain in his knee. Ryamon gritted his teeth to keep back a grunt of pain.

"What?" Valdira demanded. She made a pushing gesture in the air, and the shorbak shuffled back a few steps.

Pain made Ryamon pant as heavily as the beast. "I twisted my knee when the tree fell on me."

She offered no sympathy, but merely nodded. "All right. We'll do it this way, then."

Valdira stood back, a concentrating expression on her face. Despite her bold words, Ryamon noticed she wasn't getting too close to the shorbak.

"What do you mean?" he cried, afraid to trust her judgement. "Do what way?"

He broke off with a gasp as the shorbak gave a kind of grumble. It ambled forward. Sharp teeth pinched Ryamon's neck as it bit into the collar of his robe. Mud made sucking noises as the animal pulled him backward.

"Don't struggle," Valdira warned. "She still has her natural instincts."

Ryamon didn't even try to answer. The beast's gamy breath was enough to make him retch, if he hadn't already been choked by its grip on his clothing. The shorbak lifted his body out of the mud with a slow gasping sound. Unfortunately, Ryamon's left foot was still caught. The animal pulled harder, dragging at him with harsh jerks.

"Make it stop!" He begged as pain exploded in his injured knee.

The shorbak gave another brutal yank. Ryamon screamed and fainted.

Chapter Four

Pounding agony in his left knee dragged Ryamon back to consciousness. Something heavy and prickly braced the leg. He couldn't move. Blinking, he pushed upward on his elbows. He lay on a scratchy bed of dried sword-grass, naked except for his underwear and a rough blanket. Dried mud coated his skin from the ribs down. More crackled in his hair as he looked around.

The makeshift bed was near the back of a deep rock overhang. A row of birch trees screened the entrance. The trunks stood so close together that daylight barely penetrated. It reminded Ryamon enough of the bog in the clearing that he shuddered. He glimpsed crockery and a few utensils in the gloomy chamber. Beyond his feet was a rough pile of his waypack, hat and staff with the stone axe head still attached. Another heap nearby might have been his muddy robe and boots. There was no sign of the shorbak.

A soft noise drew his eye. Valdira knelt beside the hearth, a shallow pit ringed with chunks of stone. They were the same gray granite as the rock shelf above him. The fire's amber glow outlined a narrow rock that extended across the pit. His hostess bent over what looked like a hollowed-out turtle shell, grinding something with a smaller stone. Her back was to Ryamon, so he couldn't see her face, but there was no mistaking her intense concentration. Blood magic was thick as smoke in the air.

Ryamon watched for a moment, caught in voyeuristic fascination. He suddenly realized he was alone with a woman. This was forbidden until he had passed the three rites of initiation. Still, there was something soothing in the quiet intimacy of the scene. If it had been some other girl, he might not have minded.

Valdira gave whatever was in the turtle shell a shake and nodded to herself. She added water from a clay jug and swirled it around. The improvised pot grated as she pushed it over the fire. Then she looked toward him. Ryamon looked away. He cleared his throat awkwardly.

"You dislocated your knee," Valdira informed him without preamble. "Since you were already unconscious, I popped it back in and splinted it."

All in all, Ryamon was glad the injury wasn't worse. Through gritted teeth he told her, "So sorry to have missed that."

She rewarded his humor with a thin smile, then waved at the brew in her turtle shell.

"This is for the pain. There's more I can do, but I want the swelling to go down first." Ryamon merely nodded. "I hope you don't mind mushrooms for supper. They're in season."

"I'm not hungry," Ryamon said. His leg hurt fiercely, and he liked Valdira less with every passing moment. "Where is it?"

"What?"

"The shorbak," Ryamon snapped.

"Oh, I released her a while ago," Valdira said with a flip of her hand. She rose and stalked over to lift Ryamon's wet clothes. Mud dripped from his boots with thick splats. Valdira wrinkled her nose. Then she eyed Ryamon speculatively.

"A Stone magus," she said softly. "All the way from Polvest to see the freak, the renegade, the wild woman." She laughed again with a hard, brittle edge. "You've come to pass judgement on me."

"It isn't my place to judge," Ryamon answered. Although, he had to admit, he was feeling fairly judgmental at the moment. "I bring you a message."

"I can guess what it is."

Ryamon's anger flared. "I'll tell you anyway, and you will listen!" He was in pain, nearly naked, humiliated. Someone was going to pay for that. Conveniently, here she was.

He sat up, the better to confront his enemy, but paused as the movement made his head reel. The itchy blanket fell away. He clutched it to his chest. Valdira had the nerve to laugh again.

Just outside the shelter, the trees of the palisade rustled and swayed.

"Oh, calm down. He can't hurt me." The rogue magus wrapped Ryamon's boots in his robe and bundled them all into a basket of woven reeds. More mud seeped through the bottom. Then she knelt to inspect the turtle shell, which now steamed lightly.

"What's your name, Stone magus?" she asked without looking at him.

"Ryamon of Dalgest," he answered stiffly. "I am a novice."

"Yes, I know. I read the runes on your robe," Valdira interrupted. "Well, Ryamon, you're pretty bold for a novice, but I'll tell you now I'm not interested in any ultimatums. I do want to heal you, since you've landed in my lap. To do that, you have to rest."

"You're not qualified," Ryamon accused. "A novice must be supervised by an initiate or master."

"Do you see anyone like that around here?" she retorted, casually heartless. "I'm offering you a deal: drink this, and I'll listen to your speech."

Not waiting for him to agree, Valdira turned back to the fire. With a hooked branch, she dragged the turtle shell along the rock to get it off the flames. Using several folds of skirt as a hot pad, she swirled the makeshift bowl as she peered inside it.

Ryamon watched resentfully. He wasn't at all sure he wanted to drink a potion of Valdira's making. On the other hand, his leg was throbbing worse since he sat up. How could he refuse any relief?

Valdira leaned over to set the turtle shell beside Ryamon's pallet.

"Drink it all," she advised brusquely. "Don't burn yourself."

Reluctantly, Ryamon lifted the shallow bowl. It was unpleasantly warm, but not hot enough to actually burn him. Inside was a sour-smelling, pulpy mess. Valdira watched with a gleam of challenge in her eyes. Her expression reminded Ryamon of Akayel, the Fire Lord, whose favor he needed so badly. He wondered which of the two was more perverse.

"It's just willow bark," Valdira scolded as he hesitated. "Drink it, unless you like hurting."

Ryamon took a deep breath and raised the bowl to his lips. The brew's warmth did nothing to smooth its flavor, which was green and foul. His throat closed up on its own, refusing to admit the first gulp. He swallowed hard, forcing it down in a sour lump. Fortunately, there wasn't much of it.

"Bold indeed," Valdira mocked. She took the empty shell, offering the water jug in its place.

Ryamon drank deeply to clear the acrid flavor from his throat. Water helped, but only a little. He cleared his throat several times, trying not to burp the bitter taste back up. *Be strong as Stone,* he reminded himself. It would be nice to have some shred of dignity left after all this.

"Well, did you have something to say?" Valdira asked.

Her lack of sympathy was worse than the willow bark tea. Still, Ryamon sensed tension beneath her taunting. It could be a sign of weakness. He hoped so.

Ryamon sat up straighter, fixing her with his most baleful stare. Shame, indignation, and the memory of his purpose gave strength to his voice.

"The Collegium knows of your sin," he said, "that you have left your mentor's care to dabble in unknown magic. This is forbidden by the laws of Arkanost. Your master, Minarik, Lord of Blood, is offended by your actions. He commands you to give up your folly and return to the Order of Blood."

Valdira met Ryamon's eyes with bored patience. "Anything else?"

Ryamon fought down his fury at her insolence. He tried to think of something clever.

"Yes," he said. "Silma is worried about you."

"She would be." Valdira still sounded callous, but Ryamon was sure he was a trace of regret in her eyes.

"You owe her your life," he insisted.

"Who are you to say what I owe anyone?" Valdira snapped back. "You're just a novice, like me."

"I am not like you!" Ryamon's anger got the better of him. "I never ran away from the Order of Stone. I've kept my place and done my duty, even when—"

Ryamon stopped. He was saying too much.

"Even when what?" Valdira leaned forward, staring intently.

Ryamon looked away. He suddenly felt cold, his bare shoulders sticky with sweat. The throbbing in his knee had faded, but it seemed to take his strength with it. He felt sick and exhausted.

"Why am I so tired?" he asked, rubbing his face with a shaky hand.

Valdira sniffed, apparently recognizing that he was avoiding her question.

"Your body needs to rest and you won't let it. Lie down, you moron." Scooting forward on her knees, the rogue magus grabbed Ryamon's elbow. Her hand was chilly as melting snow. Ryamon shied from her touch, but that only made her pull harder. He gave up and let her press him back on the rough pallet. It felt amazingly good to lie down.

"You're jealous, that's what it is," Valdira fumed as she covered Ryamon with the scratchy blanket. "You want to leave your order, but you're afraid. So you come to me all high and mighty…

I'll have to put up with you for three days at least."

Ryamon was momentarily silenced by the accuracy of her perception. She was like a Shadow magus, knowing his inner thoughts. In addition to Blood magic and the heresy of her unknown powers, did she also trespass on the mysteries of a third order?

He summoned the strength to say, "I'm not the one who ran away. This isn't about me."

She gazed down at him scornfully, but her voice was almost gentle. "Don't lie to yourself. I'm going to wash your things and maybe look for those mushrooms."

She scooped up the oozing basket. The trees parted as she walked toward them. Ryamon scowled and blinked against the light that flowed in.

"Don't run off, now!" With a mocking wave, Valdira was gone.

~ * ~

Ryamon didn't think he would sleep, but eventually he dozed. When he opened his eyes again, the light from outside was different. Ruddy-gold radiance made the slender trees look pale as bone. The pain in his knee wasn't as severe as it had been, but the constant ache wore away at his heart.

He could sense the hearth fire muttering drowsily in its bed of coals. Its happy hum filled him with longing. The fire was so close, so warm and inviting. He could reach out and touch it, take that power into himself—but that was impossible. Akayel would never accept him in the Order of Fire.

It galled Ryamon to admit Valdira was right. Envy was what had driven him all along. In her defiance, she had done the one thing he wanted more than anything: chosen her own element, freely and fearlessly. The moment he heard it, Ryamon had been filled with rage. Not because of her crime, as he had thought. No, he had been furious because he would never dare to break the rules that way.

Ryamon knew he should look to Stone for courage in his time of need. He could read the strictures, if they weren't covered with mud. Yet even as he was surrounded by rocks, he felt nothing from them. Stone might shelter his body, but it was dead to his needs. So rigid and unyielding, never changing unless it was broken. And he was stuck with it. Ryamon wanted to weep.

Lying on the prickly bed, he raged at his own weakness. He

had delivered the message to Valdira, just as he promised, but it meant nothing if she didn't listen. His failure would only confirm Akayel's impression of his inferiority. The power and spirit of Fire could never be his.

Yet the fire was there, so close to him, and there was no one to stop him from claiming its magic. Valdira wouldn't argue. She had her trees and beasts. Who would ever know?

Ryamon would know. It would betray everything he believed in. He closed his eyes and turned toward the wall, trying to silence the temptation. A rustle at the cave mouth saved him. He sat up fast, eyes snapping open. The trees moved, and Valdira came in with her basket on her hip. Her sharp glance sought Ryamon. He looked away, swallowing guilt that he had even thought of being like her.

Valdira gave an exasperated sigh. Her light footsteps moved across the shelter, but she didn't approach Ryamon. He lay down slowly and dared a quick look around.

The runaway novice set her basket down with a heavy thud. She took out his robe and hung it on the wall of trees. Moisture dripped from the hem, a gentle rhythmic tapping. Bending, she placed his boots beside the fire pit.

"All right." Valdira knelt beside Ryamon. "It's your turn."

She seemed calmer. Maybe she'd worked off her anger by washing the robe. She flipped back the blanket to inspect his knee. Ryamon's stomach turned over, but he pushed up on his elbows again.

The leg was impressively purple and swollen. It had been splinted with pieces of pine branches. Rough bark dug into his skin. That caused the itching he'd been feeling.

With quick fingers, Valdira untied the rough twine that held the splint in place. She carefully rolled the twine and tucked it into her dress pocket, then put the branches aside.

"It's not too bad," she declared. "Come on."

She offered her hand. Ryamon took it doubtfully. She dragged him to his feet.

It was a hard job to balance on the rocky ground, barefoot and in his underwear. He had to lean on Valdira's shoulders, and he didn't like that. Mostly he concentrated on not banging his foot into anything as she helped him out of the rock shelter. They followed a well-trodden path a short distance down a slope to what was obviously her cess pit.

Afterward, she led him on through the brush at an angle away from the cave. The rush of water grew louder as they went. Ryamon wasn't surprised when they emerged on the bank of a creek. A small stretch of sand led down to a pool that looked perfect for bathing. Or laundry, as a nearby wet rock showed.

It seemed inviting, but Ryamon hesitated. He needn't have. Valdira stepped away briskly. "I'll be back—but don't take too long. It'll be dark soon."

Once in the pool, Ryamon discovered that he couldn't have lingered if he wanted to. The water was mountain-cold, and it made his knee hurt in a whole new way. He managed to sluice off the mud and even got most of it out of his hair before he began shivering uncontrollably. Ryamon leaned on the laundry rock, rubbing his arms and legs to dry them. Valdira returned just as he was getting his underwear back on. The evening air was chilly. He tried not to let his teeth chatter as she helped him inside.

"If you're feeling better, I'll see about your knee," Valdira announced. "Do you want to sit up or lie down?"

Ryamon didn't know what to expect. He had never been injured badly enough to need a Blood magus's healing. Still, he wanted to face Valdira as an equal, not an invalid.

"I'll sit."

She shrugged. "Suit yourself."

Valdira helped Ryamon over to the pallet and draped the blanket over his back, putting it between him and the coarse stone wall. He winced as he tried to find a comfortable position on the prickly bedding. She arranged her skirts to sit cross-legged beside him.

"This isn't supposed to hurt," Valdira told him. "Tell me if it does and I'll stop."

Again she seemed to know what he was thinking, but Ryamon tried not to dwell on that. There was nothing else to say, so he merely nodded.

Valdira laid her hands on Ryamon's leg, one below the knee and the other above it. She released a long, slow breath. Her eyes glazed as she slipped into a trance. Then he felt a rush of energy, green and cool as rain on dry land. It set his whole leg tingling. In a strange way, it felt good. He could almost see the swelling going down, the torn muscles knitting beneath his bruised skin.

Yet there was more than just physical healing. Ryamon felt Valdira's spirit within him, seeking and soothing. Once before he had experienced sharing like this. In the first months of his novitiate, when he had had trouble opening himself to the element of Stone, Cerdych had given him a pipe of *sibban*. The sacred herb had temporarily lifted his inhibitions, but Cerdych had been uncomfortable with the blending of thoughts and emotions. He had quickly broken contact. Valdira seemed to have no such fear of intimacy.

A soft, golden glow infused Ryamon's body. He let his eyes slip shut, relaxing with the wonderful absence of pain. As her power flowed through him, he saw that he had misunderstood everything about her. Valdira's spirit was kinder and more loving than he could have imagined. True, she wasn't pretty in the perfumed and painted way he knew from the women of Polvest. Despite that, her power and strength of will gave her a kind of radiance.

He was sorry when Valdira withdrew her hands. They both sat silently for a moment. Then Valdira reached forward to fold the blanket around Ryamon's shoulders like a mother tending her child. He knew he should flex his knee and make certain of her work, but he was too comfortable to move. If healing felt this good, he thought, it was a wonder Blood magi weren't besieged by patients demanding more treatments. It must be the bitter brews, like willow bark tea, that kept folk at bay.

"Feeling better?" Valdira asked.

Ryamon hesitated, ashamed of how anger had distorted his perceptions. Then he blurted, "How did you do that?"

"I can't tell you. It's a mystery of Blood." For the first time, Ryamon saw humor in Valdira's words rather than ridicule.

"I meant how you know my thoughts," he said. "You did it even before—" Ryamon broke off. As the euphoria faded, he wasn't sure what he was saying.

"Any magus can do that," she said. "You're told you can't, unless you join the Order of Shadow, so you don't even try." She straightened, strolling back toward the fire. "I never did understand why. I was always on Silma about it. 'Why can't we use all our gifts? Why only the powers of Blood?' All she would say was, we just don't."

Valdira tossed the pieces of Ryamon's former splint into the fire pit. Eager crackling greeted her gift. She settled herself on the opposite side of the hearth, facing Ryamon, and reached into her basket. First were the promised mushrooms, then a handful of herbs and a bundle of brown feathers: a grouse or quail, Ryamon didn't know which. With peasant practicality, she set to work plucking the bird, carefully saving the feathers in her basket.

"Why did you join the Order of Blood?" Ryamon asked.

Her shoulders twitched in a shrug. "Silma made me the first offer. It got me away from Father. And I didn't know better. Silly me, thinking I could follow my own magic instead of someone else's pre-set ideas."

Valdira laid the naked pink bird over the rock and started to skin it with her belt knife. Ryamon tried not to flinch as he felt the prickle of her anger within him.

"Anyway, there aren't many choices around here," she went on. "The nearest other Tower is in Kuvost, and I'm not interested in being an Ice magus. But you, coming from the big city, surely you had a choice. Why aren't you in the Order of Fire?"

Ryamon sat silent for a moment. It seemed so easy to talk to Valdira. His conscience warned darkly that this benevolence could be an after-effect of the healing, something Valdira knew about and was using against him. Ryamon was tired of questioning everything. He wanted to think he liked her because their situations were so much alike.

"I'm actually from the quarries of Dalgest," he finally said. "The only magi there were Stone, so I joined them. I guess I was in too much of a hurry."

Valdira smiled. "That's Fire for you."

"Stone didn't flow naturally for me," Ryamon continued, feeling old frustrations awaken in his heart. "I went to Polvest hoping to leave the Order of Stone and enter Fire. Stone Lord Senorith accepted it, but Fire Lord Akayel wouldn't. He said I was contaminated by my association with Stone."

"So you let him make you miserable?" Valdira turned the bird, lifted a flap of skin and cut it from the flesh with quick, angry strokes. "I'll tell you, I've never understood how the Collegium is organized. Why are there only seven Exalted Orders? And why are they so limited? Silma tried, she really tried. She looked the other way so many times. But I couldn't stand pretending to only have half my powers. That's why I finally left. I just didn't belong there.

This is my place."

She turned away, spreading the bird's skin on the ground. Then she gutted it, letting the offal drop with wet squishes. Ryamon watched, wishing he could be so sure of where he belonged.

No, that wasn't it. He knew where he belonged. He just wasn't ready to break the law. And he couldn't decide if Valdira was being naive or if she spoke from true ignorance.

"What about the king?" he pointed out.

"He's no magus," Valdira retorted. "How can he decide what magi should do?"

"The kings of Arkanost charter the Seven Exalted Orders," Ryamon explained, in case she really didn't know their nation's history. "It's for the benefit of everyone. The Collegium defends us from enemies and the people are also protected from evil spells."

Valdira frowned. "Why assume there will be evil spells?"

"Because there were in the past," he said. "Arkanost was ruled by wizard kings, but their harshness drove the people to revolt. We have all kinds of legends about it in Dalgest. Aren't there any around here?"

"I wouldn't know. I spent most of my time hiding in the woods," Valdira answered. "So they're afraid. The king is afraid. He wants to limit us so he can control us." She laughed suddenly. "I'll bet even the high and mighty Mage Lords are afraid of magic."

Ryamon hadn't looked at it that way before. Thinking back to the gloom of the Grand Collegium, he tried to remember some trace of fear in the eyes of the Mage Lords. There had been mutual distrust, certainly, but not fear.

"I don't think—" he began, but Valdira's voice over-rode his.

"Because magic is so big," she said. "As deep as the sea, as wild as a storm. It scares them. So they try to put it in boxes—fire over here, stone over there. Little boxes, to make magic smaller and weaker instead of vast and grand!"

While she spoke, Valdira sawed at the bird with angry energy, cutting it into quarters. Ryamon listened and felt her slashing at his preconceptions with the same sharp knife. It was terrifying and exhilarating at the same time.

"It's a lie, that's what it is," Valdira said. "Your Collegium is nothing but a lie."

"Magic can be dangerous," Ryamon argued doggedly. "It has to be controlled for the good of everyone."

Valdira answered with a scowl as savage as anything he'd seen on the shorbak. "Controlled, maybe. Not castrated!"

Her metaphor silenced him. While Ryamon fumbled for a reply, Valdira deposited the bird's quarters in the turtle shell with the mushrooms. She poured water over the lot and slid it over the fire. Then she rolled the offal in the skin and stalked off toward the cess pit.

Ryamon stared at the fire, wondering if Valdira was right. Had she pierced the empty facade of tradition? Or was she insane, and he, too, if he even listened to her? Ryamon couldn't help being drawn to her compelling truth. Yet wasn't it the height of arrogance to claim she was right and everyone else was wrong?

Valdira came back. She rinsed her hands and knife from the water jug.

"I don't know what to think," Ryamon confessed, as much to himself as to her.

She snorted her disgust, then added, "I don't blame you for being jealous, but magic can't be divided into neat little boxes. It isn't like that. People aren't, either. They're breaking your heart, Ryamon, denying you your proper element. Don't let them do it. Reach for what's yours."

"It isn't that simple." He felt tired again, hollow inside. The stone behind him, which should have been his strength, offered nothing.

"Isn't it?" Valdira's face was stern. Sitting by the hearth, she started chopping her herbs. The fragrance of wild sage was much better than the smell of blood.

Ryamon shook his head. There was so much he wanted to say, yet no words came.

"Well, it's your decision." She shrugged, leaning forward to add the herbs and mushrooms to the turtle shell. "Your knee is healed, but you shouldn't walk a lot for a few more days. I suggest you take the time to think about it."

He didn't want to think any more, but he had little choice. There was nothing else to do while the food cooked. Brooding, Ryamon pulled the blanket closer around his shoulders. Silma had been right. He had no hope of swaying Valdira. He had come so far, suffered pain and indignity, and he had nothing to offer the Mage Lords. Therefore they owed him nothing, and Akayel least of all.

Depression sat on his heart like a stone. Beyond the fire, his robe hung on the trees. It looked like a ghost, an empty mockery of himself. Water still dripped from the hem. The wet fabric became a focus of his irritation. This would all be better, somehow, if he was dressed. Even by morning, the heavy wool might not be dry. How long was he supposed to sit in a cave, waiting for his clothes to dry?

Frustration warred with Ryamon's sense of defeat. If he could use the fire, his robe would be dry in no time. Valdira glanced at him, perhaps sensing his agitation, but for once she stayed quiet. Ryamon let his head fall back and thump painfully against the rock wall behind him. If he wanted to knock the temptation out of his head, it didn't work. Fortunately, Valdira interrupted his slide into weakness.

"Hungry?" she asked.

Chapter Five

Despite the primitive conditions, the simple meal tasted amazingly good. Ryamon brought out the last of his hard rolls to soak up the broth and didn't even mind singeing his fingers a bit. Valdira didn't talk during the meal, but Ryamon felt her probing glances. He concentrated on eating and was genuinely sorry when the turtle shell was empty.

Even with a full belly, he couldn't get warm. It was totally dark outside. Valdira had no lamp, so the shelter was lit by the fire's hushed amber. The night's chill gnawed at Ryamon's bare toes. Valdira didn't seem to notice, but then, she was wearing clothes. After she had rinsed out the dish, she settled by the fire. Pulling off her scarf, she began to comb out her hair.

He pulled the blanket closer, trying to hold in his body heat. The night air was a piquant reminder that he needed dry clothes. It wasn't a selfish complaint, but a matter of practicality. If he had the power of Fire, he could easily dry his robe. Only Akayel's pride and indifference held him back.

Temptation whispered that he had been more than patient. Love of Fire was not some casual whim. It was his lifelong dream. The Order of Fire was the right place for him. He would never be happy anywhere else.

The unbending voice of his conscience said that didn't matter. Akayel was the Fire Lord. Ryamon had no right to step beyond his bounds.

Yet, as he shivered, his resolve weakened moment by moment. Surely when the Mage Lords sent him here, they hadn't intended he freeze. It would only take a moment, just long enough to dry his robe. Valdira wouldn't report him. She wanted him to follow his heart. And she had been right about so much else. Why not in this, too?

It was wrong, but he couldn't stop himself. Ryamon extended his trained senses, reaching out to the fire. Instead of a chill, static power he felt the thrill of forbidden heat. He opened himself to this new element easily, not forcing himself as he had had to do with Stone. Energy flowed into him, expanding in a fiery rush to fill the hollows of his heart.

He sighed aloud. Valdira turned curiously, but Ryamon didn't care about her anymore. He felt only the fire's joyous laughter echoing within him. The air trembled with heat as flames rose higher on the hearth. He leaned forward, reveling in the Fire that banished the cold from his feet. His conscience shrilled that he didn't know what he was doing. He had to stop! Its voice was a small thing, forgotten in the flames' dancing.

Ryamon gave himself to his newfound element, making the fire burn bright and high. No wood fueled it, just his own desire. This was the power he had longed for, so restless and changeable. One moment a mere spark, the next a roaring bonfire. As magic should be, and love, and life itself.

"Hey!" Valdira cried.

Ryamon turned with a start. He had forgotten she was there. The rogue magus had dropped her comb to back away from the leaping flames. Her back was pressed against the line of trees across the entrance. At the fireside, Ryamon's boots were steaming.

"You're scaring my trees," Valdira said with good-natured outrage. Through the heat-rippled air, he could see the branches tossing with agitation.

"It serves them right," he answered without thinking.

Valdira chuckled, but Ryamon could sense the trees' genuine fear. He was in too good a mood to be vindictive. He breathed in deeply, proving to himself he had control. When he lowered his hands, the flames died back. Ryamon grinned, showing off his new powers to the hostile forest—or maybe to Valdira.

"I just wanted to dry my robe," he explained. "So you can have your blanket back."

Indeed, Ryamon no longer felt cold at all. He shrugged off the blanket and started to fold it. The fire in his heart warmed him so well, he didn't think he would ever be cold again.

Valdira passed her hands over the branches of the nearest trees in a soothing gesture. Then she came to kneel at his side. Her eyes, too, gleamed with fire in the dim light.

"You see now, don't you? Not everyone fits into those neat little boxes, and the fire doesn't care what order you belong to. It only wants to be accepted. Let it live within you, love its strength and control its weakness. It will love you in return, as my trees love me."

As she spoke, she rested her hand on Ryamon's bare shoulder. A different heat crackled between them, the warmth of her healing laced with a new urgency. Valdira felt it, too. Her smile turned sensual. She didn't move her hand, but watched for his reaction.

Ryamon swallowed. How could he not have seen the beauty in her peasant ways? For she had always been beautiful, bright as a burning flame. He had been half in love from the moment she saved his life—and lying to himself about it, as in so much else.

At last he looked into her eyes without pretense. "I've been a fool. I am just like you."

"Then don't worry about the blanket," Valdira murmured. "I'll keep you warm."

She leaned closer. Ryamon smelled wild sage. He felt her kiss in his mind even before their lips touched. Their magics flowed together, just as when she had healed him, but now the power went deeper than one abused joint. Passion opened like a flower and erased all inhibition.

He had never known how alone he was, living as a cloistered novice in the Order of Stone, struggling to fit where he didn't belong. He needed so much more than the psychic pleasure of his element. Valdira was like rain falling, breaking a long drought. Her work-hardened fingers caressed his bare back and tangled in his fiery hair. His hands found the buttons of her dress, and then soft skin beneath.

"Let's not re-injure your knee," Valdira whispered.

She pushed him down on the pallet. Ryamon was beyond any argument. Valdira rode him like a wild stallion, but he didn't try to throw her off. They moved together in the fireglow like light and shadow, separate and yet forever as one.

~ * ~

"Come," Murcrys commanded.

The Shadow Lord swept imperiously past Phareth, her polished black staff rapping the pavement. Like a leaf drawn on the current of the Silver River, he followed her.

The two Shadow magi left their walled compound through its high, square gate. They strode into the city of Polvest, where tall buildings closed out the light so that they walked in gloom despite a clear sky and bright sun.

In truth, the shade was welcome; wearing black robes in the

constant sunlight was a kind of punishment. Mornings were pleasant enough, but by afternoon the sea air would lie across the city like a stifling blanket. Still, that wasn't all Phareth's worry. Murcrys had given no hint why she had summoned him from Gallitaw's lecture hall. Morbid imaginings prevented him from enjoying this rare excursion outside the tower walls.

Looking over at his mother, Phareth caught the end of a sidelong glance. Murcrys seemed to be waiting for him to do or say something, but he had no idea what it was.

They walked along a main street, where seamless pavement was clogged with ornyx carts and citizens on foot. The air was a mélange of noise, garbage odors and the dank smell of the sea. The buildings around them were all the same: tall and square with smooth sides, evenly spaced windows, flat roofs. They were built of the local tawny stone. Each had four stories and a skirt of walkway around it. At every corner, street names were imprinted in the walls and tall stone pillars supported lamps. Novice Fire magi would light them at dusk and extinguish them at dawn.

The upper levels held apartments, while the ground floors contained shops which often spilled onto the walkways. The two magi avoided the muck in the streets and wove among displays of baskets and foodstuffs, sharp steel and dainty jewelry. Even surrounded by rumbling carts and vendors calling their wares, the silence between mother and son became awkward.

"Where are we going?" Phareth asked in a carefully measured tone. Murcrys was quick to accuse him of whining these days, and he didn't want to give her more reason.

"The Grand Collegium."

"Oh?" It wasn't the usual day for a gathering of the seven Mage Lords. Murcrys' profile was white as a cameo against the shady street. It told him nothing.

"Mostly, I want to speak to you," she went on.

"Here?" Phareth gestured to take in the crowded avenue.

"Who's going to hear us in all this?" Murcrys countered.

As if to demonstrate her point, an ornyx tied to a lamp post began to screech at another of its kind hitched to a nearby cart. The two great birds raised their feathered crests to make themselves appear even taller, shrieking all the while. Phareth skipped aside in case they started kicking with their clawed feet. Even so, he wondered who Murcrys thought might be trying to overhear them.

"I don't like the way you've been acting since you returned from Logoll," Murcrys rapped out, ignoring the ornyxes' posturing.

"I've done all I could to make amends," Phareth protested.

"As your Mage Lord, I expect that," Murcrys acknowledged. Then her lips pinched into a thin line. "As your mother, I don't like it. Before you went to Logoll, you would never have hesitated to ask a simple question like where we're going and why."

Phareth paused, feeling the heaviness in his belly that never went away, not even when he was tormenting the novices in Gallitaw's lecture hall. Murcrys stared at him, absently raising her staff to shoo a vendor who rushed toward them with a bunch of watercress.

"Well?" came her exasperated demand. "Speak your mind, boy."

"Logoll changed things," he finally said.

"Things?" Murcrys countered sharply. "Or just you?"

Phareth opened his mouth, then closed it again. He groped for the words to express all he was feeling. Too many emotions tangled together, like a ball of cotton before it is spun into thread.

"I failed," he faltered at last. "The greenest, most stupid novice in Gallitaw's class couldn't have done worse. I shamed you. I disgraced our order." The image of Kylethia's dead face came to his mind. "I didn't even pay the full price for my mistakes."

Not to mention how his sleep had shattered at the mere memory of Darmosh's harsh voice. Phareth kept his shields rigidly in place. He would die himself before he admitted he was having flashbacks.

Murcrys answered coolly, "Then it's all your fault? It couldn't have been anyone else's mistake, or a lucky guess by Darmosh, or something else?"

Phareth tensed, rejecting her implication that Kylethia might have been to blame. Stubbornly, he said, "I was in charge."

To his chagrin, Murcrys laughed out loud.

"What a dramatist! You sound exactly like your father. It was always about *him*. You're no better, making sure everyone knows the humiliation you suffered."

He didn't know how to answer that. Murcrys seldom spoke of his father, who she had separated from years before. He knew Phostan was a merchant seaman who originally came from Costera, but little else.

"Everyone makes mistakes," Murcrys continued, exasperated.

"You can get beyond this, but only if you let yourself do it."

"I'll try," Phareth answered stiffly.

"See that you do."

Strangely, Phareth found comfort in his mother's words. The silence between them was more companionable.

A flicker of movement caught Phareth's eye. Glad to be distracted, he looked up toward the narrow stone bridges that connected the rooftops above. These aerial watchposts had been provided for the convenience of the town guards, who saw much from their high perches. They could move along the sky bridges with amazing speed, closing in on some miscreant. The man on duty slapped a hand to his shoulder and pointed, using hand signs to communicate with his fellows on patrol in the street below. Sometimes Phareth like to touch their minds and find out what they were telling each other. Today, with his mage lord so near, he resisted the idle impulse.

According to legend, Polvest had begun as a small fortress located at a notch where the Silver River met the Sea of Sinapos. It had been a rebel's redoubt until the revolution succeeded in overthrowing the wizard kings, whose rule was remembered with such hatred. The victor, Nickole of Shirost, had needed a new capitol. The present city of Polvest had been built at his order, raised by Stone magi in the space of a few weeks.

There were hundreds of buildings, each one exactly the same. In shifting the rock upward, the magi had created vast caverns beneath the city. Some held drinking water and others served as sewers. It all lay on a grid of perfectly square streets. Phareth found it both marvelous and depressing.

Ahead of them, however, one of the few unique structures in Polvest rose above the mass of identical buildings. The Grand Collegium lay nestled in a curve of the Silver River. It was several stories taller than anything around it, of dazzling white limestone from the quarries of Dalgest. It was also the only building in Polvest with a dome, a fantasy of pierced stone that had been the culmination of a Stone Lord's career.

Only the original Fortress Polvest rose higher. It stood directly across the river from the Grand Collegium grounds. Beside it was the residence of the current king, Sedlin of Shirost. His palace was one of many walled estates on that side of the river. As Shadow Lord, Murcrys had occasionally been summoned there.

She reported it was sumptuous inside and out, but to Phareth's mind nothing could compare with the magnificence of the Grand Collegium.

The magi's estate was also surrounded by a wall of white limestone. The flat expanse was tall enough to shield their deliberations from curious eyes. A great bronze gate controlled the entrance. It was closed and guarded by a half-dozen royal guards in uniforms of brown and gold. Some of the soldiers were spread out, keeping watch on the square. Two others stood with crossed spears directly before the gate.

The officer in charge raised his fist in salute as Murcrys and Phareth approached. "Two to enter, Shadow Lord?"

"Thank you." Murcrys gave him a bland smile. "My companion is Phareth, Initiate of the Order of Shadows."

However, the corporal wasn't listening. His gaze suddenly darted past them. Phareth instinctively probed behind himself. His pulse quickened.

"By your leave," a new voice interrupted, "make it four."

Murcrys and Phareth turned at the sound of the deep, slow voice.

"Ah, Salovik. I wondered if that was you," Murcrys said.

"Now you know," the Ice Lord replied with glacial calm.

The two Mage Lords greeted each other with formal bows. As a person of lower rank, Phareth bowed more deeply than his mother. Salovik kept his gaze fixed on Murcrys and didn't acknowledge him. Phareth tried not to resent that, nor the interruption of this rare private moment with his mother.

The two mage lords were a striking contrast. Murcrys wore black, of course, at one with her raven-wing hair and midnight eyes. Salovik, the elder, tapped a white lacquered staff as he came. His robe was so white, it hurt Phareth's eyes. His hair and beard were frosty wisps, and his eyes were pale as ice. Salovik had always struck Phareth as being rather like the frozen sculptures his novices created during winter for the amusement of the public: handsome, but too stiff and cold to be admired.

"Shall we go in?" Murcrys asked. Since she was his mother, Phareth recognized the irritation beneath her calm exterior. Murcrys didn't like the Ice Lord much more than her son did.

Salovik nodded and told the guards, "Telamar, Initiate of the Order of Ice, will enter with me."

The heavy gate was already inching open, although Phareth hadn't noticed when it began to move. The mage lords paced between the bronze leaves of the great door together. Phareth fell in behind Murcrys, taking care not to press too close in case they wished to speak privately.

Salovik's assistant, likewise, followed the Ice Lord. He was a young man, near to Phareth's age, but almost as colorless as his master. Since they were walking shoulder to shoulder, Phareth nodded politely.

"Fair day," he said. "I am Phareth, initiate of Shadow."

"I'm Telamar."

That was all the Ice magus said. There seemed no point in trying to force a conversation, so Phareth looked steadily ahead as the neatly kept grounds opened before them.

The Grand Collegium's fanciful edifice dominated the gardens, but it would not be opened today. By strict custom, no mage lord would enter unless all of them were present. This was supposed to maintain parity among the Seven Exalted Orders, but mostly it was an inconvenience. The least powerful orders were the ones who insisted on "balance," as Phareth recalled. The Ice magi were one of those orders. He was surprised Salovik even set foot on the Collegium grounds when a full session had not been called.

Salovik himself broke the silence. "How prospers your tower? Have things settled down again?"

"We are very well," Murcrys answered. Phareth heard an edge to her tone, and he felt himself coloring, too. Salovik wasn't just making conversation. He was baiting them about Phareth's failed mission. Since Phareth hadn't been spoken to directly, he couldn't respond, but Murcrys went on, "Our new novices keep us busy, but it is satisfying to build for our future."

Phareth kept a straight face, though he felt like laughing aloud. The Order of Ice had few petitions for membership. It could have been because their powers were useless for half the year, or it might have been because Ice magi had a reputation for being cold and heartless.

Although the main building was closed, the grounds were open to all magi. The gardens included a number of secluded places for meditation. Murcrys directed Salovik toward one of these, a small gazebo beside a reflecting pool. Its arched roof gave it the look of a Collegium in miniature. Phareth glimpsed movement in its shade

—a human figure paced restlessly. Since they stood in shadow, his natural element, he quickly spotted others, four in all.

"I didn't realize this was such a large gathering," Salovik murmured.

"Nor I," Murcrys responded. She smiled slightly, ignoring the hint of accusation in the Ice Lord's tone. "How intriguing."

Phareth remembered his mother telling him once that people hardly ever surprised her because she knew what they were thinking. Thus, she relished unexpected events. By Phareth's count there were eight magi present, four of them mage lords. It was an interesting situation, as Murcrys had said.

The Shadow Lord quickened her pace, striding eagerly into the cool shadows beneath the gazebo. "Fair day, Akayel," she called. "I received your message. And Klaive is here, too? My, my."

Akayel whirled at her words. "Do not make light of my summons!" His staff of office struck the pavement with an angry snap.

"Never." Murcrys placed her hand over her heart and bowed, placating her peer.

Akayel was not much older than Murcrys, yet his hair was bleached pale as dry straw. His face was withered and gaunt, while his eyes burned with a feverish light. It was as if, Phareth thought, the heat of his element had dried him out from within. His companion, a younger fire magus, also glared at the two shadow magi. Meanwhile, the Storm Lord, Klaive, rose to meet them.

"Murcrys, don't tease," he scolded, though there was a twinkle in his eye.

Murcrys permitted Klaive to kiss her cheek in greeting. Klaive was the youngest of the seven mage lords. He was wide shouldered beneath his yellow robe and carried his staff as if he knew how to use it in battle. Silver streaked his dark hair, like the lightning he commanded. Phareth knew Murcrys liked Klaive, and not just because of his good looks. Klaive, who never said a cross word, was far easier to get along with then some of the other mage lords.

As before, Phareth bowed to the two mage lords and their escorts. He glimpsed the amber eyes of Akayel's companion and wondered at the fury he sensed. It seemed out of proportion with Murcrys' slight joke. He received a more pleasant response from Klaive's assistant, a lovely young woman with bright blue eyes and hair the gold of sunshine. Curl upon curl surrounded her face, as neatly ordered as the streets of Polvest. With her many ringlets, she reminded Phareth of a child's doll, new from its wrappings. Still, the Storm initiate seemed friendlier than the other magi. Phareth bowed a little lower.

"Fair day," he murmured. "I am Phareth, initiate of Shadow."

"I am Anarinda, initiate of Storm." Anarinda smiled. Her voice was high and delicate, whispering like a wooden flute. "Well met, brother magus."

"And I'm Inigoe of Fire," the other magus snapped, annoyed at being left out. Then the Ice Lord entered the gazebo, distracting everyone.

"I trust," Salovik said with frigid courtesy, "that there is a matter urgent enough to warrant gathering so many mage lords without the knowledge of all?"

"You will find it so." Akayel scowled. Phareth didn't blame him this time.

Simple stone benches were arranged in a loose semi-circle at the edges of the gazebo. As the Fire Lord moved the center, Klaive took the middle bench. Murcrys, to his left, lounged like a sleek black cat. Phareth quickly moved to stand behind her. Telamar, Anarinda and Inigoe also positioned themselves behind their masters. Their job was to watch for eavesdroppers while the mage lords conferred. But, equally, they must also be alert for any sign of an attack from each other.

Salovik seated himself last, moving slowly to the bench on Klaive's right. Akayel fidgeted impatiently.

"Well, what is it?" Murcrys asked, not waiting for Salovik to settle in his place.

"Someone has presumed to join with the element of Fire," Akayel announced. "Someone unknown, unqualified, without my consent or the training of my House, has trespassed against our order!"

Sputtering in his agitation, Akayel started to pace again. Phareth could feel the scorching heat as the Fire Lord passed near him.

"An unsanctioned fire magus?" Klaive asked. He glanced at Salovik, perhaps hoping the Ice Lord would acknowledge the gravity of the situation. "This is dangerous indeed. Do you know who it is?"

"I can guess," Murcrys put in. "That boy, what was his name

…" She waved her hand vaguely, as if she couldn't remember, although Phareth was certain she did.

"The Stone novice from the council last month." Salovik spoke slowly, as if pondering each word. "Ryamon. He wanted to swear to you, Akayel, but you rejected him."

Phareth didn't know what they were talking about. It wasn't a feeling he liked. Carefully, he queried his mother. *"Ryamon who?"*

"If you had come to the Collegium instead of hiding, you would know," she replied. *"Just listen and try to keep up."*

"Now he's taken the element into himself?" Klaive asked soberly. "Without training, he's a danger to himself and everyone around him."

Meanwhile, Murcrys shook her head wryly. "I told you, Akayel. You should have accepted his petition. The spirit of Fire was already in him."

"I know what is best for my order!" the Fire Lord flared.

At the same moment Salovik demanded, "What business is it of yours, Shadow Lord? You have no right to lecture the rest of us."

"I guess I'm just a busybody." Outwardly, Murcrys' composure was unruffled, but Phareth could feel the knot of anger within her tighten.

"We all advise each other from time to time," Klaive interposed smoothly. "Wasn't that your purpose in asking to speak with us, Akayel?"

"I don't need advice, Storm Lord," Akayel bit back. "You all know the law. The Order of Fire has been insulted, our mysteries pillaged by this intruder. Such an outrage cannot be tolerated. The poacher much be punished."

"What do you expect us to do about it, if you don't want our advice?" Murcrys asked, all reason.

"I require assistance," Akayel said. The admission clearly scorched his pride. "The false fire magus must be returned here, to Polvest, where he will face the justice of the Collegium."

"Are you certain of what has happened?" Salovik inquired.

"Of course I am!" Akayel cried, irritated all over again. "I can sense all others imbued with the element of fire, just as you sense Ice magi. I felt the disturbance when the interloper violated my element."

"Perhaps," the Ice Lord answered disinterestedly. "Yet I fail to see how this involves the Order of Ice."

"You fail to see?" Akayel whirled, glaring at Salovik with something like hatred.

"This involves all of us," Klaive interrupted. "As Akayel says, all magi must operate within the law. If we don't act, King Sedlin will."

"You know he has people who do nothing but spy on us," Murcrys added. "He thinks we don't know about it."

Salovik's eyes narrowed at her words, but Phareth couldn't tell whether he was upset by the revelation or simply didn't believe it.

Klaive continued, "The Seven Exalted Orders are already hemmed in by too many restrictions. For myself, I will not invite any more interference."

Akayel nodded. "The Mage Lords must settle this ourselves."

"In that case," Salovik replied with cold logic, "I cannot understand why you didn't summon the entire Collegium, Akayel. This gathering smacks of collusion…"

"Not everything is a conspiracy," Klaive interposed yet again. Akayel's face was burned red with rage.

"The Collegium would spend days debating," Murcrys said. "Meanwhile, the situation would fester. The intrusion cannot be tolerated, and in any case, we're all forgetting something more important. Akayel, may I have the floor?"

Grudgingly, Akayel stepped back, followed by Inigoe. Murcrys and Phareth stepped forward to face the other mage lords.

"More than four weeks ago," she said quietly, "we sent the Stone novice, Ryamon of Dalgest, to investigate a rogue magus in Selkest. Valdira of Lornest had abandoned the Order of Blood, if you recall. Ryamon was to persuade her to return to her Order."

Inigoe gave a nasty chuckle. "I guess we know how well he fared."

Murcrys turned, one dark brow raised at the interruption.

"Silence," Akayel scolded. Inigoe bowed, his face flushed.

Murcrys nodded and went on, "We have no way of knowing if Ryamon even found Valdira, or if he seized the Fire on his own. Perhaps he did find her and she has some way to control him."

"Is that possible?" Akayel frowned at Murcrys doubtfully.

"Minarik could tell us, but he isn't here," Salovik pointed out with icy disapproval.

"Whatever the case, Akayel has acted prudently in requesting aid from the three of us," Klaive said. "We must send another group of inquisitors to take matters in hand. We don't know this Valdira's powers, but a Storm magus, a Shadow magus and an Ice magus between them should be able to cope with whatever she and Ryamon bring to the field."

"Precisely my intention." Akayel glared at Salovik.

"Perhaps." The Ice Lord shrugged. "Yet I remain troubled by your handling of this. I shall have to consider your request carefully."

As Salovik spoke, Phareth saw Telamar's smug expression. It was obvious he expected Salovik to refuse. The Ice Lord was too stuck on procedure to see the larger issue. Phareth wondered why he even pretended he would think about it.

Akayel drew himself up tall, teeth clenched to hold back hot words. "So be it," he hissed, "but I won't forget this, Salovik."

The heat of his rage made Phareth wince. Murcrys, too, stepped away from the Fire Lord's wrath.

"I fear I must yield the floor," she murmured, strolling back toward her bench. As she went, Phareth saw her give Salovik a sidelong glance, much like the one she had given Phareth as they walked to the Grand Collegium. From her expression, the Ice Lord was missing something, something obvious and important, but she disliked him so much that if he couldn't figure it out for himself, she wasn't going to warn him.

"Calm yourselves," Klaive protested. "We can ask no more of the Order of Ice."

He raised his yellow lacquered staff. All the magi's robes rustled as a strong breeze pushed Akayel's heat back.

Akayel clenched his fists before him and bowed his head formally. "Forgive me." The heat faded, and Klaive allowed his wind to die away.

"As for me," Murcrys said, sitting down, "there is nothing to think about. The Order of Fire has requested aid from the Order of Shadow. You shall have it. What remains now is to select my inquisitor."

Although her back was to Phareth, he felt the Shadow Lord's mental poke.

"Me?" Phareth's heart fluttered anxiously. She couldn't mean for him to take this on. He was still having nightmares about the ruin of his last assignment.

"You've been hiding too long," Murcrys replied. *"Besides, who is more*

motivated to redeem himself?"

"I agree," Klaive was saying, unaware of their silent exchange. "The Order of Storm will not ignore a call from our brother. We will do all in our power to find the rogues, wherever they may be."

"If Lord Klaive permits, I will go," Anarinda said. She sounded very self-assured despite her whispery little voice.

"That is well." Klaive didn't seem surprised by her offer.

Phareth squirmed internally as he felt continued pressure from his mother. *"I thought Gallitaw still needed me."*

"Are you my son or not?" Murcrys shot back.

Phareth felt her annoyance that she had offered him a chance to reclaim his honor and he wasn't grateful. As for himself, Phareth just felt manipulated. He did his best to keep his raw emotions behind his shields.

"If you wish it, I will go," he said. Murcrys was his mage lord. She could order him to go whether he liked it or not.

"Phareth will accompany Anarinda," Murcrys announced so promptly that Phareth was all the more annoyed.

"I look forward to working with you." Anarinda smiled, and Phareth felt even worse.

"The Order of Fire is indebted to the Orders of Storm and Shadow," Akayel said, still deeply angry. He had turned slightly, facing his two allies and putting his shoulder to Salovik. However, the Ice Lord ignored the fact Akayel was ignoring him.

"A Shadow magus would be particularly useful," Salovik mused. "He can report any new events to his Mage Lord instantly."

"True." Murcrys smiled tightly. "But there will be no need for you to have that information if you don't send an inquisitor."

"It has not been decided," Salovik answered. "Do not press me, Shadow Lord. I must confer with my master magi, lest hasty action bring even more regrets."

Across the chamber, Phareth caught Anarinda's eye and felt her relief they wouldn't have to work with an Ice magus. Whatever his misgivings, Phareth was wholly in agreement on that.

"Then," Klaive said, "if we are determined to do this, perhaps we have done as much as we can for today. Initiate Anarinda, Initiate Phareth, would three days be time enough for you to prepare?"

"Yes, Lord Klaive," Anarinda said. Phareth also nodded.

"And will three days be enough time for you to reach a

decision?" Akayel asked the Ice Lord with a forced smile.

Salovik refused to be goaded. "Perhaps."

"I'd say you have that long to think about it," Murcrys replied.

Chapter Six

When Ryamon woke, Valdira's rock shelter was a completely different place. The rising sun turned the leaves on the trees to translucent jade and filled the shallow cave with amber light. Nothing remained of last night's blaze, yet Ryamon felt life in the ashes. It lived in his heart, after all.

Even the granite wall that slanted against his back held a benevolent glow. Ironically, by receiving Fire as his true element, Ryamon had made peace with Stone as well. He had put aside his hopeless struggle and his pride. Here, in this secret place, no strictures chained his will. For the first time in months, he felt free. He breathed lightly, scenting wild sage in his lover's hair, and hoped nothing would disturb this perfect moment.

"What are you thinking?" Valdira asked softly.

Ryamon tensed. He hadn't thought she was awake. She rolled over, resting her head on the crook of her elbow. Years ago, there had been a girl Ryamon fancied, Mirla. She had asked that same question, 'what are you thinking?' In his folly, he hadn't realized the question was a trap. There had been something specific Mirla wanted to hear. Ryamon still didn't know what it was. The courting had been over when he gave the wrong answer and Mirla went to dance with someone else.

All this flashed through his mind. Ryamon couldn't bear it if he spoiled their bliss. Yet he had learned Valdira must always be told the truth.

"That I never want to go back," he said. Valdira's lips curved in a self-satisfied smile. He kissed her and felt a stirring of last night's passion. After a moment, she pulled away.

"But?" Valdira prompted.

He drew her warmth against him under the coarse blanket. "But I may have to," he said.

Her expression darkened like a cloudy day. "Are you angry with me?" she asked sharply. "For making you break the rules?"

Ryamon shook his head. "I think it's what I came here for, to be free of all that. I just didn't know it. And then I met you…" He trailed off, at a loss for words to describe the glory of last night's wild ride.

"Then why?" she demanded.

As he became more awake, Ryamon noticed a pink mist on her cheeks. His conscience renewed its harping. He couldn't just lie with a woman. It shamed them both, but most of the risk was Valdira's. In these peasant towns, a girl's reputation was vital, even if she lived alone in the woods.

"Ryamon." Valdira interrupted his thoughts. "Don't fret. I'm used to the things they say about me."

She tried to sound sure of herself, but Ryamon sensed awkwardness. He thought he understood why. Somewhere in Lornest, Valdira had family—including a very violent father. She might face terrible consequences for what they had done. If he didn't want her to face the village alone, the solution was obvious.

"Do you want me to make it right?" The words came out in a clumsy tangle. "We could go see your village council." Marriage wasn't something he had considered when he left Polvest, but for both their sakes, he had to ask.

Strangely, Valdira was even more tense. She met his eyes with the shuttered gaze of a rabbit sighting a fox and trying to decide whether it should hide or run.

"Will you think less of me if I say no?" she asked warily.

"Of course not!" Ryamon pulled her closer, felt stiffness in her back. "All the same, people will talk."

She stopped him with a firm hand over his mouth. *"You* talk too much."

Ryamon looked at Valdira over her fingertips, trying to understand the mix of defiance and fear in her eyes. She said she wasn't ashamed, but did she want him to leave all the same? Her hand moved, caressing his lips. Knowing when to surrender, he let her draw him down for another lingering kiss.

"You can't go," she whispered afterward. "You've touched the fire. It's in your eyes. Any magus who sees you will know."

Ryamon nodded. Valdira wasn't the only one who faced the consequences of an impulsive act. He said, "I can't just vanish. Cerdych will worry. He'll report me missing, as Silma did you."

Valdira cuddled against him, thinking. "Send a letter," she suggested. "Resign from the Order of Stone. I did, before I left Lornest."

"Minaric didn't mention that," Ryamon said.

"Silma probably hopes I'll come back," Valdira answered darkly. Then, "Would the Stone Lord be surprised if you quit?"

"Maybe not," Ryamon said slowly. "They all knew I was struggling. I was trying to transfer to the Order of Fire and Senorith supported my request."

"Then they won't be surprised at all," Valdira said, as if this settled everything. And yet, Ryamon's gut instinct was that it couldn't be so easy.

"I'm in the middle of an assignment," he said. "They would be surprised if I didn't finish my job first. Also, by the law, I would have to put aside all magic. Anything I did would be illegal."

"It isn't now?" Valdira rolled away from him and crouched on the floor, picking up her clothes with angry snaps.

Ryamon watched her. The golden moment was passing. Despite their attraction, Valdira might still leave him here in the woods if she thought he wasn't serious. That, he couldn't bear.

"Valdira." Ryamon reached out to caress her back. "Let's get one thing clear."

She froze in the act of pulling her skirt on. Hazel eyes pinned him over her shoulder, wary and vulnerable.

"I love you," he said, and he meant it. "I'm grateful. I want to stay with you. We just have to figure out how."

Valdira smiled, and it was as if the sun rose again. Ryamon reluctantly got to his feet, moving carefully until he was sure his knee didn't hurt. His gray robe was perfectly dry. It felt strange and stiff, as if he was trying to put on someone else's skin.

He would have to replace it. Smiling to himself, Ryamon wondered if he should be daring and wear the orange robe of a fire magus. He knew he wouldn't, though. It would be easier to hide if he cut his hair and put on peasant garb.

"Maybe they won't bother with us," Valdira said as they both dressed. "We're only two people, two insignificant little people. Why can't the Mage Lords leave us alone?"

"We undermine their authority," Ryamon answered, brushing the last flakes of dried mud off his boots. "If they let us get away with it, there would be no end. Everyone would start getting their own ideas."

"And what will they do?" she snorted. "Send another novice like you?"

Her harsh words should have hurt, but Ryamon only shrugged.

"They'll send someone competent," he said. "Someone stronger or sneakier."

"Well, I'll never go back." Valdira straightened the cuffs of her blouse and tied her scarf on, once more looking the quintessential peasant girl.

"You're right, we can't go back," Ryamon agreed. He, at least, could not hide the change within himself. "But we may not be able to stay here, either. It's all well and good to live outdoors in summer, but how will we survive the winter? Curl up in a cave along with your friend, the shorbak?"

"Not likely," Valdira chuckled. Then she grew serious. "I'm not sure. I've been trying to plan, but this shelter is the best I have."

"I might be able to do something about that," Ryamon said, looking around critically. "I can shape the rock, put in a fireplace with a chimney. Stone magi get lots of training in architecture. How are the winters here? My father's woodshed is bigger than this, and he'd have it completely filled with wood by fall. Dalgest is farther north, though."

"I don't cut firewood," Valdira said reproachfully. "I scavenge downed wood from the forest."

The trees, which had been silent, rustled their leaves as if scolding him. Ryamon sketched a bow in their direction.

"Granted," he said. "We can't live alone forever, you know, even with both of us having magic. We need to barter for food and tools. That means we'll have to go into the village. People will see us together."

"Let them," Valdira snapped in another mood change. "I don't care. Right now, I'm hungry. I'm going to check my snares. Do you want to come?"

"In a moment."

Ryamon bent to lace up his boots. When he took Valdira's hand, he could almost hear her complain, *"Is he always such a worrier?"*

Reflexively, Ryamon thought, *"Someone has to plan ahead."*

Not wanting to quarrel, he held his tongue. Then he realized she hadn't spoken those words. He was sensing her thoughts in her touch. Ryamon nearly dropped her hand, aghast to think he was impinging on Shadow as well as Fire. Even as he thought this, he felt Valdira tense, ready to pull away. He quickly shifted his grip, twining his fingers into hers.

With every girl he'd ever known, there had been surprises, things he had to get used to. This way of communicating was one of them. He had known Valdira less than a day, but she already meant more to him than any of the others. He wasn't going to give her up over a trifle.

When she leaned closer and kissed him, he knew she had sensed that, too. Though Valdira didn't want to marry, he felt this was a kind of honeymoon. He wanted to enjoy it. Every step of his journey had brought him to her side, even while he thought he did the Collegium's bidding. They were both so alike, he and Valdira. Both struggling to survive against a soulless hierarchy. Nothing, not man or magic, was going to separate them.

~ * ~

Like the rest of Polvest, the harbor showed the touch of Stone magi. It was a perfect rectangle, faced on all sides with seamless sheets of rock. Rows of identical piers projected inward at regular intervals. Only the noisy, messy human inhabitants interfered with its tidy precision. Even the water was fairly clear. King Sedlin insisted on a clean harbor. This was officially a measure to prevent disease. However, Phareth often wondered if he just wanted to keep the sea magi busy with trivia like water circulation.

On the third morning after the meeting at the Grand Collegium, Phareth stood near the end of a pier. His waypack and staff were propped against a stone piling. Anarinda of the Order of Storm stood nearby, watching for their boat to arrive. The water reflected late morning sunlight into their faces. The harsh glare fed Phareth's nagging headache. He closed his eyes and breathed deeply, trying to control the pain through meditation.

"Is everything all right?" Anarinda asked.

He opened his eyes. The storm magus watched him, dainty in her yellow robe and golden curls. A faint frown marred her porcelain brow.

"It's nothing," Phareth answered. "A headache."

"A difficult way to start our journey," she murmured.

Phareth nodded, acknowledging her sympathy. The pain was partly his own fault. With the discipline of a trained mind, he had been waking himself two or three times each night to listen for nocturnal chatter. He had to be sure of what he'd heard. He owed it to Kylethia's memory. Yet he had gleaned nothing more than a few stray dreams from other sleepers in the Tower of Shadow.

It had now been almost ten days since he heard Darmosh's voice in the night. The intrusion had seemed so real and dangerous at the time, but now he wasn't sure what he had detected. It could have been nothing but a nightmare. Maybe, deep inside, that was what he wanted it to be.

Uncertainty and frustration mingled with the tension of his new assignment to form a toxic brew of negative emotion. Was it any wonder he had a headache?

Unaware of his thoughts, Anarinda advised, "You should get out of the sun." She herself had covered her ringlets with a lacy scarf. "At least put on a hat. In the Order of Storm we are taught that the sun can be very destructive."

"Once we've gotten under way, perhaps I will," Phareth said. He could already feel sweat gathering under the folds of his black robe.

He folded his hands before him and tried again to meditate, but fresh questions nagged him. Maybe Anarinda was only being friendly. Or maybe she had other motives. He could have scanned her thoughts easily enough. Most magi had basic mental shields, though nothing he couldn't penetrate. However, there was a chance she would sense the intrusion. It could sour the tone of the journey if he violated her privacy for no reason. Murcrys trusted Klaive, so Phareth thought he could trust Anarinda.

"Oh, my," the storm magus breathed with dismay.

Opening his eyes again, Phareth saw her looking past him. A glance over his shoulder and he knew his headache was about to get much worse.

The pier they stood on was a private one used by the Collegium. It was quiet compared to the rest of the port. Because of that, he could clearly see Telamar stepping down from an ornyx cart. The Ice initiate wore a disagreeable, prissy smirk. His white robe magnified the sunlight enough to make Phareth's temples throb.

So the Ice Lord decided to send an inquisitor after all. Putting up with him would be a good incentive for them to work faster. Then, as the ornyx cart pulled away, a second cart stopped in its place and another passenger got off.

Phareth's lips tightened with displeasure as he took in the man's shiny dark boots and trousers, his close-fitted jacket with lace peeking from the collar and cuffs. The newcomer bowed in greeting to Telamar. He had a clever, foxy face and reddish hair that was almost as curly as Anarinda's. This was no servant. Telamar had brought along a nobleman.

Questions raced through Phareth's mind as hollow footsteps thudded on the boards of the pier. The two men approached Anarinda and Phareth, followed by a porter who carried their luggage. Phareth composed his face into an expression of bland courtesy, while Anarinda's lips curved in a fragile smile.

"A fair day to you," she fluted, and swept her yellow robe in a curtsey.

Telamar stood tall, nodding imperiously. His companion walked with a cane, its brass handle gleaming. Leaning on this, he tipped up his low, round hat.

"To you as well, kind lady."

"Will you please introduce us?" Phareth asked Telamar coolly.

"This is Lord Nepharyl, of His Majesty's court." As if they needed to be told he was a courtier. But why was Telamar still smirking? With a wave of his walking stick, he went on, "Anarinda, initiate of Storm, and Phareth, initiate of Shadow."

"The honor is ours," Anarinda replied. A gentle glance reminded Phareth of his manners, but he wasn't going to accept the blame. Nepharyl had no business being there.

"Lord Nepharyl will be joining us," Telamar said.

"Oh?" Phareth replied. "That's interesting."

Nepharyl nodded as he slipped his hat back on. "As you know, my mistress, the Countess Guilberta, is His Majesty's liaison with the Seven Exalted Orders. Naturally, she is concerned about any deviant magic. My task is to keep her informed."

In other words, Nepharyl would be spying on them. Phareth listened, but his eyes were on Telamar. From the Ice magus' smirk, it was obvious whose doing this was. Unhappy with the "collusion" of the Fire, Storm and Shadow Lords, Salovik had betrayed their secret mission to Guilberta.

"I am only here to observe," Nepharyl went on, very much apologetic. "I promise not to interfere with your work."

"I trust you won't," Phareth replied.

"You don't object, do you?" Telamar obviously enjoyed taunting Phareth, so Phareth did his best not to let his irritation show.

"If it is the king's wish, of course we are happy to comply,"

Anarinda answered. "I'm sure Initiate Phareth only meant…"

"I am simply concerned for your safety, my lord," Phareth finished when she faltered. "Since you know of the situation, you must realize you could be caught in the middle of a magical battle."

A flicker of emotion showed in Nepharyl's brown eyes, quickly hidden by innocent concern. "Goodness," he murmured.

Relentlessly, Phareth went on, "As you have no magical powers, our opponents may leave you out of the fight. Or, they could target you as a hostage. We may not be able to protect you unless one of us takes personal responsibility."

Now Phareth's dark gaze bored into Telamar's pale gray one. The Ice magus flushed slightly.

"There's no reason to expect that," he protested.

"We have no idea what scruples our quarry have," Phareth countered.

"Since Lord Nepharyl plans to stay out of the way, it shouldn't be a problem," Anarinda said. "Look, here's our boat."

Indeed, Phareth heard sloshing behind him. He turned to see a sleek craft drifting up. It stopped just short of the pier. This wasn't one of the heavy, slow barges that carried people up and down the river. It was a small cruiser with a single lateen sail. Phareth didn't see a name on it, just the number 4 painted on the stern. Crewmen moved about the ship, some jumping onto the dock and others ready to toss down ropes. On the castle, a helmsman stood at the wheel. Beside him, a Sea magus raised her hand in greeting.

"You're the party headed upriver?" she called.

"That's us," Anarinda answered cheerfully.

Phareth bent down to get his waypack and staff. Telamar awarded him one last sour glance before turning to Nepharyl.

"If you are ready, my lord."

"I'm quite looking forward to the adventure," the nobleman said with gusto. As the crew moored the boat to the stone pilings, a boarding plank thumped down on the dock. Phareth headed for it.

"Don't let them upset you," Anarinda said quietly as he passed her. Despite the perfection of her doll-like face, her blue eyes were alert and serious.

Phareth just nodded. Telamar was following close enough to hear anything he said. The plank trembled with the conflicting rhythms of their steps as they boarded the 4. Only Nepharyl lingered, tipping the crewmen to carry his luggage. He had three bags, a lap desk and two that looked like they held clothing.

Phareth kept a straight face to cover his disgust. The three magi had just one bag each. It was true that, for a courtier, Nepharyl's attire was relatively modest. Phareth had seen noblemen in much more elaborate garments, both in Polvest and abroad. Still, Phareth looked forward to tramping through the forest, where Nepharyl would snag that fine lace. If they also found some mud where Telamar could sully his white robe, so much the better.

Under the castle, six passenger cabins opened onto the deck. The ship's master probably occupied one, leaving the others for the magi. Phareth opened the door on the nearest one. Inside was a stuffy compartment, more a closet than a room, with shelves build into one wall and a narrow cot pegged up against the other wall. The penitent's cell he had occupied in the Tower of Shadow was palatial compared to this. He set his waypack down and returned to the deck.

With nothing else to do, Phareth went up the steps to the castle. The helmsman nodded in greeting. The Sea magus was an older woman whose dark hair was flecked with silver, like foam upon the sea.

"All ready?" she asked.

There was speculation on both their faces. Belatedly, Phareth realized it was unusual to see magi of several orders traveling together. They both must be wondering what was going on. Since he wasn't allowed to answer their questions, he glanced downward.

"Not yet," Phareth said drily.

Nepharyl and the crewmen he had conscripted were just coming aboard. Phareth wondered how he planned to wedge the three bags into his tiny cabin. Also if he thought he would be able to hire people to carry his things all the way across Selkest, because Phareth had no intention of helping out.

Avoiding conversation with the Sea magus, he went to the opposite rail and looked across the harbor. Ranks of barges were tied up at the docks closest to the river, while ocean vessels waited beneath a forest of masts along the seaward side. Skiffs darted this way and that, like dragonflies over a pond, ferrying magi to all the ships. Every craft in the harbor had to be piloted by a Sea magus. It was a good thing Sea was one of the largest orders.

A light step and the rustle of fabric told him when Anarinda came to join him at the rail.

"I can't believe the Ice Lord gave us away," she said, her breathy voice even softer than usual. "It's so childish."

"Akayel shouldn't have trusted him," Phareth answered in a grim undertone, "but our mission is to bring the rebels in. As you said, we can't let this distract us."

Anarinda nodded. She seemed pleased by his acknowledgment. On the deck below, Nepharyl and his baggage were finally aboard. The last crewman on the pier tossed the ropes back up to the cruiser, jogged across the boarding plank, and pulled it up after him. The Sea magus looked a question at Phareth and Anarinda.

Nobody had ever said Phareth was in charge of the expedition. By the Seven, he didn't deserve it! Telamar certainly wouldn't agree, and Nepharyl might not like it, either. All the same, Phareth knew his mother would expect him to seize the advantage.

He nodded back to the Sea magus. "When you're ready."

She replied with a slight bow. As she straightened, she raised her hands. Phareth sensed magic swirling, and then water swirled beneath their boat. Slowly at first, the cruiser slid away from the dock. On the deck below, Nepharyl and Telamar looked around, surprised by the movement.

The cruiser glided through the harbor, gathering speed. With so many vessels moving at once, the busy port reminded Phareth of a country dance. It seemed the dancers must crash into each other, but none ever did. The Sea magus was poised, concentrating on the currents she used to guide the 4. Occasionally she waved to a magus on a passing ship. The helmsman, who had no duties yet, kept a keen eye out. Twice Phareth heard him warn her of another craft moving in behind her.

Phareth was aware of curious glances from some of the ships they passed. Even though Salovik had sabotaged their mission, it would probably be better not to attract any more attention. In any case, the relentless sunlight was baking him in his black robe. His face felt slimy with sweat, and they were barely under way.

Though he didn't look forward to shutting himself up in the coffin-like cabin, Phareth told Anarinda, "We should get out of sight. There are too many of us out here."

"Does your head still hurt?" she asked.

"In more ways than one."

He had barely descended the steps when Telamar intercepted him. Scowling, he demanded, "Where are you going?"

With an effort, Phareth held himself back from snarling that their assignment was supposed to be secret and they should all avoid being seen.

"It's hot." Phareth plucked at the neck of his black robe in demonstration. "I'm getting out of the sun."

With a nod to Nepharyl, who was watching nearby, Phareth stepped into his cabin. It was even stuffier inside than he had expected, though slats in the upper door did admit a bit of air and grainy light. He pushed his waypack farther into the cabin with one foot while unpegging the bunk from the wall. There was barely enough room to sit with his feet hanging over the edge.

With quick fingers he loosened his robe and let it fall open to the waist. A thin woven pad covered the bunk. There was a small cushion for his head. When he lay back on the pad, he discovered both pillow and pad smelled like sweat, and the bunk was slightly too short for him. His skin stuck to the fabric, but he managed to turn on his side and shut out most of the light.

What he really needed was time to think. And maybe privacy for a bit of personal investigation. He needed to get nosy about Nepharyl, their unwanted comrade. Murcrys would expect no less. Phareth also wondered why Telamar had come along, since he didn't seem to like what they were doing.

Yes, Murcrys would want Phareth to be vigilant, and she would want to know about Nepharyl. She had also told him not to whine. Because of this, Phareth hesitated to contact her so soon. He hadn't even left Polvest yet.

As with Darmosh's suspected incursion, he needed solid information. As a first step, he composed himself for some quiet eavesdropping. If he wasn't satisfied, he could probe more deeply during the night, when they were sleeping.

Sighing, Phareth wondered if everyone's mother was this difficult to please.

Chapter Seven

Phareth lay in a trance, touching minds one by one. He didn't know how long the trance lasted, but when he roused the ship no longer glided gently along. It bounded at what felt like considerable speed. Faint noises filtered through the slats in the door, including rhythmic splashes that coincided with the cruiser's motion.

He stretched his arms and legs as far as the limited space allowed, then sat up to re-button his robe. Though stuffy, the cabin no longer felt like an oven. He was also glad to discover that his headache was gone. Phareth pulled a soft felt hat—black, of course—from his luggage. Straightening the brim, he emerged from his tiny cabin and put it on. The sun rode high, screened by thin clouds, while a brisk breeze filled the 4's sail. Arcs of spray glittered in the air as the cruiser cut the waves.

The Sea magus was gone. Phareth remembered her thinking about her next job when she debarked at the landing outside Polvest Harbor. Now it was Anarinda who stood on the castle. Phareth felt a frisson of power as she summoned the wind that propelled the cruiser. All the helmsman had to do was steer.

He couldn't help smiling to himself as he climbed the steps to the castle. Most likely Anarinda was also responsible for the cloud cover which made the journey so much more comfortable. There were definitely advantages to traveling in a group of magi.

Then his eye caught Telamar. The Ice magus sat in a patch of shade from the sail. He was reading something, probably his strictures. When the wind made wisps of pale hair dance around his head, he absently smoothed them back into place. It was going to take some time before Phareth discovered the advantage of having an Ice magus around.

Anarinda's blue eyes twinkled as Phareth joined her. In her mind, he saw pleasure that he had taken her advice about the hat. Once, Kylethia had smiled at him like that. His heart twisted at the memory.

"How are you?" Anarinda's breathy voice brought him back to the present.

"This feels much better." Phareth awarded her a slight bow.

Then the wind threatened to snatch his hat off. A quick grab saved it.

"We didn't bring a Blood magus with us," the Storm magus replied. "We have to take care of each other." Her smile faded slightly as she, too, glanced down at Telamar.

"It may not be easy," Phareth said.

The division in their team was all too obvious. He and Anarinda stood on the castle, while Telamar and Nepharyl kept to the lower deck. He should probably do something about that. At the moment, he just wanted to enjoy the sensation of his head not hurting.

From his vantage, Phareth could see they were well up the Silver River. Polvest was a shadow on the horizon behind them. Teams of monti pulled heavy barges upstream along the right bank. On the left, barges floated downstream with the flowing water. Lighter craft, like the 4, skimmed up and down the center. Anarinda's wind blew against the current, raising choppy waves that made the whole river shimmer like one of the king's embroidered cloaks.

Dry plains stretched out on either side of the river. Farm houses and the occasional grain mill were set near the water. Farther out, herds of sobi dotted the grass. Birds of prey soared above them, waiting for the huge grazers to scare up smaller birds or animals.

Maybe, Phareth thought, that was part of what annoyed him about Nepharyl. The man was an opportunist, like those hopeful raptors. He was taking advantage of their mission for some purpose of his own. Phareth just wasn't sure what it was.

From a cursory probe, the nobleman seemed to be exactly what he should be. He had family in Mirost, but little hope of an inheritance. His father had secured his position in King Sedlin's court. Nepharyl was wary of magi on principle, but also slightly jealous of their arcane gifts. In addition, Nepharyl's cane concealed a short sword—a typical accessory for a man of his class.

What really drove him was loyalty to Countess Guilberta. According to Nepharyl, Guilberta had been everywhere and knew everything. Phareth had never considered the Collegium's liaison so much a paragon. It surprised him such a young man could have a desperate crush on a much older woman.

Telamar, by contrast, was a solid block of icy suspicion. His strong shield suggested the Ice magus had spent time preparing to ward off mental probes. Phareth couldn't penetrate far into his mind without alerting him, but he had the impression Telamar disliked all Shadow magi, not only Phareth. Maybe it was just Salovik's influence. Meanwhile, the feeling was quickly becoming mutual.

Last of all, Anarinda. The Storm magus made no effort to conceal her thoughts. She had heard all about the disaster of Phareth's last mission and wanted to make this one a success for the sake of the alliance between Storm and Shadow. Her pity was both galling and gratifying.

However, Anarinda was also curious about Valdira. She wanted to keep an open mind about the rogue magus' unique abilities. Phareth wasn't sure how that was going to work within their mission of capturing the runaways.

For now, Anarinda focused on controlling the wind. Through her Phareth sensed the energies of the air, intangible and yet as tough and flexible as a serpent's spine. He felt her awareness of how gently the wind must be handled. Changes in the weather could affect an enormous area, and it could easily twist into something beyond any human control.

In Anarinda's eyes, the discord among their team was deeply troubling. She hoped to guide them toward unity with the same soft touch she used to shape the wind. Murcrys might say her concern for others was a sign of weakness, but Phareth didn't think so. Storm Lord Klaive wouldn't have let Anarinda accept the assignment if she couldn't hold her own. Besides, Klaive often acted as a peace maker, and he was no coward.

In any case, Phareth had to admit Anarinda was right. If Salovik was childish to sabotage their mission, then Phareth would be equally foolish to be drawn into his game. He planned to play along until he was certain what the Ice Lord was after.

He glanced again at the lower deck. Nepharyl strolled over to chat with Telamar. Then a mischievous gust of wind flipped the round hat off Nepharyl's head. Red-brown curls swept around his face as he ran to catch it.

As Nepharyl straightened, his gaze met Phareth's. He gave an embarrassed chuckle. Phareth couldn't help smiling in return. Nepharyl glanced at Telamar, who was ignoring him. With a shrug, the nobleman trotted up the steps to the castle.

"It's getting to be a nice day," he offered with a hint of a question.

"Yes," Phareth agreed, "thanks to Initiate Anarinda. We're making good speed."

"Indeed," Nepharyl made another ingratiating bow before he swept his hair away from his face and set his hat back in place.

"I can only do this for a little longer," Anarinda warned. Phareth heard her think, *"I need to keep some power in reserve."*

He wanted to follow that thought deeper, but Nepharyl was talking.

"I meant to ask, earlier, if you magi should change out of your robes along the way. I know I've been getting warm," he plucked at the lapel of his dark jacket, "and you must be, too. Also, I fear we're rather obvious. Countess Guilberta wouldn't want to start any rumors that might upset the people."

It was a little too late to worry about that, in Phareth's opinion. Still, it was a more practical consideration than he expected from a scion of the nobility.

"You are right, of course," he said. "However, the law requires magi identify ourselves at all times. Unless you can change that?"

If he did, he had a lot of authority for a junior nobleman. Nepharyl only shrugged, neither agreeing or disagreeing.

Anarinda said, "Even if we do change our clothes, I don't think we can hide who we truly are. For instance, my lord, you sound far too well bred to pass for a peasant."

Nepharyl smiled, accepting her flattery. Thinking of Telamar, Phareth added, "Not all of us are likely to agree."

"That's true, of course," Nepharyl said, "but Telamar might cooperate if I ask him properly."

Phareth would have to see that to believe it, but Nepharyl continued.

"I should be able to find us something that doesn't stand out quite so much, yet still complies with the law. Countess Guilberta did provide some funding for this journey," he added with another ingratiating smile.

So Nepharyl had money. Phareth did, too; Murcrys would never send a Shadow magus out of the tower penniless. Still, if the nobleman was trying to bribe them, it might be worthwhile to let him believe he'd succeeded.

"What do you think?" Anarinda asked.

"I'd have to see what you have in mind," Phareth said. Reaching into his pocket, he brought out a handkerchief and wiped his sweaty forehead. With a wry smile, he added, "I can't deny it's often uncomfortable to wear black on sunny days."

He was rewarded by a surge of satisfaction from Nepharyl. Anarinda still seemed to have doubts.

"I won't wear anything that disgraces the Order of Storm," she cautioned.

"Of course not," Nepharyl said immediately. "We may be delayed, but only a day or two. It should be well worth it."

Phareth nodded. He didn't like deceiving Anarinda, but he wanted Nepharyl to think he was winning them over. No magic-less noble was going to out-maneuver a Shadow magus.

Just then he sensed a prickle of anger. Turning, he saw Telamar scowling up at them. It didn't take any special powers to guess the Ice magus wondered what the three of them were talking about.

With only a hint of malice, he smiled at Nepharyl. "Have fun convincing Telamar."

~ * ~

Anarinda let her wind drop before the sun had risen to its zenith. Afterward, the crew kept busy using natural breezes to battle against the current. Phareth did his best to stay out of the way.

Near dusk, the 4 docked at a riverside inn. Nepharyl paid the mooring fee and went to eat at the inn. For the magi and crew, the ship's master passed out smoked fish, cheese, sour apples and watery ale. Afterward, the crewmen started a card game. Phareth loitered on the deck, listening to their banter with half an ear. The sun was a red satin disc setting behind black velvet plains and lavender curtains of sky. Business at the inn spilled out onto a large deck above the river. It was rowdy up there, but on the 4 all was quiet. The evening air was silken cool. Phareth didn't look forward to the hard bunk in his airless cabin.

Some time passed before he realized what he hadn't heard recently. Where was Telamar? A quick mental probe gave him surprising results. Anarinda was with Telamar, just on the other side of the castle. Apparently she was trying to unify the team.

Phareth walked that way, stepping softly as if he was merely doing sentry duty. The two magi were in a pool of lamplight on the far side of the castle, hidden from view by the crew or the noisy inn. Telamar perched primly on a coil of rope, while Anarinda sat on the deck with her robes gathered around her. Somehow, after all the wind of the day, her ringlets were perfectly in place.

Anarinda leaned forward, talking quietly. "We don't need to hurt them. After all, they are our brother and sister magi."

"Our mission is clear," Telamar countered.

"This is an unusual situation," Anarinda said. "The old ways may not work. We might have to think more broadly—"

"I won't go against my Mage Lord," the Ice magus insisted. "Especially since we can't assume all of us are acting in good faith."

As he listened, Phareth frowned slightly. Anarinda had a lot more enthusiasm for this mission than he did, that was obvious. But then, she had no reason to fear making some blunder that would worsen her disgrace.

Her suggestions to Telamar concerned Phareth all the same. He wondered if Klaive knew of her views toward Valdira, and how far she would go to satisfy her curiosity. And what did Telamar mean by that crack about acting in good faith?

Phareth had no chance to try probing the Ice magus' mind. Telamar saw Phareth coming around the castle. He tensed, gray eyes narrowing. Seeing his reaction, Anarinda turned and sighted Phareth. Her face showed no guile as she beckoned.

"Please join us, Initiate."

"Thank you," Phareth answered neutrally as he came to lean on the rail. Dark water sloshed against the 4's sides. Farther out, pale stripes reflected the dying day.

"We were just about to discuss strategies without anyone listening to us," Anarinda said.

Without Nepharyl, she implied. That wasn't what they had been talking about at all, and Phareth knew it. Telamar's pale brow quirked upward, but he didn't confront Anarinda for lying.

"Sounds like a good idea," Phareth said.

The Storm magus went on, "I was going to ask Telamar, if I raise a fog could he freeze it. That would make them colder and it would be harder to concentrate on their powers."

"It would be easier if you made it rain and I froze the water,"

Telamar said. "Since we'll be in the mountains, I will be able to call on my element more easily. Also, the plants should have a dormant response. We might be able to trigger it."

He sounded reluctant, maybe because it was unusual for magi of different Orders to combine their powers. At the same time, Phareth sensed a glimmer of intrigue at the possibilities.

"I think dormancy is caused by the length of the day," Anarinda said, apologetic. "I can't affect that."

"If Telamar puts ice on the ground, it would force them to slow down," Phareth suggested. "Or they would risk falling and injuring themselves."

If anything, Telamar sounded irritated that Phareth liked his idea. "What do we really know of their powers?" he asked.

"According to Mother, Ryamon was a Stone magus," Phareth told him. "He stole Fire without permission, although I don't see how those elements are compatible. Still, I might have to stun him first or he'd melt the ice. As for the woman, the Blood Lord said she can talk to plants and animals."

"We already knew that much," Telamar replied. "The Shadow Lord also said, at that meeting, this woman might be able to control Ryamon. Is this really possible?"

"Excuse me," Anarinda inserted. "She has a name. Valdira."

Both men looked at the Storm magus for a moment. Phareth tried to think why this bothered her. Rather than alienate his one ally, he sketched a bow.

"Valdira," he said. Answering Telamar's veiled accusation, Phareth went on, "Some of the orders do overlap, just as you and Initiate Anarinda can both manipulate moisture in the air but use it in different ways. Under some circumstances, I'm told, a Blood magus can affect people's emotions. Especially someone they have healed."

Indeed, Phareth had heard plenty of rumors about Blood magi and their awareness of the human body. They were supposed to be amazing lovers.

"Only a master Shadow magus can truly control a person's mind," he went on. "I doubt Valdira made Ryamon do anything he didn't already want to do."

Telamar eyed him. It wasn't hard to guess that he wanted to know whether Phareth had ever dominated another person's mind. Several flippant replies leapt to his tongue, but in the end

Phareth kept silent. Let him wonder.

The light of their lamp was attracting insects. Moths fluttered out of the darkness, some crawling over Telamar's white robe and others circling the lamp glass. Looking at them made Phareth feel vaguely uneasy.

"Even for a Shadow magus," he said, "it can be jarring to touch another person's thoughts, but at least other humans have similar needs and desires. I can't imagine how it feels for Valdira to share her thoughts with an animal. Their minds must be so different, without morals as we think of them. It could really warp her perceptions."

"Are you saying she's insane?" Telamar demanded.

"Until I meet her, I have no idea," Phareth replied. "At the least, we must assume she is dangerous."

"What a surprise," Telamar murmured sarcastically.

Anarinda said, "She must have some kind of influence over Ryamon. Lord Klaive said that he was taken into the wrong order. If Akayel had listened to Senorith—"

"It's not our place to tell the Fire Lord how to run his order," Telamar said, cold and angry again.

"Granted," Anarinda said soothingly. "It just seems like a pity. What do you think will happen to them?"

"The Collegium will decide," Telamar said, and he added, with cool emphasis, "the whole Collegium."

"I don't presume to speak for my mother," Phareth said, "but I believe she favors imprisonment. In the Towers, their powers would be contained. They couldn't hurt anyone there."

"But the king could demand death," Anarinda said, concerned. "That would be in line with Countess Guilberta's record in such matters, wouldn't it?"

Phareth glanced at her, surprised. It had never occurred to him that he should educate himself about the philosophies of judgement and justice in the royal court. He had enough problems of his own. Yet Nepharyl would be reporting to Guilberta, so her reaction was important.

"You're assuming we'll bring them back," Telamar replied tartly.

"Do you expect to lose?" Phareth retorted. "The three of us are fully trained and qualified. Our opponents are both failures who had to leave their orders. They're no match for us."

"Maybe, maybe not," Telamar answered.

"Although they have rebelled, they are still magi." Anarinda spoke slowly and delicately, obviously not wanting to upset Telamar. "As we are. We shouldn't be too quick to abandon our own."

"Our duty is to the nation," Telamar reminded her.

Phareth didn't answer right away. What Anarinda implied was nearly as heretical as anything Valdira or Ryamon had done. He doubted she would have said it if Nepharyl had been listening. Once again he wondered if she spoke for herself, or if the Storm Lord held the same views. He hoped they wouldn't end by fighting Anarinda, too. Storm magi were some of the most lethal fighters at Arkanost's command.

All the same, he felt his respect for her rise another notch. He hadn't expected such a fragile-looking girl to have a strong mind.

When nobody spoke, Telamar turned his cool gaze to Phareth.

"Although the Storm initiate and I have revealed some of our abilities, you haven't been so open," he said. "Will you be of any help, besides passing messages back to your tower?"

"Oh, I think so." Again, Phareth squashed his irritation. "For instance, if I can get close enough, I can temporarily block their powers."

"I didn't know that," Anarinda said, startled.

"We don't talk about it," Phareth replied. "It's like domination. The idea scares people."

Telamar's mouth twitched sourly, but oddly enough, Phareth sensed the Ice magus found his response reassuring. He glanced away, wondering how a man's opinions could be so frozen and what it would take to thaw them.

"Tell me," Phareth asked back, "since Ice and Fire are opposites, what assistance do you need from us? Will you and Ryamon be vulnerable to each other's powers?"

He expected Telamar to get angry, but the Ice magus smiled with chilly dignity.

"We know how to handle Fire magi, never fear. Frozen things don't burn, and just because it isn't winter doesn't mean I'm powerless."

It sounded like a warning. Phareth nodded, accepting it. "I'll remember that."

"Things can't burn when they're wet, either," Anarinda pointed out. "Perhaps it is we who will assist you, Initiate Phareth. Your powers may be more effective if we distract our enemies first."

"Misdirection can indeed be effective," Phareth began, but then broke off. "Just a moment."

On the other side of the castle, something had interrupted the crewmen's card game. Probing, Phareth sensed when Nepharyl had returned from the inn. Even as he greeted the crewmen, Phareth felt his concern that none of the magi were in sight.

Blinking back to awareness, he saw Telamar and Anarinda watching him, alert.

"Nepharyl is back. Much as I respect his authority," Phareth tipped his chin ironically to Telamar, "he might get the wrong idea if he sees us whispering back here."

Predictably, Telamar frowned. "We have nothing to hide."

Thinking back to some of Anarinda's comments, Phareth offered, "There's no reason to tell him everything, is there?"

"Of course not," Anarinda agreed, quickly enough that Phareth knew she understood he was protecting her. "Each of our orders has secrets to keep. I think we should try to handle this ourselves. We don't need outside help."

The Ice magus nodded, though reluctantly. Anarinda was clever, Phareth thought, to coax Telamar through his rigid sense of tradition.

"We'll be traveling for several more days," Phareth said. "Let's use the time to think of new ideas and talk again later."

Even as he spoke, he stood away from the rail and moved around the castle in the opposite direction Nepharyl was going. Anarinda got up, too. She probably hoped to intercept the prying nobleman before Telamar had a chance to change his mind and tattle after all.

As for himself, Phareth casually touched the minds of the crewmen. None of them had any mental defenses, so it was easy to make sure they were riveted by their card game when he slipped behind them and into his cabin. There was no lock, but he laid a quick ward on the door handle. If Nepharyl tried to check on him, he would have an overwhelming urge to go away. Perhaps it was arrogance, but Phareth thought it would be good for Nepharyl to not feel completely in control where the magi were concerned.

Even with protections in place, he lay silent for a while, listening for any sign of danger. The dark, cramped cabin still felt like a coffin. For no reason, he suddenly realized there was nothing to prevent anyone listening to him when he reported to Murcrys, just as he had overheard part of Darmosh's conversation.

No, that was silly. He had no evidence that incident had been anything but a dream. Phareth waited until his fears subsided before he slipped into a trance. With the ease of long training, he sent his thoughts across the distance to Polvest.

"Mother? I have a lot to tell you."

~ * ~

Proud as any woman in her home, Valdira showed Ryamon around her forest domain. As the days passed she showed him the pool where she drew water, just above the one where he had bathed. She taught him how to find mushrooms, berries, wild onions and watercress. The whisper of branches was always around them. Ryamon no longer found it threatening. He sometimes wondered if he would start to hear them himself, or if that would be treading too much on his lover's element.

He couldn't help being surprised at how many resources Valdira had to rely on in this wilderness. Deep in his heart, he knew it wouldn't be enough. They couldn't stay here in Valdira's beloved forest. All of Selkest might not be safe for them. Ryamon tried to push those fears out of his mind by concentrating on what he had.

Mostly that was Valdira, truly a prize worth fighting for. Yet increasingly it was also the land they shared. As days passed he came to love the rocky hills with their wooded slopes. He savored the cool mornings and hot afternoons, the taste of food cooked outdoors, the tang of pine in the air. He relished having complete privacy, knowing he could make love to Valdira whenever he wanted to. There were no rules to hem them in, no one to watch and disapprove.

Lornest lay east and a little north, but they avoided its pastures and plowed fields. Ryamon didn't have to ask why. The rough country continued west and south until it merged with the mountains. Despite the dense forest, the hills were dry except for a few boggy lakes. Reeds grew there; Valdira used them to make baskets and twine for her snares. Ryamon built weirs to catch fish and cooked them over the fire at the rock shelter.

He owed Valdira so much, and he wanted to repay her. Ryamon kept his eyes open for a place to build her a proper house.

He had promised Valdira some improvements, and he was afraid if he waited too long she would start to have regrets. The hills were full of shallow caves and overhangs. These were good enough to cache food in, or for an afternoon's lovemaking, but they were all too small, or too far from water, or too close to the shorbak's den. They would never be adequate for deep winter.

Finally, Ryamon decided to use the rock shelter. He wanted Valdira to be surprised by his gift, so he waited until she went out to gather bird eggs. He stood for a moment, listening to the wind in the trees beyond the ledge. Breathing deeply, he folded his hands and concentrated. The fire glowed in its pit, and he let his thoughts rest in its warmth for a moment. Then his will expanded to become one with the rocks. Ryamon still marveled at how easy it had become. All thanks to Valdira.

He breathed deeply, painting a picture in his mind of what the new house would be. Once the image was sharp, he began. Granite stretched and flowed. The back wall, which slanted so close above their bed of dried grass, rose to shape a larger room. After a critical glance, he raised the ceiling a bit higher and smoothed the floor. The fire crackled in its earthen pit, lending him more power. He left it where it was for the moment.

Excess stone flowed downward to form a front wall. He made it thick; this would be a cool haven from summer's heat, and no drafts would disturb them when cold weather came. However, he immediately noticed how the wall also blocked all the light from outside. He made a gap for a door, then opened two windows with wide ledges on the inside.

Once they were in place, he heard the trees rustling their leaves just outside. This was their alarm to Valdira. They were suspicious of his efforts.

"Don't worry," Ryamon called. "I won't hurt you."

Of course, they ignored him. He had to hurry if he wanted to finish before she came back.

Ryamon closed his eyes again, focusing hard to feel minute channels in the granite under his feet. These must be where the trees' roots ran. Eyes open again, he shaped the wall to meet the ground smoothly without exposing the roots. He gave the doorway a graceful arch, then shaped the windows to match. Their cottage would have a pleasant face behind its veil of trees.

With the rough shape done, he turned his attention to the

details. The back wall curved slightly, following the shape of the original boulders. He sank a row of shelves into the right wall. On the left, he pushed back an alcove for the bed. He built a new fireplace in the center.

No longer would Valdira have to make do with a pitiful scrape in the ground. The hearth was wide and square, a convenient height to sit on. The firebox was slightly sunken so burning wood couldn't roll out. He added a flat band of stone across it for pots to rest on. The cavity above was generous, with room enough to heat several pots or cook a medium-sized animal. Sockets in the sides would support a spit rod.

Above the cavity, he pushed a long, narrow shaft upward to vent the smoke. Then he went back to the original hearth. Since he no longer had to worry about burning himself or his clothes, Ryamon reached right into the fire. He picked up the main log, crackled black charcoal powdered with ash. It felt pleasantly warm, not hot, as he carried it across the room.

Ryamon set the fire in its new home gently, as if it was a baby animal. He added a few sticks from their wood pile. The fire fed with happy crackles. Ryamon grinned to himself. He would never get tired of that.

Brushing bits of black off his hands, he sat on the hearth, watching wisps of smoke curl upward. It was immediately drawn up the flue, just the way it should be.

With a surge of pride, Ryamon looked around. All those months he had struggled in Stone classrooms, it had seemed he was wasting his time, but he had learned something useful after all. Maybe he would do something about their cess pit next. It could definitely use a seat.

He was just starting to plan it out when the leaves started whispering more loudly outside the windows. Light footsteps came closer, crunching over the loose stones of the hillside. Valdira was coming!

Her voice reached him first, scolding the trees. "You silly things, there's nothing to get so upset about." Then the footsteps halted and there was a long silence. Finally she called, "Ryamon? Where are you?"

Ryamon's heart leapt with anticipation. "Come on in, sweetheart," he called back. His voice echoed a little in the mostly-empty room. He couldn't wait to see Valdira's face when she saw what he had made for her.

With a crisp rustle, Valdira stepped between the trees. She stopped in the doorway, silhouetted against the light from outside. He couldn't see her face, but he smelled wild sage in the basket she held against her hip.

"What did you do?" Valdira demanded.

She sounded confused and upset, not happy at all. Disappointment stung Ryamon like thorns on a blackberry cane. "I fixed it up for you," he said. "I said I would, remember?"

"It's so big," she said, "like a regular farmhouse."

"There's more rock in the hillside than it looks like," Ryamon explained. "Now we'll be warm in the winter."

"I guess so."

Valdira looked around. She stood poised, like an animal trying to decide if it was safe to graze in a meadow. Baffled, Ryamon watched her. He had poured his soul into making a present for Valdira, and she didn't like it. What had he done wrong?

"I'm sorry if I scared the trees again," he faltered.

"Oh," she said briskly, waving that away. "They're just like children. Anything new bothers them."

"I know it's still pretty bare," he said, "but it won't be hard to make us furniture. There's plenty of downed wood in the forest."

Still she didn't enter the cottage.

"I can change it," Ryamon offered. "We can have more shelves or some benches. I'll make it just the way you want it."

Valdira shook her head with a brittle laugh. Suddenly there was as much distance between them as there had been when they first met. But she did come into the cottage at last, crossing the room to set her basket on the hearth.

"I liked it the way it was," she said, sounding sharp and a little sad. "It was a special place. I know it wasn't perfect, and you couldn't stand up straight without bumping your head, but... It was mine."

Too late Ryamon understood what he had done. With a sinking heart, he looked at the smooth walls and arched windows. Even though he knew the rock shelter well, there was no way he could put it back the way it had been.

"I'm sorry," he said helplessly. "I just wanted to make you a proper house."

"We're in the wilderness," Valdira reminded him tartly. "If I wanted to live in a city, I would."

"I know, but I thought... I'm sorry," he apologized.

"It's all right," she sighed. "I can get used to it."

But it wasn't all right Ryamon had planned to give her a special gift. After all his work, he didn't want her to just get used to it. Then he caught the suppressed anger in her mind: *Why does he have to try and change me? I hate that!*

"I don't want to change you!" Ryamon blurted, and saw a flash of surprise in her eyes.

"Good," she said, still tense.

"Because you're so strong and smart," he said, desperate to make amends. "You're so beautiful. Nobody else is like you. How could I want to change you?"

Valdira gazed up at Ryamon, hazel eyes searching. At last she came closer, a sensual smile curving her lips. Ryamon knew he had said the right thing. Relieved, he pulled her into his arms.

"Keep talking," she said.

But he didn't. He just kissed her.

Chapter Eight

Valdira said she wasn't angry, but Ryamon tiptoed around her all the same. The home he had been so excited to create was a hollow shell, bare of furniture or a future. Yet he had come too far to even think of life without Valdira. Ryamon headed into the forest to cure the emptiness.

The rasp of tree-talk surrounded him as he searched for wood to make furniture. He had become accustomed to the noise, but the faces he glimpsed in the leaves were as hostile as on his first day in Selkest. Maybe it was because he had brought his stone axe along. He needed it to trim side branches off tree trunks, but the forest didn't know that. They only saw him with a weapon in his hand.

Since he couldn't communicate with the trees, Ryamon avoided the boggy areas. He stayed on the dry ridges, where there were plenty of rocks, and even then watched where he put his feet. If it came to saving his life, he did have the power of Fire, but he knew he would never use it. He could never turn his element against Valdira's.

The search went slowly. He found plenty of downed wood, but nothing he could work with. It was all either green and sticky with sap, or old and spongy with rot, or too crooked to be useful. Once he tapped on a likely log, testing how solid it was, and a cloud of bees burst out from under it. He ran, stumbling over the hem of his long robe. The trees snickered around him.

After he was clear, Ryamon leaned on his axe and laughed out loud. It helped relieve the tension. Besides, he wasn't going to let the trees upset him. Then he looked around carefully to memorize the location. When he was a boy, one of his neighbors had kept bees in her garden. He remembered her using smoke to stun them. If it meant getting a bit of honey, Ryamon was pretty sure Valdira would let him use his fire.

One by one, he dragged a few large branches back to the house. It was depressing to realize how little he knew about what he wanted to do. Furniture wasn't the same as architecture. Worse, he didn't even have any tools except for his crude axe. A hammer would be simple enough to make, but flint would be better than granite for anything sharp, like chisels, awls, and especially a saw. He would have to ask Valdira if there were any flint deposits in the area.

On the slope outside the house, he paused to rest. It worried him he was turning to things—furniture, flint—as a substitute for trust. The emptiness of it gnawed at him, hollow as the new house. Yet, Ryamon decided, there was more to it. The trappings of normalcy should help them both feel more secure.

Before he could do anything with the wood, it had to be dry. Ryamon raised a series of stone prongs along the slope and set his wood up on them. Getting it off the ground would help it dry more quickly, or so he hoped.

Just as he finished with the wood, the trees started a softer whisper. Valdira was nearby. He turned as she emerged from the forest. Her plaid scarf was tied neatly over her hair and the reed basket hung on her arm.

"Will you come with me?" Valdira asked.

"Of course. Where?" Ryamon was feeling frustrated enough he wouldn't mind leaving for a while. Brushing bits of bark from his hands, he strode to join her.

"You'll see."

Before he reached her, Valdira set off down the hillside path. Ryamon hurried to catch up. She seemed unusually somber. He held back a squirming guilt at what he had done to the rock shelter. She had already told him what she thought. Surely she wouldn't punish him with silence.

Cautiously, he asked, "Is everything all right?"

He braced himself, expecting her to say something important. That they needed to lay down some rules, or even that she wanted him to leave.

"It's fine." Shrugging, she walked on.

They reached the bathing stream, which Ryamon had privately dubbed Valdira Creek, and crossed it stone to stone. A path on the other bank led into cool shade. Falling into step with his lover, Ryamon took her hand. As they touched, he experienced another of those strange flashes of emotion. Valdira was calm and resolved, prepared for some unpleasant task, but under that darker emotions surged like hidden currents in a stream. Anger, fear, grief. He also felt a distinct twitch of discomfort; Valdira wasn't in a hand-holding mood.

Gently, not wanting to make things worse, he let go. As they ducked low-hanging boughs, Ryamon considered what he had glimpsed. He hadn't thought Valdira was afraid of anything, but these emotions were old and strong, powerful as aged liquor.

What could be upsetting her? Ryamon wanted to help. After yesterday's blunder, he was afraid to push.

Neither of them spoke as they followed the path beside Valdira Creek. It dropped down a ridge, skirted a marshy pond and cut between two folds of land. Trees crowded close, so that Ryamon couldn't see what lay ahead. The creek descended a series of cataracts, while the trail led down a steep canyon wall above it. He concentrated on sensing the path before them, making sure it was secure. The water made too much noise for them to talk anyway.

At the bottom of the ravine, the creek splashed into a wider stream. Ryamon thought it might be the young Silver River. The sun rose high overhead by the time they came to the edge of a meadow. Afternoon heat baked the grass, where insects hummed lazily. Large clusters of lacy flowers shed a subtle fragrance. Valdira reached out to pluck one.

Fenced pastures started beyond the meadow, and then peasant huts crowded up to the river. Dust rose lazily from the streets of Lornest. The river ran straight on, but Valdira stopped at the edge of the trees. She stared at the village for a long time, her expression hard and wary. Ryamon first watched her, and then watched the village.

He was glad she didn't go in. Too many troubles could find them here. The villagers had been none too friendly to Ryamon. He had no idea how they would treat Valdira. They had to know she ran away. And then there was her father, with his drunken rages.

In a low voice, he asked, "Do you want to come back here? There must be other villages where we can trade."

Her head jerked slightly, like a startled ornyx that was about to start kicking. Then her hazel eyes blinked into focus on him. Her shoulders twitched in a shrug.

"Like you said, there are things we need." She tossed her head, as if she didn't care, but there was no mistaking the tension in her voice. "Don't worry, we aren't going through the middle of town."

The retort stung, but Ryamon controlled his defensive reaction. It must be hard to come back here. For her sake, he had to stay calm.

"I know you better than that," he said. "I just hope it's safe."

"There aren't any inquisitors here," she teased, a bit sharply.

Ryamon smiled, but he went on. "I meant safe for you. Silma told me your Da used to hit you."

Valdira's hazel eyes narrowed. "I never knew she was such a gossip."

"As I said before, she worries about you."

"That was a long time ago," she said.

"She said he used to hit you a lot," Ryamon persisted.

"Not since I got old enough to hit back." Valdira smiled with a strange, cruel quirk. "He doesn't try it anymore, not on me. But I come back sometimes to make sure he keeps his hands off Mam."

"Oh. Good." Ryamon felt awkward, as if he was deliberately breaking a rule.

Valdira walked on. Ryamon was almost relieved to fall silent. Still staying behind the screen of trees, she led him eastward along the meadow's edge. Though she moved easily enough, he noticed she held the basket tight against her side, as if it could shield her from what was to come. Or just from her past.

The distant buildings shifted as the two lovers circled to come in from the southeast. Ryamon picked out Silma's olive tree and the whitewashed walls of her cottage. A low ridge rolled up between them and Lornest. Then they approached a small farm. A split rail fence separated fields of green young grain from the forest where they lurked. There was a barn, but Ryamon saw no animals in the yard, not even an ornyx to pull a cart. Tufts of weeds grew beneath the fence and from cracks in the dirt. Peeling paint on the shutters gave the small stone cottage a neglected look.

Somewhere in the distance, a squirrel chattered. Except for that and the rustling trees, it was quiet. Valdira stopped again and stared at the cottage for a long time. Her expression was intent, like an eridow sizing up a herd of sobi to find the weaklings.

Ryamon glanced around at the sound of wings. A black and white bird lit on the fence. It hopped down the top rail, tilting its head at Valdira. After a moment it gave a shrill, rasping cry.

"Shhh," Valdira whispered.

Ryamon looked around cautiously. He hoped Silma wouldn't be able to sense Valdira's magic. She had been Valdira's teacher, after all.

With a pert flick of its tail, the bird took off. It glided across the nearest field and landed outside the barn window. The shutters were propped open; it boldly hopped inside. Long moments passed. The bird soon reappeared, flying out a different window. With a flash of black and white, it landed on the cottage's thatched roof.

The bird was obviously snooping, trying to find out where the people were. For someone who claimed she wasn't afraid, Valdira was taking a lot of precautions. Maybe it was just as well. After what Silma had said, Ryamon wasn't sure he wanted to meet Valdira's father. Especially not when his relationship with her was so unsettled.

The little spy flitted down to the cottage window. It bobbed its head, peering in, then darted inside. There was a shout inside the house, a woman's voice. The bird burst back out the window and flew for the trees with something glinting in its beak.

"Little thief," Valdira chuckled, but her features were still tight.

"I hope that wasn't important," Ryamon said.

"Just a button," Valdira answered.

The cottage door opened and a woman ran out, brandishing a broom. "Bring that back, you pest!" she cried.

The bird had vanished into the forest, so there was little hope of getting the button back unless Valdira made the bird return it. She showed no sign of doing so.

Ryamon studied the woman in the yard. She was dressed exactly like Valdira, in a peasant dress buttoned up the front. A scarf covered her hair. Even from a distance, Ryamon could tell where Valdira had gotten her coarse features.

No one else followed the woman. "You're in luck," Valdira murmured, not quite looking at Ryamon. "He's not here."

She stepped out of the trees. Ryamon followed uneasily as Valdira walked along the curve of the fence toward the barn. The exasperated woman didn't see them. She shut the window shutter with a clap and stalked back into the cottage.

The lovers approached the house, silent except for the swish of their garments over dry grass. Ryamon was uncomfortably aware he was about to meet Valdira's mother. At least his face was clean, since he had brought a razor with him from Polvest. But his hair was tangled, despite his efforts to keep it back in a braid, and his robe was all too recognizable. She would know exactly who he was, while he knew nothing about her. He wondered what she would think of her daughter bringing a magus home.

At the cottage door, Valdira slanted another look around. She tapped lightly and pushed it open without waiting for permission. There was a flurry of movement inside.

"Marton?" the woman called. She sounded frightened.

"Just me," Valdira answered.

"Oh! Valdira!" Her mother rushed to embrace her. "By the Seven, where were you? It's been weeks and no one had seen you. Silma won't tell us a thing!"

Valdira shrugged, looking irritated by the scolding. Now that he saw them both together, Ryamon noticed the contrasts between them. Valdira was lean and tense, full of nervous energy. Her mother was shorter, plump and soft, her face lined with cares. The hair under her scarf was as much silver as brown. She made Ryamon think of a leather glove, so well used it was all but worn out.

The woman stopped talking when she caught sight of Ryamon. Her eyes went wide. They were brown, rather than hazel like Valdira's, and lined with heavy shadows. Ryamon shook himself into a formal bow.

"Good afternoon."

"And to you." She let Valdira go and dipped a brief curtsey.

Valdira released a short, impatient sigh. "Mam, this is Ryamon. Ryamon, my mother, Rhella." Before either of them could answer, she hurried on, "We need to borrow a few things."

"What sort of things?" Rhella asked.

Valdira set her basket on the small table, saying, "Lamp oil. Some nails. A cooking pot, if you can spare one. And Ryamon needs better clothes. Would something of Da's would fit him?"

"I was just doing some mending," Rhella admitted.

"I don't want to trouble you," Ryamon put in. If Valdira's family was like his own, they each had only one or two suits of clothes. The fearsome Marton was bound to notice if his spare shirt disappeared.

"We can trade," Valdira said. "This robe of Ryamon's, it's good sturdy wool. You haven't had a new skirt in a long time, or Da could use a warmer lining for his winter jacket. Everybody gets something."

Ryamon's robe would be cut into parts, thoroughly hidden from anyone who was looking for him. Still, he had hoped to keep it. Even if he switched to peasant garb, which he knew was more practical for roaming in the mountains, he would need a winter cloak himself. A fierce look from Valdira stopped him from protesting.

"I can say I traded for it," Rhella mused, working her way around the idea. "He doesn't have to know who I traded with."

"He can't complain about the price," Valdira added.

There seemed no point in arguing. Rhella was already picking through her pile of mending. She held up a pair of trousers with heavily stained knees and eyed Ryamon critically. Avoiding her gaze, he glanced around the cottage.

It seemed to be a normal farmhouse. The walls were stone with two small windows, one of them now closed. The wooden floor was heavily worn beneath a matt of woven reeds. An oven was built into the wall beside the fireplace and a rusty-looking water pump stood on the counter above a stone sink. It all looked hand built, not raised with magic.

The furniture was simple: a trestle table and benches, rocking chair near the hearth. A curtained alcove probably held the couple's bed. Up above was a loft for more sleeping room or storage.

After all he had heard, Ryamon had expected the home of Valdira's father to be chaotic, like a wild animal's den, but there was no evidence of his vicious nature. Everything was neat and tidy. Yet he did sense a taint in the air. Whatever had happened here, the stones of the cottage had witnessed it. They remembered.

Valdira interrupted his inspection. "Here, try these." She tossed him the stained trousers and a shirt with patched elbows.

Ryamon retreated to the alcove and dragged the curtain shut behind him. He tried not to shuffle like a brat, and also tried not to stare at Valdira's parents' bedchamber while he undid his robe. Out in the main room came the buzz of furtive conversation. He tried to not listen to that, either.

Stuffy air made his skin feel prickly in the cramped space. The sense of foreboding was even stronger close to the bed. Ryamon wasn't enough of a Stone magus to fully understand those echoes of past upheaval, but it felt less like anger than a gnawing pain and fear. The kind of torment that could drive a person to violence.

Just the idea made Ryamon nervous, so he concentrated on the clothes. The shirt was simple white linen. Its sleeves were a bit short, but that wouldn't matter if he rolled them up to the elbows. The fabric was thin compared to his woolen robe. He hoped it would be warm enough at night. The trousers were also short and slightly baggy in the waist. His belt would keep them from slipping, and his boots were tall enough to hold the cuffs in place.

Ryamon remembered how odd it had felt to put on his Stone magus robe after being naked. Wearing Valdira's father's clothes felt even stranger. When would he ever have clothes he liked? Then he felt irritated with himself for being so particular. Though worn, the garments were sturdy and comfortable. They would certainly do to tramp around the hills in.

Glad to get farther from Marton's oppressive aura, he folded his robe and took it back to the main room. The two women were now busy packing the basket. A small sack of flour and a tiny box that might hold salt were tucked into the cooking pot. A leather flask of the lamp oil Valdira had asked for. Ryamon handed over his magus robe with another little bow. Rhella stared at him with sad eyes, as if his face was a puzzle she needed to solve.

Glancing at the basket, he said, "We should pay for this. I don't have money, but I can check your chimney for leaks, if you want."

"That's kind of you," Rhella began, but Valdira interrupted.

"It's time to go. Da could be back any minute."

"We're taking so much," Ryamon said. Valdira's expression went fierce again, so he bowed to her mother again. "I'm sorry."

For the first time, Rhella's eyes twinkled. "I hope you keep this one," she said to Valdira. "He's so polite."

Ryamon was slightly dismayed by her comment, but pleased, too.

"It was them who didn't keep me," Valdira retorted. "Let's go."

She went to the door. The basket was still on the trestle table. Rhella hastily tucked a cloth over the top before Ryamon picked it up.

Valdira stopped, her fingers white on the door handle. Over her shoulder, she said gruffly, "Thanks, Mam. Give Da my greeting."

"Take care, dear." Rhella's expression was sad again as she

watched them leave.

They went back the way they had come, around the fence and into the forest. Valdira ignored the trees' rustled greeting. She walked fast, as if she couldn't get away too soon.

Ryamon didn't try to talk as they circled back to the west of Lornest. He didn't know what he could say that would not be the wrong thing. Oddly, it was Rhella who stuck most in his mind. Why had she been so surprised by simple courtesy? It made him wonder what kind of men Valdira had brought home before. And how often. He knew better than to ask such questions, ever.

They made it back to the place where they had crossed the river and started toward Valdira Creek. Ryamon paused and scooped a drink of water while Valdira watched impatiently. The basket he carried was getting heavy. He shifted it in his arms, trying to ease the ache in his shoulders. At least the forest's shade felt good.

From Valdira he felt nothing, not even her sporadic flashes of emotion. In fact, he hadn't felt anything since they stepped across her parents' threshold. She had raised some kind of mind shield, like a turtle shell to conceal what she was thinking.

At her parents' home, Valdira had been abrupt and exasperated, while Rhella had fawned and tried to make her happy. It was almost as if Rhella was the child and Valdira the parent. Rhella might love Valdira, but Ryamon thought she was afraid of her, too.

With a weak mother and tormented father, Valdira had never had anyone take care of her the way parents should. No wonder she didn't want anyone—not Silma or Minaric or Ryamon—telling her what to do. Whatever peace she had, she had fought for it on her own.

Ryamon's hands itched with the desire to hug her and swear he would protect her. He knew she would never accept his help. She didn't need it. He still wanted to give it. How could he make her understand that?

Still not talking, the started up the ravine where Valdira Creek tumbled down from the hills. Even burdened by the basket, Ryamon found it easier going as they toiled up the game trail. He no longer tripped over the hem of his robe. But he didn't like it, walking together and apart at the same time. He cleared his throat.

"So," he began. Valdira sent a wary glance over her shoulder.

Making a trying at humor, he said, "Talk about changing people." He waved the loose sleeve of his new shirt.

His lover scowled momentarily, but then gave a rusty laugh. "I suppose I deserve that."

"You deserve to be respected," Ryamon corrected. "I'm sorry I changed your house without asking. I won't do it again."

Valdira shrugged, obviously trying to decide if she should let him soothe her. "Not everything has to do with you," she finally told him.

"I know," he said, but she climbed on. Ryamon scrambled after her. The sun was harsher where the waterfalls had cut the trees away. He felt sweaty, chest and arms aching.

"I have to rest," he panted when they reached the top. He set the basket down and drank from the creek again. Afterward, he wiped his chin and tried again. "This doesn't change anything. Your mam, I mean—"

Ryamon still couldn't sense Valdira's emotions, but her sharp frown was clear enough.

"They're my family," she interrupted. "Don't try to judge us!"

"I'm not," Ryamon protested. It was true, he had been judgmental when he first came to Lornest, but he had learned better. "I already knew how your family was, Valdira. Silma told me enough. It doesn't change how I feel about you."

Valdira stared at him with piercing eyes. "You don't even know me. You have no idea." She stopped, swallowed. "If you knew, you'd hate me!"

She whirled away, striding toward the forest. Incredibly, Ryamon thought she was crying. That scared him even more than the shorbak had.

He left the basket to run after her. Trees closed around her, a wall of frowning faces, but he bulled his way through and caught her in his arms.

"I could never hate you!" he said.

With a strangled cry, she struggled free. "Let me alone!"

Ryamon watched her run for the trees. "Valdira!" he cried. "You're right, I don't know the details. I don't want to. That house is made of rocks, and they were trying to tell me things, but I didn't listen. I don't care!"

Valdira paused with one hand on the nearest tree. Tension made her hand into a claw. All around them, the forest roared and tossed as the trees felt her anguish.

"You must have fought for your life there," Ryamon said. "You had to save yourself. Do you think I don't know how it feels? I was in the wrong order. I felt trapped, too."

Valdira burst into bitter, mocking laughter. "It was never like that!"

Ryamon wanted to ask what it was like, then. But Valdira's humor suddenly turned to sobs. Trees tossed their branches in dismay. Ryamon ran to her. He tried to hold her gently, not confining her the way so many people must have done in the past. Standing in Ryamon's arms, she shook with rasping, painful sobs.

At last he could feel her emotions again, the savage moil of rage, grief and shame. He couldn't believe how much she hated herself. Valdira, who seemed so confident, kept repeating in her mind, *"I don't deserve this."*

Love and understanding, she meant. Faithfulness and trust. Ryamon tried to answer, in his fumbling way, *"Nothing you did could be so bad that you don't deserve a happy life."*

Chapter Nine

"I wish people weren't so predictable," Murcrys complained when Phareth reported Salovik's ploy.

However, there was little even a Mage Lord could do. As Anarinda's wind sped the 4 along, Nepharyl was constantly underfoot, fawning and snooping. Suspicion the magi had been conspiring together was clear in his mind, and he was determined they wouldn't have the chance to do it again. Phareth felt like telling him there was nothing to worry about. It was impossible to conspire with Telamar, who remained aloof even from Anarinda.

After six tense days, the 4 reached the river port of Elvest. Phareth was heartily glad to quit the cruiser's narrow confines. Unfortunately, they wouldn't be able to continue their journey the next day as expected. Another magus was using one of the ornyx chariots they needed. Since each ornyx could only pull one person, they had to wait for its return.

The magi took lodging at a Collegium hostel. Nepharyl, the outsider, stayed with one of Guilberta's gentle-born friends. Once those arrangements were made, Phareth returned to the dock. According to Murcrys, Ryamon had left Polvest on a montus barge. He had to have gone through Elvest on his way to Selkest. Phareth soon found a porter who recalled seeing a red-haired magus get off the barge at least ten days ago.

"Looked a bit dizzy," the man said, eyeing the silver penny Phareth was polishing between his thumb and forefinger. It was easy to pick up a picture from his mind. Ryamon was skinny and sullen, almost more boy than man. The image matched what Murcrys recalled of his appearance from the Grand Collegium.

"Did you see where he went?" Phareth asked.

"I think he took a montus train going south, but I can't be sure. So many travelers come and go. You understand."

After the fellow eagerly pointed out the train stop, Phareth handed over the penny. So Ryamon had at least started out toward Selkest. Phareth strolled across the street, but his luck ran out at the train stop. At least a dozen montus trains carried passengers south from Elvest and none of the drivers remembered seeing a

Stone magus. Nor could Phareth pick up any more psychic traces. Too many people passed through the station to isolate one person.

Satisfied he had done as much as he could, Phareth returned to the hostel. He wished he didn't have to rejoin his companions at all, but since there was no way to avoid it, he spent the rest of the day meditating in his room. With waning hopes, he listened for any foreign voices intruding on Arkanost's serenity.

The only time he saw Telamar was during meals. He liked it that way. However, on the second evening Anarinda told them the ornyx and chariot were back.

"The ornyx needs to rest," she said, "but we can leave in the morning."

"Too bad," Phareth answered drily. "I was starting to like it here."

The sarcasm drew a laugh from Anarinda, but Telamar sniffed at them both.

"We have a duty to perform," came his prissy reminder.

"Nobody wants to succeed more than I do," Phareth replied. "And you should do something about that cold."

Telamar's eyes bored into him like two sharp icicles. Anarinda's lips twitched as she restrained her mirth.

"I'm going to go pack." The storm magus edged away, leaving them to glare at each other.

Phareth contacted Murcrys again late that night. To his surprise, his mother's mind felt tired and a bit harried.

"Is something wrong?" he asked.

"I spent a lovely day at the Grand Collegium," she answered. *"Chrysen called a full session."*

It sounded like someone didn't approve of Akayel, Murcrys and Klaive acting so independently. Phareth hadn't thought it would be Chrysen. The Sea Lord was normally an amiable person.

"The Sea magi in the harbor must have noticed us leaving together," he said. Remembering what his mother had told him about apologizing for things that weren't his fault, Phareth said nothing more about blame. *"Nepharyl suggested we change into less conspicuous clothing. He said he would have something made for us. I wondered if it could be a scheme to catch us breaking protocol."*

"Clothes don't matter," Murcrys answered immediately. *"Still, if you can, perhaps you should let him think he's won you over."*

"That was my thought, too."

Murcrys went on, *"You might as well know, there were a number of comments about me sending you to Selkest."*

It was a good thing Phareth's shields were solid. Blandly, he asked, *"What did you tell them?"*

"That it was none of their business." She projected a broad imitation of Salovik's prudish manner. Phareth laughed in his mind. Telamar's attitude at supper made the mimicry even funnier.

"I wanted to know what they would say," Murcrys went on. *"And who would say it."* Phareth sensed a grim purpose in his mother, but she only added, *"Go on with your work. I've been trying to learn more about your new friend, Nepharyl. So far, his background seems legitimate."*

"I appreciate it," Phareth said. He didn't ask her to warn him if she learned something alarming. He knew she would.

"Be well, son," Murcrys said.

Phareth felt an unexpected wave of affection and concern as the connection between them faded. He sat up for a while longer, thinking about that.

~ * ~

Nepharyl arrived at the hostel the following morning in a chariot piled high with luggage. A quick mental probe told Phareth he had borrowed the ornyx and cart from his wealthy host, and that Telamar had sent a note telling him the magi were ready to travel on. Phareth wasn't surprised, but he felt a twinge of disappointment all the same. He would have liked to leave the prying nobleman behind—purely by accident, of course.

Meanwhile, the three collegium orynxes screeched at the new bird. They ruffled their feathers and flashed blue patches around their eyes. Their dominance displays expressed Phareth's mood quite well.

Nepharyl cautiously tied his bird at a distance from the others. "Have a look at this," he called as the three magi came to meet him. Beside the driver's seat were three parcels wrapped in delicate paper. Nepharyl tore the topmost package open.

"Count Aisleng has a hunting estate not far from Lornest," he explained. "He says this is what the local people wear. I asked his tailors to make a few small alterations."

Aisleng must be Guilberta's wellborn friend. Nepharyl's admiration for Guilberta and everyone connected with her beat outward so strongly Phareth had to raise a shield and block it out.

To distract himself, he looked at what Nepharyl wanted them to wear.

It was hardly peasant garb. The jacket and trousers were of a nubby, light brown fabric. A plain white shirt went with them. At least the jacket was short and sensible, without the long tails and lacy cuffs Nepharyl's had. The lapels were turned outward to expose a lining of white satin. Phareth wondered about that until Nepharyl handed the bundle over to Telamar.

"For you," he said, clearly enjoying his role as gift-giver. "And for the lady…"

He opened the next package to reveal a full-skirted dress in the same brown homespun. A line of black buttons marched up the front. The cuffs and trim were of yellow satin.

"I'm sure this will be fine," Anarinda said politely.

The last bundle held another suit, this one with black lapels. Phareth reached for it without being told. White for Ice, yellow for Storm, black for Shadow. They were still identified by order, though you'd have to look closer.

"I'll go get changed," Phareth said. Inside he sighed with resignation. His robe was more comfortable than trousers, even in hot weather.

"You will?" For once, Telamar let honest doubt show through his chilly manner. He held his new clothes as if Nepharyl had given him a live skunk. "This isn't authorized."

"We brought Lord Nepharyl along to advise us," Anarinda pointed out in her delicate voice. "What's the point if we ignore what he tells us?"

Smirking a bit, Nepharyl bowed to her. Since it was Telamar's own Mage Lord who had gotten Nepharyl sent with them, Telamar couldn't even argue. Savoring his rival's chagrin, Phareth went inside to change.

In his hostel room, he studied his reflection in the small mirror on the wall. It wasn't a bad fit, all in all. He still didn't think anyone would mistake the magi for peasants. No commoner would ever have such a soft, clean shirt, nor did farm folk dress in identical jackets. These could be uniforms borrowed from Lord Aisleng's own staff. Nepharyl probably thought he was sending a clever message.

When he came out, Anarinda was standing just inside the hostel door. Even in the drab brown skirt, she looked dainty as a child. A lacy scarf embroidered with sunflowers covered her perfect golden curls. Phareth couldn't help wondering how long she would be able to keep her hair so neat.

The dress must have been intended for a woman with a heavier build. As he drew near, Anarinda adjusted the buttons down the front, trying to make the fabric lie flat.

"It suits you," Phareth said.

Anarinda smiled, crinkling her nose a little. "I'll have to get used to these buttons. My own robe is much more convenient."

"I agree," Phareth said. He turned sideways and flexed his arms, showing how the jacket tightened across his shoulders. In a low voice, he added, "We are not Guilberta's lackeys, no matter what Nepharyl makes us wear."

Anarinda leaned toward him, seriousness contrasting with her childlike appearance. "Since his lordship thinks he knows everything about Selkest, should we have him lead off?"

With a tight smile, Phareth said, "I like it." Nepharyl couldn't follow them around if he was in front of the line.

A surly slam announced when Telamar joined them. The ice magus stopped when he saw Phareth and Anarinda. His trousers were too long, making him seem to shuffle with every step. The dull brown leached color from his already pale face, except for an angry pink flush in his cheeks.

"It isn't that bad," Anarinda offered gently.

"We're both better looking than him," Phareth put in. "I think he wants to make us look homely."

Telamar's irritated scowl yielded to a reluctant quirk of smile. "I don't suppose you brought along a needle and thread?" he asked Anarinda.

Her blue eyes sparkled like sun on the river. "Of course. I can take them up for you tonight."

The ice magus nodded. Then he pushed past them with an air of surrender. "Let's go before someone sees us and makes a complaint."

Outside, Nepharyl waited, scuffing his black boots in the dusty street. He brightened when he saw them.

"Perfect," he declared.

Telamar didn't say anything, but his dragging trousers sounded like a disapproving sniff as he walked by. Hiding his smile at the wordless comment, Phareth surveyed the three ornyx chariots.

Wild ornyxes still lived in Mirost, where they were called "terror of the plains." Their wings were too small to lift them in flight, but their long, strong legs gave them speed in exchange. Long necks helped them spot prey over the tall grass and weeds. Luckily, they preferred to eat reptiles and rodents. People were in no danger unless they got close to a nest.

These tame birds were all females, easier to manage because they were only half again the height of a human being. Except for their colorful eye patches, they were covered with speckled brown feathers. There seemed little difference between them, so Phareth went to the one farthest away from Nepharyl. The ornyx snapped her head around as he approached, putting her sharp beak in profile. Pale gold eyes blinked alertly. Perhaps, he thought, there was a bit of wildness left in them yet.

The ornyxes were harnessed to the chariots by wide leather bands that buckled over their backs and around their chests. The reins looped over their wings. The chariot itself was a low, open cart with large wheels. It had a wooden frame and leather siding around a single seat. On the back was a metal rack with more straps for securing luggage. Ornyxes were fast, but they couldn't pull much weight. Phareth wondered how Nepharyl's bird would fare with the lordling's extra bags. Not that it mattered to him, except tiring the ornyx could delay their journey.

As Phareth tied his bag down, he heard Anarinda say, "My lord, you have already helped us, but if you could do one more favor? You seem familiar with this area, and I know I've never traveled here before. Perhaps you could guide us onward."

"That would be my honor," Nepharyl said. Glancing over his shoulder, Phareth saw another of his oily little bows. "If we are all ready?"

Ornyxes were social creatures, and the collegium birds were quick to follow Nepharyl's despite their initial spat. Phareth tried to get comfortable as his chariot rolled over smooth stone streets. The ornyx's head claws clicked on the pavement. Elvest was too crowded to move faster than a walk, but at last they passed the city's gate. Nepharyl shouted a command, and suddenly they were skimming along at speeds that put Anarinda's wind to shame.

It was interesting, at first, to watch the hills roll by. Green-gold grain fields and montus mills gave way to endless stretches of weeds and wildflowers. The ground cover appeared seamless at first, but Phareth soon realized there several types of grass. The shorter tufts had a bluish caste, while another kind was yellower and twice as tall. Feathery seed heads made all the land look hazy.

Then Phareth chuckled. If he was reduced to studying the grass, he must be bored indeed!

Mostly he pondered what had happened, and what was still to come. Murcrys' instinct had been correct that Nepharyl coveted the leader's role. Phareth was curious to see where Nepharyl planned to lead them.

~ * ~

Four days later, he no longer enjoyed feeling the wind in his hair. His hat wouldn't stay on in the open car, and relentless sun left him parched despite the waterskin he kept under the seat. A hot breeze blew over the plains. He constantly blinked against the dust. Flat, magus-made roads had long since given way to rutted gravel. The chariot continually jolted and bounced between Selkest's rocky hills.

Yes, Phareth was heartily tired of having tangled hair, itchy eyes and muscle cramps from sitting still all day. The only relief came when forest sprang up on the hillsides. He relished the shade. Mountains loomed through every gap in the trees. That meant they were approaching the border. Phareth hoped they would reach their goal soon.

Unfortunately, the road had narrowed enough the ornyxes no longer had room to run. As they plodded by one of the occasional pull-outs along the trail, something he sensed jolted him out of his boredom.

"Halt!" Phareth called with his mind, because he didn't know if the others would hear him in their separate chariots. Nepharyl gave a startled yelp, and Telamar stopped his ornyx fast enough to raise a cloud of dust. Phareth tugged on the reins to guide his ornyx into the clearing.

"What's wrong?" Anarinda called from the chariot behind him.

"I sense something." Phareth jumped out of his chariot, trying not to hobble on his stiff legs, and looped the reins over a convenient branch. "Stay where you are."

He walked forward slowly, surveying the area. The pull-out held little but a stretch of dusty ground and a circle of stones full of charred wood and ashes. The fire had obviously been cold for many days. He was vaguely aware of Nepharyl sneezing as he pushed through the brush beside the road. Telamar swung his arms and legs to ease their stiffness.

"What is it?" the ice magus asked irritably.

"Someone used magic here. It could be Ryamon," Phareth said. "I need to scan for his traces. Don't come in here or your auras will cover his."

Telamar folded his arms with forced patience. Nepharyl finally struggled through to the clearing, but Anarinda intercepted him.

"We must let Initiate Phareth work," she said.

Nepharyl answered with more, louder sneezes. Pressing a handkerchief to his nose, he complained, "I will be so glad to reach a town where we can wash."

Anarinda made sympathetic noises. Phareth ignored his companions. What he sensed lay farther back under the trees. Stretching out his senses, he homed in on a place where magic permeated the ground.

Within moments he looked down on a long trench of solid stone. He crouched to examine it. It was definitely a stone magus' work. Rusty-brown pine needles lined the trench, which was just the right size for a man to stretch out. Phareth reached out one arm until his fingertips brushed the stone bed. He drank in the maker's aura, and with it shadows of his identity. Satisfaction rushed through him.

It was definitely Ryamon of Dalgest. Phareth recognized the young man's thin face, red hair and hot blue eyes. There was a smokiness to his aura that Phareth had always associated with Fire magi. Frustration and pain turned it acrid. Ryamon's spirit throbbed in the stones, his drive to find Valdira and punish her. He had wanted to hurt someone as badly as he himself had been hurt.

Phareth sat back on his heels. This was the first time he had directly felt his quarry's personality. Ryamon was desperately unhappy—or he had been, those many days ago. He had been so committed to duty, almost obsessed. What could have turned him from his cause?

Phareth straightened and went to untie his ornyx. Seeing him move, Telamar called, "Well? Was it him?"

"Yes." Nepharyl looked baffled, so Phareth explained, "I got a good sense of his aura. There's no way he can hide from me now."

Anarinda looked distressed at Phareth's words, but he had no pity to spare for Ryamon. The Stone novice had failed. He would pay the price, because Phareth had no intention of failing. Not again.

~ * ~

The sun was sinking low when they finally reached Valdira's home village. Nepharyl wasn't the only one disappointed by what he saw. Of course, every peasant village the magi had passed through seemed untidy compared to the orderly, planned city of Polvest but Lornest was the smallest one by far. In the outskirts, juvenile ornyxes stalked the grain fields, hunting mice. In town, streets curved unexpectedly and houses were built haphazardly, no two alike. They crowded around a central plaza like a herd of animals huddled together for warmth.

Villagers turned to watch as the four ornyx chariots bumped their way into the cobblestone square. There was a kind of fountain at the center. One side had a large watering trough, which the ornyxes went straight for. Women were filling jugs of water from a tap on the opposite side.

They halted the chariots, and Telamar went to stop the ornyxes from kicking each other in their eagerness to drink. Anarinda greeted the women with a pleasant, "Good evening." Phareth held back, watching, as Nepharyl looked around at the ramshackle town.

"Good evening." Nepharyl bowed to the women at the well, his courtly manner out of place in the rustic setting. "Is there an inn here?" he asked plaintively.

"No, lord," one of the women replied. She and her fellows tried to back away while curtseying nervously.

"Does anyone rent rooms?" Anarinda asked.

All the women shook their heads. Meanwhile, men started to wander out of the shops along the plaza. In such a small town, Phareth realized, any unexpected event could draw a crowd.

"Is there even a barn we could use?" Telamar demanded coldly. Though he tried to control the ornyxes, they and the chariots were getting into a tangle at the watering trough.

The townsfolk stared at him doubtfully. "Tyteb has a montus," a woman ventured from the back of the group.

"Isn't anyone in charge?" Nepharyl asked. "We need official

support." He tried to come off lordly and gracious, but his gritted teeth spoiled it.

Much as he enjoyed watching the nobleman flounder, Phareth realized it would be truly dark soon and he, too, wanted to sleep in a proper bed. He rifled through the thoughts of the crowd, looking for someone who had a spare room.

He found the mind of a dark-eyed woman, she who had been brave enough to answer Nepharyl's first question. Gritl was her name. She stopped backing away after Phareth inserted the idea that Nepharyl might pay for her assistance.

"We have a mayor," Gritl said. "Tyteb, your lordship."

Someone added, "He's coming there," and several villagers pointed across the square, as if Gritl's cooperation had given them permission to do the same.

Mayor Tyteb was a stocky man with a lot of nose and very little hair. He wiped his hands on a dusty apron as he came. It seemed that Tyteb was also the town miller. This must be why he had a montus, to turn the millstones.

"Now then, what's to do?" Tyteb asked as the crowd let him through to the fountain.

"His lordship need lodgings," Gritl announced. Nepharyl looked slightly startled she had suddenly become their spokesman.

Tyteb's eyes darted, taking in the four of them. Phareth heard the flicker of his thoughts: *"Nice chariots. They must be rich. Who are they, a caravan? But where are the wagons? No, their hair's too long. Magi? They should be wearing robes."*

All this flitted through his mind as a free hand smoothed the fringe of hair behind his ears. "What's your business in Lornest?" Tyteb asked, neither offering nor denying hospitality.

"We are on Crown business," Nepharyl began importantly.

Telamar turned sharply, frowning, but Phareth spoke first.

"Say rather, the Collegium." He didn't want to argue in front of the villagers, but this was going too far. Their mission was, and always had been, at the command of the Mage Lords.

"We're searching for Valdira and Ryamon," Anarinda added.

"Ah. Indeed? I see," Tyteb said.

Phareth felt a new crackle of interest in the air. The villagers stopped retreating. A few even started to press in closer. Phareth watched them dart glances first at Tyteb and then among themselves.

Flushing slightly, Nepharyl gave Phareth a curt little bow. "The Collegium, of course. Anyone who helps us will be rewarded, but first we must have a place to stay for the night."

"I'm sorry to say we don't have an inn," Tyteb began.

"Perhaps each of us could stay with one of your families," Anarinda suggested. "It would be less of an imposition."

"It might," Nepharyl agreed doubtfully. Phareth guessed he didn't want the magi to separate. He couldn't watch them if they all went to different houses.

"Anarinda's idea has merit," Phareth said smoothly. "We have been in close company for several days. It might do us good to have a bit of time apart."

Anarinda looked pleased, while Nepharyl's eyes glittered with annoyance. Across the crowd, Phareth saw Telamar nod slightly in acceptance.

"Well, if that's your wish, sir magus," Tyteb said, although he didn't look much happier than Nepharyl.

"I have room if it's only one," Gritl volunteered.

Once again, the villagers followed her lead. The guesting of all four travelers and their ornyxes was soon settled. Phareth felt the villagers' curious thoughts around him all the while, silvery glints like fish in deep water. It was maddening that he couldn't focus on them.

However, it might be something they could use. As the crowd began to break up, seeking their homes in the gathering dusk, Phareth called his companions to him with a light mental touch. He included Nepharyl, since it might mollify him.

Or perhaps not. "You wanted me?" Nepharyl demanded.

Pretending to separate the wheels of two chariots, Phareth leaned toward his companions.

"I have an idea," he said in a low voice. "Most of these people know Valdira. Try to talk to them. We might learn something important."

"You're right," Nepharyl agreed, though grudgingly. "This is a small town. There's sure to be gossip."

"I want to know more about her," Anarinda said.

"I thought we might have been staying with Silma, the Blood magus," Telamar complained. "She was Valdira's mentor. Who would know more than she does?"

"Yes, I was surprised she didn't come to meet us," Nepharyl

said. "Maybe she's ashamed that her novice ran away."

"We can look for Silma in the morning," Anarinda said.

"Good," Phareth said. "We'll meet here and compare notes, then go to Silma's. Agreed?"

"Agreed," Anarinda said. Nepharyl stared daggers at Phareth, then reluctantly nodded.

"As long as I don't have to sleep in a montus barn," Telamar said.

Phareth blinked at him, distracted from the jumble of half-formed plans in his mind. "Did you just make a joke?"

"No," Telamar answered stiffly. "I don't want to sleep in a barn."

Phareth smiled all the same and clapped him on the shoulder. "Nor do I, brother magus. Nor do I."

Chapter Ten

Phareth went with Gritl, who had volunteered to host him. It didn't surprise him she lived in one of the larger cottages facing onto the plaza. He could already tell Gritl enjoyed playing an influential role in village life. This was exactly why he wanted to lodge with her.

The cottage was of field stones, whitewashed in imitation of a nobleman's house, with a thatched roof. There was a bit of bustle as Gritl moved her son, Evritt, out of his loft room so Phareth could sleep there.

Supper was dry bread, sour ale and peas porridge freshened with a few vegetables. Phareth ate enough of the crude fare to satisfy his immediate hunger and tried to ignore Evritt's resentful stare.

Evritt was a strapping boy with dark hair slashed off across the back of his thick neck. At sixteen, he could be considered a man, but Phareth sensed he was in no hurry to make his own way.

During the meal, Gritl proudly explained that her son was Tyteb's apprentice. The miller had no sons of his own, and her husband had passed away, leaving Evritt fatherless. It seemed a natural fit.

"You have connections, then," Phareth said, knowing Gritl would tell him more if he flattered her.

"I don't like to brag," Gritl said, but Evritt cut her off with a chuckle.

"My Mam, she knows everyone." There was a lurid undertone in his voice.

"Now then." Gritl gave his shoulder a shove, partly playful but partly a warning.

"What can you tell me about Valdira?" Phareth asked.

"Her." Gritl's eyes glittered, hard and sharp as obsidian glass. "Is someone finally going to do something?"

Evritt took a quick drink, hiding his face behind a wooden cup. Phareth wondered why he was avoiding his mother's gaze, but didn't want to drop the conversation with Gritl in order to probe her son's thoughts. Marking the reaction in his mind, he answered Gritl's question.

"Word has reached the Mage Lords," Phareth said, "but we need more information before we can proceed."

"Well," she said sourly, "if you want to know about Valdira, you have to know about Marton. He's her father."

Gritl said the word with a bitter snap. Phareth wondered why she said it that way, Father instead of the more casual da.

"Tell me about Marton," he said.

"Nothing but a brute, that man." Gritl's lips pressed tightly together. "A drunkard and a brute. Many's the time I saw his wife, Rhella, with black eyes and bruises. The girl, too."

Through Gritl's disapproval, Phareth glimpsed a mental picture of a girl child with tangled blonde hair and frightened eyes.

"They kept to themselves, but they were always over at Dama Silma's having some hurt looked at," Gritl said. "Valdira hid in the woods, I think."

"What made Marton act that way?" Phareth asked.

"How should I know?" Gritl snapped, outraged. "There's no reason good enough to lay hands on your loved ones!"

"Of course not," Phareth soothed her. "Could no one act?"

Gritl shrugged uncomfortably. "Daverel spoke to him. That was my husband. They were friends, him and Marton, before we wed. Once I saw what Rhella had to live with…"

She broke off, shaking her head. Phareth nodded. Gritl must have insisted her husband end the friendship.

"We all felt sorry for her," Gritl went on a bit defensively, "but we had our own families to think of." She laid a protective hand on her son's shoulder. Evritt kept eating, as if their conversation was of no interest.

"I see," Phareth murmured. "What about Tyteb or the other village elders?"

In her mind, Phareth heard a snort of contempt. *Them. Strutting around all the time, but when you need them…*" He also sensed when she swallowed the words. Gritl wouldn't say anything that might affect Evritt's future career.

"Marton never listened to anyone," she replied.

"You said that his family spent a lot of time with Initiate Silma," Phareth said. "When did Valdira become her novice?"

Gritl frowned, thinking. "Two or three years ago, when the girl turned thirteen. We all thought it would be good for her. Get her away from that man and let her blossom on her own." She didn't say who 'we' was; the other village women, Phareth assumed. Once again he felt fury rush through Gritl. "She blossomed, all right."

Evritt chuckled into his cup with the vulgar familiarity Phareth had noted before. His mind whispered, *"She can hide in our woodshed any time."*

Keeping his eyes fixed on Gritl, Phareth took a moment to probe Evritt's mind. He saw Valdira, several years older. Her hair was neatly plaited and she wore the red robe of a Blood novice. She smiled, a secretive smile, and Evritt followed her into a dusty, dimly lit shed. Without flirtation, without permission, he pinned Valdira to the wall and kissed her violently. And then he discovered she wasn't wearing anything under her robes.

Phareth jerked away from Evritt's lustful memory. Everyone had such experiences, of course; Phareth preferred his own to those plundered from strangers. But Gritl was watching him, obviously waiting for a response to her acid statement.

He took a sip of his beer before asking, "Was she not called to her element?"

"I'm not sure what you mean by that," Gritl said, baffled by the Collegium jargon. "The girl never had a serious mind like Silma. We started hearing rumors right away that she was seducing the young men, and some of them," her voice was deadly now, "young men with no morals or standards, lay with her in sin. They even fought over her, as if she was a sobus to be bought and sold. It was disgusting."

Suspicion was razor-sharp in Gritl's mind. She suspected Evritt was one of those young men without morals, but didn't know for sure. Phareth saw no reason to meddle between mother and son.

"As a novice, she should have remained celibate," he said quietly. "It is a small thing, however, compared to her other offenses."

Curiosity flared in both Gritl's and Evritt's minds. They truly didn't know what Valdira's abilities were, or what she had done by running away. Phareth fought to keep disappointment out of his voice.

"What happened then?" he asked.

"Some of us talked to Tyteb, and he talked to Silma," Gritl said. Dissatisfaction seethed within her, so Phareth wasn't surprised by her next words. "Nothing more was said, but then I heard that Valdira lay with Tyteb, too. And him a married man. Poor Kathlen could hardly hold up her head."

"Silma did nothing?" Phareth asked.

"Nothing that stopped Valdira," Gritl said. "She should have sent the girl home, but I suppose, knowing what she would go home to—" Gritl trailed off, teeth gritted, and then burst out, "It may be wrong of me, but I was glad when she ran off. Let her live with the beasts if she wants to act like one!"

"I'm afraid it isn't that simple," Phareth said.

Evritt spoke for the first time, his voice thick with food. "What's going to happen?"

Gritl glared at him, suspicious again. Phareth didn't sense any real worry about Valdira. Evritt only wanted to know if he was going to get in trouble.

"It depends on what she does." Since Phareth had no intention of discussing magical policy with two ignorant peasants, he stood up, making it clear the interview was over.

"Thank you for the meal and for your honesty," Phareth said. Somehow, he kept the irony from overflowing in his voice. "Now I must rest, for my journey continues in the morning."

Phareth made a little bow, just the way Nepharyl would, and climbed the ladder to the loft. Below, he heard muffled voices discussing what he had said, then crockery rattling as Gritl cleared the table. In a moment of spite, Phareth planted the notion in Evritt's mind that he should make up for lying to his mother by helping with the supper dishes. Clumsy clinks and splashing came from downstairs as Gritl made sure Evritt did the job right.

Phareth sat on the bed he was borrowing. Evritt's reactions nagged at him until Phareth recognized the farm lad as a dark reflection of himself.

Once, he been that eager for Kylethia's company. His feelings had been fresh and hot, impossible to ignore. Still, he hoped he had never been so selfish, using Kylethia for his own pleasure and not wasting a thought on her welfare.

Then there was Gritl, who clung to self-righteous morality and refused to help someone who desperately needed it. All at once, Phareth despised them both. He couldn't decide who was worse, so he closed his mind to both of them.

~ * ~

Breakfast was a boiled ornyx egg, big enough to divide among the three of them. Phareth left as soon as he sensed his fellow magi at the fountain in the square. He was still hungry, and he had a bit of hard sausage tucked into his bag. He didn't feel like sharing. Telamar and Anarinda were taking turns drinking from a dipper when Phareth joined them.

"How was your evening?" Phareth asked.

"The bed was hard and the food was terrible," Telamar reported with no particular feeling.

"I agree, except you left out the bed bugs." Nepharyl was just coming to meet them. He walked with fast, irritable steps. One arm twisted behind him as he tried to scratch a spot between his shoulders.

"Oh, dear," Anarinda said. She passed the dipper to Telamar and stepped over to rub the back of Nepharyl's jacket.

"Lower," the nobleman said, and then sighed with relief. "You are a true lady."

Telamar set the dipper on a ledge above the tap where the women had been filling their jugs the night before. Phareth felt a wave of cold annoyance from him. He glanced at the Ice magus with mild interest.

"At least it wasn't a barn," he said.

Telamar ignored the teasing. "You were right," he told Phareth. "They wouldn't stop talking about the woman."

Anarinda stopped scratching Nepharyl's back. "You mean Valdira?" She spoke very politely, but with an edge worthy of Gritl.

"Tyteb said the village women complained about her attitude. He said they were jealous of her," Nepharyl said, still shifting his shoulders. "He told me they would say the same about Silma if she was twenty years younger."

Phareth shook his head. "Tyteb said that to protect her. She was his paramour."

Nepharyl looked startled, but Anarinda nodded soberly.

"Levalia thought so, too—and Tyteb wasn't the only one. Her daughters grew up with Valdira. They said she came and went in the forest as she pleased. She would be gone for days, then suddenly reappear. When she got older, she lay with anyone who would hide her from her father."

"I heard that wild animals attacked the father," Telamar said, unconcerned by these sordid tales. "Yorec works the farm closest to Marton's. He moved his kin into town because he feared they would be next. He hasn't seen Valdira since."

"Wild animals?" Nepharyl murmured. "But this looks like such a peaceful village."

Ignoring him, Telamar said, "They want her contained."

Anarinda sighed lightly. "None of the villagers seem to know what her element is. Maybe that's best."

"It'll help limit the scandal," Phareth said, nodding.

"We'll have to be careful." Nepharyl clutched his sword-cane as if wild animals might spring out at them.

Telamar and Phareth shared a glance over the shorter man's head. Valdira was a rogue magus; no one had to tell them to be careful. Yet Phareth also sensed prickles of curiosity from houses around the square. Even though it was perfectly normal and understandable, he was getting tired of being stared at.

"People are watching," he told the group. "Let's see if Silma will talk to us. If anyone knows more, it will be her."

"Quite right," Nepharyl said. "It's this way, Tyteb said."

Phareth let the nobleman lead. He wanted time to think. Gritl hadn't mentioned an animal attack. Since she didn't like Marton, maybe she didn't care whether he got hurt.

Phareth chewed on the end of his sausage, connecting details in his mind. The abused child hiding in the woods had grown into a wild adolescent who would do anything to feel safe. She might be too damaged to control her magic, especially if her spirit had been molded by animals. Valdira might, indeed, be the beast in human form that Gritl called her.

"Silma may not be there," Anarinda cautioned as they left the plaza. "One of the village women is near her time, Levalia said. Silma could be at the birthing."

"I hope you're wrong," Phareth said. "I'd like to see the inside of her house. Since Valdira once lived there, I may be able to pick up her traces."

"She's been gone for months," Anarinda pointed out.

"Nor should we trespass in a place consecrated to Blood," Telamar added stiffly.

"I don't intend to," Phareth said. "We can wait. Unless you have a better idea what we should do?"

The Ice magus said nothing and Phareth didn't press him. Although it would have been easier, he didn't actually have to enter Silma's house to do his work.

The cottage of the Blood magus was beautiful, in a humble way. Plastered walls gleamed white in the morning sun. The fountain splashed lightly, bees hummed, and a breeze whispered in the rows of fragrant herbs. Already he could tell there was no one in the house. He stopped the others.

"Anarinda is right," Phareth said. "Silma isn't home. Wait here and I'll see what I can learn from outside."

Telamar shrugged. Anarinda bent to inhale the fragrance of a *sibban* plant. Nepharyl perched on the fountain's edge, fidgeting with his shiny black hat.

Phareth went to stand on the shadowed porch. The dominant aura in the house was a woman's, steady and kind. Initiate Silma, he assumed. He also caught an acrid whiff of Ryamon's presence, but the porch was heavily used. Too many traces overlapped on the boards.

Moving slowly and deliberately, he descended to the level of the garden and walked alongside the house where there was less foot traffic. Only vague impressions rewarded him: Valdira, in her novice robe, picked olives from the tree. She walked between the rows of herbs, singing softly as she brushed them with her hands. Then, in a vivid flash, she dove to hide behind a lavender bush just as someone banged in through the gate.

Phareth shook himself out of his trance. He was standing beside that same lavender bush. Looking around, he saw no sign of whatever confrontation had unfolded in Silma's garden. Then the voices of his comrades reached him faintly across the morning stillness.

"You shouldn't get so attached," Telamar was saying to Anarinda. "It may cause you to doubt at the wrong moment."

"I won't have you speak of her as if she has no identity," Anarinda replied. Her sweet, soft voice was stern. "We aren't after some woman, somewhere. We're after this woman, Valdira, in this place, Selkest. Where, I might add, she knows everything about the people and the landscape, and we know nothing. We mustn't let prejudice about her origins blind us to her capabilities."

"Even if she has the advantage," Nepharyl countered, scratching over his shoulder, "surely three magi can overcome one."

"Two, my lord," Anarinda corrected. "Ryamon is with her."

Telamar waited a moment longer to answer. When he spoke,

his voice was cool and dispassionate.

"You have a kind heart, but you can't save her. Valdira is a lawbreaker. We have to bring her down."

Phareth turned. A pink flush colored Anarinda's face, and fury sparked in her eyes. "She is our sister magus. Look what she's had to live with!"

She seemed to have forgotten Nepharyl was there, listening. Everything she said might be used against her and even against the Order of Storm itself.

"We have to find them first." Phareth strode across the garden, hoping to interrupt before Anarinda brought any more trouble on herself.

"Yes," Nepharyl demanded, "when are we going to do that?"

"It isn't as easy as you think," the Storm magus' voice was unusually sharp.

"Alas, my sister magus is again correct," Phareth said as he joined the team. "It's been too long since Valdira lived here. I can't get a strong impression of her. We'll have to start by finding Ryamon."

"Then why haven't you already done it?" Nepharyl asked impatiently. Phareth was getting tired of his complaints, but he managed a courteous reply.

"We can't be sure Ryamon has anything to do with Valdira. We think they're together, but they may not be. We could waste our time if we rush off—"

He broke off as a new sensation scratched across his mind. Someone approached on a side street. A man, agitated. Phareth instinctively turned toward the source. He was just in time to see someone emerge from between two huts.

"What is it?" Telamar asked.

"I'm not sure," Phareth muttered.

The man Phareth sensed had a slight frame and sandy brown hair cut something like a haystack. He walked with a jarring limp. At every step, Phareth sensed a sharp ache in his right leg.

With his leather trousers and rough-woven plaid shirt, he seemed no more than another peasant. Yet the man had a powerful presence, almost like a magus, except no pure element shone in his aura. He slammed through the gate and Phareth experienced a moment of double vision. It was the man Valdira had tried to hide from.

"Marton," Phareth breathed in warning.

Valdira's father limped to a halt a few steps away. Nepharyl winced at the reek of beer that came with him. Telamar was at Phareth's shoulder now. One hand was slightly cocked, ready for whatever might happen. He might have wanted to shield Anarinda, but she came around to Phareth's other side and offered a girlish apology.

"If you need Silma, she isn't here."

Phareth could tell that Gritl had been right about Marton's drinking. His skin was deeply tanned, but his face had a pinched and wasted look. Hazel eyes, surprisingly pale, flicked over Anarinda.

"I'm not looking for Silma." His voice was a coarse growl, not slurred as Phareth expected. "You're looking for my daughter."

Emotions came off him in waves: frustration, fear, rage. Marton seemed unable to conceal them. Or he simply wasn't trained to. It hurt to be near him, like shoving his arm into a blackberry bush, but Phareth didn't raise a shield. Painful as it was, he had to learn what he could.

"Will you help us find her?" Telamar asked warily.

"No, I just came by for a little chat," Marton sneered. "Come on. We can't talk here."

He whirled and lurched off. After a moment of shock, they followed him. From Telamar's and Anarinda's expressions, Phareth was sure they also picked up Marton's agitation. Just being in Silma's garden seemed to upset him.

Nepharyl, who had no such sensitivity, said, "It's about time we had some cooperation. Thank you, my good man."

Marton snorted and kept walking. *There's nothing good about it,* Phareth heard him think. After a moment, Marton rasped, "She's out of control. Someone has to do something."

Anarinda watched his back with dismay. Phareth saw in her mind that she couldn't believe a father would betray his own child. After a moment, she breathed to Phareth, "Do you have any idea where he's taking us?"

"He's not leading us into an ambush," Phareth replied just as softly. He was still pondering the way Marton said 'someone has to do something,' in almost exactly the same words Gritl had used.

"As if he could hurt us," Telamar sniffed.

Nepharyl, who had been trying to match Marton's stride,

dropped back as if the ambush idea had just occurred to him, too. Phareth could hear him wondering whether Marton's limp was a result of Valdira's attack.

"He's uncomfortable near Silma's house," Phareth murmured. "I don't think they agreed on how his daughter should be trained."

Marton slanted a glance over his shoulder, mocking their muffled discussion. Everyone fell silent.

Lornest was not a large village and they soon left its houses behind. The tapping of Nepharyl's cane on cobblestones turned to earthy thuds as they followed a wagon track cutting through a copse of trees. The sun was behind them, so Phareth thought they were heading west and a bit south. Around a low shoulder of land, the woods opened up onto farm fields and pastures where sobi grunted peacefully to each other.

A worried-looking farmer stood up from his vegetable patch as they went by. A clump of weeds dangled from his hand. Telamar raised his hand in greeting, and Phareth realized this must be Yorec, who had moved his family for fear of wild animals.

Marton didn't acknowledge his neighbor. He led them on to the rail fence bordering another farm. On one side, grain fields rustled in the wind. Vines climbed tall lattices on the other. The house and barn were rough-hewn, ordinary and anonymous. Beyond them was only forest and rocky hills. Marton paused to ease open the gate leading into his yard.

"This way," he ordered. "Fast and quiet, or the bitch will hear us."

"Who?" Anarinda asked with knife-edged courtesy.

"My wife," Marton bit out, and somehow the plain word held more contempt than if he had insulted her again. "You don't want to talk to her. She cries."

He limped off and the magi followed, though Phareth felt the sizzle of Anarinda's indignation in the air. After a glance toward the house, Marton opened one of the big barn doors and jerked his thumb to direct the magi inside.

Once he shut the door, the interior was dark and almost chilly. Side windows admitted little daylight. There were no animals in the stalls and only a faint odor lingered to suggest there had ever been any. Instead, rows of barrels and vats lined the stalls. They were surprisingly clean and orderly compared to the rest of the farm.

Marton stumped into one of the stalls, leaving the others to cluster in the center aisle. Nepharyl turned in a circle, annoyed at finding no place to sit. Phareth seized his moment of confusion to brush close to Anarinda and Telamar.

"His wife's name is Rhella," he whispered, remembering Gritl's story. "Keep him talking. I'm going to be busy."

Telamar eyed Phareth, suddenly uncooperative, but Anarinda nodded gratefully. In a high, clear voice, she asked, "If Rhella is Valdira's mother, wouldn't she also have useful information?"

"Useful?" Marton snarled. His hands bunched into fists. "None of this would have happened if she'd kept her promise!"

Such rage swept through him that Phareth thought he might strike Anarinda. Telamar took a half-step forward, and the barn got even colder as he prepared to defend his companion. Nepharyl backed away, hand on his cane. Then Marton whirled and snatched up a wooden tankard from somewhere in the stall. A single keg sat near the back of it. Everyone jumped as Marton banged at the tap to fill his mug. He slammed the tap shut and gulped at the foaming brew.

There was no need to probe his mind. Emotion poured off Marton like beer from the keg. Phareth watched, analyzing. Marton needed the drink, craved it to quiet his rage. Yet although he had already smelled of beer when he came to meet them, he seemed steady on his feet. It must take a lot of beer to really make him drunk.

Marton drained the tankard in one long pull. He finally stopped with a gasp that sounded almost painful. Then he turned, glaring at all of them.

"Don't think to judge me, you fine and fancy lords! I told her, that bitch. I told her no kids. When we were courting, I said I never wanted any kids and she said that was fine."

He spoke with desperate certainty, fury blazing inside him. Marton couldn't forgive his wife for ignoring the one thing he had asked of her. He went on, his face twisted with frustration.

"But what did she do? Gave me that brat anyway. Oh, did she cry. Swore she ate her lace flowers every time. Said I would come to love the girl in the end. Ha!"

Marton slammed at the tap again, splashing more beer into his tankard. Phareth sensed confusion from Nepharyl.

"What's lace flower?" he hissed.

Telamar shrugged. "I've heard women speak of it, but…"

"Herb lore," Anarinda snapped. "To keep from quickening."

Phareth saw a pale glow in her eyes, little sparks creeping over her hair. She no longer looked like a toy, but almost as dangerous as Marton.

He spared a moment to murmur, "Stay calm, sister magus."

She glared at him.

Marton drank again, his back to all of them. When he paused to breathe, Telamar asked, "Why did you not want children?"

The cool question made muscles bunch on Marton's shoulders. His hand tightened on the rim of the barrel but he didn't look at them.

"To end the curse," he grated, his voice barely human. "It's been in my family for generations. Skips a few now and then, but it always comes back. It came to me." He gulped again, sucking in beer as if he never wanted to stop.

When the brew ran out, he panted, "It's disgusting, unnatural." Phareth couldn't tell if he was describing himself or Valdira. Marton stared into the empty mug, his expression bleak. "I swore it would stop with me. That I would end the curse. But she… That bitch… She undid my choice and spread the curse into a new generation."

So that was it. Phareth took little joy in understanding. He had been correct that Marton was an untrained magus. He had the same gift Valdira did, but knowing it was illegal, he had hidden and denied it. His drinking was a way to block the flow of a magic he couldn't understand or control.

"What is this curse, exactly?" Telamar asked.

"A bond with beasts." Marton shuddered. "To feel what they feel and command their obedience. I didn't want it. Sold all my livestock to keep them out of my head."

And turned to brewing as his profession, Phareth saw, because no animals were involved but also because it ensured a steady supply of beer.

"Her, she liked it. Valdira." Marton all but spat his daughter's name. "She was rotten from the start."

"And the trees?" Anarinda asked in a strained voice.

"Not I," Marton denied feverishly. "That girl, though, she was always in the woods. Who knows what she got up to."

"You never told her to stop?" Nepharyl asked with more than

a tinge of indignation.

Marton roared out an ugly laugh. "Of course I did! For all the use it was. Didn't I say she was blighted from the start? She never listened to anyone."

Marton's face worked, his fists opened and closed, and he panted with rage. From his wild eyes, Phareth could see how easily he could slip into violence. Even Nepharyl realized that he had said too much. The lordling edged away, trying to put the magi between himself and Marton.

"And you punished her?" Phareth asked, carefully trying to redirect the men.

"Beat her good and proper," Marton said, without shame or remorse. "Whenever I caught her, or just when it felt like she was thinking about it. And when her bitch mam cried, I beat her, too. Never did no good, though. They had no respect for me or the law."

"What about Silma?" Telamar asked.

"She made it worse," Marton growled with contempt. "She promised to set the brat on the straight and narrow, but all she did was train her to make the curse stronger. Then we had years of trouble, her stirring up the young men, luring them to her like a bitch in heat. Because Valdira never meant to give up the curse. She liked it when they fought over her. She's a beast at heart, that one."

"Surely…" Anarinda started to protest. She fell silent when Marton wheeled to glare at her.

"When the animals attacked you," Telamar inserted, cold and relentless. "Was that Valdira?"

Unexpectedly, Marton went pale. Phareth caught jumbled images in his memory: snarling eridow, rank animal breath, the flash of white teeth, searing pain as the pack tore into his leg. His own power, so long denied, exploded outward and sent the eridow running, but Marton was left bleeding and hating himself for giving in to the curse.

In present time, sweat trickled over his wasted face. His chin twitched as he nodded.

"She finally grew strong enough to defend herself," Anarinda said, not bothering to hide her disgust. "People in the village were complaining. When you went to discipline her, she called the beasts to save herself."

"It was my duty," Marton snarled back at her. "I didn't want her, but she's my kin. It's my responsibility."

Phareth's head ached with the onslaught of emotions, but he maintained his composure.

"Not anymore," he answered. "The Collegium has sent us. We'll see to it now."

Marton's knuckles clenched white on the tankard handle. His fist trembled, as if he wanted to throw it, but he mastered himself and set the tankard gently on top of the keg.

"Find her," Marton grated out. "Stop her. No one will ever be safe as long as Valdira runs free."

Chapter Eleven

As the magi left Marton's farm, Anarinda's mind crackled with questions. She wanted to find Rhella and ask her about Valdira. Phareth did sense the woman in the house, but she seemed unaware of their presence. He was glad. He already had so many conflicting viewpoints and extreme emotions to absorb, he thought his brain would crack open if he had to make room for one more person's ideas.

If Anarinda broadcast her frustration, Telamar was a coldly brooding blank. Nepharyl radiated his own fears and suspicions. Phareth, meanwhile, tried to bring the bigger picture into focus. Gritl had painted Marton as a brute. His own words confirmed it, yet Marton was also a tortured soul, driven to violence when everything in his life went wrong. Gritl and Marton both called Valdira a beast, while Evritt knew her as a temptress. Which of these images was real?

Phareth was almost glad to have his thoughts interrupted when Telamar remarked, "Too bad Marton couldn't tell us where the girl is right now."

"Valdira!" Anarinda snapped back. "And you can't blame her for hiding."

"Nor do I." Nepharyl shuddered dramatically. "Peasant or not, that's a scary man."

"He's an untrained magus," Phareth said, in case the other magi hadn't figured it out.

"I thought as much," Telamar said.

"Is that the curse he was talking about?" Nepharyl demanded. Phareth nodded and the nobleman frowned in alarm. "That's unsanctioned magic. Should we arrest him?"

Telamar answered with a bleak chuckle. "I wouldn't want to try it."

"The village might safer without him," Anarinda countered.

Phareth glanced at the nobleman, watching worry and indignation flit around in his mind. This wasn't the job Guilberta had sent Nepharyl to do. He could send for another group of inquisitors, but that might take weeks. Meanwhile, a dangerous, illegal sorcerer would be at large. What would the countess expect Nepharyl to do about it?

Inside himself, Phareth muffled a sigh. Nepharyl and his spying was just one more problem he had to solve. Telamar's shields couldn't hide his distaste at the thought of returning to the village empty-handed, and Anarinda was still spitting mental sparks after meeting Marton. Phareth wasn't sure what to do, yet, but he didn't want the villagers to see them so confused and upset.

"Let's stop here." He suited action to words by halting in the middle of the dusty track. Telamar scowled and Nepharyl scratched. Even Anarinda looked charmingly impatient.

"Have you detected something?" she asked.

"We need to plan," Phareth said, "and I hope we can all agree it would be better to talk here, where no one can see us. Besides," he added flippantly, "it's shady here."

"There is that." Nepharyl sat, loosening his jacket, though Phareth still saw resentment and suspicion in his thoughts. A low stone wall stood between one of Yorec's onion fields and the copse of trees. Anarinda brushed the top lightly before she settled, dainty as a bird on a branch. Only Telamar stood tall and stiff, his gray eyes hooded.

"Perhaps you'd like to start," he with chilly courtesy. "You haven't said whether you learned anything new from Marton. Since the…Valdira grew up there, I would think you could detect her traces."

"Marton's presence was a distraction," Phareth admitted, "but never fear. Now that I've met him, I can find his daughter. Their auras will be much alike. What we need to decide is how to approach her and Ryamon."

"I suppose talking is out of the question." Anarinda shot an accusing glance in Telamar's direction.

"Her father said she doesn't listen to talk," the Ice magus replied.

"He only talked with his fists," Anarinda flared.

"Even considering that," Nepharyl interrupted, "it will take too much time to try. Now, Lady Magus," he said to Anarinda, "you can make it rain, can't you? If they have a Fire magus, we want to wet the forest down."

Phareth caught quick flash of contempt from Telamar, that Nepharyl thought he was so clever. He had no idea the magi had already discussed this tactic.

"Of course, my lord," Anarinda said, calmer now. "It will take me several hours to prepare. The weather has been dry, and we're far inland. I'll have to shape the wind to bring in moist air from the sea. Although, if Phareth will agree to help, he can pass the word back to Polvest. I'm sure the Storm Lord would be willing to assign a few initiates to speed the work along."

"My pleasure," Phareth said.

Anarinda nodded, then added, "I might as well tell you that I can't use my full power here."

Nepharyl frowned, discontented.

"What limits you?" Phareth asked.

The Storm magus gestured over the wall, where onion stalks swayed in a gentle breeze. "It's almost harvest time. A light rain won't hurt anything, but a hailstorm or a tornado would be too dangerous. I can't do anything that might harm the people or ruin their crops."

"Surely this is an exception," Nepharyl argued.

"I must be true to my vow." Anarinda's voice was soft and apologetic, but Phareth felt a core of steel inside her.

"Let no one question it," Telamar said. "For my part, I can help reduce the fire danger by drawing in cold air from the mountains. This will also take time, but not as long; the mountains are closer than the sea. It will also enhance the power of my own spells."

"And it may take a while for Phareth to locate your targets," Nepharyl mused. "If you all start at once, that works."

"Except for one thing," Phareth put in. "My lord, you must remain here, in Lornest."

"I will not!" Nepharyl protested. His mind whirled with angry thoughts, sharp as thrown daggers.

"You must," Phareth repeated. He had no intention of letting some toady tell the magi what to do. "It's for your own safety. We magi have our powers to protect us. You, my lord, have no such defense. I would not place you in harm's way."

"But I must go," Nepharyl insisted. "I must observe…" He broke off, realizing what he had been about to say.

"We know why you came," Telamar told him flatly. "It's only logical to assume part of your duty is to assure we operate within the bounds of the law."

"I'm sure Countess Guilberta wouldn't want you to be in danger," Anarinda added.

"Quite so," Phareth agreed. He could feel Nepharyl's anger weaken. Once again, Guilberta's name carried weight.

Phareth went on, "More important than that, I need you in Lornest as our anchor point. We'll be heading into wild country." He swept an open hand toward the west, taking in the rugged hills beyond Yorec's farm. "We're sure to get lost, but I can find our way back by seeking your mind. If one of us is injured, you can guide a rescue party. If the worse happens and we all disappear, you'll be able to report it more quickly."

"But I'm part of the team." All at once, Nepharyl sounded like a whiny child. "I want to help."

With some difficulty, Phareth held back a sarcastic laugh. Nepharyl was a last-minute addition, sent along solely to spy for the king. He had never been one of them. Fortunately, Anarinda spoke before Phareth did.

"We do need your help," she said sensibly. "Each of us must do his part if our mission is to succeed. Your part is to support us here in Lornest."

"Or," Telamar said, "Phareth can force you to do as you're told."

"You wouldn't dare!" Nepharyl sputtered.

"I would rather not have to," Phareth answered. He didn't appreciate Telamar using his powers as a threat. It was exactly the kind of thing non-magi feared the most. Yet Phareth also knew they wouldn't get Nepharyl to cooperate unless they presented a united front.

"Please listen to reason, my lord," Anarinda said. Her doll-like face radiated sincerity. "I know it must be hard to trust us, given the history of sorcery in our land, but that is what we need most: your trust. We have all taken vows to our own orders. Among those is the sacred promise to protect Arkanost and uphold its laws. If you have come to know us during our journey, you should be able to believe that none of us will take any action we know King Sedlin or Countess Guilberta would not approve."

Phareth, watching, tried to keep a sober and respectable face. That was clever of Anarinda, repeating Guilberta's name. Much better than Telamar's clumsy threat, because it worked.

"All right," Nepharyl sighed. "I'll stay behind." His shoulders sagged with defeat, but he drew the comfort of his patroness' approval around him like a warm cloak. Then he flared, "But I expect you to keep me informed!"

"Certainly," Phareth replied.

Nepharyl nodded, a sulky jerk. His mind still fluttered with panic at the idea of being controlled. The fear seemed out of proportion with Telamar's threat, but the matter was settled and Phareth wasn't in the mood to ask questions. At last they could begin their real job: finding the rogue magi.

"If we're all agreed," Phareth said, "we might as well get started."

~ * ~

A wind moaned through the rocky crown of the ridge above Ryamon. He stopped walking to listen. He was used to the rustling noise the trees always made when Valdira was nearby. This was different, a foreboding steady whistle. The change made him nervous.

Change. He and Valdira hadn't stayed at the rock shelter since he changed it. Looking on his work with unbiased eyes, Ryamon had recognized part of his mistake. It was a proper house now, spacious and secure, but the bare walls echoed with every step. Rhella's generous gifts only made the emptiness more obvious. Their possessions were so pitifully few. How could they hope to survive a mountain winter with a turtle shell, a wicker basket, worn clothing, a dull knife?

But retreat was not possible, so Ryamon had to make some furniture. To do that, he needed flint. As soon as he mentioned it, Valdira had been eager to start prospecting. She had packed a few more things and they were off. Ryamon was so glad to see her recover her personality, he didn't even mind carrying the heavy basket.

After a week of roaming, searching for flint, they were farther from Lornest than Ryamon had ever been. Mountains loomed before them, but they weren't the sturdy peaks Ryamon had imagined. A broken land lay ahead of them, great slabs of rock tilted skyward. Exposed layers painted the sides with ocher and cream. All the jutting rocks pointed south.

He folded his hands for a moment, focusing his mage-trained senses. Whatever he sensed, it wasn't in the rocks. Nor was there any fire nearby. Yet the air tingled with power.

Here in the hills, wind usually came in broken gusts reflected from one rock face or another. This wind flowed without stopping. It tugged at branches and raised a veil of fine dust. And—he breathed deeply—it carried cold air from those peaks in the south.

Long ago, when he had been a boy, he had heard a wind like this. It had been a clear day, the mountains of Dalgest blazing white with snow. He hadn't understood why all the adults hurried the sobi into their sheds and set the older boys to cutting extra firewood. A blizzard had struck the village before nightfall and lasted for six days.

Under this cool wind, Ryamon felt the same expectancy in the air. A storm was coming. He peered through the trees toward where he thought Lornest was. In the hazy distance, white clumps dotted the horizon. Clouds.

Ryamon turned to look for his lover. Valdira had been just down the hill, gathering raspberries. Now she stood up from the berry patch, listening alertly. Ryamon picked his way down the slope toward her.

"I haven't lived through a summer here," he remarked when he was close enough, "but is it normal to have snow at this time of year? Because if this was Dalgest, I'd say we're going to get some."

"No," Valdira answered, absently pulling one sleeve loose from a bramble. "Rain, maybe, but not snow."

"I was afraid of that," he said.

They looked at each other, needing no more words. If a storm was on the way, it was being brought by magic. And that meant the Collegium was coming.

Valdira's eyes flashed with defiance. "Give me a moment."

She strode out of the raspberry thicket, and this time none of the thorns snagged her dress. She knelt to slap her palm against the ground, the way she had done when Ryamon was trapped in the mire. A faint prickle ran over his skin, and a whisper that wasn't truly sound tickled inside his ears. Valdira was using her magic. Last time, she had called a shorbak. What was she summoning now?

Ryamon paced nearby, trying not to make any noise that would disrupt her trance. He watched the rocky ridge for signs of danger. There was no reason to panic, he told himself. He and Valdira were far from Lornest. Far from anywhere, really. Whoever was coming would have a long trek to reach them. Maybe they would wear themselves out.

On the other hand, he had to admit the inquisitors would find them eventually. Even Ryamon had been able to find Valdira, and he had been a wretched excuse for a magus. They might be found sooner than he expected. Still, unless the inquisitors were already well out in the wilderness, it wouldn't happen today.

They did have time. A few days. Valdira was powerful and she had the advantage of unknown abilities. The Collegium magi would have a general idea of everything Ryamon could do, but they wouldn't be able to predict Valdira. She would give them a hard battle.

Even so, Ryamon was the thinker of the two. He had to be smart, try to plan—and hope Valdira would listen to him.

"Huh," Valdira muttered. Ryamon whirled toward her. "Four of them, three men and one woman. They're standing in the trees, like they don't even know that helps me. I think they're near my da's house."

"Can you see their robes?" Ryamon asked. If he knew what orders the other magi belonged to, it might help him think of a strategy.

"They aren't wearing any." Valdira frowned to herself. "One of them has black breeches and a long jacket. The others have matching jackets, not as fancy. None of them have robes. I thought that was against the law?" She glanced up at Ryamon, who shrugged. "They're definitely the source of what we sensed. I can tell from how they're standing there, concentrating."

"Does the black jacket have lots of lace?" Ryamon asked, trying to piece these details together. Valdira nodded. "He's a nobleman. I guess he must be in charge. I don't know why the magi are out of uniform. Maybe they're in disguise. Can you see any other details?"

Valdira was silent, but then she said, "The fronts of... Oh!"

She jumped and fell sideways, one hand flung out for balance. Ryamon grabbed her elbow to steady her.

"What's wrong?" he demanded.

~ * ~

Phareth stood in the shade of the trees. Sending Anarinda's message had only taken a few minutes. He had also requested time for a longer consultation with Murcrys in the evening. The rest of his searching had to wait until the other magi finished, so he shielded lightly against the invisible storm of magic that swirled around him.

Telamar's power felt like a cool draft, unexpected in summer's heat. Anarinda emitted a sharper tingle. Nepharyl slouched on the wall, feeling sorry for himself.

Among so many currents of power, Phareth almost didn't notice the intruder. Slowly he recognized that another magic had penetrated the grove. The new presence was sleek and stealthy, yet muscular. Phareth stretched his arms casually, faked a yawn, wandered a few steps as if bored. He looked around casually. The unfamiliar power felt close, yet spread out. As if there wasn't one active source, but many.

The stone wall was to the west, with the onion field beyond it. A grove of birch trees grew up the hill to the east. Anarinda's wind blew a hiss through the leaves. Slim, straight white trunks blended together in the dappled light, so many that they confused the eye. Anything could be in there and he wouldn't see it.

What had Marton said? That his mind joined with animals and he felt what they felt. Phareth didn't see any creatures moving, but that didn't mean nothing was there. He breathed lightly, extending his senses with slow caution as if he himself was a beast stalking its prey.

Phareth scanned the area. The intruder was everywhere, yet nowhere. His gaze ran over a broken stump, then jerked back. The shape was wrong somehow. He squinted. The stump blinked. Suddenly it came into focus. The 'stump' was a small feline with yellow eyes and tufted ears. Its coat was dusty brown flecked with black, perfect camouflage against the fallen leaves that covered the ground.

They stared at each other. If Valdira was using the animal to watch them, that meant Phareth could attack her through it. He probed hard. There was a moment of contact, the startled awareness of another mind behind the bobcat's. He tried to pin the stranger, to dominate her will and bring her under his control. The rogue magus exploded in his mind, twisting and lashing back at him with animal ferocity.

"Ouch!" Phareth cried out in pain. Valdira wrenched away. He blinked back to himself. In the birch grove, the bobcat vanished in a flurry of dry leaves.

"What's wrong?" Nepharyl demanded.

And Telamar asked, "Got something?"

Phareth rubbed his forehead, recovering his composure. Only Anarinda didn't stare at him. Her eyes were still unfocused as she held her trance.

"Valdira," Phareth told them. "She knows we're here."

Telamar looked thoughtfully in the direction the bobcat had run. "That was fast."

Phareth nodded, understanding what he meant. So far, the magi had done nothing but move air, yet Valdira had noticed them right away.

"Should we go back to the village?" Nepharyl asked nervously.

"No need," Phareth said. "She was just watching. We tangled, but it was nothing. I'll sense it if she tries to spy on us again."

"As long as you're sure," Nepharyl grumbled. He reached behind himself to scratch again, and brooded over Yorec's onion field.

Phareth could still feel Nepharyl's annoyance that he couldn't go with the magi. Also that he had to spend more time with Tyteb, whose company was beneath him and whose hospitality was so lacking. Nepharyl preferred a long, hard hike to any more bug bites. Of course, Phareth thought sarcastically, it was easier to think about hiking than to actually do it.

Phareth settled back to consider his psychic skirmish with Valdira. His first direct contact wasn't what he had expected. Gritl and Marton called her a beast. That wasn't wrong, but neither was it true in the way they meant. She wasn't wild and undisciplined. She was strong. His attack hadn't frightened her. Nor was she insane. Compared to Marton, she seemed quite stable.

Further, Phareth had the impression Valdira wasn't very close to Lornest. That meant she could extent her power over a distance. She was very alert to have sensed them from afar. Phareth rubbed his forehead again. Her psychic strike had left him with a slight headache. He hadn't expected her to fight back, so he hadn't kept his shields up. It wouldn't happen a second time.

Nepharyl suddenly sat straighter, distracting Phareth. The nobleman stared toward Yorec's farm. The stone cottage was shuttered, its chimney smokeless. Little birds hopped around the dusty yard. Nepharyl jumped to his feet.

"I have an idea," he announced. He strode off, cane under his arm, before anyone could object.

"Now what?" Telamar murmured.

Phareth lifted one shoulder. Nepharyl marched along smartly, trying not to stumble in the furrows as he cut across Yoreck's onion field. The confused farmer bowed anxiously.

"I think I know what he has in mind," Phareth said. "You said Yorec moved his family into town. That means this house is empty. Nepharyl wants to rent it to use as a base."

Telamar considered. Even Anarinda looked around with some interest.

"It seems roomy," she commented, "and it will be private."

Phareth watched for a moment as Yorec led Nepharyl toward the vacant farmhouse. The way he held his cane was both ridiculous and grand. Phareth didn't want to like Nepharyl, but there were days when he just couldn't help it.

"Sometimes he impresses me," Phareth admitted. "We need a safe place to store our supplies. The chariots will fit in that shed, and the ornyxes can stay with Tyteb for the time being. It's not a bad idea."

"What if Yorec has bed bugs?" Telamar asked with cool humor.

Phareth chuckled. "Nepharyl can see to it. We'll need someone to cook and clean, and he should enjoy bossing the staff around."

"It will keep him busy while we're gone," Anarinda added quietly.

"Exactly." Phareth smiled. Finally, their search was having some results

~ * ~

"Sweetheart?" Ryamon persisted. "Are you all right?"

"I'm fine." Valdira straightened, rubbing at the back of her neck. "One of them saw me. He tried some kind of mental hold, but I broke it."

"Thank goodness," Ryamon said. For some reason, he had never thought the Collegium magi could really hurt Valdira. It was foolish, of course, but he didn't know what he would do without her.

Then the meaning of her words penetrated his alarm. He asked, "Was it a Shadow magus?"

Valdira nodded. "I wish he hadn't seen me, but at least I got a good look at them. It isn't easy to tell, but their jackets have colored linings. The one who spotted me has black lapels. The other man's are white, and the woman's bodice is trimmed with yellow."

"Then we know what we're up against," Ryamon said.

The Storm magus was probably the most dangerous. Ryamon had heard many tales about how lethal that order could be. The Ice magus was less of a problem, since the summer heat would work against him. In a way, the Shadow magus was the worst. He wouldn't be much of a threat physically, but they wouldn't be able to get rid of him once he caught their trail. At least, not without getting physical themselves. That was something Ryamon didn't want to think about. Not yet.

"Well," Valdira said with a wry smile, "I guess we might get that snow after all."

"Then we'd better find shelter," Ryamon said.

They moved fast, staying close together. Valdira summoned an elgus from somewhere nearby and used it to search from the air. Ryamon ducked under ledges and between boulders, hoping to find a good camp site without shaping the stone. Any magic he used would draw the other magi, and he saw no reason to help them.

Eventually they found a natural overhang near a small lake. There would be mosquitoes, but a bit of smoke would hold them at bay. Ryamon scraped out a fire pit and hurried up and down the slope, gathering wood and cutting it into useable pieces. Valdira found branches for bedding. She set up a snare and found more berries.

It struck him as absurd to do all these mundane chores when their foes were on their trail. Yet he knew they still needed to rest and eat. All the while, the wind whistled in the reeds on the lake shore. Clouds drifted closer and darker, closing in on them like vultures.

Chapter Twelve

A thin tang of wet dust flavored the air as night settled over the hills. Rain hung a sheer curtain over the rock shelter's opening. Ryamon shaped the stone at the back just enough to make a shelf, where he placed a small oil lamp. He concentrated and the wick flared into life, a golden pearl in the shadows. This was Rhella's gift to them: light. It made the raindrops glimmer against the darkness outside.

The night was getting cold. Ryamon was aware of the faint mist from his breath, though he didn't truly feel the chill. His inner fire protected him. He glanced toward the crude hearth, where Valdira crouched with her arms wrapped around her knees.

"Are you cold?" he asked quietly.

"It's all right," she said. Valdira seemed intent, focused on her own thoughts, but her voice held a faint tremor.

Ryamon knelt and put his arm over her shoulders. Ever so gently, he summoned the fire in his heart, creating warmth he could share. After a moment, she relaxed. The evening meal had been quiet, and not nearly enough of it. Ryamon was used to being a little bit hungry, out here in the hills, but tonight it worried him. Maybe the silence as much as the hunger. Valdira didn't want to talk, he could tell. On a normal night, he would have let her have her way and waited until she felt like speaking.

This night wasn't normal, as the chill in the air demonstrated. They had only a few days—no time to waste. It would take more than hope or denial to save them from the Collegium.

"What do you think they're planning?" he asked.

Ryamon felt Valdira's irritation that he wouldn't let her brood in peace.

"I didn't get any details," she bit out. "That Shadow magus tried to take over my mind! I'd guess they're wetting down the forest to keep you from burning it around their ears."

"I wouldn't do that," Ryamon protested. "It's your forest. That would be like attacking you."

Valdira rewarded him with a strange smile. He wanted to kiss her, bring humanity back into her eyes, but he was afraid to try it.

"Can I ask something?" Ryamon hesitated, not sure how to put his question into words.

"What I'll do to them?" The hint of darkness was stronger in her eyes.

"No," he answered, puzzled that she would think of that. "I wonder how bound you are to this place, your forest. If we have to flee, will you lose some of your power?"

He felt the prickle of anger even as she cried, "I'm not leaving!"

"If it means being captured," he reasoned.

"This is my home," Valdira insisted, her fey mood replaced by determination. "I won't be chased away!"

It was exactly what Ryamon expected her to say, though he wished she would at least consider some alternatives.

"All right, then we'll fight," he said. "And I'll be at your side."

Valdira regarded him, one eyebrow angled upward. "But?"

This was what he had been trying to avoid thinking about. When he joined with Fire, it wasn't because he craved violence. Even so, he knew his natural element could be deadly.

"How hard do we fight?" Ryamon made himself ask the question. "Am I allowed to burn the forest? A tree or two, to slow them down? And what about the magi? Do I burn them?"

"Are you afraid to?" Valdira challenged.

Ryamon looked into her eyes, appalled by her ruthlessness and yet understanding it. Valdira knew, even better than Ryamon, that important things must be fought for. Things like freedom and one's true Element.

"I don't want to," he said honestly. "As a Blood magus, won't you feel their pain if I burn them?"

"Only if I choose to." She was silent for a moment, then unexpectedly said, "I don't want to fight, either. I just want them to go away. But I think we'll have to do it. They're city folk, right? They won't like pain. If we make it hurt to bother us, then they'll go away."

"I'm city folk, and I stayed." Ryamon said, stung by her assessment.

"I know." Valdira answered softly. Her shoulder dug into his side as she shrugged. She didn't look at him. She seemed focused on the fire flickering in its pit. Ryamon felt emotion moving in her, some fear or regret he couldn't identify.

"This isn't your fight, you know," she said to the fire. "I'm the one they want. If you'd rather surrender…"

"No!" Ryamon burst out. He didn't want the escape she offered. "I won't leave without you. If you're staying to fight, then so will I."

"Not so much!" Valdira shifted, pushing his arm away from her body.

"Sorry," Ryamon mumbled. He had forgotten how heat boiled within him when he got upset. The last thing he wanted was to burn Valdira. He breathed deeply, controlling his emotions.

After a moment, he joked, "You know what a tenderfoot I am. I couldn't find my way back to anywhere without you."

"I know," she agreed. "You're hopeless."

"Hopelessly in love with you," he answered.

Valdira looked up at Ryamon with the mocking smile that always set his heart on fire. The invitation in her eyes was unmistakable. This time he didn't hesitate to kiss her. Whatever uncertainty he had sensed before was gone, swept away by rush of their desires.

On their bed of pine branches, Ryamon did not feel the prick of needles or the occasional waft of rain from outside. Only Valdira mattered, her legs wrapped around him in the passion that blazed so brightly. The Collegium might try to separate them, but Ryamon would never give her up. More even than fire and freedom, this kind of love was worth fighting for.

~ * ~

Despite Telamar's misgivings, the farmhouse was in good condition. In the loft, Phareth listened to rain slithering over the thatched roof. At least there were no leaks—and no bed bugs. Actually, there were no beds. Yorec's family had taken their furniture with them. Sleeping on floorboards was no worse than sleeping along a dusty trail, however.

Phareth and Telamar shared the loft, but Telamar had reluctantly granted Phareth a few minutes of privacy to contact his order. Now he sat cross-legged on his bed roll, eyes closed, breathing lightly. Far away, in Polvest, half a dozen magi snapped to alertness as his probe touched them. Tendrils of thought came in reply, then dropped away as they learned he wasn't looking for them. Phareth felt something like a handshake from Gallitaw, and then Murcrys reached back to him.

"*What news?*"

"*Everyone has an opinion,*" Phareth said, and he launched into his report. First; he repeated the rumors among the villagers, which of them he could confirm and which he couldn't. Then he told Marton's story, and ended with his encounter with Valdira. "*The Blood magus who trained her is the only one we didn't talk to.*"

"*Interesting,*" Murcrys said at the end. "*So Valdira's gift is hereditary?*"

"*That's what Marton said. Does it make a difference?*"

"*It may.*" Murcrys spoke slowly, thinking it through as she went. "*If one person acquires a new Element, that's an aberration and must be rejected. Yet when several people develop the same Element, even if it's rare…*"

"*It still wouldn't be part of the Seven Exalted Orders,*" Phareth pointed out.

"*Magic is mysterious,*" Murcrys replied. "*Even now we don't understand all it can do. And I don't believe we should be too quick to reject new ideas only because they are new. If the girl's power breeds true, we'll have to deal with it sooner or later.*"

"*What do you think the Collegium will do?*" Phareth asked.

"*I guess I'll have to ask them,*" Murcrys answered with a sweet sting. "*It will be my turn to call a full session.*"

"*Salovik will be thrilled, I'm sure.*"

Phareth felt his mother's sarcastic chuckle. Then she said, "*You said you sparred with the girl. What did you think of her?*"

"*Valdira,*" Phareth corrected automatically.

"*What?*"

"*Anarinda wants us to call her by name.*"

"*Really.*" Murcrys sounded thoughtful.

Phareth went on, "*It's a rough comparison, but I would say she's equivalent to an Initiate. She hasn't tried to deny her magic, as Marton does. She's used it a lot, she's sure of what she can do. Rather like the three of us, actually,*" he said, meaning the magi presently in Lornest. "*Ryamon is probably weaker because he struggled with his Element.*"

As he explained, Phareth felt his mother probing. His instinct was to raise shields and resist, but he controlled the impulse. He had nothing to hide from his Mage Lord. On the other hand, he didn't have to tolerate mental intrusions like some untrained novice.

"*Is there something else you want to know, Mother?*" he asked boldly.

"*Whatever it is you're not telling me,*" Murcrys shot back. She didn't like being corrected, yet Phareth sensed she was pleased that he confronted her snooping.

"All right. I'm not sure we can trust Anarinda."

"Oh?" Murcrys she stopped probing to focus on what Phareth was telling her.

"I know Klaive is your friend," he said cautiously, *"but Anarinda has really taken Valdira's side. She was upset by meeting Marton—and I don't like him either, I have to say—and she insists on treating Valdira with respect, as if she was one of us. I don't know what she'll do when it comes to battle."*

"Shouldn't you respect your opponent?" Murcrys countered.

"She's…Valdira, that is. She's a lawbreaker," Phareth argued. *"Remember the rumors, that she provokes men to fight over her and lures them away from their wives. That she set wild animals on her own father. How can I respect someone who abuses her powers?"*

"Son," Murcrys cut in, unexpectedly serious. *"You were raised within our tower. As soon as your magic stirred, I was there to explain what it meant and there were many others to help train you. Valdira had no one. She was alone with a power nobody understood. Do you wonder that she's made mistakes?"*

"It isn't a few mistakes," Phareth said, thinking back to Evritt's memory. *"It's a pattern of behavior that doesn't accept boundaries."*

Murcrys brushed that aside. *"Speaking of boundaries, I've been asked to remind you how close to the border you are."*

"I know where the border is," Phareth retorted. Now he did conceal his feelings, the residual shame and fear of entering Costera. Either he succeeded or Murcrys let him get away with it.

"No matter what happens, you must not cross," she said. *"The king won't support any ventures onto foreign soil. Our dear friend Guilberta made that very clear."*

"What if Valdira crosses the border?" Phareth asked. *"If she isn't in our country, she isn't our problem?"*

"If only it were so easy," Murcrys answered drily. *"Costera is always our problem, as you well know. I would rather not drive her into the service of our enemies."*

"Agreed." Darmosh had enough sorcery at his command without adding Valdira to the mix.

"Your instructions are to bring the renegades back," Murcrys went on. *"If you can persuade them to come without fighting, so much the better."*

"I thought Akayel wanted justice," Phareth said.

"Him," Murcrys snorted. *"He's just annoyed having to take responsibility for a magus he didn't choose. However, Akayel is not your Mage Lord. I am, and I want to talk to this woman. It's been decades since a new Element emerged. We need to study it, not crush it."*

Phareth considered. *"That day in Polvest, when we spoke at the Grand Collegium, that's what Salovik didn't understand, isn't it?"*

"Exactly." Murcrys let him feel her pride that he had figured it out. *"Klaive also believes Valdira's abilities should be brought into one of the Seven Exalted Orders. Try to work with Anarinda, because Telamar isn't likely to be as flexible."*

She was probably right, but that still didn't mean Phareth could fully trust any of his comrades.

"What should I tell them?" he asked.

"That the Collegium is discussing the situation and not to do anything fatal," Murcrys said. *"Or whatever else you think will work."*

Phareth smiled to himself. *"Nepharyl would do anything if I told him Guilberta agrees with you."*

"So I hear," Murcrys answered slyly. *"His fascination with the countess has raised a few eyebrows in the capital."*

"He's obsessed with her," Phareth said. *"Have you learned any more about his background?"*

"Guilberta sends him out to a lot of places. Either she trusts him completely, or she doesn't want him around."

"Guilberta doesn't have to keep people around if she doesn't want them," Phareth observed.

"True." Murcrys was silent long enough that Phareth began to wonder if he should end the interview. Finally she said, *"It may be nothing, but Nepharyl was with Sedlin's ambassador, Korwynt, when they visited Estrona."*

"Estrona?" That was an island on the Sea of Sinapos, another wizard kingdom that was strong enough to maintain its neutrality in the ongoing feud between Arkanost and Costera. *"You mean during the negotiations that went so badly?"* He felt his mother's assent. Though any mention of Costera made his blood run cold, Phareth quipped, *"It wasn't my fault."*

"We're discussing Guilberta's lackey, not you," Murcrys snapped, annoyed by the reminder. *"It was five years ago. Nepharyl was only a diplomatic page then, but it could explain why he seems so suspicious of all magi."*

"I suppose," Phareth said.

Over the years, he had heard all sorts of rumors in the Tower of Shadow about what happened to Korwynt and his aides. There had been few survivors, which put Nepharyl in fortunate company. Since then, tensions between Arkanost and Costera had only grown worse. The incident had led, indirectly, to his own debacle in Logoll.

Murcrys interrupted, *"I should go, if you've nothing else to report?"*

He didn't. Murcrys released Phareth, leaving him with more questions than he'd had before. He sighed lightly and opened his eyes. And jumped, startled.

Telamar stood at the top of the ladder up into the loft. He had obviously been there for some while, watching Phareth communicate with his tower. The cool gray eyes showed interest, even amusement, as if the Ice magus had overheard him talking in his sleep.

"Yes?" Phareth suddenly felt ridiculous sitting on the floor.

"I want to go to bed," Telamar replied indifferently. "We're traveling tomorrow, unless you've received new instructions."

"Fine." Phareth ignored the veiled question. He had been trying to overcome Telamar's hostility for the sake of their mission, but moments like this didn't help.

Saying no more, Telamar knelt to lay out his bedding. Phareth felt stiff after sitting motionless through the long conversation. He stretched his arms and lay back on his blankets, hoping the Ice magus wouldn't snore.

~ * ~

Several days later, Phareth looked back on the loft in Yorec's farmhouse with distinct nostalgia. When he had scorned Nepharyl's desire to travel with them, he hadn't considered that he, too, would find a long hike easier to say than do.

There were no trails in the hills, not even game tracks to follow. Nor could they bring pack animals, since Valdira might be able to subvert them. That meant the magi had to carry everything themselves. The terrain was so rough, it was hard to find camp sites. There were plenty of trees to hang tents from, but nowhere to stretch out that rocks or roots didn't poke them; nowhere to build a fire, cook food or heat water for washing.

Carrying out the strategy they had agreed on, Anarinda made it rain every night while Telamar kept the ground frosty. He claimed the temperature didn't bother him. Anarinda didn't mention being uncomfortable, so her element must have protected her, too. Phareth resented being the only one who was damp, cold and muddy. Fortunately, they eased off during the day or travel would have been even more miserable.

Now Phareth struggled along the latest in an endless series of steep hillsides, pushing through brambles and stumbling over loose rocks. The others followed him. No one spoke except to pant with effort. Suddenly Telamar muffled a curse. Phareth turned to see what was wrong. The ice magus rubbed his cheek, where a red welt stood out against his fair skin.

"I'm sorry," Anarinda apologized. She must have let go a branch that whipped back at Telamar.

Ignoring her words, Telamar turned a cold sneer on Phareth. "I thought you said you could find them."

"We're getting closer," Phareth retorted. "Or perhaps you think you can do better."

They glared at each other until Anarinda snapped, "Stop it, both of you. We aren't getting anywhere standing here. Let's keep moving."

Phareth shrugged and turned away with an irritable jerk. He struggled onward, though the hills were steep and the rocks slippery. It was better than trying to get through the dense forest.

Even Anarinda didn't understand. Finding the renegades should have been easy, but it wasn't. Not that he couldn't sense Valdira—her presence seemed to radiate from every tree—but there were so many of them. He had never imagined there could be this many trees growing so close together. Because her aura was everywhere, Phareth couldn't pinpoint Valdira's actual location.

Then there was the forest itself, which surrounded them like a living wall. Huge conifers hung curtains of sharp needles in every direction. The magi pushed through the trees toward what should have been clear ground, only to confront another solid wall of greenery. Half the time, Phareth couldn't even see the sun to keep his directions straight.

Even when there was no wind, the branches constantly rustled and swayed. The susurrus grated on his nerves. Phareth remembered thinking, back in Polvest, that the tower garden was peaceful because plants didn't think. Yet he couldn't deny what he sensed. The trees did have awareness, though an alien one. They knew why the magi were there. And the trees felt emotion: hostile to the magi, protective of Valdira. They were doing their best to slow the magi and divert them from their course. Phareth was starting to think a nice forest fire might be the answer after all.

Lungs aching, legs burning, he finally led the others to the rocky crown of a hill. "Take a breather," he said.

Leaning against the nearest boulder, Phareth caught the end of a sour glance from Telamar. The Ice magus was too tired to block well. He clearly thought Phareth was delaying on purpose, enjoying a lovely view of the woodlands. The Shadow magus felt his scalp prickle with irritation. Or maybe it was just sweat.

Anarinda pulled a waterskin over her head and drank deeply before offering it to Telamar. "Water?"

"Thanks," he grunted.

Phareth sensed Anarinda's annoyance at Telamar's coldness. All this hiking was hard work. The magi were tired. That was why they were all so cranky. If she hadn't been maintaining the cloud cover, Phareth was sure they would have been even hotter and in worse moods.

"Water?" Anarinda broke into his thoughts.

"Thank you." Phareth drank gratefully, though the fluid had a slightly musty flavor. He returned the skin with a small bow.

After several days in the woods, all of them looked rumpled and dirty. Nepharyl's brown suits were looking like a practical solution, as they showed less mud. Long hair, a sign of status in the cities of Arkanost, was hard to take care of out here. The two men had soon tied theirs back into ponytails. Even Anarinda had given in and plaited her golden curls into a neat crown.

Movement caught Phareth's eye as he looked over the landscape. High above the hilltop, a bird turned lazily in the air. It was a big one, an elgus or perhaps a condor. Another of Valdira's spies? He couldn't tell. Farther off, mountains rose in a jagged line, the rows overlapped like a shark's teeth.

Phareth felt a moment's alarm when he saw how close they were coming. Those mountains were the border. Was this a ploy of Valdira's, challenging them to follow her? How could she know he had orders not to cross into Costera?

Phareth stared at the mountains without seeing them. He gritted his teeth in frustration. If only he could find her! It was bad enough to be eluded by an untrained rogue, but he couldn't believe they were being held off by trees. He was tempted to call on Murcrys for advice, but the situation was ridiculous. He couldn't face the embarrassment.

Strangely, thinking of his mother steadied Phareth. Murcrys had sent him here to do a job. She wouldn't expect him to give up so easily. He could practically hear her saying, *"If what you're trying isn't working, stop it! And try something else."*

He closed his eyes to shut out Telamar's suspicious regard.

Try something else. What could he do differently?

With his mind magic, he had quickly found the cabin Ryamon built. It was nice work, well laid out and hidden by trees. In a way, it was sad the couple would never get to use it. Locating it was about the last thing that had gone right for Phareth. The farther into the woods they got, the stronger Valdira's aura became. By now, it was strong enough to cover up even Ryamon's traces.

He sighed to himself. Ryamon. Somehow he had managed to find Valdira out in this wilderness. How had he done it, and why couldn't Phareth do the same? After all, he was a Shadow magus, his mind honed to perfection. Ryamon was nothing but a half-trained novice.

Half-trained.

The phrase echoed in Phareth's mind, halting the baffled grind of his thoughts. Maybe that was the problem. Ryamon had only basic skills, while Phareth was so skilled and sensitive he felt every trace of every personality in the area. Maybe what they needed was someone *less* trained, someone able to sense only the strongest vibrations.

He opened his eyes. Anarinda sat on a nearby rock, chewing a bit of jerky. Telamar stared at Phareth with open impatience. As before, Phareth held back a rush of annoyance that the Ice magus was so quick to find fault. Yet if his idea was to work, he couldn't let that influence him.

"Telamar," he said through gritted teeth, "I need your help."

~ * ~

Ryamon and Valdira remained at their new rock shelter, leaving only to search for food and staying close to each other at all times. Ryamon had thought they might try to get farther away from their enemies, but Valdira showed no interest in moving. He didn't argue with her decision. Even though she had sworn she wouldn't run away, he still had a hunch they would have to break for safety in Costera.

Valdira spent a lot of time crouched with her hands on the ground. Ryamon assumed she was communing with the creatures of the forest. He built another weir and caught a few small fish, then spent hours practicing how to release heat through his hands. He wanted to cook the fish without fire. This would mean no smoke to give their position away. Mostly he burned the fish. At least it gave him something to do besides jump at every noise.

Despite this, Ryamon felt his tension increasing as the morning wore on. It was still damp, the air harsh with last night's chill rain. A heavy overcast added to his sense of foreboding. No wind blew, yet the treetops rustled and churned. The faces he glimpsed there were angry, but also worried.

Ryamon glanced at Valdira, making sure he knew where she was. At the same moment, she looked over to him. Neither one spoke, until finally Ryamon couldn't stand the silence.

"Are they getting close?"

She nodded, her lips pinched into a thin line. "I'm going to have to get pushy."

Ryamon fought the urge to tell her to be careful. That would be stupid, and Valdira wouldn't listen anyway. She knelt, pressing one hand flat to the ground. The other made an odd circling in the air before her.

Moments passed. Then, somewhere in the distance, eridow began to howl. It sounded like dozens of them, barking and shrieking up and down scales in a whirl of noise. It was hard to tell, but he thought they were north of the rock shelter. Ryamon knew eridow lived in packs, sometimes more than 20 animals. He thought of the big canines charging through the woods, weaving between trees, closing in on their quarry. He almost felt sorry for the magi.

Ryamon wanted to ask, *"Do you have to?"* But that was stupid, too.

Valdira did have to send the eridow. They both knew why. There was no more time to delay this battle. The day he had been dreading was here.

Chapter Thirteen

It galled Phareth to admit that another magus could search more effectively. Especially Telamar, whose suspicion prickled through his patchy defenses. He still thought Phareth's confusion was a ruse, though Phareth had no idea what benefit Telamar saw in not completing an assigned task. Anarinda's pitying expression didn't help, either, but at least he had some assurance of her friendship.

At first, Telamar's progress was no faster than Phareth's had been. The forest was still dense and the hills were just as steep. Yet as the Ice magus settled into his new role, he chose his direction with increased confidence. Circling bramble patches and crossing streams, he headed always south. Like Phareth, Telamar stayed on rocky ground when he could. The trees creaked and swayed, dropping pinecones on their heads, but they couldn't stop the magi.

Near mid-morning, they emerged on a knoll overlooking a shallow valley. At last no more trees surrounded them. A small lake reflected the rocky bluff on the far side. Its dark waters were marked by the bright wakes of swimming birds. The valley continued on past the bluff, curving southeast between the ragged peaks.

"It feels like she's close," Telamar said. "We might be able to spot them from here."

Phareth told himself not to let the Ice magus' success grate on his nerves. Finding their quarry was the most important thing. At that moment, distant howling came to their ears.

"Eridow?" Anarinda sounded nervous. No doubt she, like Phareth, remembered the stories they had heard of wild animals attacking Valdira's father.

"Do you think it's her?" Telamar asked.

"Probably," Phareth replied. "Maybe we'd better hurry."

"You first," Telamar retorted.

He pointed to the rugged slope before them. Rocks jutted every which-way, with no clear path. Phareth was glad it wasn't raining. As if to mock him, a grumble of thunder echoed over their heads.

"That won't help," he told Anarinda.

He tried to be polite, but she turned stormy eyes on him. "My tower is still pushing moisture in from the sea. How long do you think it can stack up with nothing happening?"

"Don't blame her because your magic is useless," Telamar added.

Phareth had just about had enough of the stubborn, obstructionist Ice magus.

"If you're looking for a fight—" he let the challenge hang for a moment "—help me find Valdira."

He started to pick his way down the treacherous slope.

~ * ~

Ryamon busied himself packing, dividing their belongings between his waypack and Valdira's basket. It was depressing how little they had.

The less we have to carry, the faster we can run, he told himself.

"There they are," Valdira announced from just outside the overhang.

"Where?" Ryamon stepped toward her, but her head snapped around.

"Stand still or they'll spot you!"

"Sorry," he muttered.

Ryamon searched the rocky valley with his eyes. He frowned. Hadn't there been more trees yesterday? Only a dark fringe circled the valley, leaving open ground around the lake. They trees must have moved, crowding in between Valdira and her enemies. People on foot could still walk faster than trees, however. Once they got through the living wall, they would be here all too quickly.

Ryamon finally picked out a scratch of movement across the valley. Two distant figures stood at the top of a knoll. A third was trying to scramble down. Their brown clothing blended into the rocks, making them hard to see.

"I thought there were four of them," he said.

Valdira shrugged. "The nobleman must be staying out of the way. It's only the magi now."

Ryamon wasn't sure if that was helpful or not. He asked, "What should we do?"

Her lips curved in a grim smile. "Change their minds about coming any closer."

~ * ~

Phareth picked his way between the boulders, moving slowly to keep his balance. A fall on this rough ground could end the battle before it began. Eridow were still wailing in the distance. He paused, trying to judge how close they were. Echoes bounced off the rocks until the beasts seemed to be on every side.

Distracted by the howling, he failed to perceive the real threat until Anarinda gave a yelp of pain.

"What's wrong?" he called back up to them. Up above, he heard a new noise, something he couldn't name that still made his skin crawl.

On the brow of the hill, Telamar was cursing. Anarinda whirled, ducked, slapping at her arms, her shoulders and hair. Phareth couldn't see anything, but the Storm magus continued to cry out.

"Ow!" she cried. "Get them off! Oh!"

Frustrated, Phareth reached for her mind. He sensed Anarinda's pain, a dozen points that throbbed and burned. Through her ears he heard it more clearly: the low hum of angry bees. Now that he knew, he could see hundreds of golden motes crawling over the magi's clothes. More swirling in the air around them.

Phareth stayed where he was for a moment, pinned by surprise. Since these creatures had no minds, his Shadow powers were useless against them. The bees hadn't come after him yet, but that wouldn't last.

On the hilltop, Anarinda whirled and slapped, trying to brush off the tiny attackers.

"Don't run!" Telamar commanded. "Stay close to me!"

When she didn't respond right away, he reached out and dragged her to his side. Phareth felt the Ice magus' power come to life. With a crackle, a glittering sphere formed in the air. The rocks where Telamar stood suddenly twinkled with ice crystals. He maintained the globe of frost for a few heartbeats, then let it drop. Tiny objects pattered down the slope. One landed near Phareth and he saw the glittering shape of a wasp, frozen as it flew.

"Show-off," he muttered.

"Thank you," Anarinda said in a trembling voice.

More yellow jackets already buzzed toward them. Telamar

extended both arms as Anarinda huddled against him.

"This should keep them back." More fog swirled around them. A fresh rain of insects came down to Phareth. These ones still twitched, barely alive.

"Careful!" he protested.

Anarinda's hands trembled as she brushed bits of frost and dead bees off her shoulders. Icy air flowed down the slope, bathing Phareth in its chill. The cold wasn't as extreme, but he could still see pale fingers of frost creeping over the rocks.

"If you're going to do that, we'll need a rope," he called up to them.

Telamar frowned, perhaps resenting the intrusion on his triumph. Anarinda peered down at Phareth.

"I'll get it," she said.

Phareth waited while she got a rope from her waypack and tied it to a projecting rock. He carefully pulled to test its hold before he started down. The rope creaked ominously but it did its job and steadied him when his boots slipped on slick rocks.

"Come ahead," Phareth called once he stood on level ground.

Anarinda began her descent. Phareth looked around for trouble as he steadied the rope. Above them, Telamar calmly froze anything that buzzed near him.

When she reached the bottom, Anarinda called, "Ready!"

Only then did Phareth see how many welts dotted her face, neck and hands.

"I can help, if you like," he offered.

"Could you?" Anarinda continued to shiver with pain.

"You'll still feel the stings," Phareth said, "but they won't bother you as much."

He touched her forehead lightly with his fingertips. She probably didn't feel his thoughts penetrate with hers. Finding a particular part of her brain, he gave a quick tweak.

"All done."

"That is better," she sighed with relief.

Meanwhile, Telamar jumped and slid down the slope with aplomb. Apparently, he didn't have to worry about losing his footing. Other things still worried him, however.

"What are you doing to her?" he demanded.

"Helping," Phareth snapped back. "You might be too frozen to feel the bee stings, but…"

"Stop it!" Anarinda cut in. "I'm all right, thanks to both of you. Can we please go on?"

Telamar sniffed as he stalked past the two of them. His breath came in clouds of cold mist. There were no more trees at the base of the knoll, just blackberry thickets bristling with thorns. Telamar's power flowed again, and Phareth sensed a bit too much pleasure as ice made the brambles glisten. With a chorus of sharp pops, the Ice magus strode on through, shattering canes as he went.

"Don't be so rough," Anarinda scolded as she hurried after him. "These creatures are just pawns."

Phareth didn't bother arguing. Somewhere, the eridow continued to howl. He kept an eye out for Valdira's next attack.

~ * ~

"It didn't stop them?" Ryamon asked. While the magi were busy, he had chanced coming out of the rock shelter. Now that they were moving again, he knelt beside Valdira.

She shrugged. "I didn't think it would."

She glanced toward the lake, where several dozen geese glided across the dark water. They had been flying in all morning, big gray birds with black necks and heads. To Ryamon they looked like living pieces of the leaden sky.

Following Valdira's gaze, he saw how the geese had drawn into a tight cluster near the shore. They didn't look around or dabble for food as they usually did. The whole raft just floated, barely moving.

Valdira gave no sign, but the geese burst into a chorus of honks and squeaks. Suddenly they were in motion.

~ * ~

The air pulsed with the whir of wings as a dark column rose from the lake.

"What's all that?" Phareth asked.

"Birds," Telamar said with frigid contempt.

Phareth glared at him. Of course he knew they were birds! That wasn't what he was asking and Telamar knew it.

Anarinda glanced at Phareth anxiously while Telamar strode ahead, smashing the foliage on his path. Phareth held onto his feelings. If Telamar said one more word, he would tweak his brain a lot harder than he had Anarinda's.

The flock rose high, then twisted and broke into bunches all heading toward the magi. Lines of individual birds came into clearer focus as they got closer. Some kind of wild geese, and they were coming fast.

"Any suggestions?" Phareth felt the sour taste of humiliation in the back of his throat. Once again, his powers were no help.

Telamar smiled, as if he enjoyed Phareth's predicament. Then he turned pale, measuring eyes on the approaching horde. Anarinda hastily stepped forward.

"Let me do it," she said.

The wind rose even as she spoke, a powerful blast from behind the three magi. It pulled their hair and ruffled their clothing. Bits of dust and broken blackberry canes lifted from the ground to pelt Phareth's back. Thunder rumbled overhead as Anarinda made a broad pushing gesture. Geese squawked with alarm as they met the gale. The flock scattered, wing beats faltering as they fought the wind.

Phareth was tired of feeling useless. He projected his mind toward the geese, hoping to catch Valdira unawares. He found her, but her will wasn't only in the geese.

"Take care!" he shouted, almost too late.

With a crackle of canes, an animal stood up from the blackberries. Shorbak! It shocked him to think a predator had been lurking there, watching as they passed.

The beast was huge, like a mountain moving. Through a frozen moment Phareth took in details of its coarse black fur and sloping shoulders, massive paws with terrible sickle claws. It stared back at them through tiny eyes in a vaguely canine face. With a deep whuff, it dropped to all fours and charged.

The shorbak came at them as if the brambles weren't even there. With a startled shout, Telamar jumped back out of the way. Not that Phareth blamed him, but it left Anarinda right in the shorbak's path.

His only hope was to attack through the animal. He sent a mental thrust into the shorbak's mind, hoping to stun it. The animal paused, shook its head, then charged on with a guttural roar.

Behind its animal psyche, Phareth sensed his real enemy, Valdira. He made a grab, contacted the rogue magus. She fought, and he tried to hold her. If he could reach the right part of her brain, the battle would be over.

Concentrating on the mental battle, Phareth barely saw Anarinda's horrified face as the shorbak rushed her. Then she turned and set her feet.

"Cover your eyes!" she cried.

He had no time to react as her right hand snapped in a throwing gesture. A flash split the air, lightning that turned everything to white and fire. Thunder shook the whole world. Phareth and Valdira's combat was split apart. Through the buzzing in his ears, Phareth heard the shorbak's moans. It suddenly sounded pathetic rather than frightening.

Yet he hadn't neutralized Valdira's powers. "This isn't over," he warned.

~ * ~

Valdira bit off a cry. Kneeling beside her, Ryamon asked, "Sweetheart?"

In a strange, choked voice she said, "Oh, no, you don't."

Ryamon leaned back, wondering what he had said to make her so angry. Then he felt the power in the air. Her face was flushed, eyes focused across the lake. He could make a good guess who she was fighting.

"Hold him off," he whispered. "You can do it." There was little else he could do to help her.

Across the lake, lightning blazed. In the same moment, Valdira screamed. Ryamon caught her as her head jerked back.

"What happened?"

"They killed the shorbak," she growled, and then, "I'll get you for that."

This time he knew she wasn't talking to him.

~ * ~

The afterimage of Anarinda's lightning blotted out Phareth's vision, a shape like a black tree against a white sky. His head throbbed and he could barely hear through the ringing in his ears. When he could see again, the shorbak lay in a black heap surrounded by flickering sparks. A choking stench of burnt fur rose from its smoldering body.

"Are you all right?" Anarinda asked, not specifying who she meant. On the other side of her, Telamar blinked and rubbed his eyes.

"A little more warning," he snapped.

"I did warn you," she protested. "Should I have waited for that thing to gut me?"

The ringing in Phareth's head broke into weird squawks and hoots. The sounds faded when he pressed his hands to his ears. If his ears weren't ringing, what was the noise?

He looked up and shouted again, "Take care!"

It suddenly got dark as the first flight of geese descended. Phareth ducked and covered his head. He heard an angry shout from Telamar and Anarinda's startled shriek. There was a moment of milling confusion, wings buffeting and bills pinching. The birds were bigger than they looked from a distance. Even through clothing, the bites hurt.

As quickly as they had descended, the storm of geese lifted. Phareth dared a look just as another river of geese streamed from the sky. Then, in the midst of the feather-storm, he heard something that made his heartbeat falter: a high, shrill trumpeting.

Crouching nearby, Anarinda moaned, "Oh, please, don't let that be what it sounds like."

When he could stand without being knocked over, Phareth straightened. Across the valley, a dark form came around the bluff behind the lake. It seemed to move slowly only because it was so large. The gloomy sky muted its reddish fur, but its tusks still gleamed as it raised its trunk to trumpet again.

"It's a lesser montus," Phareth reported. An answering shriek rang off the flanks of the mountains. "Monti," he corrected.

Then more geese descended. By the time they flew off, all three magi were bruised, their clothing torn, and hair pulled into loose strands. Three monti pounded along the lake shore, kicking up clumps of turf. Another two were just rounding the bluff.

"She's pinning us down until they get here," Phareth warned.

"I told you we're close," Telamar snapped back, smoothing his fair hair. "She must be getting desperate."

"Can you flush her out?" Phareth asked Anarinda.

She nodded, eyes alight with power. "Which way?"

"Straight across the lake," Telamar said.

"Give me room," Anarinda commanded.

Phareth jumped back, despite a fresh wave of geese. The Storm magus extended her arms and a gale blew past them. With an ominous whistle, the air formed a circular wall around the magi. Any geese that didn't veer off were flung away in clouds of feather.

Oddly, Phareth also noticed the smell of smoke. He looked around to see a gray pall rising from the shorbak's corpse. Sparks struck by Anarinda's lightning flared to life under the wind's urging.

Anarinda didn't seem to notice. She brought her hands together as if pressing something into a ball. The wind's roaring went lower and louder. Phareth didn't think Telamar would hear a spoken warning, so he tapped the Ice magus' shoulder. Telamar turned with a jerk. When Phareth pointed at the small fire, he nodded stiffly.

Bits of debris lifted from the ground as Anarinda shaped the wind. It was hard to tell through the smoke and grit, but Phareth thought the clouds above them had started to rotate along with their wind-wall.

Eyes narrowed in concentration, Anarinda raised one hand and lowered the other. The wind's noise changed again. Glancing upward, Phareth saw that the clouds had taken on an eerie glow. A dark finger poked downward, writhing as it descended.

There was no longer anything doll-like about the Storm magus as she exerted her full power. Phareth was extremely glad she was on his side.

Slowly she brought both hands back to level, now only a finger's width apart. She made a deceptively gentle pushing motion. The tornado moved off, feeling for the ground like the trunk of an enormous montus. When it touched down, the noise was indescribable, even louder than the crash of lightning. Yet somehow Phareth had no trouble hearing Anarinda when she spoke.

"If this doesn't scare them, I don't know what will!"

~ * ~

"A tornado?" For the first time, Ryamon heard a suggestion of fear in Valdira's voice.

"Should we leave?" he asked.

"I told you we're not running away!" she flared. Monti trumpeted on the lake shore as if emphasizing her words.

Every moment that passed only convinced Ryamon that Valdira was wrong and they ought to retreat, but he had already pledged to fight at her side. He wouldn't abandon her.

He fought back crushing helplessness as the tornado roared toward them. The noise changed when the cyclone reached the lake, but it didn't slow down. It writhed its way toward them, slick and gray with water sucked up from the lake.

Beyond that, smoke was rising near the magi. Smoke meant fire, which Ryamon could use. He studied its placement, then stretched his senses across the distance to touch the spirit of the fire.

The idea of burning someone still appalled him, but maybe it didn't have to be that way. Valdira was fighting hard; Ryamon preferred to fight smart. If he could make it more difficult for the magi to tell where he and Valdira were, that would be helping, wouldn't it?

"I'm going to try something," he said.

~ * ~

Telamar gave a shout of alarm and suddenly Phareth couldn't see the tornado. Smoke was all around them, shifting layers that blocked out everything. His eyes burned and he coughed as harsh vapors clawed at his throat. More sparks flew in the wind. One landed on Phareth's hand. He slapped at the sting.

"I thought you could handle it," he choked at Telamar.

"What do you expect with this wind?" the Ice magus snarled back. His sleeves flapped violently as he tried to kick dirt over the flames. All he did was add dust to the veil of smoke.

"You can't have it both ways," Anarinda called through the wind. "Do you want me to do this or not?"

Actually, Phareth was surprised she had taken such extreme action. Anarinda had always been sympathetic to Valdira. She must have changed her mind when she saw the shorbak coming at her.

Somewhere in the valley monti were shrieking, either in terror or rage. Phareth had to stop Valdira before the giant mammals reached them.

He shut his eyes and folded his hands before him. Power rippled around them, but it wasn't Valdira's. It was Ryamon. So the fire-thief had finally taken a hand. Even better—Ryamon was the weaker of the two renegades.

Phareth struck without hesitation. He felt Ryamon's shocked awareness of the intrusion, but the man had no mental shields to speak of. In a moment Phareth took in his turbulent emotions, his intense love for Valdira, the need to protect her and his revulsion at the idea of hurting the magi. Through Ryamon's eyes, Phareth saw the thing he needed: Valdira, close at hand. She was unaware of his presence, therefore vulnerable.

Before Ryamon could cry a warning, he struck again. The leap from Ryamon's mind to Valdira's took but an instant. He pierced the rogue's defenses before she was fully alert and drove to her core. The source of her magic pulsed like a beating heart. Phareth seized it, squeezed, twisted hard. He felt her scream, mind and body together, then nothing more.

Triumph surged through him. Valdira was unconscious. At last, he had won!

~ * ~

It happened so fast, Ryamon couldn't respond. It felt like drowning; the stranger's presence filled him like water in his lungs. Then, just as suddenly, it surged out of him. Even as Ryamon's breath came back, Valdira screamed. Her shoulders arched in a terrible spasm. Then she collapsed on the ground.

"Valdira, no!" Ryamon cried.

He scrambled to her side, pressed a desperate hand to her throat. A pulse still flickered there, and her breath came in strangled gasps. She wasn't dead, only stunned.

Rage scalded through Ryamon, more poisonous even than the anger he had once felt toward her. He wouldn't stand for this, being used by the Shadow magus to strike his own lover down.

"Never," he snarled with a fury worthy of Valdira herself.

~ * ~

"You did it?" Anarinda asked.

Phareth nodded, sighing with relief as he saw the monti falter in their headlong charge.

"It's about time," Telamar said.

Phareth found it easier to ignore him now that he had finally succeeded.

"Thank goodness." Anarinda let the tornado dissipate in a spray of falling water. Robbed of Valdira's control, the monti dropped to a lumbering walk and wandered aimlessly. Geese winged overhead without guidance, honking fear and confusion to each other.

"Let's go get them before she recovers," Phareth said. He had no doubt he could find the rogue magi now; Ryamon was so helpless.

Phareth knew from bitter experience what it was like to be helpless as his lover died. Having seen Ryamon's devotion to Valdira, Phareth couldn't help feeling a bit sorry for him.

~ * ~

The water-filled tornado collapsed in a swampy-smelling spatter. Ryamon crouched beneath the falling water, glaring at the Collegium magi who headed toward him with casual strides. They thought he was finished. They were wrong.

He cradled his fallen lover and scrambled for a plan. He couldn't use fire. The Shadow magus would expect it and the Storm magus could quench it too easily now that she wasn't focused on the tornado. What they had forgotten was that they were approaching over rocky ground. Ryamon had full control of that Element.

Through the stones, he felt each step. He concentrated on their footfalls, sensing their path and gauging the moment. He struck as swiftly as the Shadow magus had. With a supreme effort, Ryamon sheared the rocks and wrenched them wide. Across the valley, a pit opened up to swallow his foes.

~ * ~

A sink hole yawned under their feet, too sudden to avoid. With startled cries, all three magi went in. Arms flailing, Phareth fell. He saw flashes of torn stone and stormy sky. Then his head struck the side of the pit. He didn't feel it when he hit the bottom.

~ * ~

They wouldn't get out of there any time soon. Ryamon hoped he had stopped them. No, he hoped he had *hurt* them.

He swept one arm through the handles of Valdira's basket. Summoning the strength of Stone into himself, he gathered his lover to him. Ryamon faced south, deeper into the mountains. And he ran.

Chapter Fourteen

A searing headache dragged Phareth awake. The ground beneath him was all lumps and prickles. Scents of pine and wet earth clawed at his sinuses. He was damp and cold and surrounded by an endless, shuddering roar.

As his senses cleared, the noise separated into individual drips and splashes of water. He tried to open his eyes, but something stuck his eyelashes together. With a flutter of panic, he forced them open.

He was beneath some kind of overhang, lying on a bed of pine branches. Rain pounded down outside. That explained the noise. Under a dreary sky, Phareth saw a lake shore and sharp peaks half hidden by mist. Dry needles crackled as he raised a hand to wipe his eyes. He blinked at a sticky, dark smear on his fingers. What was that… Blood!

He sat up fast and regretted it. Everything whirled, and the pain in his head got so much worse that he thought there must be a shard of rock sticking out of his forehead.

"Ow," someone moaned in a weak voice. After a moment, Phareth realized it was himself.

The rock ledge was long and narrow, barely wide enough to stretch out his arms. There was a crude fire pit near his feet. Anarinda and Telamar knelt on the other side of it. The Storm magus had a sleeve ripped off her blouse and Telamar was using strips of cloth to wrap her left wrist. He barely glanced around at Phareth's complaint. Anarinda attempted a wan smile.

"Sorry about the rain." She tried to sound cheerful despite her obvious pain. "I landed on my wrist, and I think it's broken. I lost control of the storm."

"Don't apologize," Phareth said. Heavy clouds muted the daylight. He was pretty sure that any more light would have made his headache even worse.

Cautiously, he felt his head. No rocks were sticking out, but the right side of his face was scratched and tender. On the same side of his forehead, he found a painful lump. It felt enormous and was still seeping blood. That was what had sealed his eyelids.

Phareth struggled to remember. He had beaten Valdira. He was sure of that. Then the rest of the tale came crashing back and he thought he might rather be out in the pit.

That fast, the ground dropped out from under them. They had fallen with it. Phareth's whole body ached, especially his knees. It remembered the heavy landing, even if his mind had blanked it out. His companions must have brought him to this rough shelter. Probably Telamar, if Anarinda had a broken wrist. Phareth wondered how long he had been unconscious after hitting his head.

It hardly mattered compared to the bigger disaster. There was no sign of any captives, only Phareth, Anarinda and Telamar. That meant Ryamon and Valdira had escaped.

Gloom settled over him, darker than any storm. He lifted his knees enough to lean his forehead against them. All that gained him was a blast of pain, until he turned his head to stare at the back wall of the shelter. His stomach felt sour and his headache tightened into a band of fire. He knew this feeling all too well, the bitter dregs of shame. They had come so close to achieving their goal, and yet they had lost.

Phareth had sworn he wouldn't fail. He had expected to win back his honor and the pride of his order. Now his boast was ashes, less than the cinders in the fire pit. His mother had trusted him. She had given him a job to do, and he had let her down. Again.

Softly, Anarinda said to Telamar, "Let me have that."

Phareth watched without caring as she took the last strip of cloth from the Ice magus. Using her injured hand gingerly, she folded the bandage into a neat square. This she held under the rim of the stone ledge, so it was drenched with dripping water. Even short as she was, Anarinda had to walk bent over before she could kneel beside Phareth. She leaned forward to dab at the blood on his forehead.

"Stop!" He winced, and not only because the bruises hurt. Phareth could feel Anarinda's concern, just as he sensed Telamar's hostility from across the shelter. Too many emotions, too much conflict scraped against his raw nerves. He tried to raise a mental shield but it only made his headache worse.

"Sit still," Anarinda scolded.

"I'll do it. Please." Phareth tried not to be too rough as he grabbed the bandage from her hand. Anarinda meant well, but he didn't want anyone to touch him.

The Storm magus sat back with an exasperated sigh. Phareth pressed the folded bandage to his right eye, which was most crusted with blood. Anarinda watched critically. After a moment, he began to wipe at the half-dried smears. The smell of blood suddenly assailed him and his stomach did a queasy flip-flop. Swallowing heavily, Phareth held the bandage into the rain, wrung it out, and set to work on the other eye.

"See? I'm fine," he said.

Anarinda crooked one eyebrow at him. "You were unconscious for a long time. Even Telamar was getting worried."

On the far side of her, the Ice magus gave a muffled snort: "Beh."

Phareth went on cleaning the blood from his face. Part of him—no doubt the wiser part—wanted to ignore Telamar. The man only cared about himself. His hostility pinged off Phareth's tattered shields like a shower of invisible hailstones. Phareth was in no mood to put up with his attitude.

"You're a fool," he muttered back.

"Don't," Anarinda protested, but Telamar sat up straighter, his pale face frozen in icy disdain.

"I'm sure you'd like to think so."

"You would never have found them without me." Both eyes clear, Phareth started dabbing the blood from his forehead.

"I did all right," Telamar retorted. "Better than you, Shadow magus."

"After I told you what to do!" Phareth said.

"Oh, yes, you're our noble leader." Telamar's lips curled in a cold sneer. "Just because your mother is a mage lord, you think you're so much better than the rest of us. You're the only one who has any ideas…"

"Stop this!" Anarinda cried. "I know everyone is upset, but…"

"You think the rest of us are fools who can't see through your plan." Telamar went on, ignoring her.

"What? I don't…" Phareth broke off. He tried, but couldn't keep his voice from shaking. "My only plan was to do my job."

"Oh, yes, your job." Telamar nodded with fake wisdom, but his eyes blazed with silvery light. Wisps of fog curled off his shoulders as his power leaked into the surrounding air. "I know all about that."

"What?" Phareth felt stupid repeating himself, but he really didn't know what the Ice magus meant.

Anarinda said, "Explain, Intiate."

"It's all just a game," Telamar explained with frigid logic. "The Shadow Lord is moving us like pieces on a chess board. You know how close Murcrys and Klaive are. She's had him eating out of her hand for years. But Lord Salovik isn't fooled. Murcrys is up to something. She has allies outside Arkanost who…"

"What?" Phareth shouted, appalled by Salovik's twisted version of Murcrys' motives. His hand jerked and bumped the lump under his hair. He bent forward with a groan of pain.

While Phareth cringed, Telamar went on, "He meant for us to lose this fight. Murcrys wanted the renegades to escape. Just like he planned to lose in Logoll."

"Shut *up!*" Phareth raged, the words torn from his soul. "People died in Logoll. Kylethia died!"

"While you survived. Convenient?"

Phareth felt something warm and wet trickle between his fingers. Without realizing it, he had been squeezing the bandage hard enough to force the water and blood back out of it.

"There was no secret plot." Phareth's voice was a harsh whisper as he tried to control his emotions. "It was a mistake, something I can never live down. This mission," he tapped the damp ground, "was my chance to make it right. If I could do it, this one thing… But now that's gone, too. How can you even think I wanted this to happen?"

Telamar looked back at him, perhaps realizing he said something too cruel and personal. If so, he refused to admit it.

"Don't try to pretend you don't know," he scoffed.

"How can I know something that isn't true?" Phareth hissed.

"Excuse me." Anarinda didn't shout, but her delicate voice held the fierce crackle of lightning. "The Storm Lord does not eat from anyone's hand, Telamar. He makes his own decisions for the good of Arkanost and our Order. Just because he doesn't agree with your mage lord doesn't make him a traitor or a pawn. You will never say this to me again!"

For the first time, Phareth sensed a crack in Telamar's sour certainty.

"Don't you see?" the Ice magus argued. "Phareth was in your

mind. He made you believe his lies!"

"Stop saying that!" Phareth burst out. His forehead throbbed wildly. "I never tried to dominate Anarinda!"

Beside him, Phareth could feel the sizzle of power that betrayed Anarinda's fury. Now she did shout: "I'm still talking!"

Glaring between the two of them, the Storm magus said, "I'm ashamed of you both, shouting like children when things go wrong. We didn't lose this battle because of Phareth or anyone else. *They won it.* Because of their love for each other, because they protected each other and worked as a team.

"We—" she glared at both of them "—have never worked as a team. You two insulted each other and tore each other down every chance you got. Of course we lost. We didn't deserve to win!"

Both magi stared at her, speechless. In Telamar's stunned silence, Phareth could hear the crash of illusions shattering. He couldn't tell if those illusions related to Anarinda, Salovik, or Telamar himself.

Yet Phareth had to admit that he, too, was part of the problem. The rivalry between the Seven Exalted Orders was ancient and tenacious. Always they watched each other, wary of any change and jealous of any success. If one order became too powerful, the others brought it down. That was the way it had always been.

However, Phareth could see the petty divisions had their price. If the Collegium magi had fought as one, who knew what the outcome of the recent battle might have been? Humbly, he bowed his head to Anarinda.

"You are right, sister magus." There was more he wanted to say. Perhaps he could even admit he had been trying to out-shine the others by defeating Valdira on his own. Looking at the Ice magus, he couldn't quite force the words out. Telamar remained silent and bewildered.

"What's done is done," Anarinda said in a more normal voice, "and pointing fingers does no good. We're out in the wilderness, it's cold and wet, and we have to take care of ourselves."

Even she, Phareth noted, didn't go so far as to suggest they take care of each other. It was too soon for that.

"You," Anarinda pointed at Telamar, "are going to go back out to the sinkhole and make sure we didn't leave anything behind. We need all our equipment."

Still silent, Telamar nodded and gathered himself to stand up.

"Also," she went on, "my lightning should have killed some of those geese. See if you can find one and bring it back with you."

Finally Telamar found his voice. "You want to eat that?" he asked, disgusted.

"It's food," she replied, stern in her bandages and smudged clothing. "Go find it, unless you prefer the shorbak. It's already partly cooked."

Shuddering, Telamar straightened. He barely missed hitting his head on the low overhang. Then he was gone in the rain.

"I'm going to clear this weather," Anarinda said to Phareth. "Then I'll see if there are any embers left in that fire pit. We're going to need heat tonight."

"What do you want me to do?" Phareth asked.

"Stay here and meditate," she said. "That was a bad fall. Make sure you don't have a brain injury. After that, contact Nepharyl and get a rescue party on the way to us."

"All right," Phareth said.

Anarinda left the shelter, and he teetered between resentment that she had seized control and amazement at the sudden turn of events. The Storm magus seemed so dainty and childlike, yet her spirit was worthy of a mage lord.

Also, of course, it was a relief to know he didn't have to report to his mother yet. He knew he would have to tell her what had happened soon. If he didn't, he would be deceiving her, and Murcrys wouldn't stand for that. Still, Phareth wouldn't mind waiting a little longer.

He looked around the little rock shelter with its low roof and dirt floor. Except for one small shelf above his head, it hadn't even been shaped. Not up to Ryamon's usual standard of workmanship.

Suddenly Phareth realized how quiet it was, just him with the bare hearth and drumming of rain. After several days in close company with Anarinda and Telamar, he found it strange to be left alone. It was almost like the penitent's cell he had occupied in the Tower of Shadows.

With that, all the emotions he had been fighting off came crashing down on him. Maybe he should never have left the Tower of Shadow. He had lost again. Failed again. Phareth couldn't stop repeating it to himself. Then came the grief he could hardly endure, that Kylethia was dead because of his mistake. He tried to bury it, had never spoken of it even to his own mother, and then he yelled it at Telamar? The Ice magus, with all his accusations, had no idea how the loss tore at Phareth.

His eyes burned and his throat felt too tight for breath, but there was no time for self-pity. Anarinda wanted him to do something. It would be better to concentrate on that be trapped by his grief.

Phareth sat up straighter. His head still pounded, but he breathed out and relaxed. It felt good to let his eyes slip shut. Sounds came clearer as he eased into a trance. The wind whispered outside the shelter. Rain chattered onto the rocks. To his dismay, Phareth was assailed by erotic images rising from the pile of pine branches he sat on. Valdira and Ryamon must have shared this bed.

Phareth needed no reminders of their rutting at this moment. He crawled over by the fire pit and tried his trance again. Just moving the short distance woke many aches and pains. He examined each one, looking for serious injury, and wondered whether Murcrys, if she had seen him, would accuse him of wallowing in guilt the way she had when he confined himself to the penitent's cell.

Last of all Phareth focused on the lump on his forehead. Fortunately, only the skin was swollen. He sensed no breaks in his skull. Phareth traced his own nerve endings and tweaked the proper spot. The pain eased.

The blow to his head hadn't affected his powers, then. He was grateful for that much. Returning to awareness, Phareth saw the rain was slackening off. He tasted the ozone tang of Anarinda's magic, and farther off Telamar's revulsion as he touched the sodden feathers of a dead goose. They were both doing their parts. It was time Phareth did his.

He extended his powers to search for Nepharyl. It galled him to admit they needed help from the meddling nobleman. Maybe that was why he couldn't connect right away. Phareth reached, but found nothing. He concentrated harder, drawing in his mind the image of Nepharyl's curly brown hair, his brown eyes and deprecating smile. Then he added the dapper black suit and the fancy way he held his cane when he walked.

"Nepharyl." He spoke the name clearly in his mind and still

didn't sense even a glimmer of Nepharyl's presence.

Even in his trance, Phareth felt a frown tighten his forehead, creating pressure on the swollen lump. Patiently, he called on even more detail. The little village of Lornest with the fountain in the square. Then the farmhouse they had commandeered. The onion field and birch woods surrounding it.

"Nepharyl."

In response he heard only silence. No answering awareness, not even the murmurs of a dreaming mind. Nepharyl simply wasn't there.

How could he not be there? The magi needed help. Nepharyl was supposed to wait for them to call him.

With growing concern, Phareth pressed his powers farther. He reached out across the hills of Selkest and on toward Elvest. Dozens of times he felt flickers of other minds, but not the one he sought.

Eventually he came back to himself. The rain had stopped. Anarinda was trying to coax the fire back to life with dried needles from the pile Phareth woke up on. Just outside the shelter, Telamar was wrestling the feathers off a slightly singed goose. Bits of fluff stuck all over his brown suit, and crimson smeared his hands. Clearly, Anarinda was punishing his rash words about the Storm Lord. Yet watching Telamar's humiliation no longer cheered Phareth up.

Hesitantly, he said, "Anarinda?"

She glanced across the fire, all her usual cheer restored. "Are they coming?"

Phareth shook his head. "He's not there."

"Nepharyl left Lornest?" Anarinda asked, puzzled.

"No, I've been searching. I can't find him anywhere between here and Elvest. He's just gone."

"What?" Telamar interrupted. Then, with a wary glance at Anarinda, he went on more respectfully. "How can he be gone?"

Phareth silently shrugged.

"We only left Lornest a few days ago," Anarinda said. "He shouldn't have been able to travel farther than Elvest, even if he left as soon as we did."

"Why would he go anywhere?" Telamar pressed. "He wanted to come with us."

"Could he have been attacked?" Anarinda asked. "Maybe he's

unconscious."

"Who would do that?" the Ice magus replied. "The villagers weren't hostile."

"I would sense if he was asleep or unconscious," Phareth said. "No, he's gone. Really, completely gone."

"Gone." Anarinda poked at the fire, obviously thinking hard.

Telamar burst out, "You mean we're on our own out here?" He lifted the half-naked goose by its neck in a gesture of demonstration. If he was still upset, at least he didn't seem to be blaming Phareth.

"I can reach others in the village," Phareth offered. "Gritl or Tyteb, for instance. It just won't be as easy because they don't expect me to call on them."

"Two of us are injured," Anarinda said. "You'd better try to find Silma, the Blood magus, even though we never met her. The villagers would probably listen if she told them to head into the mountains."

"All right," Phareth said. Nepharyl's disappearance still baffled him, but it felt good to have a plan.

"Then," the Storm magus went on, "you'd better report to your order."

Phareth's reluctance must have shown on his face. With some sympathy, Anarinda went on, "The Mage Lords will want to know what has happened. Even beyond that, something strange is going on. Nepharyl has no magic to let him vanish like this. There's something we don't know. Murcrys will be the best one to find out what it is."

Phareth nodded. He didn't like it, but he knew Anarinda was right. It gave him little consolation that, for once, Telamar didn't snort at the mere sound of the Shadow Lord's name.

~ * ~

With Valdira in his arms, Ryamon ran up the long curve of valley and over a low saddle of land. Tilted slabs of rock pointed the way. He followed them southward, into the unknown.

Only when he was sure they were out of danger did he slow to a steady stride. The sun traced its arc behind clouds and rain, yet he felt neither fear nor fatigue. Nor did he feel Valdira's weight. The spirit of Stone made him strong.

All the while, his lover lay slack in his arms. She breathed, so he knew she was alive, but that was all. Ryamon didn't like the way her head rolled loose against his arm, so he shifted to let it rest on his shoulder. The basket bumped his ribs and still Valdira didn't stir.

Concern began to penetrate Ryamon's bond with Stone. Valdira was so strong and full of spirit. What had that Shadow magus done to knock her out so long?

It had been mid-morning when Ryamon began his flight. Now the rain had stopped and the sun stood well past its zenith. Even in his altered state, he knew he was going to hurt himself if he went on this way. Who would take care of Valdira then?

He found a small spring surrounded by ferns and birch trees. The surface of the pool trembled as strings of tiny bubbles rose from the depths. Ryamon let the basket drop, then trampled the ferns to make a bed. Carefully, he knelt to lay Valdira down near one of the birch trees. Maybe its presence would help her.

With a shrug, he swung his waypack off and set it beside the basket. Then, at last, Ryamon released the spirit of Stone. Strength left him as suddenly as water draining through sand. For the first time he felt the chill of wet clothes and stickiness of sweat in his hair. He was dizzy and sick, his lips split by thirst and throat rough as sandstone.

With a trembling hand, he drank from the spring. The water had a strange, tinny flavor but he sucked it in anyhow. Groping in his waypack, he found the one fish he had managed to dry. Then, before vertigo overcame him, he stretched out beside his lover.

Ryamon lay in a daze, chewing on the fish very slowly. He had no idea where they were. Through the treetops, he glimpsed the mountains. They still angled upward, striped with shades of paler or darker gold, but the peaks no longer pointed away from Ryamon. Some pointed toward him. They must be in the middle of the range, or even on the other side. He was too exhausted to have a clear opinion about whether that was good news or not.

As he slowly recovered, Ryamon's concern for Valdira also revived. It scared him that she lay so close and he couldn't catch flashes of her emotions. Her mind was silent, empty as a forest buried in snow. He dragged himself back up to a sitting position.

She hadn't moved since he put her down. It tore his heart to see her lying like a rag doll in her threadbare dress. He hoped he managed to pay that Shadow magus back for doing this to her.

Valdira would need water just as Ryamon did. Spotting a bush with broad, shiny leaves, he reached over and tugged a leaf free. This he used to scoop water from the spring. Gently, he pulled Valdira's mouth open enough to let a few drops trickle between her lips.

"Drink it, sweetheart," he murmured, although he didn't know if she could hear him.

Her breathing caught. Then she blinked. Ryamon let go a breath he hadn't even known he was holding. She was awake!

Her gaze was still blurry and unfocused. Remembering how dry his own throat had been, Ryamon quickly offered her more water. She drank, but then coughed and feebly pushed his hand away.

"What is that?" she croaked.

"Water from a spring," he said softly. "I know it doesn't taste very good."

Valdira struggled to get her elbows under herself, so Ryamon helped her sit up.

"Where are we?" she asked.

"I'm not sure," Ryamon admitted. "What do you remember?"

"We were fighting." Valdira's voice was still weak and slurred. "That man, the shadow... He did something to me. I was locked inside myself, trying to get free. My Blood magic should have fixed what he did, but none of my powers worked. I felt..." She trailed off, looking around with fresh confusion.

"Thank goodness you came out of it," Ryamon said, sickened. He could only imagine what Valdira had suffered, trapped within her own mind. He could never bear to lose his magic, even temporarily.

"Where are they?" Valdira's voice was getting stronger, tinged with alarm.

"I dropped them into a pit," Ryamon told her with satisfaction. "They would have to climb out, and we got away in the meantime."

"Wait... We left?" Anger flared in her hazel eyes.

Finally he could sense her emotions again, but they weren't what he had hoped. Hurt, betrayal, then fury flared within Valdira.

She exclaimed, "I told you I wouldn't run!"

"You were unconscious," Ryamon protested. "I couldn't fight all of them by myself."

Valdira glared at him, her bosom heaving and face flushed. Ryamon sat back, stunned by the pain of his blunder. He had meant to help, but somehow he had made a mess of things again.

"They would have captured you!" he said.

Still she didn't answer, just stared at him as if he was the one who had struck her down by the lake.

"As long as we're free, it will be all right." Ryamon desperately hoped it was true. In his mind, he wondered if he would ever do the right thing, or if Valdira would ever appreciate what he did for her. Still, the thought of being separated from her in this wild country was terrifying.

"You have your powers back," he said, trying to soothe her. "And, look, there are trees. Birch trees, just like at home."

Reluctantly, Valdira glanced at the forest around them. It was a calm day, no wind to stir the branches, but then came a tremor in the lacy leaves. A shy rustle spread through the grove and along the slope behind them. Ryamon dared to relax a little.

"Do you want some food?" he asked meekly. Valdira didn't answer. "Sweetheart?"

He reached out, but her quick hand brushed him away before he could touch her shoulder. Valdira's expression hardened; hazel eyes pinned him, wary and alert. Ryamon wondered what else he had done wrong.

In a low voice, she said, "Someone is coming."

Chapter Fifteen

At Valdira's words, Ryamon froze like a hare in a thicket. "That's impossible," he whispered in protest.

No one could have followed him. He had walked for hours, taking no time to rest. Exhaustion was a dull, burning weight in his chest. Yet there was no reason for Valdira to lie. He held still, listening.

Birch leaves rustled. The spring simmered with minuscule bubbles. Farther off, a bird's song echoed faintly from the peaks. Silence stretched tight as a snare. Ryamon tried to sense approaching footsteps in the ground, as he had at the lake, but there weren't enough rocks in the ground here. His magic felt flaccid, stretched out of shape by his pushing it so hard. He didn't even have enough energy to summon a spark.

Ryamon hated feeling so helpless. He breathed to Valdira, "Where?"

Valdira, too, sat poised to run or fight. She answered by moving only her eyes, a steely glance back up the slope to his left. That way led back to Arkanost. Ryamon had definitely been followed.

"How many?" he murmured.

"One man and an ornyx."

He held back a curse that one of the magi was free so soon. And with a pack animal, too. Valdira must have sensed Ryamon's thoughts. She shook her head, a tiny jerk.

"It's the other one. The nobleman."

Ryamon tilted his head, confused. He had forgotten about the nobleman. The man hadn't even been there during the battle at the lake. He must have waited farther back, out of danger, and then started tailing them.

No, that didn't make sense, either. He should have stopped to help the magi.

"Why come on his own?" Ryamon asked.

Valdira's shoulders twitched in a shrug. Slowly she shifted in place, bringing her knees under her so she could jump up if she had to. Ryamon did that same. Soft green ferns whispered beneath them. Together they stared up slope, watching his back trail.

He could hear something else now, a faint crunch of footsteps over earth and dried leaves. It definitely sounded like a human's stride, a quick one-two-one-two with an odd tapping in between. Then the slower rhythm of the ornyx's long strides. He could picture the tall bird pausing between steps, looking around with innate caution.

That gave Ryamon an idea. Maybe Valdira could get control of the ornyx. If she made it run away, and the hunter would have to chase it.

Before he could suggest this, Ryamon spotted movement above them. Their pursuers approached from the opposite side of the hill. First came the bobbing crest on top of the ornyx's head, then its blue face, beady eyes and cruel beak.

In front of it, lower down, the crown of a round black hat appeared. Under that was a pale face surrounded by curly brown hair. The newcomer wore a black jacket with shiny buttons and lace at the throat. With one hand he led the ornyx; with the other he used a polished cane to probe the ground. He looked like exactly the soft city dweller Valdira had predicted would give up the chase if they made it hard enough for him. Whoever he was, the man was far more determined than she had believed.

The stranger jerked on the lead to stop the ornyx and stood on the brow of the hill, searching the forest with his eyes. His fine boots were muddy and the jacket stained by hard travel. Yet the bits of leaves in his hair were little consolation when he stood so close, clearly looking for them.

Twice his gaze passed over their hiding place. Ryamon was just wondering if they could successfully evade him when his eyes jerked back. The nobleman frowned slightly as he focused. Then, incredibly, he bowed toward their hiding place.

"My lady of the trees, we meet at last," he called out.

"Do we," Valdira replied in a tight voice.

Ryamon jumped to his feet, ready to defend his lover. He wished he had a weapon, and that his knees wouldn't wobble underneath him.

"What do you want?" he yelled back.

"I am a friend," the nobleman answered warmly. "I can help you if you let me."

"Help us straight to prison," Ryamon challenged. He hoped

he could summon fire if he had to.

"Not at all," the nobleman answered smoothly. "Perhaps you didn't realize we are no longer in Arkanost. Thus their laws, which have treated you so unfairly, no longer apply."

Ryamon glanced at Valdira, who listened in tense silence.

"You have crossed into Costera," the man went on. "Here you are free. Your powers do not make you outcasts, but nobility. Let me be the first to welcome you, Dama Valdira and Dom Ryamon."

"Who are you to welcome us?" Ryamon asked.

"My name is Nepharyl. I speak on behalf of my mistress, Dama Yolie." Bracing his cane on the hillside, Nepharyl made an even more elaborate bow.

It was tempting to believe him. Who wouldn't want to be honored instead of hunted? Yet Ryamon didn't see how the man could promise them anything out here in the wilderness.

"You were with them," Valdira countered warily. "In Lornest. I saw you with the magi from the Collegium."

"We did travel together for a time," Nepharyl admitted easily, "but only to serve my lady's purpose."

"What purpose would that be?" she asked.

"That is for my mistress to say," Nepharyl replied. "Dama Yolie is presently dwelling in her estate at Laceto, beyond the Valley of White Sand. It isn't far, but a few days' journey. If you wish, I will take you to her."

Ryamon glanced at Valdira again. It was true, they knew nothing of Costera and its customs. Having a guide could be useful. On the other hand, this purpose which Nepharyl referred to but wouldn't define, made Ryamon nervous.

Valdira didn't look at him. She pursed her lips, eyeing Nepharyl with an expression Ryamon couldn't read. It might be distrust, but it could just as well be ambition.

"You say we're nobles now," Valdira said.

"Indeed, Dama."

"And you have no magic of your own, so you have to do what we say?" she went on.

Ryamon thought he saw a flicker of alarm in Nepharyl's eyes, but the nobleman bowed again. "True, Dama, unless my mistress should command me otherwise."

Valdira smiled, a strange twist of the lips. Ryamon shifted in his place, wishing she would take a moment to talk this over. Still she refused to look at him.

"Do you have any food?" she demanded.

"Naturally, Dama." Nepharyl smiled obsequiously. As if he had carefully set a snare and Valdira was about to step into it. Since Ryamon couldn't survive alone in the wilderness, he had to step in with her. He had no choice.

~ * ~

It took hours for Phareth to arrange a rescue party. First, he had to find the Blood magus, Silma. Since he had never met her, all he could do was make himself still and listen for the pulse of magic over the distance. Silma had no skill with mental telepathy, so even after he located her it took time to explain what he wanted. There were moments when Phareth wondered if she was deliberately misunderstanding. After all, Silma had been Valdira's mentor. She might want to protect the rogue magus despite her crimes.

He finally made an impression by emphasizing that two of the Collegium magi were injured. For Anarinda's sake, Silma promised to bring help.

Afterward, Phareth fumed with frustration. He rested for a few minutes, watching Telamar break Valdira and Ryamon's bed into pieces and feed it to the fire. It was childish to take pleasure in the sight, but Phareth couldn't help it. It was the only revenge available to him.

When he could delay no longer, he composed his mind and cast his thoughts across Arkanost, seeking the one mind he could never mistake. Murcrys' answer came at once, as if she had been expecting to hear from him.

"Son?"

All the fancy words Phareth had been trying to arrange to soften the truth deserted him. Nothing could make his failure less than it was. Bluntly, he told her, *"They got away."*

Silence came back to him, her reaction so completely concealed that for a moment Phareth wondered if Murcrys had deliberately broken contact.

"I'm sorry," he said, hearing how inadequate the words were.

"I'm not surprised," Murcrys said. Phareth winced, but she went on tartly, *"I'm still your mother. I sensed earlier that you might have been injured. Were you?"*

"Yes, I was knocked out." Phareth followed her lead in keeping to the facts rather than groveling or dramatizing. *"I'll be fine, but they escaped while I was unconscious."*

"Where are they now?"

"I haven't been able to search for them yet. We were very close to the border when we caught up with them, but I don't know which way they went."

Murcrys didn't answer right away, and Phareth could no longer resist trying to explain.

"It was a near thing, Mother. I had her. Valdira's powers were bound. She was helpless. But then Ryamon dropped us into a pit." Phareth couldn't keep the resentment out of his tone. *"That's what knocked me out."*

"I told you not to underestimate him."

"I thought his stonecraft was supposed to be no good," Phareth complained.

"No one said he couldn't *shape Stone,"* Murcrys retorted, *"only that he didn't want to."*

Phareth was in no position to complain, so he went back to the bare facts.

"Since I recovered, I've been arranging for a rescue party to come from Lornest. Anarinda was injured." He sensed his mother's concern and quickly said, *"Her left arm. The wrist is either broken or badly sprained. Silma will put it right when she gets here."*

"I'll let Klaive know," Murcrys said.

"Tell them they can stop sending the rain. Anarinda doesn't need it any longer." As an afterthought, Phareth added, *"If Salovik asks, Telamar is fine."*

"The Ice Lord will be pleased, I'm sure," Murcrys said sourly.

"Speaking of him," Phareth went on, *"there's something else you should know."* He quickly repeated what Telamar had said, that Salovik believed Murcrys was in league with someone outside Arkanost and manipulating the Collegium.

"He said what?" Phareth felt her anger like the jagged edge of a broken jug.

"Anarinda was furious," Phareth said, and added indignantly, *"Telamar thinks I let Valdira escape on purpose."*

"That fool."

Phareth wasn't sure if Murcrys meant Telamar or Salovik. *"There's more,"* he went on, gratified that he could divert his mother's anger toward someone else. *"Nepharyl has disappeared."*

"Disappeared?"

"He was supposed to be my anchor, so I could find my way back to Lornest, but now I can't find him. I've searched, and you know how careful I would be. He's just not there."

"Guilberta's pet, the snoop Salovik insisted go along with you?"

"That's the one."

"And now he's gone?"

Murcrys fell silent once more. Phareth could feel her mind racing, connecting facts and discarding unlikely ideas.

"Yet Salovik thinks I'm part of a conspiracy," she said at last, her thoughts prickling with contempt. *"I wonder who could have told him that?"*

"The real conspirator?" Phareth suggested. *"Everyone knows you and Salovik don't get along. It would be easy to drop a few hints and let him invent the rest."*

"Perhaps. Well, my brother magus is going to regret his rash words when I proclaim them to the Collegium. I need a few more answers about our friend Nepharyl."

Phareth tried not to flinch, knowing his failure would be spread around all the more quickly. Resigned, he asked, *"What do you want us to do?"*

"Return to Lornest, but don't come back to Polvest yet. If there's any chance Valdira is still in Arkanost, we want you within striking distance. I'll let you know if the Collegium makes some other decision."

"All right." Phareth hesitated. Before he could lose his nerve, he stammered out, *"Mother, I…I really am sorry. I failed you."*

"Then so did Telamar and Anarinda," Murcrys interrupted. Her mind vibrated with strong emotion, not all of it focused on her son. *"Valdira is a powerful magus. So is Ryamon, of course, but she has abilities we don't understand and cannot anticipate. Not the way you could have predicted what Telamar or Anarinda would do."*

"Even so," Phareth began, but she cut him off.

"This was a difficult mission, son," Murcrys insisted. *"You three are the best your orders could bring to the field. It's possible that no one could have beaten them on their home ground. That's what I will tell the Collegium."*

Her presence was gone, suddenly and completely. Alone in his own mind, Phareth felt vaguely disappointed. It was foolish, really. Murcrys had just told him he was one of the best magi in the Order of Shadows. Did he want her to rage at him, instead? To make him feel even worse?

Yes, he had to admit that he did. Phareth wasn't worthy of kindness. He was a failure. And, like Valdira, he deserved to be punished.

~ * ~

Nepharyl led his ornyx down to the place where Ryamon and Valdira had been resting. They soon learned there was more than just food in the ornyx's pack. Nimble as any butler, Nepharyl laid down a sturdy cloth with pillows to sit on, extending his hand to help Valdira move over. Ryamon caught Valdira's hand first, but immediately sensed her annoyance. As soon as she was seated, he let go. Still smiling, Nepharyl managed to turn his offered hand into a graceful gesture.

"A soda spring," he explained, pointing to the bubbling pool beside them. "There are many in this area. One of Costera's interesting natural features. You will find the Valley of White Sand even more impressive."

"What makes it bubble like that?" Valdira asked.

"Ah, Dama, that is a mystery." Nepharyl seemed to dismiss the spring with his glance. Ryamon, who had chosen this spot to rest, also felt dismissed. "The water will not harm you, but why suffer the unpleasant taste?"

As he spoke, Nepharyl brought out a pair of silver goblets. He poured wine from a skin and offered the first cup to Valdira. She accepted it regally, without thanking him. Ryamon felt a twinge of guilt over being waited on. Once again, he wished Valdira would talk to him about this.

Nepharyl offered the second cup to Ryamon. He sniffed it cautiously, looking for some hint of danger in its ruby depths. He wasn't sure why he found the nobleman's presence so threatening, but he did. A sip proved it was a very good wine, rich and flavorful. Better than soda water, he had to admit.

As the wine spread its warmth through Ryamon's weary body, Nepharyl brought out food: a hard, smoked sausage; oat cakes, crisp but sweet; soft cheese to spread with a little silver knife; dried apple rings. As Ryamon ate well for the first time in weeks, he could almost overlook his distrust.

Once they had eaten, Nepharyl had more gifts to woo them with. With yet another groveling bow, he presented new clothing to replace their worn garments. For Valdira, a knee-length dress in soft green, trimmed with silvery embroidery. For Ryamon, a waist-coat and breeches in deep blue. Nepharyl allowed them to admire these presents while he hung their picnic blanket between two trees to make a changing area.

"You came prepared for everything," Valdira said as she stepped behind the blanket.

"My lady would be displeased if I did not," Nepharyl answered with a winning smile.

Ryamon glanced at him, hungry for information about who-ever had sent Nepharyl to intercept them. If there was anything sinister in her plans for them, nothing in Nepharyl's brown eyes betrayed that fact.

Meanwhile, Ryamon heard sounds behind the partition, the rustle of fabric and crackle of ferns as Valdira moved. Nepharyl glanced over slyly, obviously wondering why they didn't change together. Embarrassed, Ryamon waited. Valdira was his lover, yet he had clearly not been invited to join her. He knew better than to enter without permission.

Valdira's cool voice interrupted his thoughts. "It seems a little tight."

Ryamon turned toward her and tried not to stare. The cut of the gown from Costera was unlike any he had ever seen. Its deep neckline would have caused a scandal in Arkanost. The sleeves barely clung to her shoulders, while the bodice was tight enough to push her bosom upward in a way he couldn't help appreciating. The full skirt emphasized her slim waist. Ryamon had to admit that green suited Valdira more than the dark colors favored in Arkanost. Only her well-worn boots and unkempt hair didn't fit with the ensemble.

He cleared his throat and said, "You look beautiful."

Valdira smiled at him. Then she turned a stern glance toward Nepharyl. Ryamon caught the tail end of a lecherous smirk as the nobleman bowed his apologies.

"Forgive me, Dana. I could only guess at your size."

Valdira swished past him. Almost defiantly, she came to Ryamon and kissed him. Though startled, he was happy to respond.

All too quickly, she leaned away. "Your turn." She pointed at the hanging blanket.

Reluctantly, Ryamon took his new garments behind the screen. The fabric was sturdy, with a subtle sheen he had never seen before. Otherwise, there were no surprises for him. Trousers were trousers and a shirt was a shirt, even if softer than he was used to. The cut of the jacket was only slightly different from Nepharyl's. At least there was no lace on the cuffs.

A few feet away, on the other side of the blanket, he heard Nepharyl say, "Dama, may I help you with that?"

Ryamon scowled, imagining the nobleman with his hands on Valdira's waist.

"I think I can manage," she answered drily.

Ryamon wasted no more time stamping into his boots and rejoining them. Curtly, he asked, "Do we have enough daylight to travel farther today?"

Nepharyl put on an expression of polite surprise. "If you wish it, Dom."

"Yes."

Nepharyl set to work taking down the blanket and packing away the remaining food. This time, Ryamon felt no urge to help with the chores. He quickly folded their old clothing into his way-pack and went to stand with Valdira.

Already, he could see that he would miss the intimacy of traveling with her, just the two of them. Part of him feared their magical time together was already over, like a dream he was waking from. But Ryamon wouldn't give up on his lover so easily. He reached out to take her hand, hoping their empathic link would permit them to have something like a private conversation. Her fingers twitched a little, but then slipped into his.

Ryamon sensed turbulent emotions, chiefly annoyance at Nepharyl for ogling her but beneath that was anger and a keen sense of loss. He tried to focus on calm feelings, that they were safe, however temporary it might be, yet also communicate that he, too, didn't like Nepharyl.

In return he received the tart accusation, *You were the one who wanted to come here.*

Stung, Ryamon protested, "I didn't have any choice. Arkanost is too dangerous for us."

Valdira's simmering anger suddenly erupted. Around them rose the familiar susurrus of birch trees swaying without wind. He felt the sting as she squeezed his hand, crushing his fingers against each other. Her silent rage blazed in his mind.

"You didn't listen to me! You ignored my decision and did what you

wanted!"

"Sweetheart," Ryamon protested. Weeks ago, Silma had warned him about her father's violent temperament. Now he was seeing it for himself.

Nepharyl glanced curiously over his shoulder. "Dom?"

Then something else happened, almost too quick for Ryamon to follow. A shudder ran through Valdira, body and spirit. Her rage evaporated. In its place was something else—not anger, but sickening fear.

Eyes fixed on the trees, she whispered to herself, "No, I won't do this. I'm not like him."

"Sweetheart?" Ryamon repeated, baffled by her words. Why was she so upset?

Valdira had already dropped his hand. "Leave me alone!" she cried, despairing. Lifting her skirts, she ran from him and vanished among the trees.

"Dama, if there is anything I can do!" Nepharyl started to follow Valdira, but Ryamon caught his shoulder.

"No, don't follow her," he said. "It's been a difficult day. Just get us ready to go."

"But," Nepharyl sputtered. "Alone, in this wilderness…"

"She said to leave her alone," Ryamon snapped. "Leave her alone! She'll come back when she calms down."

Even so, a part of him focused outward, trying to hear some trace of Valdira's presence in the sighing trees.

~ * ~

Although Ryamon couldn't see where Valdira was, she must have been watching them. Not long after Nepharyl buckled the last strap on the ornyx's back, she reappeared on the hilltop where the nobleman had first stood to look for them. In the green dress, she looked like the forest itself come alive, Ryamon thought.

Valdira didn't say anything, just walked down toward the soda spring.

"Dama!" Nepharyl sounded relieved. "It's good to have you back."

Valdira didn't acknowledge his concern. In a flat, hard voice, she asked, "Were we going somewhere?"

"Of course, Dama. This way," he answered smoothly.

Taking up the lead, Nepharyl started off down the hillside,

weaving through the birch grove. Valdira followed, her expression stormy, and then Ryamon. His legs were still heavy with residual fatigue, so he didn't try to talk. Valdira maintained her silence. Walking with her was a bit like walking next to a porcupine; Ryamon didn't know when he might be pricked.

Eventually he fell in on the other side of the ornyx, where he could see his lover without being glared at. He wished she would tell him why she was so upset. He could only guess it was because of how the Shadow magus had beaten her, binding her powers and making her helpless. Ryamon himself had been used to attack his love, and the humiliation still gnawed at his heart. He kept wishing Valdira could come back and walk at his side, the way she always had. They could talk about the battle, try to ease each other's pain. But she didn't.

Once they emerged into a clearing, he could see it was midafternoon. Nepharyl kept to stream sides and meadows, where the going was easier. Sometimes they saw squirrels and jays, but no larger beasts. Always he led them south, deeper into Costera. Angled shelves of rock jutted skyward on either side, but gradually Ryamon realized there was nothing rearing up in front of them.

Shortly after that, Nepharyl brought them onto an exposed ridge where rocky cliffs fell away, revealing the land below. A long valley stretched in either direction with jutting peaks pointed inward from both sides. It looked like a mouth full of fangs about to snap shut. What was really striking, though, was the bare ground beneath them. This had to be the Valley of White Sand.

It wasn't really sand, Ryamon could tell at once. The cliff they stood on was yellowy-tan and the valley floor didn't match that. It was a strange gray-white, almost a chemical color. Trees grew down the flanks of the mountains, but nothing lived on the valley floor. Only a few snags stood up, silvery and dead.

Because there was no cover, they could see a river flowing in sluggish curves. Dozens of shallow pools lay scattered across the ground. Some were an attractive blue-green color, others brilliant orange, yellow, or sickly brown. In other places, piles of slick, grayish stones steamed ominously. Vapors rose from the pools, even in the warmth of afternoon, and a faint, foul odor came up on the wind. Ryamon wondered how many soda springs were down there.

The view was startling enough to bring even Valdira out of

her dark mood. Hands on hips, she looked down for a moment.

"What a lovely spot," she observed sarcastically.

Like a good sycophant, Nepharyl chuckled. "In its own way, Dama, I suppose it is. Yet the Valley of White Sand is also very dangerous. We can hike down to the valley floor, but night will come soon. We need daylight to cross."

Costera suddenly seemed a lot less promising as their new home.

Chapter Sixteen

Ryamon slept restlessly and dreamed of fire. He was surrounded by the dance of flames. The comforting glow called to him, yet vanished into mist when he opened himself to take them in.

He woke to wan light and the misery of sore muscles. Ryamon slept alone, wrapped in his travel cloak. There had been no question of Valdira sleeping beside him, and Nepharyl had given her most of the blankets. He wasn't truly cold, for his Element protected him, but loneliness made for another kind of chill.

Stiffly, he moved over to the campfire. Not a trace of warmth there, either. For all his simpering, Nepharyl was a poor manservant.

Ryamon reached over to the pile of wood he had collected the night before. He arranged a few small pieces around a charred section of log and stretched out his hand. With a soft pop, flames curled into life. Something inside him relaxed as it burned with soothing noises. After his strange dreams, Ryamon had been half-afraid he was losing his connection to Fire along with Valdira's respect. As long as he still had the Fire, there was hope for Valdira, too.

An odd rumble nearby distracted Ryamon. He both heard it and felt the vibrations in the earth. The sound grew louder, then softer, then louder again, then softer. As he traced the sensation through the ground, Ryamon realized he also felt heat, just as in his dream. He turned to stare at the source.

A short distance from their camp, one of the enigmatic piles of gray rock steamed in the pre-dawn light. He was sure it was throwing off more steam than it had when Nepharyl chose this spot for their camp. The rumble became a sputtering hiss. Ryamon watched, amazed, as the steam hardened into a fierce jet. Foaming water suddenly shot skyward in angry billows. He instinctively scrambled backward. Ryamon smelled hot mist, thick with a rank stench of sulphur.

So this was what he had sensed during the night. It wasn't true fire, but hot water under the ground. Reaching deeper, he sensed a much larger mass deep below the earth, something heavy and hot like metal ore in a furnace. The rising heat must have killed the trees in the valley by cooking their roots in the ground.

The incredible spectacle drew Ryamon back to himself. Though Valdira was annoyed with him, he didn't think she would want to miss it. He crept to her side and touched her shoulder.

"Sweetheart," he murmured. "You have to see this."

Valdira sat up, blinking. She tensed and looked around, fixing her eyes on the hot fountain. She stared at it, dismayed, and then glared at Ryamon.

"What did you do?" she accused.

"Nothing," he answered, his sense of wonder deflating. "That's water. I'm a Fire magus. I couldn't—"

"It's called a geyser," came Nepharyl's voice behind them. He yawned, then continued, "One of the chief dangers in the Valley of White Sand, Dama. They erupt without warning. Animals cannot bear the noise."

Ryamon glanced over at the ornyx, which had run to the furthest extent of its tether. Its frightened squawks were hardly audible through the geyser's roaring.

"Dama Yolie sometimes sends her serfs to gather the minerals that collect near the springs," Nepharyl went on. "If they aren't careful, they fall through the ground into hidden pools, where the water is hot enough to boil the meat from your bones. That's why we must cross in daylight."

Valdira glanced at Nepharyl skeptically. Ryamon tried not to resent the interruption, and the implication that they were helpless without him.

"You forget, I'm a Fire magus," he answered. "I can feel the heat beneath the surface. We'll make it across the valley, never fear."

"Indeed, Dom." Nepharyl raised one eyebrow in what might have been either surprise or mockery. "Then I shall be at ease. Dama, are you hungry?"

He went to get food from the ornyx's pack, which meant he had to get close to the agitated bird. Ryamon could have suggested Valdira calm the creature, but he decided he would rather watch the geyser.

They sat together in silence until the steam and water lost its power. Just as when the eruption started, the boiling plume dropped and rose again and dropped even farther. Soon there was nothing but a pile of wet, steaming rocks. The water that had been expelled from the geyser ran off in shallow channels. Curls of steam chased it toward the river.

"That's something you don't see every day," Valdira admitted.

"Amazing," Ryamon murmured. The geyser's power and turbulence reminded him a bit of Valdira, although he didn't say so. She might not like the comparison.

"Can you really sense hot water under the ground?" she asked dubiously.

He shrugged modestly. "Can you really keep that ornyx from gutting Nepharyl?"

Just for a moment, he thought she would smile. She must have remembered that she was angry, for she tossed her head. The ornyx stood still as one of the trees on the hillside.

"My thanks, Dama," Nepharyl called, panting slightly.

Valdira tossed her head at him, too.

The breakfast Nepharyl offered was exactly the same as last night's supper. If Ryamon hadn't put his hand on the kettle to boil the water, even the tea would have been cold.

"Forgive me," the nobleman apologized. "In my mistress' house you will see true hospitality."

"You said you serve Dama Yolie," Ryamon asked, hoping to gather more information. "What is she like?"

"Ah, Dom, she is the most beautiful of the witch queens," Nepharyl said. "A powerful sorceress, to be sure, feared by her rivals, yet the most marvelous dancer, a brilliant gambler. She adores all sorts of games…"

He trailed off, running short of superlatives. Ryamon watched him for a moment, amazed to see the suave courtier grin like a moon-struck swain.

"Not *the* most beautiful," Ryamon put in. He glanced at Valdira, but she didn't notice his compliment. Nepharyl merely smirked.

"When you meet my lady, you will understand."

Ryamon didn't answer. Valdira seemed lost in thought, her gaze fixed in the distance. As he watched, she scowled faintly at something no one else could see.

"Dama, would you like more fruit?" Nepharyl leaned forward to offer Valdira the dried apples. She jumped, startled. For a moment she stared, as if she didn't recognize him. Then she winced and rubbed her forehead.

"Sweetheart?" Ryamon asked, concerned.

She pushed his hand away and jumped to her feet. "Aren't we ready to go yet?"

"I need but a moment, Dama." Nepharyl scrambled to pack away the food and blankets.

Ryamon extended a hand to absorb the fire, leaving nothing but ashes in the fire ring. Valdira had never stayed angry this long before. But, he consoled himself, they were about to cross the Valley of White Sand. That should give him ample opportunity to display his magic. After the previous day's debacle, a bit of showing off might not be a bad idea.

~ * ~

By the morning after the battle, Phareth felt rested enough to try finding Valdira or Ryamon. Though not completely gone, his headache was much better and it was frankly boring to sit under a cramped ledge waiting for the villagers to rescue them. After an all-too-brief breakfast, because they didn't have much food left, the Shadow magus settled himself to work.

Since he had already been in contact with both rogue magi, they weren't difficult to locate. Phareth immediately perceived, with a deep inner sigh, that they had fled southward into Costera. Already they were well into hostile territory. Unless the royal court authorized an outright invasion, it would not be possible to physically retrieve them.

That didn't mean Phareth had no options, however. It was still possible, if he was careful, to persuade the runaways to come back. They might even think it was their own decision if he did it right. Phareth considered suspending his trance long enough to let Anarinda know what he had in mind, but quickly decided not to. Telamar would take the plan as more proof of his evil mind control. Another argument would only waste energy.

Valdira was the one he needed to influence, he decided. And, as he recalled, his quarry was alert enough to realize what he was trying to do. He would have to be very, very careful.

Phareth renewed his contact with Valdira. At first he just listened, trying to figure out what was happening around her. Sights and smells confused him: hot mist and water shooting into the air? He kept a psychic silence lest she pick up his puzzled reaction.

Ryamon was nearby, Phareth sensed. Hovering, as Valdira saw it. His attentiveness annoyed her. Phareth wondered if he could use her emotions to drive the lovers apart. Alone, they would be easier to capture. No, the Mage Lords wanted both rebels. He needed to keep them together.

Ever so cautiously, Phareth whispered a reminder of Arkanost. He sent the whisper of birch leaves and fragrance of pine into her mind. Wasn't she homesick, he suggested? Perhaps she should turn back.

Irrational rage exploded within her. He froze as emotions swept over him, hot and raw. Had she already detected his presence? No, she didn't raise any shields. Valdira was already homesick, he realized. She loved the wilderness of Selkest and was furious with Ryamon for taking her away from it. Indeed, she was terrified to leave the land where she first came into her powers.

Feeling her wild passion, it was easy to believe this was Marton's daughter, but getting her angry at Ryamon wasn't what he wanted. Feeling slightly bruised, Phareth waited for the firestorm to pass. He mulled what he had learned and tried to think of a new approach. There had to be some way of bringing her back to Arkanost without making her hate Ryamon. Who, Phareth readily admitted, didn't deserve her scorn.

While she struggled to control her emotions, Phareth heard voices nearby. Ryamon and another man. The second voice sounded familiar. Straining, Phareth caught a name, Yolie. He recognized the name, too, but couldn't placed it. Phareth frowned to himself. Where had he heard this man's voice before?

"Dama, would you like some fruit?"

Someone Valdira wasn't looking at offered a small silver plate loaded with dried apple rings. Phareth saw a man's hand in a dark sleeve with a lacy cuff. He froze in mind and body. That looked like Nepharyl's jacket.

Valdira ignored the food and the plate withdrew from her sight. He listened, barely breathing in his trance. Nepharyl? Yes, the nobleman was missing. Phareth couldn't find him in Lornest. Yet how could he be with the renegades?

It was agony to keep still when every nerve shouted that he should slice into Valdira's memory and seize the knowledge he wanted. Ever so delicately, trembling with urgency, Phareth probed for information about the man who was talking.

There they were, the face and the name. In Valdira's memory, Nepharyl strode out of the woods leading an ornyx packed with supplies. It was the same animal he had borrowed from Lord Aisleng. Phareth could see the badge embossed in its harness.

Valdira jerked and gasped. Instantly Phareth dropped his link, hoping he had been quick enough that she wouldn't know he had been in her mind. He opened his eyes and blinked against the daylight outside the shelter. His breath came in deep gulps as he grappled with what he had seen.

Just outside the shelter, Telamar was stacking pieces of trash wood for the fire. The Ice magus scowled, still tense from yesterday's scolding. "Something wrong?"

Phareth couldn't even answer at first. Anarinda came to crouch beside him, concerned.

"Did you find them?" she asked.

"Yes," Phareth told her. "I found them. And I found Nepharyl."

"What?" Telamar demanded, incredulous.

"He's with them," Phareth said. "Nepharyl is guiding the runaways."

Silence filled the shelter. Then Telamar dropped what he had been stacking. He knelt to enter, even as Anarinda sagged into a sitting position.

"Nepharyl is a traitor?" Her soft voice trembled with shock. "We told him all our plans."

Phareth nodded. His mind whirled with the implications.

"It can't be," Telamar insisted.

Phareth shrugged. "He isn't where he was supposed to be."

"How could he follow us without our knowing?" the Ice magus argued.

"The same way he kept me from homing in on him," Phareth replied bitterly. "We drove Valdira right into his hands."

"I thought you couldn't find Nepharyl," Anarinda cut in.

"I didn't, but I found Valdira," Phareth answered. "She saw him and talked to him. I tell you, it's Nepharyl. He's in Costera and he's taking them someplace called Laceto, to meet his mistress."

Telamar settled across the fire from them. His face was pale and set. The three magi looked at each other in silence before Anarinda spoke again.

"This must be where Lord Salovik got his ideas about Murcrys leading a conspiracy," she said.

"Guilberta told him that," Telamar protested.

"Who do you think told Guilberta?" Phareth made an effort to speak quietly. This wasn't the time to rub Salovik's errors in Telamar's face. "Anyone who watched the Collegium would know our mage lords don't get along. It would be easy to drop a hint to Salovik and let him take it from there. The Collegium is always divided, suspicious of each other. Now Mother and Klaive are angry and Salovik will be humiliated when he finds out he was tricked. Arkanost is weaker, and Nepharyl... We don't even know what he's up to."

"Or who else he's working with," Anarinda added.

"This is all guesswork," Telamar said. From his expression, even he knew it was a weak excuse. Phareth just shrugged.

"Unless you feel like taking chances," Anarinda said, "the three of us had better start getting ready."

"For what?" Telamar asked.

"Whatever is coming out of Costera."

The Ice magus looked around, taking in their pitiful shelter and the few materials they had to work with. Finally he nodded.

"I suppose it wouldn't hurt to prepare for trouble."

~ * ~

"What's taking so long?" Valdira complained.

Ryamon looked up cautiously. While Nepharyl packed their supplies onto the ornyx, he sat facing out over the Valley of White Sand. Both hands were pressed to the ground, helping him sense the network of hidden channels and pools beneath the pallid soil. It was a complicated array, interconnected like a spider's web, but he knew he could get through it. However, Ryamon wanted more than mere survival.

"I'm trying to choose our path," he said, "but I also want to mark a safe route for others who come here."

"It's a big valley." Valdira had been pacing for several minutes, arms crossed defensively.

"I have to do what I can," Ryamon said. He glanced over his shoulder to make sure Nepharyl was still busy. "Do you remember how he said the serfs come to collect minerals, and sometimes they fall into boiling water?"

Valdira nodded, rubbing her forehead absently. She had been

doing that a lot today. Daring her wrath, Ryamon asked, "Headache?"

She shook her head, an angry twitch. "That Shadow magus, I think he was trying to spy on me. I blocked him," she added, seeing Ryamon's concerned expression.

"All right," Ryamon said. "Well, Nepharyl might not care what happens to the serfs, but I do. I know we don't have time to map out the whole valley, but at least I can mark our trail across."

"Why bother?" Valdira asked. "They're just serfs."

Ryamon's heart sank at her words. How could he make her see how callous she sounded without destroying their relationship?

"Sweetheart," he said quietly. "We're serfs, too."

"Not anymore," she interrupted. "We're nobles now, remember? He said so. We don't have to follow a bunch of rules and serve the common good." Her voice took on a mocking sing-song as she repeated what was evidently a stricture of the Order of Blood. "We can make our own rules."

"Maybe," Ryamon said, though he didn't see that they had gained any money or property to go along with their supposed rank. "Don't you think Nepharyl could just be saying that to get you to cooperate? He never has told us what he wants."

Valdira gave a light snort. Before she could answer, Nepharyl called, "I'm ready if you are."

His tone was smooth and cheerful. So cheerful that Ryamon was sure Nepharyl had heard what he was saying.

"Yes, let's go." Valdira went back to pacing, arms folded angrily. Bracing to battle the Shadow magus at any moment, Ryamon guessed. Ready to battle something, at any rate. He was tempted to tell them both to try and cross the valley without him, if they didn't respect what mattered to him.

Even as he thought this, he knew he wasn't ready to let Valdira go. Slowly he stood up, brushing grainy white dust off the seat of his trousers. Nepharyl led the ornyx toward them.

"Dom, if you still wish to lead the way?" He asked with another of his insufferable bows. Ryamon was sure Nepharyl meant to mock him, but he was determined not to act the fool in front of Valdira.

He stretched out his senses, finding rock beneath the coarse soil of the valley. With a low grumble, half a dozen stone pillars split the earth in a half-circle around their camp site. They weren't large, only knee height, but too big to erode away very easily. As an afterthought, he squared them off to make it obvious they weren't natural stones.

This marked their starting place. Ryamon moved off from there. Concentrating on the subterranean hazards, he barely heard the shuffle of Valdira and Nepharyl following along, nor the occasional squawk from the ornyx. The sun was just rising over a ridge. Its rays lit the pale gray dirt to brilliant white.

Contrary to his first impression, the Valley of White Sand was not a barren landscape. Tufts of grass rose from the chalky soil. An occasional fallen tree trunk sheltered communities of colorful wildflowers. The ground was streaked with channels, some dry and others gaudy with algae as steaming water ran from various pools and vents. Although no more geysers erupted nearby, the chemical stench gave its own incentive to hurry.

Ryamon walked slowly but with confidence, threading a path between subterranean hazards. He raised a new marker every thirty paces or wherever his route took a turn. Nepharyl and Valdira followed closely, saying nothing. Nepharyl showed his impatience by constantly adjusting his hat to ward off the sunlight. The ornyx pulled on its lead, trying to get farther away from whichever pool or geyser they happened to be passing.

As for Valdira, she kept her arms folded and face set in a petulant frown. From time to time, she rubbed her arms. He wondered if she was cold in the low-cut dress or just anxious about being in strange country. It tore his heart to see her turn away from him, but he couldn't give in on this. He had to do what was right and hope she would come to understand.

~ * ~

Once again, Phareth had to wait until he was calmer before he called on his mother. It took her longer to respond this time. From the snippets of talk echoing in her mind, he could tell she was in a busy area.

"Is this urgent?" Murcrys sounded sharp. *"Guilberta is about to address the Collegium."*

"Excellent. It will save you having to summon them all back again." As quickly as possible, Phareth explained what he had learned.

Murcrys gave a kind of hiss in her mind. Then, faintly, he sensed her speaking aloud. "Your grace, forgive me, but this cannot wait. Nepharyl has been located." A brief pause. "Certainly. I will ask."

To Phareth, she said, *"Didn't you say Nepharyl was obsessed with Guilberta?"*

"I thought he was."

"Yet now he swears loyalty to… What was the name?"

"Dama Yolie." Dama was only a title, Phareth knew. Once again, he was certain he had heard the name, Yolie, before.

Before he could unearth that memory, Murcrys said, *"I think I understand. It's a very advanced technique. Yolie established such powerful control, she could manipulate Nepharyl from any distance. Then she concealed her domination by substituting the image of Guilberta in his mind. All those times you thought he was fixated on the countess, but he was actually thinking of Yolie."*

"You mean," Phareth said, *"Nepharyl told everyone he escaped from Estrona, but he never really did."*

He sensed his mother's agreement. *"This is valuable information, son, but I must go. The council is waiting and I think—"* he sensed her ironic smile *"—I would like to know who else came back from Estrona and what positions they now hold in our government."*

"Check on Count Aisleng of Elvest," Phareth suggested.

"I will. Wait where you are. Do nothing. You will hear from me again soon."

"Mother, wait." Phareth held the connection a moment longer. *"I know the name, but I can't place it. Who is Yolie?"*

"You should know her name," Murcrys said grimly. *"She's the sister of your old friend Darmosh."*

"What?" Phareth demanded, but Murcrys was gone, leaving him terribly alone.

~ * ~

"Well done, Dom," Nepharyl said. The praise came out flat and indifferent.

Ryamon shrugged his shoulders and rolled his head from side to side. His muscles felt pinched and tight. Crossing the valley had taken several hours, including a long pause while he created a bridge over the river. Valdira and Nepharyl had taken a nice rest, loitering on the riverbank and watching another geyser erupt. Ryamon had worked the whole time.

He glanced over at Valdira, wishing she would rub his neck.

With her healing powers, he knew she could soothe his cramped muscles in a moment. She was watching him, her expression thoughtful. He almost thought he could see a return of respect in her eyes, but she didn't offer to ease his pain.

"Shall we go, then?" Nepharyl cut in officiously. "I know the way from here."

"How much farther is it?" Valdira asked.

"We can be there by evening if there are no more delays."

Ryamon was irritated by the slighting remark, but his labors had left him too tired to debate the point. Nepharyl pushed to the fore, tucking his cane under his arm importantly. Since he was leading the ornyx at the same time, he only looked ludicrous. Valdira followed and Ryamon trailed behind them. Despite the dangers he knew lurked in Arkanost, he really wished they weren't going to Laceto.

Nepharyl led them eastward, skirting the edge of the valley until they came to a road. It wasn't much, a double scratching of wagon tracks that led into the forest. He turned up it, and they began to climb a narrow canyon between two of the jutting, tooth-like crags. The three of them walked through the afternoon, stopping only to drink from small streams as they passed.

The road crossed a steep pass, then angled southwest in the shadow of tall peaks. Even as they climbed, Ryamon sensed the land dropping away before them. It felt strange to him, but Valdira didn't seem to notice. The trees along the road were neither birch nor pine, but some type Ryamon didn't recognize. It was gloomy in their shade, at any rate. He began to wonder if the sun ever shone in Costera.

The trees thinned out at last, allowing a ruddy glow to reach them. A breeze brushed between the tree trunks. It felt warm compared to the cold air in the mountains.

"Ah," Nepharyl exclaimed. "We're almost there!"

He yanked on the lead to make the ornyx go faster. Ryamon glanced at Valdira, hoping she wouldn't like the man abusing the bird. She looked ahead with wary eyes, as if she was trying to sense what kind of land this was. Then the woods opened up and they caught their first glimpse of what lay ahead.

Ryamon wasn't sure what he had expected Laceto to look like. Perhaps a frowning crag and a keep with many towers. What he saw instead were fields of ripening grain, the level ground a surprise after the rugged mountains. A montus team trudged slowly across the fields. Set in the center, a lake shimmered with afternoon sunlight. A man in a canoe cast a fishing net into the water. There was a village farther back, neat houses clustered behind a high stone wall. On a hilltop beside the lake, a great house dominated the landscape.

The mansion was nothing like the buildings of Polvest, which stood in their hundreds, each one exactly like the others. It had a high, peaked center and two wings spread wide like arms ready to embrace them. Columns lined the edifice, giving it an open, airy look. A garden of flowers ran down to the lake shore, where a dainty gazebo stood poised above the water.

Columns and flowers shone back, reflected in the water. Ryamon thought the mansion looked like a woman bent over a mirror, admiring her reflection. Nepharyl paused, letting them take in the view.

"Laceto," he declared proudly. "Now you will see the wonders of Costera. You shall sleep on silk and dine on the finest. Come, we must hurry. Dama Yolie is waiting."

To Ryamon, his words sounded more like a threat than a gift.

Chapter Seventeen

Beckoning eagerly, Nepharyl led the ornyx down the road. Ryamon followed slowly. Valdira stayed where she was, eyes sweeping the country before them. She seemed interested, yet distrust also flitted across her face. Ryamon wondered if she was going to show her spirit and just stand there until Nepharyl noticed she wasn't coming. When she saw Ryamon looking at her, Valdira finally strode forward.

"We don't have to go with him," he murmured. "The mountains are close by. We could…"

"Don't be stupid," she hissed as she passed.

Ryamon sighed and trailed after her, wondering if he would ever say the right thing again.

The crude track led down a slope and beside the closest field, which was enclosed by a wooden fence. Soon it met a wide circle of packed gravel. The area looked large enough for a montus wagon to turn around in, but nothing so familiar waited for them. Instead, there was a low-slung carriage, long enough for two rows of open seats. It was lacquered bright blue with extravagant brass rails and fittings. The front and back ends curved upward like flower petals.

An unfamiliar animal was yoked to the front. It stood short and wide, with heavy shoulders and stocky legs ending in thick pads. The hide was tough and wrinkled. It had little eyes, scooped ears, and a horn on its nose that looked as if it had been filed down considerably. The beast wasn't pretty, but it did seem powerful.

"Ah!" Nepharyl exclaimed. "You see, Dama? My lady is prepared."

At his cheerful whistle, a group of liverymen sprang into action. The driver stayed where he was, on a platform behind the beast, but another man leaped down and jogged toward them. When he got closer, he stopped and stood aside, bowing deeply. Nepharyl tossed the ornyx's lead to him. A third man opened the carriage door with a flourish. They were all dressed the same way, in rust-colored breeches and loose white shirts that looked something like smocks. As they passed the man who now held the ornyx, Ryamon tried to catch his eye and nod in greeting, but the man held his bow and did not look up.

Behind the vehicle, four more men jumped to attention. In addition to their livery, this group wore leather jerkins. They carried narrow bladed swords and bucklers. Each had a small red hat with a white plume sticking up from the front. As they got closer Ryamon could see that not only their clothing was the same. All the men had olive skin and dark hair. Their eyes were black, sharp and serious.

It made him wonder what kind of place Laceto was. True, magi wore matching robes in Arkanist, but you didn't need protection to travel. Why had Yolie sent an armed escort in what seemed to be quiet countryside?

They reached the carriage, where the footmen were now bowing and the guards stood straight and stiff with their bucklers clasped across their chests in salute. Nepharyl offered Valdira his hand.

"Allow me, Dama," he all but purred.

Ryamon couldn't help clenching his fists in anger as Valdira let the traitor help her into the carriage. She settled into the seat as if it was her birthright. Whatever doubts Valdira might have felt, she seemed to have put them from her mind, but Ryamon didn't want to get in. He felt as if he would be giving up control of his own fate if he did. Delaying, he turned to the footman who stood at the chariot door.

"What is this animal?" Ryamon asked.

The man glanced up at him, startled, but didn't answer. He held the door, still bowing. Ryamon wondered how long he could do that before his back started to hurt.

"Pardon me, Dom." Nepharyl was back in the chariot's doorway. "He will not speak to you. A servant does not address his betters, and Dama Yolie's staff are very well trained. If you will be seated, I'll be happy to explain that fascinating creature."

Nepharyl spoke condescendingly, as one would to a foolish child. Again Ryamon's fists clenched with embarrassment. He felt heat building there and took a moment to exhale, controlling his reaction. Behind Nepharyl, he thought he saw a flicker of anger in Valdira's eyes. Ryamon clung to the hope that she was irritated with Nepharyl, not him.

Ignoring Nepharyl, he said to the servant, "I'm sorry."

Ryamon supposed it was also against the rules for a "dom" to apologize, but he didn't care. Like Valdira, he had learned to question the rules. Especially when they were stupid. Or cruel. Or both. His legs felt stiff with anger as he stepped into the chariot and took the seat beside his lover.

Smiling, as if well pleased with himself, Nepharyl sat in the front seat and tapped the driver's shoulder. "Take us home."

The servant said nothing, but shook the reins. The strange animal jerked to alertness. The man who had held the door now sat beside the driver. He rang out a warning on a small brass bell. Just as the carriage lurched into motion, the four soldiers leapt up to cling on the side rails. Behind them, the last servant led the ornyx in the same direction they were going. Ryamon soon lost sight of his lonely figure in the dust.

Once they were moving, Nepharyl turned to face Ryamon and Valdira. He held his hat in his lap, but the wind of their motion continually blew stray curls into his face.

"The animal is called a twyeron," Nepharyl said. "You don't have them in Arkanost. The climate is too cold. They are rare beasts native to southern Costera. As you can see, twyeron are large and difficult to manage. Only the most powerful wizards own them."

Having started this conversation, Ryamon felt obligated to ask, "Are they born with horns?"

"That is true, Dom." Nepharyl paused to smooth the loose hair away from his eyes. He went on, in a reassuring tone, "I believe this animal was taken as an infant to help tame it. The horn is cared for during normal grooming. In the wild, they are much more dangerous."

Ryamon could imagine. Such a creature could trample to splinters whatever it didn't ream with its horn. He wondered how non-magi handled a twyeron if they didn't have Valdira's gift. Ryamon also wondered if Valdira saw the pattern that was emerging, that the wizard-kings subjugated everything around them, whether that meant silencing their servants or cutting off an animal's horn.

"It does seem fast," Ryamon said. Although the twyeron had taken a while to get its bulk moving, it was now pulling the chariot and ten passengers at considerable speed. Ryamon hadn't had the chance to ride in an ornyx chariot very often, but he thought the twyeron might be even faster.

"They are like monti," Nepharyl said. "Useful creatures if handled properly."

The twyeron pounded down the gravel road, grunting deep in its chest. Fields of grain or vegetables flashed past on both sides. All the fields were bordered with wooden fences. Red and white pennants fluttered on posts at the gates to each one. The footman in front continued ringing his bell at intervals. Ryamon wasn't sure why until he saw a group of women emerge from one of the fields carrying baskets heaped with some kind of vegetables. He caught a glimpse of rusty red skirts and white smocks, red scarfs tied over dark hair. The bell clanged its warning. The startled women leaped over to the roadside. They bowed and stayed bent over as the carriage thundered by.

The twyeron raced on, unaware of the near miss. The road curved leftward to follow the lake shore. The carriage leaned significantly as the twyeron pulled it around the bend. Momentum pressed Ryamon against Valdira's side, though he clutched the arms of his seat for balance. Her hazel eyes flicked up to meet his, and he saw she was unsettled by the vehicle's speed.

Ryamon fixed his eyes on the road ahead, but he slipped his hand under the chair's arm. He touched Valdira's hand lightly, in case she objected. The carriage straightened out until they both sat upright again. Valdira was shielding her emotions. Ryamon couldn't tell what she was thinking. He waited for her to twitch her hand away, but she didn't. Hand in hand, neither one speaking, they rode between banks of colorful flowers on the lake shore.

The road rose toward the hilltop, forcing the twyeron to slow down. The gravel road ended in another wide circle, just the right size for the twyeron and carriage to turn around. The mansion stood just above them on the crest of the hill. Ryamon gazed up at it.

A grand sweep of stairs led up to the columned facade, which was taller than he had expected from a distance. To Ryamon's surprise, it was built of limestone blocks rather than raised with magic. He wondered if it was as solid as it looked.

As soon as the carriage stopped, the servants and soldiers sprang into action. The man who had held the door reappeared, bowing as he opened it. The soldiers formed a line beside the carriage, bucklers across their chests as before. The footman beside the driver rang a new pattern on the bell. This must have announced their arrival, for the mansion doors opened at once.

Bowing, a pair of maidservants in red skirts and white smocks held the doors open. A lady in shimmering pink stepped out behind them. Feeling her presence, Ryamon paused in the act of helping Valdira down from the carriage.

From Nepharyl's description, he had been expecting a radiant young woman, but the lady of Laceto was at least fifteen years older than Valdira. She had a plump frame and dark hair. Regardless, Nepharyl rushed up the steps to meet her. Yolie paused while he knelt at her feet. With his cane cradled in the crook of his elbow, Nepharyl lifted the hem of her gown and kissed it reverently.

Valdira breathed the lightest snort of disgust.

Yolie was clearly posing to be looked at. Her gown was cut in the same style as Valdira's, though Valdira's wasn't covered in gold embroidery or studded with pearls. The tightly laced bodice pushed her bosom upward until she seemed about to overflow her gown. More pearls ringed her neck and draped over the edge of the bodice. Her hair swept upward into what reminded Ryamon of wings on either side of her head. Silver strands glinted among the dark. These were placed as carefully as the pearls.

Still kneeling, Nepharyl murmured something to Yolie. She stroked his head absently. "You have done well, my pet."

However, she didn't look at Nepharyl. Her dark eyes were focused on Ryamon and Valdira. Something brushed past Ryamon, a wind he didn't quite feel. Valdira tensed, but nothing more seemed to happen.

Yolie started down the steps. "Welcome, Valdira and Ryamon," she said as she descended. Her voice was sweet and light, yet strangely without emotion. "I have heard so much about you."

Ryamon expected Valdira to make some kind of sarcastic retort, but she merely dipped in the start of a curtsey. Feeling her move, Ryamon also began to bow. A trilling laugh startled them both into stillness.

"Oh no, no. You must not bow to me." Yolie hurried down the last few steps, pearls clicking together softly as she moved. "No longer are you prisoners of your power. In my country, this is how we greet our guests."

Before Valdira could react, Yolie embraced her lightly and kissed first one cheek, then the other. Though startled, Valdira managed to kiss the air as Yolie moved past her. Ryamon could clearly see how cosmetics covered the lines around her eyes. He smelled a heavy floral perfume and wished for the clean simplicity of wild sage.

Fabric rustled as Yolie turned to Ryamon. He was much taller, so she stood on her toes and pressed against him to kiss his cheek. It might have been enticing except that the pearls on her bodice felt hard even through his jacket.

"I can see we have a lot to learn here," Valdira said with a trace of tartness.

"We're sorry to impose on your hospitality," Ryamon said. "In our country, it's considered polite to wait for an invitation."

"But I'm so happy to have you," Yolie said. In an expert motion, she twirled in between Ryamon and Valdira and took each of them by the arm. Ryamon was forced to release Valdira's hand. "You have traveled so far. You must be exhausted. Do please come in. My servants are waiting to refresh you."

Even as she spoke, Yolie propelled them up the stairs in a swirl of pearls and perfume. Ryamon heard faint tramping as the soldiers marched toward the back of the house. Gravel crunched as the twyeron cart turned to go.

"It would feel good to wash up," Valdira said. She sounded subdued, not at all her usual willful self.

"I heard there was a battle," Yolie continued with a dramatic shudder. "Dreadful. My dear brother lives just down the valley. He'll be joining us for supper. I'm sure he'll want to hear all about it."

"There isn't much to tell," Ryamon demurred. He didn't want to remember how the outcome had turned Valdira against him.

They reached the mansion. Yolie's laugh echoed slightly beneath the columned porch.

"You are too humble, my pet," she fluttered up at him. "Obviously you survived the struggle, so all is well."

Ryamon noticed she didn't have any trace of a foreign accent. Either Yolie had spent years studying the language of Arkanost or both countries spoke the same tongue. He wasn't sure which would surprise him more.

The house's door was wood, double-leaved and heavily ornamented with brass trim. Inside was a foyer two stories tall. A pair of stairs rose in graceful arcs to make almost a perfect circle. The floor was white limestone, polished to such a shine that the stairs reflected in it just as the mansion had reflected in the lake outside.

"Now you go along with Nepharyl," Yolie said to Ryamon. "He'll see that you're properly taken care of. Valdira, my pet, you must come with me. I'll set you right."

Ryamon halted. He was being separated from his lover, like a sobi cut out of its herd by a pack of eridow. He didn't like it. Valdira glanced at him behind Yolie's extravagant hair and shrugged. Since she wasn't concerned, he reluctantly stepped back and let Yolie bustle Valdira up the left hand set of stairs. After all, if they had been in Polvet, he wouldn't have expected to bathe with Valdira. Apparently Costera also had some customs in common with Arkanost.

"I'll see you tonight," he called, trying to sound sure of himself.

Swallowing a sigh, he turned to face Nepharyl, who trailed along after them with his hat and cane. The man hadn't said a word since they entered the house. He gazed after Yolie, no longer arrogant but stricken at being left behind. For some reason it irritated Ryamon.

Then he paused. He hoped that wasn't how he looked, fawning on Valdira despite the way she had been treating him since the battle. Was he really that much of a fool?

Yet he also felt like a fool standing at the bottom of the stairs and watching the two women walk away from him. Ryamon was getting tired of that feeling. And he was tired of the servants standing there, bent halfway over and waiting for him to do something.

"Which way do we go?" he asked.

A blink, and Nepharyl was himself again, poised and slightly condescending. He gestured to the right-hand staircase, which was lined with a deep red carpet.

"This way, Dom. Now you'll see true hospitality."

Nepharyl headed grandly up the steps. Since both stairways met at the top, Ryamon couldn't help wondering why it mattered which one they used. Nevertheless, he followed his guide. Despite the claim that there were no rules in Costera, Ryamon was fairly sure he wouldn't be permitted to just wander around at will.

At the top landing, Ryamon heard the faint echo of Yolie talking to Valdira. Then Nepharyl led him into the mansion's right wing. They came into a large room where tall windows gave an expansive view. Mountains dominated the scene, familiar jagged peaks aglow with sunset's rose. There were more farm fields and the walled village at the base of the hill. The floor was polished here, too, so that the setting sun filled the chamber with its fiery rays.

Two fine porcelain tubs steamed invitingly behind an arrangement of folding screens that gave them privacy to change clothes. Two dark-haired women dressed as servants bowed beside each tub. Ryamon was surprised to see women. In Arkanost, only men worked in a men's bath.

While Ryamon hesitated, Nepharyl wasted no time ducking behind the nearer of the two partitions. "Don't let it get cold," he warned with barbed cheerfulness.

Ryamon peered cautiously behind the other screen. He saw nothing sinister, only furniture: a chair with a bath robe laid over the back, a tall mirror in a gilt frame, a rack of towels, a large empty basket. After sliding his waypack under the chair, where he could keep an eye on it, he quickly stripped and dropped his clothing into the basket. Then he stopped at the sight of his own image in the mirror.

He was grimy all over, of course, even in places his clothes had covered. Living outdoors was dirty no matter how often one dipped into cold mountain lakes. More bits of twig and leaf than he had expected were tangled in his long coppery hair. What startled him was to see himself so thin and tanned.

True, Ryamon had always been skinny. But he had lost weight living in the hills, where meals were always too few and too small. Yet he didn't look gaunt or sickly. Living rough also meant constant walking and hard work with his hands. The new Ryamon was lean and muscular. Blue eyes were pale in his brown face, alight with his inner fire. Life in the hills had suited him more than he realized.

He had to be honest—that was only because Valdira had been with him. Yet, in some way, Valdira also needed him or they would never have become lovers. With a sinking heart, Ryamon wondered if that was all at an end. They were in Laceto, a more civilized place. Did they still need each other, or by leaving the hills had they also left each other behind?

A series of sloshing noises and a long sigh told him Nepharyl was into his bath. Ryamon felt foolish again, just standing there and looking into the mirror. Irritably, he shook himself into motion.

Ryamon glanced around the side of the screen. His two attendants weren't bowing any more, to his relief. They stood looking straight ahead with their hands folded in front of them. The older of the two noticed him. Barely moving, she nudged her companion and they instantly faced away.

It was ridiculous, but Ryamon was relieved not to be stared at. He went to the tub. The water was faintly amber and smelled of musk. It steamed invitingly. He quickly stepped in and sat down. The bath wasn't as warm as Ryamon had expected. Maybe he'd spent too much time thinking. Summoning his inner fire, he released heat from his body until the temperature was right. He ducked below the water to wet his hair, then surfaced and leaned back to soak away the aches of his long journey.

The two women approached with timid, mousy steps. The younger one held a small cloth, comb and long-handled brush. The older had a wicker basket and a towel hanging over her arm.

"Yes?" Ryamon asked warily.

Without looking directly at Ryamon, she bowed and offered him the basket. Inside he saw a selection of soaps wrapped in dainty paper, and small bottles that might have contained skin oils.

"You have to let them wash you," Nepharyl called around the partitions. His voice sounded lazy and content, like someone... What had Yolie said? Someone who was being refreshed.

"I can do it," Ryamon protested. No one waited on a magus of the Seven Exalted Orders. The maidservants appeared slightly flustered, although they still didn't say anything.

"They're servants. It's their job. Be nice to them," Nepharyl advised. Indeed, Ryamon heard gentle splashing and trickling, so Nepharyl was obviously being washed even as he spoke.

Ryamon couldn't think of any more arguments, so he gave in. "All right," he sighed.

The older maidservant bowed slightly lower and extended the basket a fraction closer to Ryamon.

"Do I have to pick one?" he guessed. Already this pampering seemed like more trouble than it was worth.

She gave a tiny nod. Feeling foolish all over again, Ryamon studied the contents of the basket. The toiletries were color-coordinated, either yellow, green or pink. He lifted the soaps and smelled them in turn. The pink and green fragrances were extremely floral, but the yellow was musky again.

"This one," he said, deciding it would be best if his perfumes didn't clash.

Somewhat nervously, Ryamon sat in the water and let the servants get started. The younger one poured an amber liquid into his hair while the older one soaped up the cloth. Both began to scrub mightily. The dirt they were removing quickly turned the water milky gray, effectively concealing his nakedness.

The two women did know their work. Much against his own wishes, Ryamon began to relax. The cloth was a strange fabric, soft and yet scratchy. The scalp massage that went along with having his hair washed also felt amazingly good.

"You see?" Nepharyl called over to him. "Life is good in Costera."

Ryamon thought about that for a moment, then answered, "I haven't made up my mind."

"Once you get used to our ways, you'll like it here," Nepharyl insisted. "There's no place better for a wizard."

A gentle pressure on Ryamon's head let him know the serving woman wanted to rinse his hair. He obediently slid down below the water and felt her brisk fingers swishing through his hair. He surfaced, and the other woman deftly blotted his eyes with a towel. Then the first one began to comb through the wet tangles of his hair. He felt frequent tweaks as she picked out the larger bits of bracken.

"What about you?" Ryamon called over to Nepharyl. "Without magic, how do you support yourself?"

"I don't have to," Nepharyl replied. "My lady is everything to me."

His voice sounded different—thick, almost drugged. Ryamon glanced toward Nepharyl's tub, wishing he could see through the partitions. Caution re-awoke, reminding him not to trust so easily. Not the women of the bath, or their mistress, Yolie, or Laceto itself.

In the corner of his eye, Ryamon caught a movement as the older serving woman bowed to him. He turned to look as she offered the glittering length of a razor on another dry towel. She wanted to shave him.

Ryamon ran a hand over his chin. He had a small razor in his waypack. Though the geyser had distracted him enough to forget that morning, the stubble wasn't too bad. No matter what Nepharyl said, Ryamon didn't trust these women with a blade at his throat.

"No thank you," he said firmly. "I'd simply like to rest for a moment."

The women bowed and slowly backed away, leaving him to his own thoughts. Once they were outside the partitioned area, he leaned back into the warm water. Although his muscles were nicely loosened up, his mind wouldn't relax. Too many emotions mixed with his impressions of this new land.

Yolie seemed to be all hugs and kisses, shuddering at the very idea of combat. Yet Nepharyl had described a powerful sorceress who loved to gamble and take chances. Was Nepharyl confused, or was Yolie trying to hide who she was? It reinforced Ryamon's suspicions. She had to want something in return for her hospitality. He just didn't know what it was.

Then there was Valdira. He loved her so much, it hurt to breathe, but since the battle against the Collegium magi, she had no use for him. Even now, she might be bathing in the company of handsome men who would wash her hair and rub her back and tempt her—

Ryamon cut off that thought. Valdira wasn't such a fool. The question was, what she wanted from Ryamon. What he wanted from her. If they could ever really be that, to each other. What would he do if they couldn't? He cut that thought off, too. He had to, because it was impossible to make a decision until he talked to Valdira. If he could get her to talk to him.

Something drew him out of his brooding. He sat up, tense and dripping, searching with his trained senses to discover what had alerted him.

Someone was approaching. He could feel it the same way he had sensed he was getting closer to Valdira in the hills. A powerful personality. Ryamon wondered who it was.

Alerted by the splash, the two silent women reappeared at the gap in the screens. Ryamon wasn't surprised to see that one was holding a thick towel and the other neatly folded clothing.

"I can do this part," Ryamon told them as he reached for the towel. Whatever was coming, he definitely wanted to be dressed when he confronted it.

~ * ~

Evening came on, and with it a chilly draft from the mountains. Phareth shivered as he tried to meditate. By unspoken accord, the three magi had returned to their original clothes. Woolen robes would be warmer than Nepharyl's thin garments, but it was still going to be a cold, uncomfortable night with not enough to eat. No matter how they hurried, Silma and the villagers wouldn't arrive for two or three more days.

Until then, Phareth had little to do but brood. Darmosh. The name rang in his mind like thunder in the mountains. Every echo held a new meaning.

Darmosh. Phareth had spent months trying not to think that name, even to himself, because he had assumed what happened in Logoll was his fault. That some slip on his part had brought about disaster.

Now he knew there hadn't been a mistake. It had just been an elaborate lie. There had never been a network of rebels in Costera. No oppressed peasants begging for help in their struggle toward freedom. It had all been a ploy to lure the Collegium into Costera. A trap set by Nepharyl, under Yolie's command. Which meant the orders had come from Darmosh.

This knowledge brought Phareth no peace. Instead of shame, he seethed with grief and fury. Nothing could change the past, he knew. Nothing he did would bring Kylethia back from the dead. It didn't matter. Phareth had a new purpose.

Wait in the hills, Murcrys said. So he waited. Stomach growling empty, shivering in the cold, Phareth listened into Costera. He waited for some hint of his enemy's presence. When he heard it, the time for waiting would be over.

In his mind, he vowed, *"Kylethia, I will avenge you."*

Chapter Eighteen

"Ah, there you are. Come in, my pet, come in."

With a silken rustle, Dama Yolie sailed over to where Ryamon stood hesitating in the doorway. Tucking her hand into the crook of his arm, she drew him into a small dining room.

No windows here showed the evening sky. Instead, portraits of men and women in antique costumes adorned the very white limestone walls. Lamps burned in sconces, their flames reflected in yet another highly polished floor. At the center of the room was a small table set with a glittering silver service. Four chairs sat around it.

Beyond that, a cheerful fire crackled in the fireplace. Another lord and lady stood silhouetted against the flames. Valdira was so changed after her bath, Ryamon almost didn't recognize her. She wore a different gown, the bodice a sparkly brocade, and her hair was pulled up on her head.

The man with her was a stranger. In the crook of his arm he cradled a small erid with short yellow fur and lively dark eyes. Valdira was just reaching to stroke its head when Yolie spoke.

"Allow me to present my brother, Dom Darmosh of Olalu. This is Dom Ryamon, recently come to our country." She patted Ryamon's arm as if he was a new possession. "Of course, you have already met Dama Valdira."

"A pleasure, dom." Darmosh strolled forward. The erid let its ears fold back as he caressed it.

Even if Yolie hadn't said so, Ryamon would have known she and Darmosh were related. They had the same dark hair and eyes. He was surprised to find out he was quite a bit taller than Darmosh, though not as broad-shouldered.

Ryamon hesitated, having no idea what kind of greeting the nobleman expected. Though he smiled politely, Darmosh didn't look as through he wanted to be hugged. After a moment, Ryamon put out one foot and made a quick bow.

"For us as well," he said.

"But my pet," Yolie tittered, "did I not say bowing is…"

"You did, Dama," Ryamon answered as he straightened, "but

I know only the customs of my own land. In time, perhaps some-one will show me how a gentleman should greet a person of equal rank in Costera."

Darmosh studied him for a moment, then bent to set his pet on the floor. The erid immediately circled to sit silently at his left heel.

"It is thus." Darmosh reached out with both hands, waited a moment for Ryamon to reach back, then clasped Ryamon's right hand briefly with both of his while tipping forward very slightly. Ryamon copied him. It was almost, but not quite, a bow.

"Lovely," Yolie crooned. "Now if we are ready, let us sit and eat. Our guests have traveled far. I know you must be famished."

Tugging gently on Ryamon's arm, she led him toward the table. With some regret, he watched Darmosh escort Valdira. The little erid followed them with a quiet click of claws on stone. Swishing and swirling her gown, Yolie seated them all. She took the seat on Ryamon's left. Darmosh was seated across from Yolie, which meant Valdira sat across from Ryamon.

While everyone settled into place, Ryamon studied the group. Darmosh wore trousers and a deep blue jacket, as thick with embroidery as Yolie's gown but without the glittering beads. His hair was shoulder length with a slight curl, frosted in silver like his sister's. Overall, the man's bearing made Ryamon think of an eridow in the mountains, fearless and supremely confident. The effect was somewhat spoiled, however, when Darmosh patted his knee and the little erid jumped up to his lap. Its head was just above his plate, eyes bright and ears folded back meekly.

Ryamon decided he would rather look at Valdira, even if a private conversation was impossible. Her gown was in the Costeran style, low cut and tightly laced with sweeping skirts. It was orange, a little deeper than the color of a pumpkin, and lavishly embroi-dered with beads that sparkled as Valdira breathed. It might have been one of Yolie's gowns, for the intense color would have favored the dark-haired lady. On Valdira it leached color from her face. A small bird made of white feathers had been pinned into her upswept hair. In her new finery, Valdira looked like a stranger to Ryamon. He had much preferred her old clothes, threadbare as they were.

Naturally, Ryamon wore clean garments as well. The maidser-vants had insisted on dressing him. They hadn't argued, of course, just stood there bowing until he gave in and let them do it. He still felt a bit uncomfortable in fabric so stiff with stitchery and boots that rubbed when he walked. Luckily, men's clothing in Costera seemed to favor more subdued colors—in Ryamon's case, a muted lavender that set off his coppery hair but clashed with Valdira's orange. It was probably foolish, but he wished their hostess could have found them outfits that went well together.

Yolie herself hadn't changed out of her pink gown, although she seemed to be wearing more pearls than Ryamon remembered. Her perfume was so strong, he was sure he would taste flowers when he ate. Glancing around, he belatedly realized one of their party was missing.

"Pardon me, Dama, but where is Nepharyl?" Ryamon asked.

"Resting in his quarters," Yolie replied carelessly. "In the morning he travels back across the border. He left in secret, you see, and he's useful to me there."

Ryamon caught an odd expression on Valdira's face as she asked, "No one will have noticed him missing?"

"Then he can say he was waylaid by bandits and had to get away." Yolie waved casually, as if the question was a bothersome fly. "The mountains are full of them, you know. Besides, those people are fools. They'll believe anything."

That wasn't a safe assumption at all, in Ryamon's opinion. He hadn't heard any rumors about bandits when he stopped in Lornest.

"Don't tell me you miss his company," Darmosh added, giving Ryamon a droll eye. "He's a toad, you know."

"He's devoted to me," Yolie countered. She and her brother shared a smug smile. Ryamon shrugged. He didn't like Nepharyl, yet it bothered him that someone so loyal had been pushed aside this quickly.

Meanwhile, Yolie lifted a little silver bell from beside her plate. As the delicate notes rang out, a cadre of servants swarmed into the room. They came in pairs, one bearing a covered tray and one holding utensils. To Ryamon's surprise, they went first to Darmosh rather than Yolie. He would have expected the owner of the house to be served first.

Silent as always, the servants with the trays bowed low and lifted the lids. Those with the utensils served from the trays, watching carefully for a sign that Darmosh wanted more. If he didn't, the servants moved behind him, offering their trays to Valdira, and then Yolie. They were skillful; not so much as a drop spilled. As steam rose from the trays, Ryamon discovered he was ferociously hungry. He tried not to stare as the servants worked their way toward him.

While Ryamon waited to be served, Valdira turned to Darmosh. "You were going to tell me about your erid?"

"Ah." He smiled at Valdira with almost exactly the same self-satisfied expression he had recently turned on Yolie. "This is Toki." Darmosh plucked a morsel from his plate and fed it to the erid. It licked its muzzle and gazed up at him adoringly.

Not to be left out, Ryamon asked. "What kind is it? I haven't seen one like it."

Indeed, all the erids Ryamon had ever seen were working animals. Large and shaggy as their wild cousins, the eridows, they guarded the mines and homes of Dalgest. He had never imagined one small enough to sit on its owner's lap, let alone share a meal.

"I'm sure you haven't," Darmosh replied. "They are our particular breed in Costera."

"We call them spirits of the wind," Yolie added. "Do you see how long and slender his legs are, and yet how broad his chest is?"

"I guess they're fast runners," Valdira said.

Darmosh nodded. "We use them to hunt rodents in the fields or hares for the peasant tables, but we have our share of friendly races."

"His kennel is famous." Yolie leaned forward, her voice dropping to a whisper as if she was sharing a special secret.

Darmosh shrugged modestly. He and Valdira started eating. Evidently it wasn't the custom in Costera to wait until everyone had been served. Ryamon's stomach growled anxiously as the first of the servants tended to Yolie.

"Do you also race erids?" Ryamon asked her.

"I prefer ornyx chariots," the lady of Laceto demurred. "My drivers are some of the best in Costera, if I do say so."

A few days before, Nepharyl had mentioned how much Yolie loved contests. Odd that she avoided competing with her brother.

He was distracted by the arrival of the first servants. There was some kind of red meat that didn't seem to be sobi, mashed turnips, greens with oil and vinegar, several types of sliced cheeses and small, hard rolls. He nodded yes to all of these and hoped they wouldn't take the trays out of the room. He was sure he would want seconds.

The servants seemed startled when Ryamon thanked them. No one corrected him, but he caught a shrewd glance from Darmosh. It made Ryamon a bit self-conscious, but he wasn't ready to give up his principles.

While Ryamon tucked into his meal—and tried not to attack his food like a wild ornyx—Valdira cleared her throat.

"Yolie said your estate is called Olalu," she said to Darmosh. "Is that far from here?"

It sounded like casual conversation, but Ryamon caught an edge of tension in her voice. Valdira hadn't called Yolie 'Dama' or by any title. He wondered if she was deliberately baiting them, wanting to see if they would scold her.

The last servant had just poured wine for Darmosh, a pale pink liquid that twinkled with tiny bubbles. He sipped it before replying, "Not far, no. If the day is clear, you can see my manor from the upper balcony."

"So you can keep an eye on each other?" Ryamon suggested cautiously. "The way the Seven Exalted Orders do?"

Yolie gave another of her silvery chuckles. "Not at all, my pet. It's so we can reach each other quickly if need be."

"What do you mean?" Valdira asked.

"Costera is peaceful, but there are sometimes...incidents." Darmosh spoke slowly, as if considering his words.

"What kind of incidents?" she persisted.

"Bandits, rebellions, challenges." Yolie flicked her fork in the air, dismissing these as unimportant.

Conversation tapered off for a time as they all ate. Ryamon found the food delicious, though unfamiliar. He soon learned that merely glancing at the servants would bring additional servings. Valdira, too, ate quickly and looked around for more. Yolie and Darmosh, who hadn't been living in the wilderness for several weeks, picked at their plates and chose only the finest morsels. Once the Costeran Dom had satisfied his hunger, many of these went to the erid.

"La, my pet," Yolie trilled as Ryamon finished his third helping of meat and turnips. "That should be enough, surely? You'll hurt yourself if you eat another bite."

"The pain would be worth it," Ryamon said. He felt much

more relaxed with a full stomach. "I would never criticize my sweetheart, but I haven't eaten so well since I left my tower in Polvest."

Valdira gave him a sharp look, but admitted, "I don't mind eating a meal I didn't have to catch myself. Please thank your staff for me."

"You are both so kind," Yolie said with a grand shrug. "It is only their duty, but I shall inform them my guests were pleased."

As soon as they set their utensils down, a servant came to whisk the plates away. Another replenished the wine. Across the table, Ryamon became aware Darmosh had been silent for some time. Stroking his pet, he watched them both. Ryamon wondered what the man was looking for.

As if he sensed Ryamon's feeling, Darmosh remarked, "I had heard of your exile. A sad tale, but all too common."

"We're putting it behind us," Valdira replied firmly.

Ryamon was relieved she had spoken, because he had no idea what to say. He hadn't thought his predicament was very common at all, and he'd never heard of magi fleeing Arkanost for Costera or anywhere else.

Of course, it was possible the Exalted Orders had suppressed reports of such defections. They wouldn't want their magi getting any ideas.

"Understandable," Darmosh said. "I must admit, I'm curious about your country. It's been an interest of mine, living close to the border as we do."

"But first," Yolie put in hastily, "is there anything else you would like to know about Costera? You must ask us anything that puzzles you."

Darmosh shrugged, accepting the interruption, but when he looked away Ryamon caught a flash of irritation in his eyes.

"All right," Valdira promptly answered. "I'm wondering why, if you're brother and sister, you each have your own estates. Why don't you share?"

"In Costera we prize our independence." Yolie fluttered a smile at Darmosh. "I adore my brother, but I wouldn't be happy with him bossing me around just because he's older."

"Nor should I be responsible for my little sister," Darmosh retorted with a dry smile. "In Costera, each wizard has his or her own estate. Even when we marry, the properties are not combined."

Ryamon wondered if that was meant to keep any one family from acquiring too much land, but Darmosh was still talking.

"Each is supreme within his or her own domain. We have alliances, of course, but only between equals."

"And you make your own rules?" Valdira asked intently. "No one can tell you what to do?"

"Absolutely not," Yolie said.

"That would be grounds for a challenge," Darmosh added.

They were telling Valdira exactly what she wanted to hear, Ryamon thought. And bringing in the erid, when Valdira was so connected to animals. He wondered how they anticipated her needs so precisely. Surely even Nepharyl didn't know that much.

"How do you establish your estates?" he asked, hoping to stop them from snaring her too easily. "Do you need permission from the Wizard King, or…"

"We have a looser association with our rulers than you do," Yolie replied. "Anyone can open up a territory in the wilderness and drive out the bandits and wild beasts. Since these explorations expand our borders, Domen Terlith looks upon them with favor. Of course, one must pledge loyalty. Defend the realm from invaders and so forth."

"One may inherit an existing estate," Darmosh added, "or purchase one, or challenge the current holder for possession. That's how I assumed control of Olalu, actually."

"Since he and I could not both rule over Laceto, Darmosh sought his fortune elsewhere," Yolie simpered. "Wasn't that noble of him?"

Ryamon wasn't sure the previous owner of Olalu would have agreed with her.

"What kind of challenge is it?" Valdira asked. Ryamon was relieved to hear her ask a sensible question.

"A magical duel, my pet," Yolie said with another of her dramatic shudders. "But—forgive me—since you both have such limited training, I fear you would not be equal to the task."

Valdira smiled slightly. "Maybe not yet."

"As long as you are allied with Yolie and myself, no one will dare to challenge you," Darmosh added. He spoke with a casual arrogance worthy of the Wizard King himself. Ryamon didn't remember making any alliances, but he decided not to mention it.

Yolie went on, "In order to inherit an estate, one must have magical power, of course. Sadly, not all are born with the gift."

"Excuse me for asking," Ryamon said, "but do both of you have heirs?"

"I do have a son who will one day become a wizard," Darmosh said. "He is but young, and lives with his mother in Logoll."

Darmosh didn't mention marriage, Ryamon noticed. He wondered how inheritance could be established without some sort of legal agreement.

"Sadly, my two children are both lacking," Yolie said. She didn't seem to care very much. Ryamon wondered what had happened to the rejected youngsters. To his surprise, Yolie angled a sly glance toward Valdira. "That being so, I am free to choose any heir I please, so long as his or her power is proven."

"Really." Valdira sipped her wine, hazel eyes glinting.

Darmosh considered her for a moment, stroking his erid. Then he said, "If you have no more questions, I believe it is my turn. I mentioned I have an interest in matters to the north."

Ryamon's stomach tightened over the huge meal he had eaten. Guests or not, their hosts were about to demand payment for their hospitality.

"It is a matter of our heritage, you see," Yolie said sweetly. "Our ancestors once lived in Old Arkandor—or Arkanost, as you now call it. At that time we were all one country. It was a terrible time, during the revolution. Our ancestors were forced to flee."

"Those were the wizard kings?" Valdira half accused.

"They were born to power," Darmosh corrected. "Fortunately, some found refuge here in Costera, where the old ways were never abandoned."

"This must be why we all speak the same language," Ryamon said.

And it was consistent with the way Yolie treated her servants. Ryamon had grown up with legends of the wizard kings' cruelty. Yolie didn't seem to be as vicious as that, but she clearly had no respect for the serfs who shared her estate.

"Correct," Darmosh said. His dark eyes were hooded, but the little erid in his lap was suddenly shivering.

"What is your interest now?" Ryamon asked warily.

"The old wrongs must be righted." Yolie leaned persuasively toward Ryamon. She pressed her hand over his, her fingers warm and slightly sticky. "The ancient ways should be restored."

"Nowhere else in the world do commoners rule over magi," Darmosh went on. "A sword cannot be used as a butter knife. Just so, no wizard should be forced to labor in a tower, wasting his mighty powers on humble tasks. Nor should she serve the commoners like a beast. Our kind are meant to rule."

Ryamon sat stiffly, trying not to see Yolie's tempting cleavage or feel her shoulder pressing against his. What Darmosh said went against everything he had ever been taught. Yet Yolie's perfume surrounded him with sweetness. Between that and the wine, his head was swimming.

"You haven't said what you want us to do about it," Valdira interrupted, and there was an edge in her voice. With a flare of hope, Ryamon thought she might even be jealous of Yolie's attention to him. He was relieved when Yolie sat back.

"Any information could be useful," Darmosh answered. "Locations of the towers, what powers they have, where the army is based and who commands it."

His questions made Ryamon's heart drop yet again. Darmosh seemed to mean what he said about restoring the ancient ways. He wouldn't ask these questions unless he was planning a war. Ryamon opened his mouth to ask if Domen Terlith had sanctioned an invasion, but his lover spoke first.

"We don't know anything about those things," Valdira's voice was brisk and flat. She sent Ryamon a sharp glance, warning him not to contradict her.

"Surely there is something," Yolie protested, sounding slightly stern.

"I grew up in the hinterlands of Selkest," Valdira said. "That's how I liked it—open space and privacy. I could have gone to Polvest and trained in the Order of Blood. They wanted me to, but I refused. Nepharyl must have told you I ran away rather than give up my independence. So I really don't know anything about the Collegium or who's in charge of what and where."

"Even a small detail can be helpful," Darmosh reasoned. "You might not even realize it. For instance, I've heard there was a battle?"

Now he looked straight at Ryamon. Despite Valdira's sharp gaze, Ryamon couldn't bring himself to lie outright. He nodded reluctantly.

"Tell me about it." Darmosh spoke mildly, but it was clearly a command.

"It was just a skirmish." Ryamon swirled his wine, delaying. "You probably know from Nepharyl that we're fugitives. The Mage Lords sent a few magi to retrieve us, that's all."

"How many?" Darmosh asked bluntly.

Valdira bristled on the other side of the table, but Ryamon could hardly evade such a simple question. "Three."

"Three to two, and you escaped?" Yolie patted his hand again. He wished she would stop doing that. "You are too modest, my pet. Or perhaps those tame sorcerers aren't as powerful as they give out."

Ryamon shrugged. In his mind, the memory of a tornado filled the leaden sky. Yolie could think it was modesty if she wanted, but he wasn't about to reveal how the Shadow magus had used him to attack his lover.

"These three magi," Darmosh pressed. "Which orders did they belong to?"

He had no trouble using the correct terms, Ryamon noted.

"Ice, Storm and Shadow," he replied. Valdira sighed audibly. Ryamon looked at her helplessly.

Darmosh's pet erid must have sensed her frustration, for it suddenly jumped down off his lap. With a rapid click of claws, it scurried over the polished floor and made itself even smaller on a cushion near the fireplace. Darmosh didn't seem to notice its departure.

"Shadow?" He and Yolie shared a significant look across the table. "Was it a young man, dark hair, dark eyes?"

"They were a long way from us," Ryamon said. "He was dark haired, but I couldn't tell you his age."

"This just gets more interesting," Darmosh said. He smiled, and something about it made the small hairs stand up on the back of Ryamon's neck.

Both Darmosh and Yolie also had dark hair and eyes. Ryamon wondered if that was significant. Valdira must have noticed the same thing.

"A relative of yours?" she inquired in a stinging tone.

"Unlikely," Darmosh snapped.

Yolie gave a nervous giggle. "What a thing to suggest!"

Valdira shrugged. "You said you had roots in Arkanost."

Darmosh chose to ignore her. Turning again to Ryamon, he said, "Dama Valdira may not have trained in Polvest, but I understand that you did."

Ryamon nodded again. This time he couldn't back down—and not only because Valdira was giving him another of her razor-edged glares.

"That's true, although I never advanced in the hierarchy. Nepharyl must have told you my gift was unsuited to the order I was placed in," he said.

"But you were there, my pet," Yolie urged.

Ryamon cleared his throat, which had suddenly gone dry. "I must be honest with you. I'm not ready to answer these questions."

Yolie looked up at him with wounded eyes, while Darmosh sat stiff and silent.

"We're grateful for your hospitality," Ryamon hurried on with all the sincerity he could muster, "but so much has happened. It's all new to us. We haven't had time to think about what to do next. I won't try to speak for Valdira, but Selkest is home to me. It may be foolish, but I still hope there's a future for us there."

Just for a moment, Valdira gazed across the table with luminous eyes. Then Darmosh shattered the moment.

"You wish to consider before you decide," he said slowly, thoughtfully. "I respect that."

Surprisingly, Ryamon felt it was true. Darmosh and Yolie had both said they thought the magi of Arkanost were weak in will and power. By standing up for himself, Ryamon had risen above that low standard.

"A future can still be yours, even in your beloved Selkest. But," the Costeran noble said, and his voice fell dangerously low, "do not take too long to decide. Events are already in motion. The time for thinking may pass more quickly than you realize."

~ * ~

As they rose from the table, Yolie offered her brother a guest room, since night had fallen. There was a bit of confusion over the sleeping arrangements for Ryamon and Valdira.

"I didn't know your wishes, so I've prepared a room for each of you," Yolie said with a sly gleam in her eye.

Ryamon suddenly found Valdira at his side, her arm twined with his.

"Perhaps I should escort her." Ryamon kept his face as straight as he could, though his heart fluttered with pleasure at Valdira's touch and relief that she seemed to have forgiven him at last.

Yolie shrugged innocently. "Sleep well, then."

At her gesture, one of the maidservants stepped forward to lead them out of the dining room. After saying goodnight, they followed their silent guide down a polished hallway lined with gilt-chased doors. The maidservant stopped at one of them, though Ryamon couldn't tell what set it apart from the others. She pushed the doors inward and stepped aside, bowing.

"Thank you," Ryamon said as they entered. After a moment he turned back to her. "Will you just show me where my room is?"

The maid stepped across the hallway. She bowed as she rested her hand on the handle of another door.

"Thank you," Ryamon repeated. "That will be all."

She bowed a fraction lower and silently walked away. Then Valdira spoke from the room behind him.

"I could get used to this."

Ryamon followed her in. Lamp glow revealed a spacious chamber decorated in gilt and creamy velvet. There was a settee with plump cushions, a bed with a thick comforter, a small chest of drawers and table with two chairs. A cozy fire warmed the room. Its smoke had a mild, spicy fragrance after Yolie's cloying perfume.

In the midst of this luxury, Valdira's old basket sat on the table. It looked crude and lumpy compared to the dainty furnishings. Still, after sleeping on sword grass and eating from a turtle shell, the comforts of Laceto were almost too much.

"Yolie seemed to take to you," Ryamon ventured.

"She's jealous." Valdira suddenly sounded tired and jaded. "I'm younger and prettier, and she hates it, but she doesn't want to cross her brother, so she covers her feelings with sugar."

"Are you sure?" Ryamon asked, faintly alarmed. Maybe this explained why Yolie had given Valdira such an unflattering dress. "She didn't act jealous."

"You really are dense, aren't you?" Valdira snapped. "Why do you think she was trying to lure you away from me?"

Stung, Ryamon protested, "I have no interest in her."

Valdira prowled the chamber, looking into drawers and peering behind the curtains as if she expected to find some hidden danger.

"The only other man there was her brother," Ryamon pointed out. "Or she might have hoped to recruit me the way she must have done with Nepharyl. I can't believe she sent him away so soon after he brought us to her."

"That's the least of our problems," Valdira said in a dark tone. Reaching up high, she plucked the tiny bird off her hair and tossed it onto the table. Ryamon heard her tongue click irritably as she struggled to free her hair from the chains Yolie's staff had bound it in. "No wonder she needs a lady's maid."

"May I?" Ryamon asked.

When Valdira didn't object, he came to stand behind her. After a moment's study of the complicated arrangement, he untucked a few ends and gently pulled out the flexible wooden comb which had been supporting it. He set it on the table. Valdira sighed with relief as her hair tumbled around her shoulders.

Ryamon asked, "Then what do you want to do? We don't have to stay here. Really. Especially now that we know what they want from us."

"We can't go back," Valdira said, her voice taut. "You were right all along, don't you see? There's no place for us in Arkanost."

She started pacing again, jerking irritably at the gown's tight laces. Ryamon watched her, trying to understand. He didn't like the atmosphere of Costera so far, but Valdira seemed more upset than that.

"That doesn't mean we're stuck here," he said. "From what Darmosh said, there are lots of wizard lords in Costera. We could try to find someone who wouldn't expect us to betray our homeland."

"How long would that take?" Valdira retorted. Laces undone, she sank into a chair near the fire. Suddenly she looked like a child with her loose hair and rumpled dress. Ryamon sat down and took her in his arms. For once, she didn't push him away.

Softly, almost to herself, Valdira said, "I'm so tired of laws. And everyone telling me what to do. And running away. I want to have my own place and make my own rules, and tell anyone who doesn't like it to get lost. I could never do that at home."

"I know," Ryamon murmured. Valdira hadn't said 'our own place, our own rules,' but 'my place, my rules.' It hurt to think he wasn't included in her plans, but he knew better than to make demands. Valdira would reject them along with all the rest.

At the same time, he realized he couldn't feel his lover's thoughts and emotions the way he was used to. Confused as she was, he couldn't even tell if she was hiding from him or from herself.

"I guess we'll have to stay," he said heavily.

Valdira frowned up at him. "Why don't you just run home if it's such a bother?"

"I'm not leaving you alone with a woman who hates you," Ryamon said firmly.

Valdira's angry eyes suddenly softened, just as they had in Yolie's dining room. She raised her head to give him a lingering kiss. Ryamon sensed her tenderness, but no passion, and he knew they wouldn't be sharing a room tonight.

On the other hand, they were still a couple. It would have to do for now.

Chapter Nineteen

"We need more firewood."

In his trance, Phareth barely heard Anarinda's delicate voice. He had been meditating almost constantly for the past three days, trying to spy on the rogue magi. Mostly he watched Ryamon, since the former Stone novice wasn't as alert to intrusion. Unfortunately, Ryamon was distracted by his confusion over Valdira. He knew nothing of Darmosh's plans. It was maddening for Phareth to have this intimate contact and yet receive no useful information.

At least he could be sure the runaways were still in Laceto. Monitoring them gave Phareth something to think about besides how hungry he was.

Vaguely, he heard Anarinda ask, "Telamar, can you gather wood again? I'm sorry, but my wrist—"

"It's Phareth's turn," Telamar answered.

Phareth's concentration wavered as fabric rustled near at hand.

"Phareth," Anarinda said. "Come back to us."

Without opening his eyes, Phareth asked, "Are they here yet?"

"No, but we need you."

"To gather firewood?" Even in a partial trance, Phareth knew he was coming across sullen.

"Why should I have to do it all?" Telamar reasoned with glacial cool.

"You haven't moved in hours," Anarinda said. "This isn't good for you. Please open your eyes."

She obviously wasn't going to let him alone, so Phareth complied. Mid-morning sun glared over the small, reedy lake and mountain crags. A campfire smoldered under the rock ledge while black, white and yellow tents clustered nearby. Anarinda knelt nearby, lowering her unsplinted hand with a guilty jerk. Phareth wondered if she had been about to shake him out of his trance.

"I'm moving," Phareth grunted. "See?"

"That's better." Anarinda pouted prettily at his rudeness.

Farther back, Telamar watched them with something almost like concern. Seeing Phareth respond, he gave a little nod and walked down toward the lake shore. The Ice magus' white robe was liberally smudged with dirt. Bits of bark and pine needles clung to the weave. It wasn't nearly as entertaining as it once had been.

When Phareth moved his head, stiffness grabbed his neck and back. He had been sitting in one position too long. The pains had been there all along, of course. He just hadn't felt them while he was meditating. The gnawing in his belly was equally real.

"And now I'm hungry again," he muttered to himself.

Phareth stood slowly, resenting the tightness of his muscles that showed Anarinda was right. Even now he wasn't to be left alone. The Storm magus rose along with him.

"Before you go," she said, "tell us what's happening."

"Nothing."

"Really?" She arched one fine eyebrow. "You haven't been acting like yourself since we fought Valdira and Ryamon. Before that you were organized, always planning ahead. Now it's like you've stopped thinking about anything."

Phareth's jaw tightened. He stared out over the lake, refusing to acknowledge the accuracy of Anarinda's observation.

"Has Lady Murcrys told you something else?" she persisted. "Events we should know about?"

"No," he answered. "I've told you everything Mother relayed to me."

"It's been three days." Telamar looked up from strolling beside the water. He sounded like his normal self, wary and accusing. There was something comforting in that.

"Gathering information takes time," Phareth told him. "Weeks, even months. When the Collegium decides what to do—or rather, when the king tells them—Mother will let us know."

"If you know all this, it shouldn't be bothering you," Anarinda said.

Her prying annoyed Phareth even more than her giving him menial chores. "It's nothing to do with Mother, and it's none of your business."

"Rot!" Telamar said, surprising Phareth with his cold force. "As long as we're stuck out here, your business is our business."

"We're a team," Anarinda added. "If anything is wrong, we deserve to know."

Their arguments only hardened Phareth's resolve. "Not this."

"If we can help…" Anarinda began, but Phareth cut her off.

"You can't. It's personal."

Tottering on stiff legs, Phareth walked off before she could argue. He wasn't lying, he told himself. His business with Darmosh was highly personal. Ryamon and Valdira were only involved by the accident of being in Costera at the moment.

Behind him, Telamar told Anarinda, "He has to want our help."

What did they know about it, Phareth snarled to himself. It still hurt just to think about what Darmosh had done. To Kylethia, to Phareth's reputation. Much as he liked Anarinda, she couldn't just demand information. That level of trust had to be earned, and they were still members of rival orders. They weren't supposed to trust each other.

At least his muscles loosened as he kept moving. Long, angry strides carried him around the side of the lake. They had to keep the fire lit day and night, and it took an amazing amount of fuel. Even with all the debris Anarinda's tornado had tossed around, they had to go farther every day to collect enough wood. Well, that was fine. Phareth didn't feel like sitting there, being quizzed by his companions.

The growling of his stomach reminded him they were also out of food. Telamar had only brought back one of Anarinda's storm-killed geese, and it hadn't been as large as it looked once they got the feathers off. Scavengers had taken the rest, even the shorbak's carcass. Ryamon had built a weir during his time at the rock ledge, and the fish it provided were keeping the magi alive—but that didn't make Phareth feel any better.

He roamed aimlessly until he reached a clump of pine trees across the valley from the magi's camp. Downed branches littered the ground. Phareth snatched them up and shook them well to get rid of insects. It was a long walk, so he loaded his arms well before starting back with his prickly load.

Only two things could make him happy right now. One was taking revenge on Darmosh. The other was getting out of this valley, where he had once again failed his mother. He was tempted to stop waiting for the rescue party and just start walking. Phareth knew better than that, but he was beginning to wonder if Silma was deliberately moving slowly in her quest to bring help.

That was hunger talking, Phareth knew. Hunger made him so cross with Anarinda and suspicious of Silma. And there was nothing he could do about it. Not until the cursed villagers arrived!

Phareth stopped where he was. He was being stupid as well as surly. Of all the magi, he had the power to find out exactly where the rescue party was. Murcrys would have been disappointed with him.

He shut his eyes, cleared his mind of hunger and the weight of prickly branches. Instead of sending his thoughts into Costera, he now reached back toward Selkest—and had his answer almost at once.

"Thank goodness," Phareth sighed.

Silma's mind was closer than he had expected. Just a ridge or two away, actually. However, not all the news was good. Along with the Blood magus and a band of hardy villagers, one more mind approached. It took no effort to recognize the churning ball of rage and pain that was Marton. Phareth groaned to himself. Why was Marton coming? Bad enough he'd mishandled his daughter so completely. His belligerence would only make things worse.

Phareth suppressed his sour mood long enough to contact Silma.

"Is everyone well?" The Blood magus thought back to him.

"We're pretty hungry," Phareth replied. *"You're nearly here. Turn a bit more to the south."* Carefully, respecting her privacy, he pressed a picture into her mind of the long, shallow valley, the lake and the bluff. *"We're right there."*

"I think I can find it."

"Good."

Phareth let the connection drop and resumed his walk. By the time he got back to the camp, his arms and shoulders were throbbing with his heavy burden. Outside the ledge, he dropped the wood with a dramatic crash.

"They're almost here," he announced.

"That's wonderful news." Anarinda's dainty features were pinched with exhaustion. Phareth knew her wrist still hurt despite his repeatedly numbing the part of her brain that felt it.

Telamar was crouched on the shore near the weir, cleaning the guts from a pair of small trout.

"I hope they have real food," he remarked.

"We all do," Anarinda said.

Phareth got to work breaking the tangle of branches into useable pieces.

"I gave Initiate Silma a clear picture of where we are," he said. "They should be here in an hour at the most, but there's one thing you should know first."

"What is it?" Telamar asked over the stomping and cracking of branches.

"Our favorite person is along for the trip."

They both gazed at him, perplexed. Anarinda said, "I thought you couldn't find Nepharyl."

Phareth gave a grim chuckle. "Not him. The other one."

"Don't be so mysterious," Telamar snapped.

Anarinda figured it out. "Marton?" she asked with a frown.

"The very same."

"I thought he hated Silma," Anarinda spoke softly, more to herself than her companions.

"He must hate Valdira more," Phareth said with a shrug. He knelt and started tossing pieces of wood into piles according to their size.

"It's his family, it's his problem," Telamar said, approaching with the cleaned trout. "He told us that before."

"That could be it," Anarinda said doubtingly.

Telamar knelt at the fireside and laid the fishes skin side down on a flat rock which had been serving as the magi's main cooking surface. He scraped at the fire to clear a gap in the ashes, then carefully placed the rock into it.

Phareth watched without really seeing him. Telamar was absolutely right. Marton felt responsible for what Valdira did. It really was amazing how the Ice magus could point out vital information and not think about what it meant. Phareth was thinking, though.

As the trout began to sizzle, he decided Marton's presence might not be the problem it first seemed. Perhaps, instead, it was an opportunity. As Anarinda had said, it was time he stopped moping and started to plan again.

~ * ~

Two small trout made a most unsatisfactory meal when shared between three people. Still hungry, Phareth resumed meditating until a faint hallo told him the rescue party had finally arrived. He rose to his feet and peered toward the feeling of new minds approaching. People and ornyxes stood on the knoll in almost exactly the same spot where the three magi had been when the battle began. A red-robed figure with a staff was clearly visible at the fore.

"At last," Telamar said. "Hallo!" he called back to them.

The rescue party waved and halloed again before they started down the slope, avoiding Ryamon's pit at the base. The ornyxes screeched in protest at the steep terrain.

Even over the distance, Phareth could feel the ferment of Marton's anguish. He easily picked out the brewer's jarring limp, and the way he kept to one side of the group. Probably staying as far from the animals as he could. Phareth stiffened his mental shields to resist the onslaught. Doing this reminded him how much he had relaxed his defenses around Anarinda and Telamar. Well, the time for such familiarity was past. Especially if Marton was to play the part Phareth had in mind for him.

He especially didn't want Anarinda to guess his plans. To distract her, Phareth jabbed a thumb at the approaching Blood magus.

"That must be Silma," he remarked.

"At last," Anarinda sighed, anticipating relief from pain.

"I'll go get her." Telamar strode off to meet the group.

Together, Phareth and Anarinda watched as Telamar intercepted the rescue party near the lake shore. Listening with his mind, Phareth heard one of the men ask Silma if they would be making camp or leaving again.

Silma's voice was soft and a bit slow. "I'll have to see how severe the injuries are. What do you recommend?"

"The day's more than half spent," answered the man, whose name was Partren. "We'd barely get anywhere before we had to stop at dusk. Here, there's water for us and the birds."

"Fairly level ground," another man added. "I wouldn't mind that for sleeping on."

"The fire's already lit," Partren said.

"Very well," Silma agreed. "We'll camp here tonight and be on our way in the morning, well rested. Will you see to it?"

"Aye, Dama."

Interesting the locals addressed her with a title of the nobility. It sounded a little too Costeran for Phareth's liking. However, Telamar was at Silma's elbow. While Partren ordered this man to unload the ornyxes and that one to clear brush for tents, the Ice magus gave a brief bow.

"This way, Initiate."

"Certainly."

Phareth studied the Blood magus as Telamar led her toward them. Silma was neither short nor tall, with dark hair and a solid frame under her crimson robe. She didn't hurry, but walked slowly and leaned on her staff. Not like Nepharyl, showing off; Silma was limping slightly. Her impairment wasn't as severe as Marton's, but it still surprised Phareth.

As they got closer, Telamar noticed it, too. His pale eyebrows drew together in a frown. "Pardon me, Initiate, but if you're a Blood magus, why are you limping?"

Phareth expected Silma to be annoyed, but she only shrugged.

"I have arthritis," she replied in her slow way. "I can heal it, certainly, but the pain always returns. We in the Order of Blood can do many things, but even the Blood Lord cannot stop aging. We must accept our limits."

"I see," Telamar replied.

With a rueful smile, Silma went on, "This journey has irritated my hip more than usual. I believe I will have to heal myself, but not until I've seen to your wounded."

Just then Marton jolted past, helping another man carry a roll of canvas and poles that would soon become a large tent. He glared at Silma, but turned away with a sneer when he met Phareth's eye.

Yes, Phareth thought, Marton would serve his purpose nicely.

"What about him?" Anarinda asked in a low voice.

Silma didn't have to ask who she meant. With a mixture of sadness and distaste, she replied, "Marton wouldn't let me heal him."

There was a story there, Phareth was sure, but Anarinda put on one of her sunny smiles. "Well, I will be happy to accept your aid."

Silma's eyes twinkled with understanding. "Then let's begin."

Within moments, she and Anarinda were sitting by the fire circle. There wasn't room for Telamar and Phareth, so they stood outside, in front of the tents. Phareth kept one eye on the villagers as they set up camp. He was especially interested in the three ornyxes being led in with baggage strapped to their backs.

"Aren't those ours?" he asked Telamar. There were only three ornyxes—Nepharyl had taken the fourth, as Phareth well knew.

The Ice magus shrugged, not caring about livestock. "Makes sense to bring them. The people need their own animals at home."

Silma unwrapped Anarinda's injured forearm. The fair skin was mottled with bruises and reddish grooves where swelling had caused the bandages to dig into her skin.

"You fell?" Silma asked. Phareth could feel her wondering if Valdira had caused this injury.

"Yes, in that big hole at the bottom of the hill." Anarinda offered no other details.

"It's good that you wrapped it right away," Silma replied. She turned Anarinda's hand, looking at both sides, then probed gently with her fingertips. Anarinda's shoulders went rigid.

"Phareth helped numb it." Her voice sounded slightly choked with pain.

Silma looked up to nod appreciation at Phareth. Turning back to her patient, she went on, "Luckily, the bone is only cracked, not broken. I'll set you right in no time."

Still touching softly, Silma folded her hands around Anarinda's swollen wrist. Phareth felt her power swirling around them like a warm mist.

Anarinda relaxed almost at once. "That's so much better," she sighed.

The Blood magus smiled, still concentrating. "That's that," she said a moment later.

"Thank you, Initiate." Anarinda rubbed her wrist and rotated her hand experimentally.

"The bone is still weak," Silma cautioned. "Don't lift anything heavy until ten days have passed."

Anarinda nodded, her eyes bright with relief. Phareth watched with interest. Murcrys had suggested several weeks ago that a Blood magus could influence people she had healed. Before he could probe for evidence of that, Silma looked around.

"Wasn't there also a head injury?"

"That was me," Phareth said. "It doesn't hurt much now."

All the same, he knelt before Silma and held the hair back so she could see the lump in his forehead. Only a ghost of the original pain now stirred. Phareth held his shields tighter as the Blood magus' power trickled through him, probing skin and bone.

"As you say," Silma said a moment later. "It's healing well

without my help."

"His head's too hard to crack," Telamar added with cool humor. Phareth squinted up at him, but couldn't think of any clever retorts.

"If that's it, I suppose we can all relax," Silma remarked.

"Not quite," Phareth answered. He scooted over and beckoned for Telamar to crouch beside him. Softly, he said, "As long as we're here, there's something else we need to discuss."

"Valdira?" Silma asked, resigned.

"Not the way you think," Anarinda said reassuringly. "Initiate Phareth has news from the Collegium."

At her gesture, Phareth outlined what Murcrys had said about Valdira's power being hereditary rather than a freak deviation. Silma raised her eyebrows in surprise. She shot a quick glance toward Marton, then leaned closer to the other three magi.

"Are you telling me that her father..."

"Phareth believes he's an untrained magus," Anarinda said.

"He suppressed his magic because it didn't fit within any of the towers," Phareth said.

"Of course. That will be why he hated that Valdira accepted her gifts," Silma finished softly. "He wouldn't want anyone to know about the family's secret and Valdira was giving it away."

"Did you ever suspect he could be a secret magus?" Anarinda asked.

"No!" Silma gave a wry laugh. "All anyone knew was that he answered every question with his fists."

Phareth nodded, remembering his Gritl had spoken of her husband's former friend with his terrible temper and tendency to violence.

"He called it a curse upon his line," Phareth said. "Were there any stories in the village about his relatives having a special way with animals?"

"Alas," Silma answered with a shrug, "I don't come from Lornest. I was born in Mirost and trained in Polvest. Even if someone did suspect, they wouldn't have told me."

"They obviously respect you," Anarinda countered. "Any village would want an Initiate of Blood. They need your good will."

"I've been assigned in Lornest for twenty-three years, and I'm still an outsider," Silma replied. "Marton is one of them. For all his flaws, they won't betray him." She looked to Phareth, "Now you say the Collegium is discussing this?"

"Yes, though I haven't been informed of any decision," Phareth said. "Other things are happening. Not just our battle with Valdira," he added, seeing Silma's concerned expression. "You might have heard about a nobleman named Nepharyl who was traveling with us when we got to Lornest."

"The one who was bossing our mayor around?" Silma smiled momentarily. "Tyteb can be a bit bossy himself. There were a few who enjoyed watching him take orders, I assure you."

"That may be," Telamar said. "Nepharyl left without telling anyone. He was supposed to be Phareth's anchor in Lorest, but after the battle he couldn't locate his mind."

"Yes, I remember," Silma said. "That's why Initiate Phareth called on me. No one told me they saw him leave, if that's what you were going to ask. The village women were watching you—"

"Naturally," Phareth put in drily.

"They were quite disappointed when you rented Yorec's house and they couldn't see what you were up to," she finished.

"We wanted our privacy," Telamar said.

"I'm not criticizing," Silma assured him.

"Nevertheless," Anarinda said, "it sounds like the only one who could have seen when he left was our dear friend Marton."

Telamar gave a sarcastic chuckle, but Phareth said, "It doesn't matter. We know where Nepharyl went."

"You told me you couldn't locate his mind," Silma objected.

"Ah, but—" Phareth held up one finger. "During our battle, I fought Valdira mind to mind. I've been able to keep track of her since then."

The question Silma had been longing to ask burst out. "Is she all right?"

"She's fine," Phareth said sourly. "Better than we were. I blocked her powers temporarily, but they're back now. She fled to Costera, and who do you think is with her?"

The Blood magus stared at him for a moment, then ventured, "That Stone novice, Ryamon? He must have made that pit you fell into. I wondered what had happened to him. No one in the village knew anything."

"Well, yes," Phareth said. "Ryamon is with Valdira and he's deeply in love. But Nepharyl is there, too."

Telamar snorted to himself, apparently unable to believe any man could fall for a woman like Valdira. Silma looked confused.

"Lord Nepharyl went to Costera?"

Phareth nodded. "I gather it caused a bit of commotion when I reported this to the Shadow Lord. It appears Nepharyl is part of a conspiracy. The Shadow magi have been backtracking him, trying to find out who else is involved and what their goals are. Valdira's situation had to be put aside."

"I see." Silma stared at the fire, thinking.

After a moment, Anarinda reassured her, "It sounds like things may work out for her. If the Mage Lords accept that her power is a legitimate variant—"

"There's no guarantee of that," Telamar pointed out.

For once, Phareth agreed with him. Ice Lord Salovik would not easily be persuaded to accept any change in the Seven Exalted Orders.

"I know," Anarinda said impatiently.

"If the Mage Lords call upon Marton or Valdira to testify, there's no way to know if either of them will trust the Collegium enough to answer the summons," Silma added.

"Do you think it will make any difference?" Phareth asked.

"With Marton?" Silma asked. "It's hard to say. He's so committed to hating Valdira—and himself, if what you say is true. It may be impossible for him to change his mind and view his magic as a gift rather than a curse.

"Valdira is different. She only wants to be left alone, but she's so angry with her father." Phareth felt a snap of shields closing around some painful memory. Aloud, Silma said, "I'm not sure what she would."

Phareth nodded, pondering these insights and how they might affect his private plans.

"We'll just have to hope," Telamar said. From his tone, it wasn't clear exactly what he hoped for.

Anarinda turned to Phareth. "I want you to talk to Marton. Explain the situation and see if you can find out how many of his family also have this gift."

Since this was what Phareth planned to do anyway, he shrugged. "I'll do what I can."

"There may be more unknown magi than you expect," Silma said to Anarinda. "Most of the locals are related to each other. Don't look like that," she added, scolding Telamar. "It's a small town. They don't all marry cousins, but it's hard for the young men to attract brides from outside."

"I can't argue with you," Anarinda said with a rueful smile. "Is there anything else we need to talk about?"

"Yes, something important," Telamar said calmly. Looking over his shoulder, where the villagers were raising their tents, he demanded, "Did they bring any food?"

Chapter Twenty

Ryamon sat near a window in Yolie's library. A history book lay open on his lap. He looked through the glass without really seeing Laceto's green fields and fences.

"There you are," Valdira said.

"What's wrong?" Ryamon turned, worried by her mildly accusing tone.

"I'm running away," she announced, a gleam of mischief in her eyes.

"Not without me." Ryamon put the book aside and strode to join her. No dusty tome was as interesting as Valdira.

His lover was back in the pale green gown Nepharyl had originally given her. Her hair was loose, with only a white ribbon holding the golden locks back from her face.

"You look beautiful," he said.

"You always say that," Valdira answered, but she sounded pleased.

"Only because it's true."

He offered his arm and Valdira took it. Together they walked down the gleaming hallway. The door to Valdira's chamber was ajar, and Ryamon glimpsed a maidservant inside. From her guilty pout, he suspected Valdira had bullied the girl into dressing her down instead of up. Farther along, another maid stopped dusting between the banister rails to bow as they passed. Ryamon wondered if he would ever get used to that.

The maid looked startled to see them. And, just as they reached the foyer, he thought he heard someone scurry away behind a closed door. Yolie hadn't said they were supposed to stay in their rooms, but Ryamon wondered if they were breaking the rules by walking around without her. From her impish expression, Valdira definitely thought she was breaking the rules—and she enjoyed it.

"Where are we going?" he asked as they descended the curving stair.

Valdira shoulder rolled in a shrug. "I don't care, as long as it's outside."

"Good idea," Ryamon answered with feeling.

"I know," came her smug reply.

Beautiful as it was, the manor was starting to seem like a prison. They had scarcely been outdoors in the three days since they arrived in Yolie's domain. Ryamon hadn't realized how accustomed he was to open spaces. He missed the freedom of the wilderness.

Valdira appeared to enjoy being pampered, so Ryamon had found the library where he could study Costeran history in the afternoons while their hostess tended to administrative matters. Unfortunately, Yolie's collection was small. He found few answers to his questions about this country's customs.

There was no mention of the nobles getting married, though they frequently had liaisons for the purpose of getting children. In several cases, civil wars had been sparked when different wizards fought for the title of Wizard King. Ryamon couldn't understand how this society survived when every relationship was temporary.

Yolie did eat with them in the evenings. She had taught them several card games as entertainment. Most involved gambling. Since the exiles had no money, Yolie provided a store of buttons to wager with. She usually ended up with most of them.

Curiously, she hadn't invited any other Costeran nobles to meet them. It was almost as though she wanted to keep them to herself. Ryamon couldn't see what advantage this brought her. As days passed, he waited with increasing dread for Darmosh to visit again. The man was going to demand an answer, and Ryamon didn't have one.

The big doors in the foyer were closed. A pair of guards with rapiers and bucklers flanked it. Both men watched nervously as Ryamon and Valdira approached. Ryamon hesitated, not sure he wanted to cause a confrontation, but Valdira pulled him onward.

"Excuse us," she said.

Her loud voice echoed off the polished walls. One of the soldiers shifted, his hand dropping to his sword hilt. Valdira whirled to face him.

"Were you going to *say* something?" she asked sweetly. The man's face burned as she taunted him with his enforced silence.

"Sweetheart, that's not fair," Ryamon murmured. Valdira didn't answer. She grabbed the door handle and turned, pushing it briskly outward.

Neither man tried to stop them, so they went down the steps to the gravel circle. The lake shimmered at the base of the hill, and a light breeze carried a sweet medley of fragrances from the flower garden.

"Smell that," Valdira said, drawing a deep breath. She sighed. "Ah—isn't that worth it?"

Ryamon leaned closer to whisper, "You're prettier."

"You…" She leaned upward to kiss him lightly. Before he could really enjoy it, she tugged on his arm to lead away from the manor house. "Come on, let's walk around."

Arm in arm, the two exiles strolled down the gravel drive to the base of the hill. Afternoon sunlight lit the jagged mountains as they turned right, onto the main road. Yolie had taken them around Laceto once, in her twyeron coach, so Ryamon knew the road circled the estate like the bars of a cage.

The village walls soon came into sight. Another cage, perhaps, within the larger one. Yolie hadn't taken them inside, dismissing the area as "a few peasant hovels." Ryamon wondered if Valdira meant to stride in and explore it.

"It isn't really much of an estate, is it?" Ryamon ventured, hoping to divert her. "Compared to what we had in Selkest…"

Valdira's hand tightened against his arm. "I know," she answered tightly, "but we can't look back. Not all the time."

"I'm not sure what I see ahead of us," Ryamon persisted. "The sanctuary they offer comes at a high price."

"This isn't only about us," Valdira said.

"You're right." Ryamon said. The people in Lornest and hundreds of other villages would be kept in smaller and smaller cages if Darmosh succeeded in reconquering Arkanost.

Valdira didn't seem to be listening. He caught the jerk of her head as she looked over her shoulder. Without a word, she pulled him left, down a lane between two turnip fields. It was obviously too narrow for the twyeron coach. That must be what Valdira had intended, to avoid being chased down.

"What's wrong?" Ryamon asked.

"I think someone's following us."

With an effort, Ryamon fought back the impulse to turn and stare behind them.

"One of the soldiers?" he murmured. "I suppose it's only to be expected."

Valdira answered with a vague murmur. Ryamon thought she might be trying to contact the local wildlife and see what was behind them. They walked on in silence. He sighed to himself. It would have been nice to enjoy Valdira's company without these complications.

On their left was a small birch grove, green-gold against the darker hues of spruce and pine. The trees sighed restlessly, no doubt longing for Valdira's attention as much as Ryamon did. The familiar noise soothed him because it meant she had all her magic back. Still, he noticed his lover constantly looking from side to side. Her expression was alert and tense.

"Are you looking for something?" he asked.

"Maybe."

Ryamon definitely felt a lurking purpose, but he couldn't tell what. Valdira still blocked him out.

As if she sensed his thoughts, Valdira gave Ryamon a sharp glance. Then he realized she wasn't looking at him, but past him. He waited a moment and glanced over to his right.

Several serfs in red and white livery watched nervously from a turnip field on that side. Ryamon supposed they were wondering if they should stop weeding the turnips and bow. Just in case, he raised his hand to acknowledge their presence. Valdira snorted lightly.

"Troublemaker," she murmured, but she was smiling again.

"You're one to talk."

Valdira smiled up at him, and he saw a grim sheen of mischief in her eyes. "Watch me."

"Sweetheart?" he asked.

She raised her left hand just as a flash of black and white caught Ryamon's eye. A bird flitted in from the birch grove and perched on her hand. She drew it closer to her body, where the serfs wouldn't see it. The bird gave a harsh chirp and flicked its tail. She stroked its round head with a gentle finger.

"I've been thinking about what that Darmosh said." Valdira looked up at Ryamon, her green eyes narrowed. "How he thinks magi should take over Arkanost."

"You can't want to help him," Ryamon protested. He gave a guilty glance at the serfs and lowered his voice.

Valdira rolled her eyes, her mouth twisting with disgust that he would even think this. The black and white bird gave a shrill, rasping cry.

"Don't you want to know if he has anything to back up his bragging?" she asked. "My friend here is going to get us some answers."

With a final glance at the serfs, she flicked her wrist. The bird flitted off and disappeared into the birch grove.

"You're going to spy on him?" Ryamon asked. It was probably a good idea, but he still worried. "Isn't that dangerous? He's a wizard."

"So are we," Valdira patted his arm. "How can they prove I'm controlling the bird? Now, it will take him a while to fly down to Olalu, and I may have to help him find the way. We need to go back to Yolie's house, where you're going to put me to bed. I have a terrible headache and I just want to sleep, understand?"

"If you're sure," Ryamon said.

Any number of things could go wrong, but Valdira was a clever woman and she wouldn't take foolish chances. If what she learned convinced her not to stay in Costera, the risk might be worth it.

~ * ~

Phareth felt his exhaustion and ill temper melt away as he devoured the sour beer, dried fruit and cheese Silma offered. Even Anarinda, who was a fastidious eater, attacked her food like a hungry shorbak. Three days of short rations would do that.

They sat around their original campfire under the rock ledge. Silma chuckled occasionally at their voracity. An assortment of canvas tents now rose nearby, including a scarlet one for the Blood initiate. A larger fire pit was being dug near the center, and three of the men were stringing bows to hunt small game.

Watching this activity, Phareth mulled his options. What should he do about Valdira? From his surveillance, he knew she missed the forest and despised her hostess, Yolie. Valdira was sure to come home if given the chance to return honorably.

However, Silma was undoubtedly correct that she wouldn't have any faith in an offer from the Collegium. Nor, since their battle, would Valdira trust Phareth if he contacted her directly. Even Ryamon was unlikely to believe if an offer came from Phareth.

Nor could he rely on Ryamon to persuade Valdira, even if he

placed the idea in his mind very subtly. The couple was still together, but their relationship seemed tenuous. There was something Valdira wasn't telling Ryamon, and Phareth couldn't find out what it was without alerting her.

Even considering all that, he wasn't sure bringing Ryamon and Valdira back to Arkanost was what he really wanted. To strike without being seen was appropriate for a Shadow magus; it was what Murcrys would want him to do. Yet, as a man, Phareth could never be satisfied with such an oblique revenge.

No, he needed more. He wanted to hurt Darmosh, deeply and personally. Through Ryamon, he had seen the full scope of his enemy's ambition. Phareth wanted to snatch those dreams away and smash them. More, he wanted Darmosh to know who had done it.

Which meant Phareth wasn't going to contact his mother for instructions, as Anarinda wanted. Stand or fall, he would do this on his own. He'd have to make his move before his team started back to Lornest, too, or he'd waste time getting away from them and backtracking through the wild lands.

Phareth swallowed the last of his beer and considered the man who had brewed it. Marton was somewhere on the other side of camp, chopping wood. They could hear his axe biting at the wood. He probably thought he was being clever, showing everyone how agitated he was.

Valdira's father was no more likely to convince her to come home than Ryamon, but persuasion wasn't what Phareth wanted him for. How to use the man without being bitten, that was the question.

Anarinda cleared her throat purposefully. Phareth looked around and saw her watching him. Still chewing on a strip of jerky, she tilted her chin and focused her gaze on the side of the camp where Marton was.

If Anarinda wanted to think she was in charge, Phareth would let her. He nodded briefly, as if accepting her instructions, and rose.

"Excuse me," Phareth said.

Silma looked mildly surprised, and Telamar's wary eyes pricked at him. Phareth slapped dust off his black robe as he strolled toward the sound of chopping.

He found Marton hobbling between a pile of firewood and

the large, flat rock he was using as a base to cut it on. Phareth watched for a bit, assessing again the man's work-worn clothing and the painful injury he refused to let Silma cure. Even with the limp, Marton seemed steadier on his feet than he had been before. What could cause this change?

The brewer swung his axe with fast, angry jerks. He split half a log into neat sections—surprising for a man who was obviously in a foul mood.

Marton must have glimpsed Phareth standing there, for he turned to glare with hard, green eyes. As their eyes met, Phareth sensed what was different: Marton was sober. It clearly pained him to not be drunk. He wondered why the man had come along for the rescue if being there was such a problem. What did he hope to prove, besides that he was in control of his daughter?

Marton snarled, "What do you want?"

Phareth kept a blank face. "Need any help?"

"From you?"

Phareth could hardly avoid picking up the man's opinion of himself, a pampered magus from the big city who was looking thin after his forced stay in the woods. There was no way cutting wood interested him.

He shrugged. "I have something to tell you, and not everyone needs to know."

Marton glared at him a moment longer, but then his eyes flicked behind Phareth, where the other villagers were gathering around the new fire pit. In a strangely dexterous movement, he balanced on his axe to kick the last section of wood onto the pile.

"Let's go, then. We have a couple of fires to feed, and those twigs you have here won't do the job."

Still armed with the axe, Marton stalked off along the lake shore. Phareth ambled after him. Once again, he felt Telamar's suspicious gaze. Phareth kept his shoulders straight. There was no need to slink around. He was doing what Anarinda wanted… mostly.

He pointed toward the grove where he had found wood earlier in the day. "I think we can get what we need over there."

"Huh." Marton grumbled, but he did adjust his direction. After a moment, he demanded, "Where is she?"

"Valdira?" Phareth asked blandly. "She went south."

"Got away from you," Marton sneered. In his mind, Phareth

heard the unspoken: *So much for the mighty Collegium.* Despite himself, Phareth tensed.

"We fought, and yes, she escaped us," he admitted. Because it was what Marton wanted to hear, he added, "For now."

"Fool," Marton grunted. Phareth couldn't tell whether Marton meant himself or Valdira.

"She wasn't alone," Phareth said. "It was her boyfriend who dumped us all in a hole."

Suddenly ferocious, Marton snapped, "Her what?"

"Didn't you know?" Phareth asked coolly. "Silma reported her and the Collegium send an inquisitor. But he fell in love with her instead…"

"Does this fellow have a name?" Marton interrupted, hostile as any father who finds a young man in his daughter's company.

"Ryamon," Phareth answered. "He was a novice in the Order of Stone, but he has problems of his own now. You really didn't know?"

"I don't listen to gossip," Marton growled. "Bunch of stupid nattering."

Actually, Phareth could believe that. With his nasty temper, Marton wasn't the kind to draw confidences. His wife might have heard something, but Marton would never ask her for news of the town. He was still too angry over Valdira's birth. Phareth spared a moment of pity for Rhella, tied to a man who wouldn't let go of a grudge after so many years.

"Huh," Marton went on growling, and then, "Fool."

This time Phareth was certain he meant Ryamon. Painful as it was, he opened his mental shield to hear to Marton's thoughts more clearly.

Ryamon, eh? The brewer's scorn scraped on Phareth's nerves. *"She'll finish with him soon enough, like every other lad she's used and cast aside."*

"He might surprise you," Phareth remarked, remembering Ryamon's devotion to his lover.

"That's what I'm afraid of," Marton bit out.

Phareth walked on as if he didn't care, but he was sufficiently intrigued to press further into the maelstrom of Marton's psyche.

"A bitch, like her bitch mother," Marton raged to himself. *"Always running after some young fool. I have to find her, bring her in line. Stop her before she spreads the curse any further."*

Feeling slightly battered, Phareth withdrew. The family curse again. That was what Marton cared about, not the welfare of his rebellious daughter.

It was a perfect opportunity to tell Marton the Grand Collegium might decriminalize his "curse." Phareth considered keeping the knowledge to himself. If Marton gave up his anger, Phareth would lose his perfect tool.

In the end, he knew he couldn't hide the truth. Anarinda was sure to ask what the man had said. He didn't have to hurry about it, though. Phareth wanted to think a little bit more.

They reached the copse of trees he had visited that morning. Stopping, he gestured around him. "See anything we can use?"

Marton limped to a halt and looked around without much hope. It seemed to Phareth that he, too, was glad to stop thinking about Valdira for a while. The farmer raised a hand to hold his hat on as he looked upward. Pine trees loomed over them, gaunt shapes bristling against the sky. Marton kicked his away over the layer of brown needles that covered the ground.

"Not much," he grunted. A few of the fallen branches that Phareth had left behind rattled as he passed them. "This stuff is too small, but I don't want to take a tree down. We're only here the one night."

"What about this?"

Phareth beckoned Marton to follow him behind a large tree. Some long-ago storm had snapped off the top half of a pine tree. The dry crown was propped at an angle between two smaller trees. A thicket of vines grew around them.

"It's not green wood," Phareth pointed out. "Can we shift it between us?"

Marton eyed the tangle with grudging acceptance. "It'll do to start."

Together, the two men approached the deadfall. Phareth quickly fell back, giving Marton room. The wood was completely dry, brown needles crumbling as the brewer swung his axe. After a little bit of hacking and a lot of cursing, he freed the trunk from the thicket. It fell with a thud, raising coarse dust from the forest floor.

Phareth swallowed a sneeze and went to grab a stub of branch. Bark dug painfully into his bare hands as they dragged the log back toward camp.

Once they were in motion, Phareth asked, "Would it matter if I told you the Collegium is taking another look at your daughter's situation?"

"What do you mean?" Suspicious again, Marton glared at Phareth over the top of the log.

"After Valdira subverted Ryamon, the Collegium sent the three of us to collect them both," Phareth explained, panting slightly with effort.

"I remember," Marton growled.

"But you told us Valdira didn't develop her magic on her own. You said it was something that ran in your family."

The tip of the log caught between two stones and stopped them both with a jerk. For a moment, the two men wrestled to twist it free. Once they had the tree trunk moving again, Phareth continued.

"One person with a strange power would clearly be an illegal abuse of magic, but a hereditary power implies continuity. One thing they want me to find out is how often this curse appears in your family. Because if it's a magic that can be duplicated—"

"Just say what you mean," Marton interrupted. He didn't answer the question about his family.

"The Collegium might acknowledge Valdira's gift and make it part of an existing order," Phareth said. "You wouldn't have to hide your abilities any longer."

"Me? I don't have any magic." Suddenly Marton was sweating, and Phareth was sure it wasn't just from dragging a treetop across the valley.

It was Phareth's turn to sneer. "Don't lie to me. I'm a Shadow magus. It's obvious what you are."

Marton stopped pulling on the tree. Seeing his knuckles whiten on the handle of his axe, Phareth modified his tone.

"It's also clear that you've contained it and not used it," he reasoned. "You followed the law. That's an honorable solution. The Collegium won't punish you."

Marton's fist relaxed. He turned away and started yanking on the tree again. Phareth joined him.

"I have to be honest with you," Phareth said as they started off again. "The mage lords don't make changes easily. It could take months to reach a decision."

Marton sent him a wary glance, but he no longer radiated

murderous fury.

"I can't promise," Phareth stressed, "but it seems most likely they'll bring Valdira and any other relatives you identify into one of the Seven Exalted Orders."

Thinking back, he was sure this had been his mother's plan all along. Valdira's mental link with nature could logically be taken as part of the Order of Shadows. However, Murcrys might not be the only one who wanted her. Any Mage Lord could desire the new possibilities that came with Valdira's unusual gifts. Blood Lord Minaric, for one, had a claim on Valdira even though she had tried to leave his Order.

On the other side were Salovik and Akayel, who were sure to resist any change within the Collegium. To say nothing of King Sedlin and Countess Guilberta.

"What about me?" Marton grated. "Will I have to leave my farm?"

Ironic that he shared a love of home with his prodigal daughter. Phareth laughed wryly, and Marton scowled at him.

"No one will want you. You're too old," Phareth assured him. Although it was certainly amusing to picture Marton in novice robes, fasting and memorizing Strictures. "They'll just watch you to make sure you don't abuse your magic."

Marton nodded stiffly and continued dragging on the tree trunk. Phareth wished he would hurry. The log felt heavier by the yard. His lungs ached and shoulders burned with the effort. From time to time, Phareth glanced aside, watching his companion nervously. Marton still frowned, mostly out of habit. His fury seemed to turn inward as he grappled with his new information. Phareth felt the jagged edges of his emotions even though he was fully shielded.

The man was angry, because Marton was always angry. He wanted to reject what Phareth had told him. It couldn't be easy to accept that he had been wrong all his life, about himself and his family. Marton had never accepted his magic the way Valdira did. He hated that his daughter reveled in what he despised. No amount of calm explanation could change these gut reactions.

All the same, Phareth did sense some remorse for the way Marton had treated his family. He had been cruel to his wife for no good reason. He had demanded Silma do what he himself never could: change Valdira's behavior.

Marton wasn't a deep thinker. He wasn't used to feeling regret, didn't know how to express it. In his confusion and denial, Phareth saw an opportunity to shape the man's reaction as he wished it.

Bracing himself for the violent emotions, he infiltrated Marton's thoughts. The brewer already felt obligated to control Valdira. She was his blood, therefore his responsibility. With great care, Phareth modified this idea. If Marton was really a man, he suggested, he would make things right with the women in his life.

Phareth slipped back out just as Marton dropped the log at his chopping rock. In his concentration, he hadn't realized they were already back at camp. Gratefully, Phareth let go. He stood rubbing his sore shoulder and shaking his stinging hands. His mouth felt tight and dry.

In a way, Phareth was as bad as Ryamon and Valdira. What he had done to Marton was exactly the kind of manipulation Telamar had always believed him guilty of. Well, fine. This was what he had to do, for Kylethia and himself. If he had broken the strictures of Shadow, so be it.

The last needles on the tree trunk crackled as Marton leaned over the log. In a low voice, he asked, "You say she's in Costera?"

Phareth suppressed a surge of triumph.

"That's right," he answered in an equally soft tone. "What are you going to do about it?"

Chapter Twenty-One

"Valdira isn't feeling well, I hear?"

At the supper table, Yolie leaned toward Ryamon with sympathy and concern. Her gown was of ivory silk studded with garnets. The pale fabric set off her dark hair, which had been left loose. Curls ran over her shoulders in artful strands, like serpents basking on sunny rocks.

"It's nothing," Ryamon said. "A headache, and her stomach was troubling her a little."

He tried to speak in a normal tone. Even though he understood Valdira's reasons, Ryamon didn't like lying.

"A headache?" Yolie arched her brows with sly understanding.

"I'm sure she'll be herself by morning." Ryamon rubbed his neck, where sweat tickled under the collar of his jacket. The room felt overly warm with a fire blazing on the hearth and high summer outside. Such temperature variations didn't usually bother him, but Ryamon knew the fire wasn't the real problem. He had never been a very good liar. The deception felt so obvious to him. At least the nausea was true. Valdira had mentioned it as they were climbing the spiral stair to her room.

"Too much exercise, perhaps," Yolie suggested with a hint of coy bite. Ryamon chuckled nervously.

"Pardon me, Dama," he politely corrected. "Valdira and I have been living in the hills for several weeks and we walked everywhere. To us, it was merely a refreshing stroll. You've been so kind, we didn't think you would mind."

Inside, he wondered how Yolie even knew they had been outside the manor. With her servants were forbidden to speak, who was going to tell her?

"I make it a point to know what's happening in my land," Yolie chided. "You could have taken my coach. One mustn't become too familiar with the serfs, my pet. They might begin to take us for granted."

So there were rules after all. Valdira would be interested in that, Ryamon was sure. Even as Yolie spoke, her servants circled the table, setting out food. He couldn't help wondering what they thought of her viewpoint.

Food was a welcome diversion. Tonight it was meat and vegetables in thick gravy, all topped by a flaky crust. Ryamon found it ironic Yolie's fancy supper looked so much like a peasant's pot pie. There was also soft bread, a sharp reddish cheese, and some kind of dark blue berries.

Ryamon knew he didn't have to wait for Yolie to eat before he began, so he tucked into the hearty meal. The taste of the herbs was unfamiliar. He wasn't sure he liked it.

"Must you eat like a wild man?" Yolie teased as she picked up her own fork.

Ryamon smiled ruefully. Living in the hills had had its pleasures, but he didn't think he would ever forget the pinch of perpetually short rations. He swallowed a mouthful to answer, "It's a compliment to your staff."

"What a sweet boy you are," Yolie murmured. As the last maid poured their wine, she waved all the servants toward the door. "That will be all."

Ryamon watched, startled, as the servants bowed in eerie synchronicity and filed from the room. He chewed his latest bite slowly. The idea of being alone with his hostess was faintly alarming. The fire's crackle seemed loud. Its heat was oppressive. Ryamon sipped his wine, trying to cool himself. He focused on his plate, avoiding Yolie's gaze.

She leaned toward him anyway. The cut of her gown made her bosom glow softly in the lamplight. A garnet pendant on a golden chain glittered as she breathed. It seemed she was trying to make him stare.

Guiltily, Ryamon jerked his eyes away from Yolie's chest and looked her in the face. Her dark eyes were warm with concern as she asked, "Is everything all right, my pet?"

"Of course," he fumbled. Ryamon had no interest in Yolie, not really. How could he tell her without insulting her? He lifted his spoon, pretending she had meant the food. "It's delicious, as always."

Yolie gave one of her trilling laughs. The garnet pendant twinkled at him.

"You know that's not what I mean. Perhaps it's not my place, my pet, but I do worry. It seems your sweetheart isn't taking very good care of you."

Ryamon's cheeks burned as Yolie reminded him that he and Valdira were sleeping apart. Was it so obvious, the distance between them, and that he was doing his best to hold their love together?

"So much has changed all at once," he stuttered. "We're still adjusting…"

"You poor dear," Yolie murmured. She reached across the table for the wine bottle. "She really is neglecting you."

Yolie's perfume seemed to mingle with the wine fumes as she refilled his goblet. Her bosom glowed like twin moons half-hidden by clouds. It was almost repulsive, yet Ryamon couldn't seem to look away. He drank deeply to shut out the sight of them. It had been so long since Valdira really touched him.

"Everything is fine," he mumbled.

"I've seen it so often," Yolie said sorrowfully. "A couple in love, but circumstances change. She meets someone new, or he loses at the gaming tables and there is less money."

"Well—" Ryamon wished she wouldn't mention how he always lost at cards.

"Suddenly she has more options," Yolie mused, sipping her own wine. "Should she stay, or move on and cut her losses?"

"Pardon me!" he cried, stung by the suggestion Valdira was ready to leave him. "Relationships in Arkanost aren't so disposable."

And yet, he had just been thinking that he was doing all the work to make their love last.

"Oh?" Yolie smiled up at him with something like pity.

Ryamon looked away, embarrassed. She patted his hand, and he did his best not to pull away from her.

"That isn't what's happening," he went on, weakly.

Valdira wasn't trying to get rid of him, Ryamon reminded himself. She had sent him here to keep Yolie busy. And it was obvious Yolie wouldn't mind being kept busy, in a certain way. Despite himself, Ryamon felt his heart pound in his throat. His groin was tight and hard. It had been so long since Valdira slept with him.

Still Yolie leaned closer. Her hand was on his shoulder, though he didn't remember her putting it there.

"But she does neglect you," Yolie crooned. "Such a fine young man, so sweet and strong. She doesn't appreciate what she has."

"I think…" Ryamon stammered, but she was starting to make sense. His thoughts tumbled wildly, as if by saying the words Yolie had set him free him to think about these things. Ryamon was the one who had to pursue Valdira, begging for her approval. He never knew if he would say the wrong thing. Could Yolie be right? Was Valdira looking for a way out? And how long did she expect him to go without satisfaction?

Yolie's hand slipped up to his shoulder, then curved around his neck to tangle gently in his hair. Ryamon looked into her face, stunned by the flood of desire that blazed through him. Yolie pressed against his head, gently tipping his face downward.

Everything blurred around Ryamon. Fire thundered in his veins. Ryamon's hands moved without his wishing it, seeking her ripe bosom. Yolie moaned in his ear.

"Be my wild man," she whispered, her lips barely brushing his. "I can take care of you. Valdira won't mind. She won't even notice."

Her words sent a shock through Ryamon, burned away the haze of wine and lust. Somewhere in his memory, Valdira's voice echoed: *She hates me.*

An instant later, he realized the desire he felt was not all his own. Yolie was in his mind. Somehow she was feeding him this emotion, forcing her desires upon him, weakening his will—

"No!" he shouted.

Ryamon jumped to his feet, knocking his own chair out from under him. Crockery clattered as he bumped the table. Yolie gave a startled cry as he pushed her away, and then a true scream as the Fire within Ryamon exploded outward.

Flames were everywhere. He couldn't see past them. Ryamon felt dizzy—had he really had that much wine? —and he fought to straighten his wobbling knees. He smelled steam and smoke. Then the techniques he had learned in the Tower of Stone came to his rescue. He breathed deeply, calling on all his control. Flames flow-ed back into him.

Nothing was actively burning, although a scorched odor hung thick in the air. The tablecloth where he had been sitting was singed. The wine goblets were tipped over, remains of food cook-ed brown on the plates. Yolie's dress was also charred in places. He could clearly see a reddish print where his hand had burned her. Ryamon's clothing, however, was unaffected.

"Why did you do that?" Yolie shrilled, her voice no longer a tempting whisper.

"I… This is wrong…" Ryamon's mind whirled. How long

had Yolie been in his mind? How deep had she gone? Did she know he was only buying time for Valdira to spy on Darmosh? He pushed all that to the back of his mind. Yolie couldn't be allowed to see how much he suspected. Better to pretend he was merely ashamed of his loss of control. Which, actually, was true enough.

In a choked voice, he went on, "Even if you're right, I can't..." He swallowed. "It's for Valdira to tell me we're through."

"You fool," Yolie hissed, glaring at Ryamon. One hand groped for a napkin, soaked with spilled wine, which she pressed to her burned skin. Her face was flushed and eyes blazing with intense emotion—humiliation, frustration, or perhaps simple fury.

Before he could answer, they both heard the thud of footsteps outside. The door burst open and one of the guards cried, "Dama!"

The man stopped in the doorway. His rapier flashed in his fist. Wide-eyed maidservants clustered in the hallway behind him.

Ryamon had to get out of the room before someone came after him. He had no grudge against the man, even though he served such a mistress. Upset as he was, afire with lust that couldn't be shared, Ryamon didn't trust himself not to hurt someone.

He straightened and faced Yolie with his quaintest, most old-fashioned bow. As he did so, he saw his footprints had burned into the carpet where he stood.

"Dama, please forgive me," he said with stiff formality. "My lack of control is inexcusable. I must go and meditate."

Without giving her a chance to argue, Ryamon strode for the door. The maids jumped back at his approach, as if his nearness might contaminate them. The guard held his ground, glaring, but he must have seen something in Ryamon's face. He also gave way.

Escaping into the hallway, Ryamon paused long enough to tell the maids, in a clipped voice, "Dama Yolie is burned. She'll need salve and bandages."

The women scattered. He wondered if they were more afraid of him or Yolie. Inside the room, he could hear his hostess berating the guard for entering without her permission. He walked faster. He was pretty sure he didn't want to know how angry Yolie really was.

~ * ~

With the meal complete and camp set up, the villagers sat

around their fire. They talked softly as the evening air grew brisk. Silma and Anarinda joined them. Telamar went to bed. Phareth sat alone, silently planning the night ahead.

The Shadow magus froze in place as a faint sound reached him through the murmur of voices. A high screech echoed across the valley and suddenly cut off. Not eridow this time—that was an ornyx.

Phareth's pulse raced, but he didn't want to give his discovery away. Feigning boredom, he turned his head to track the sound. Nothing moved in the small valley. Only a line of rocky hills loomed against the darkening sky.

He glanced toward the bottom of the hill, where the ornyxes were picketed. They sat alert, listening. So Phareth hadn't imagined the ornyx call. The birds had heard it, too.

With them in plain sight, there was only one other possibility. And it could change everything.

~ * ~

Ryamon walked blindly, not even sure where he was going. He needed Valdira. Fire blazed inside him, and he wanted to hold his sweetheart, kiss her, feel her body beneath him. Yet he was afraid to face her.

What had Yolie been trying to accomplish? Did she think he would tell her what Valdira was up to, alone in her room, or did she think she could ensnare him the way she had Nepharyl? Ryamon might have walked away from her, but he couldn't escape the ideas she had planted in his mind. Nor could he guess how Valdira would react. She might blame him for Yolie's attempted seduction. Worse, she might have expected him to go along with Yolie, since that would give her more time to spy on Darmosh.

Despite all his fears, Ryamon found himself standing at Valdira's chamber door. He didn't know what was happening with her. He couldn't tell if she loved him or wanted to be free. He had been avoiding these questions, trying not to ask them even of himself. Yolie had sensed that weakness and exploited it.

Now he stared at the carved gilt of Valdira's door and braced himself to enter. No, he couldn't guess what Valdira would say about Yolie. She was never so predictable. All he could do was tell the truth.

The metal door handle felt cold under his fevered hand. He

pushed it down and entered the room. The chamber was dark. No fire burned in the grate and the lamps were unlit. Ryamon saw only shadows of the furnishings. Valdira sat near the window, a black outline against the wan gold of the dying day. She jumped at the sound of the door opening.

"You're back early." It was half question, half accusation.

Emotion flooded Ryamon at the sight of her, shame and desire mixed together. A few steps carried him across the room. He swept her into his arms and buried his face in her hair. Ryamon reveled in her slender strength and the smell of her, slightly oily with no hint of perfume. Valdira let him hold her for a moment, then struggled against his grip.

"You smell like smoke." Alarm flashed in her eyes. "What's wrong?"

"I—" Ryamon began, shamefaced. "I exploded."

"What?" Valdira demanded, incredulous. "You've never had trouble controlling your Element."

Ryamon shook his head, groping for words to explain. "It was Yolie. She—" Lust raged within him, a flame too hot to endure. Valdira yelped as he grabbed her and kissed her hard, crushing her against him. It helped, a little.

Breathing hard, Valdira broke the kiss. She stared up at him. Ryamon felt the faint brush of her power through his body.

"She did something to you," Valdira said in a fierce voice. "What did she do?"

"I didn't want her. I only want you," Ryamon pleaded. He lunged to kiss her again. Valdira pulled completely away and stood with both hands braced against his chest.

"Stand still," she ordered, concentrating. Her power felt cool now, a flood that swept away the dizziness of wine and soothed his lust. Ryamon felt relief, yet also regret. It had been a powerful feeling, to know what he wanted so clearly.

As he grew calmer, shame sank its claws into his soul. He babbled to explain.

"She was forcing her feelings on me. It was her magic or something, I don't know. When I sensed it… That she was trying to twist my feelings… That's when I lost control."

"She tried to seduce you?" Valdira demanded angrily. "It serves her right!"

Ryamon was pathetically glad she was angry with Yolie and

not him.

"I should have guessed," Valdira went on acidly. "She probably thinks you can give her a baby with power."

"A what?" Ryamon stared at her. This wasn't something he had ever thought of, although it was true, Yolie had mentioned her own children lacked wizardly potential. "Isn't she too old? At her age, she could die in birthing."

"She's a sorceress. Who knows what she can do?" Valdira pushed away and paced the room, rubbing her arms in agitation. Then she snapped, "No, that's not it. I told you before, she wants to cut me down."

"Like a rival?" Ryamon ventured.

"Because I'm not afraid of my own power," Valdira said angrily. "At home, the women always hated me for that. It would be just like Yolie to take the one good thing I have and soil it."

"Oh. But..." Ryamon trailed off. He was absurdly glad to know Valdira thought of him as something good in her life. Best not to spoil the moment with questions.

Valdira was still pacing and scowling. "No, that's not right, either. I'll bet she wanted to drive us apart. If we were alone, we'd be more likely to go along with whatever she has planned. Well, it didn't work." She smiled triumphantly.

Ryamon sank down on the settee. Much as he hated it, questions were what he had come here for. Yolie might have wanted to manipulate him, but there was still truth in her words. He couldn't ignore it. Ryamon stared at his lover, struggling to find words.

Valdira's smile faded as he stared at her. After a moment she looked away, rubbing her arms again. Her face still showed anger, and something else—fear, maybe, or guilt.

"What, is there more?" Her voice was acid again.

"Valdira," he fumbled. "What she said to me, that... That you're tired of me and you don't want me any more..."

"You'd believe her?" Valdira whirled back, furious now.

"No! But you can't deny, you've kept me at a distance since we got here. I mean, since we fought the magi and had to run. I understand why you were angry then, but you've hardly spoken to me. I don't know what to think."

Valdira faced the window. She stood silent and he couldn't see her face at all.

"There's something you aren't telling me." Ryamon's throat felt dry as ash. "I can feel it. When Yolie said all those things… It just seemed like it could be true."

Valdira turned to look at him with a haunted expression. He hated to see her look so trapped.

"Sweetheart," Ryamon stammered, "you have to tell me. Whatever it is, or whatever you want. I love you, but I'll go if that's what you want. You just have to tell me."

Valdira stared at him through another long silence. Then, slowly, she walked over to the settee and sank down beside Ryamon. Her face was pale and she licked her lips. If it had been anyone else, he would have thought she was afraid, but that couldn't be. Valdira never got scared. She just got angry. Yet now he felt a tremor in her arms where their shoulders touched. He waited, dreading what she would say.

"You haven't asked what I found out." Her voice was crisp, like ice that might break if he stepped on it. "While you were dallying with Yolie, my little friend flew down the valley to Olalu."

"I wasn't dallying! And I didn't forget—"

"Let me finish!"

He broke off.

"Darmosh isn't just dreaming of conquest," she said, hard and precise. "He has an army."

That did get Ryamon's attention. "How many? Did you see what kind of weapons they have? Are they all wizards?"

She shrugged, shoulders still tense. "I don't know. The bird couldn't count. All I saw were rows of tents. They seemed to go on forever."

Valdira looked at Ryamon. Her gaze was flat, like that of a hare hiding in a thicket and hoping the bobcat hadn't seen it.

"We can't stay here," she said.

"Not if Yolie's going to throw herself at me," Ryamon agreed. His words startled a brittle laugh out of Valdira.

"That's not what I mean. This place isn't home. I thought it might become one. If we could be safe here and do things our own way—but there are still rules," she finished bitterly. "I can see that."

Ryamon darted a glance toward the door, making sure it was closed. They couldn't just ignore an army. Arkanost's way of life had its shortcomings, but no one deserved to be abandoned to the wizards of Costera.

"What do you want to do?" he asked quietly. "Should we go back and warn them, even though they might throw us in prison?"

"I don't know." Valdira's face was tight with a wary expression. "But, Ryamon, there's something else. It's even more important."

"What do you mean?" Ryamon burst out. He didn't want to shout, but he couldn't help it. "Just tell me what's going on!"

"What's going on," Valdira said, her voice choked, "what Yolie doesn't know, is that there already is a baby with power."

She watched his face anxiously as she spoke. Ryamon had thought he was prepared for anything, but now he sat stunned.

"A baby?" he repeated stupidly.

"Our baby." She shifted in place, ready to jump for safety.

"How?" Ryamon choked.

For a moment Valdira was her old self. Her shoulders slumped and one eyebrow raised in exasperation. Ryamon hastily corrected himself.

"Well, I know *how*, but you ate the lace flowers. I saw you," he said. The image was clear in his mind, Valdira striding through a sunlit meadow, snapping off clusters of the tall blossoms. When she chewed them, she made faces at the taste.

"I know." Valdira's shoulders were hunched defensively. "It must have been while the Collegium magi were chasing us. I couldn't always find lace flowers. Or maybe they were past their season, not as potent." She was still staring at him, waiting for him to get angry. "I'm sorry. I didn't mean for it to happen."

"Don't be sorry!" Elation surged in Ryamon's veins. The woman he loved was carrying his child. Even with things getting so complicated, it seemed too good to be true. "Sweetheart, I'm not angry. This is wonderful news!"

He moved to embrace her, but Valdira scooted away on the settee. Clearly she didn't want to be held.

"It's just that, the last time…" She trailed off.

Ryamon let his hands fall to his sides, his joy deflating. Last time? He remembered Valdira's mother mentioning other suitors, but had she really been pregnant before? His shock must have shown in his face.

"It didn't quicken," Valdira quickly told him.

She must have had a miscarriage. Ryamon decided that, this time, he wouldn't ask any more questions.

"The boy I was with, he was so angry. He said I was trying to trap him and make him marry me." Valdira gave another bitter laugh. "As if I would have a fool like that."

Ryamon sat silent, at a loss to respond.

"My father used to say that to my mother, all while I was growing up," Valdira went on. "That she had trapped him. He said she promised not to have any children, but she went back on her word. She had me."

She said the word, *me*, as if it was a choice insult.

"He said that in front of you?" Indignation surged through Ryamon's veins. He took a deep breath to control the heat.

"When Pa was angry, he didn't care what he said or who heard him." Valdira glared at Ryamon as if he was to blame.

"Well, I'm not that stupid," Ryamon said, and he reached out to hug her before she could pull away. "I know what I have. You might not be a perfect woman, but you're perfect for me."

This time Valdira let him hold her, but she still looked away, defensive and shamed. Ryamon felt the thoughts racing in her mind. *"What am I supposed to do with him? All the other men only wanted one thing, and once they got tired of that, it was over. But Ryamon won't go away!"*

Ryamon winced at the way she classified her former lovers, although he had to admit he knew young men who fit the description. Given how their relationship had started with such passion, he could see how Valdira would think the same of him.

"That's right," he said gently. "I'm the one you can't get rid of."

"It's all such a mess," Valdira moaned.

"Is that why you didn't want to get married?" he asked. "Because you thought I would hit you?" She shrugged within the circle of his arms. "Real men don't beat their wives."

"I can't help it. I'm still afraid."

"One thing at a time," Ryamon said.

He wanted to tell her, flat out, that she was going to marry him as soon as they found a village elder or some kind of authority. For the sake of their baby, who deserved to be born with a family who loved it. Of course, that was what Valdira's father would do—give orders enforced with violence.

With a shuddering breath, Valdira drew away. She repeated, "We can't stay here. If Yolie keeps me prisoner, she can take our baby and raise it as one of them. She said she can pick her own heir, remember? There's nothing to keep her from stealing a baby."

The thought of anyone threatening his family filled Ryamon's veins with fire.

"Oh, yes there is," he said with angry certainty. "I'll burn her whole house down if she tries it."

He was startled by a silvery laugh. "Do you really think it will be that easy, my pet?"

Ryamon spun toward the voice, pushing Valdira behind him—or tried to. The very air seemed to congeal around them. It dragged him to a stop. Ryamon was suspended in the strangely solidified air, unable to complete the motion of turning.

Yolie appeared inside the closed door in a slow shimmer of light. She strolled forward, a cruel smile curving her lips. Weird colors rippled around her, thick as syrup. Yolie's ivory dress turned yellow-green. Her hair was black as charcoal. Artful silver streaks blazed like lightning painted onto a stormy sky. Her face was skull white, and the handprint on her chest glowed red as hot coals.

"I fear you will not be leaving my house," she purred to them. Her voice was faint, oddly distorted by whatever power made the air congeal. "Did you think you stood a chance against me?"

Chapter Twenty-Two

Ryamon tried to answer, but he couldn't make his tongue move. Panic blazed through him, as it had when he was mired in the birch grove, yet no fire answered his call.

With obvious effort, Valdira grated out, "He marked you once."

"A mere trifle." Yolie waved her hand as if flicking an insect. "I'm sure it impresses you, but then, you're both so young. Inexperienced. Confined by your training to small spheres of influence."

In his mind, Ryamon raged that they weren't as helpless as she thought and she had no idea what they could really do. It did no good, since his tongue refused to obey him and speak. Yolie strolled a little closer. The swish of her skirts sounded like snake scales scraping on the polished floor.

"Sad, really. I'm sure, with your limited training, you never considered this," she bragged, gesturing to whatever it was that imprisoned them. "It's a specialty of mine. Time is moving, but you are outside of it. You cannot escape to act against me, nor can your pathetic magic touch the world."

So Yolie's spell was a time trap. Ryamon had to admit she was partly correct. He had no idea how she did this, or which of the Exalted Orders might have been able to counter it.

She didn't get too close to it, he noticed. If only his power could reach beyond the pocket of stopped time, he might be able to tip her into the morass. If she got stuck, she would have to take the spell off. Ryamon concentrated, trying to push his will into the polished stones of the floor. He felt no reaction.

"Your loyalty to your sweetheart is touching," Yolie went on, her voice nearly as acid as Valdira's had been. "But I can see I should never have made you welcome here. Your wills are too weak, your magic stunted. You could never be worthy to rule." She sighed dramatically. "Darmosh said this would happen. He'll be impossible to live with now."

Silently, Ryamon ground his teeth in frustration. It was all he could do.

Yolie continued, "Even if you will not join our cause, you can still be of some use. You must have come here for some purpose. All the questions you asked and the way you tried to stir up my serfs…I do believe you're spies!"

She proclaimed this as if it was a great surprise, but her mocking smile made the "discovery" a lie. Yolie must have planned this all along. If she couldn't get them to cooperate, she would brand them as enemies. His suspicions were confirmed as Yolie continued, her eyes blazing with triumph.

"Arkanost has sent spies into Costera! This is a provocation that cannot be ignored. I'm sure Domen Terlith will agree, when we tell him, that we could not let this assault on our borders pass unchallenged. And how fortunate that we are prepared to retaliate immediately."

She strolled around to the side, where she could turn her vicious smile on Valdira.

"Don't worry, my pet…"

Somehow Valdira hissed, "I'm not your pet!"

"Yes, yes, I know. You're savage and untamed." Yolie rolled her eyes mockingly. "Well, I won't keep you there too long. We must show you to Domen Terlith as proof of your treacherous attack. I'm sure he'll want to punish you." She looked at Ryamon, clearly savoring the idea. "But I'll let you out in good time. The babe must be allowed to grow."

Yolie leaned a bit closer and smiled a deadly smile. "I hadn't thought of that, you know. It's amazing how many wonderful ideas my prisoners think up all on their own. And now I can look forward to meeting my new heir."

Ryamon realized he was still touching Valdira inside the time bubble when he sensed her despairing, poisonous hatred for Yolie.

"It's all right," he thought to her. *"It won't happen."*

He couldn't tell if Valdira heard him.

Yolie turned toward the door. Over her shoulder, she said, "I don't know how you discovered my brother's secret, but it doesn't matter. Darmosh and I will take back what is rightfully ours. There is nothing you can do to stop us."

Still smirking, Yolie strolled out the door and left them there.

~ * ~

Night fell and the moon rose over the nameless valley. Phareth pretended to sleep. Though he was heartily bored with meditation by now, he made himself do it. He needed to be strong and alert for what lay ahead.

The magi's tents faced the stone ledge and the villagers' tents spread out around them. Phareth sensed when sleep claimed them. Even the sentry was drowsy. It was easy to convince the man he heard nothing as Phareth slipped out of his tent.

The moon glowed faintly behind thick clouds and the mountain air was cold in his lungs. Phareth breathed lightly, willing himself not to cough. He had no trouble seeing—Shadow was his element, after all—but he wasn't sure about Marton. Some magi had these extra gifts. He could only hope for the best.

Phareth circled outside the camp to avoid crossing directly in front of the farmer on watch. He stepped carefully as he approached Marton's bedroll near the wood pile. The brewer was fully dressed, boots on. Phareth knelt beside him. He felt as much as saw Marton's eyes snap open. His mind, which had been quiet for once, burst into something like a startled shout. Luckily, he controlled the impulse to lash out.

When Marton was truly alert, Phareth beckoned. He would have preferred to communicate by telepathy, but he didn't think Marton was ready for that. The man rolled stealthily to his feet, grabbing his axe. Awake, Marton spewed anger and anxiety again. Perhaps, Phareth admitted, he wasn't ready for a mental bond with Marton, either.

Shielding himself, he scanned the camp once more to assure no one was aware of their departure. Then he jerked his chin to indicate which way, and crept off. Marton followed.

It would have been faster to walk along the lake shore, but the reeds would make too much noise and hold an obvious trail. The two men had to circle around again, moving behind the rock ledge and then following the rim of the shallow valley as if they were going back to Lornest. When Phareth thought they were far enough from camp, he chanced speaking.

"We need to change our plan," he whispered.

"Why?" Marton snarled. At least he had the sense not to shout.

"I heard something earlier. Maybe you did, too," Phareth replied. "It sounded like an ornyx."

Marton stood silent for a moment, then nodded grimly. "No wild ones in these hills. We need to look for it."

"Exactly," Phareth said, cautiously pleased that Marton was taking the change of plans so well.

"Get on with it," the brewer bit out.

Phareth shrugged and led his companion across the narrow end of the valley, taking care to avoid the pit Ryamon had left there. On the opposite side, they turned southward again. The ridges were steeper here. Soon the lake was a considerable distance below them, glittering faintly in the night. Phareth wasn't as familiar with this side of the valley, so he moved cautiously.

The two men followed a narrow crack that led over a ridge, out of the valley. Whatever Phareth had heard ought to be somewhere in this area. Marton grabbed his arm, startling him. Now it was Phareth who froze, smothering a cry. Marton jabbed a finger in front of them. Heart beating hard, Phareth looked where he was pointing.

Just to their left was a small hollow, sheltered from the wind by rocks. What he had taken for a stunted tree was actually the long neck of a sleeping ornyx. A thin slant of line showed that it was tied to a stone. Its pack had been removed. Nearby, a man lay up against the rocks, his head pillowed on the baggage.

"I thought so," Phareth breathed. Even from this close, he couldn't sense Nepharyl's mind. He glanced behind them. If the fellow crawled up to where they were standing, he could easily watch the magi's camp without being seen.

Beside him, Marton bristled with impatience. Phareth studied the scene for a moment longer. Nepharyl must have tied the ornyx close to the path, hoping it would detect intruders. Foolish. Had he forgotten who he was dealing with?

Marton muttered, "Do you expect me to handle that bird?" He sounded disgusted, as if Phareth had suggested he should go for a midnight swim in the freezing mountain lake.

"I've got this," Phareth whispered back.

Now that he could see his quarry, there was no more hiding. He breathed out, extending his mind. He reminded himself to be cautious. The traitor might not be as helpless and undefended as he seemed. Yet Phareth's mind easily penetrated Nepharyl's. He skirted layers of dream and found the part of Nepharyl's brain he needed. Phareth paused, alert for any sign of Yolie's awareness. He felt nothing. The Costeran witch must not be monitoring her plaything too closely.

All the better. Phareth twisted, hard. The sleeping man spasmed, then lay still. Nepharyl was unconscious, paralyzed, and he probably hadn't felt a thing.

Moments later, Marton slung the helpless nobleman over his shoulder. "You say this fool is the key to finding Valdira?"

"To bringing her safely home," Phareth corrected, reminding the brewer why he had come on this adventure.

"Huh." Marton tramped easily out of the hollow.

It was a good thing he could manage Nepharyl by himself. Phareth had his hands full with the ornyx. Unlike himself, the bird couldn't see well in the dark and was none too happy about moving from its warm spot. It kept stopping and squawking irritably. Phareth yanked on its lead.

"Come on, you," he demanded.

"This had better be worth it," Marton grunted.

Luckily, it no longer mattered if they made noise. Once they got down to the flat valley bottom, they slogged through brush and reeds with abandon. Phareth was aware of time passing with each ornyx screech and every beat of his heart in his chest. As yet, there was no sign Yolie had sensed her puppet was prey, but he had no idea how long it would last.

Considering the noise they made, it wasn't surprising that everyone in camp was awake by the time they got back. As they got closer, he could see the farmers running around with torches. The night echoed with voices calling for Phareth and Marton. Up by the rock ledge, the magi were clustered together. Telamar seemed to be talking. He stood tall and white, outrage visible in his gestures. Phareth smiled mockingly as he yanked the balky ornyx forward. Trust Telamar to take his little foray as a personal insult.

Adding to the din, the ornyxes in camp shrieked their own alarms. Nepharyl's bird finally moved forward when it heard them. Everyone in camp stopped running and looked around as its eager cry rang in the night. Torch-bearing farmers converged on them.

"Help me with this," Marton snapped to no one in particular. A pair of men helped roll Nepharyl off his shoulder. Marton straightened his back with relief. Phareth passed the ornyx's lead to another man.

"Put it down with the others?" the fellow asked.

"That's fine," Phareth said, and to the men carrying Nepharyl, "Bring him up this way."

He led them to the fire near the rock shelter. The three magi watched them come. Anarinda rubbed her eyes, her hair in disarray. A frown wrinkled her pretty forehead. Silma radiated concern upon seeing them carry an unconscious man. Telamar stood aloof now, but his stare was cold enough to create frost on the rock ledge behind him.

"Did you miss me?" Phareth quipped. His dry lips cracked as he spoke. It stung.

"Where were you?" Anarinda cried, exasperated. "The sentry got up for more wood and realized Marton was gone. Then we couldn't find you, either."

"I brought you a present." Phareth swept a mocking bow as the farmers set their burden on the ground by the fire.

"Is that Lord Nepharyl?" Silma circled the fire and leaned on her cane to kneel beside him.

"Let him be," Phareth warned. "He's an enemy."

Perplexed, Anarinda asked Silma, "How do you know Nepharyl?"

"He paid me a courtesy call," Silma said. "He seemed quite the gentleman. It's hard to believe you found him all the way out here."

"I told you, he's a puppet of Costera," Phareth said. "I'll bet he asked all kinds of questions about the town's defenses and where the nearest mage towers are."

Stricken, Silma murmured, "Why, so he did."

Even the whispering farmers fell silent. For a moment, everyone gazed down on the fallen nobleman. The dark suit, once so fine, was pale with dirt. Its lacy cuffs were torn. In unconsciousness, Nepharyl's face was thinner than Phareth remembered. His cheeks looked hollow, as if he had been eaten away from inside.

Telamar's cold voice shattered the moment. "Is this supposed to make everything all right?"

Phareth glanced up to meet the Ice magus' stare. He fought down a moment of embarrassment, followed by indignation that no one appreciated his accomplishment.

Phareth stiffened his resolve. Jerking his thumb to take in Marton, he answered, "A small team had the best chance to catch Nepharyl unaware."

"A team?" Telamar repeated coolly. "I thought *we* were supposed to be a team. Maybe I was wrong."

Phareth glanced at Anarinda, expecting the Storm magus to defuse the tension as she usually did, but she only listened intently.

"You acted on your own," Telamar accused.

"It's called taking the initiative," Phareth retorted.

"It's showing off," Telamar corrected. "You didn't tell us what you had planned. You didn't give us the chance to help."

Nor would he, Phareth thought rebelliously. Not until he had his revenge. Behind them, he heard the ornyxes screeching at each other and thought that at least the birds were honest about their rivalries.

"As if you would have," he snapped back. Telamar's own accusation of treason was vivid in his memory. "How can you talk about teamwork when you act like everything I do is a threat to your order."

In response, Telamar's mouth got even thinner. He, too, evidently remembered what Phareth was speaking of.

"What you did was dangerous," Anarinda said seriously. "We couldn't have helped you if we didn't know where you were."

Phareth scowled at all of them. He didn't need help. What he needed was for everyone to stop interfering. He was doing this for Kylethia, and he refused to feel guilty for it.

Unaware of his thoughts, Anarinda asked softly, "Would it have been so hard to trust us?"

Silence stretched between them again. Phareth felt the prickle of anger and rebellion from the magi, the confusion of the watching farmers. He also felt the bite of Marton's sarcastic amusement to see the vaunted magi bickering like children.

"Is this all for tonight?" Marton asked. "Maybe we should try to sleep."

"Yes, get some rest," Anarinda told the farmers. To Marton, she added, "You should stay. This is your battle, too."

The farmers gratefully shuffled toward their bedrolls. Marton shrugged. "Whatever you say, lady magus. I just want my daughter back." He sent a dark glance toward Phareth, who felt the prick of his impatience that they were getting sidetracked from the search for Valdira.

"Don't change the subject," Telamar said. "If Phareth sensed Nepharyl was nearby, he should have told us."

"I don't answer to you," Phareth snapped.

"No, Telamar is right," Anarinda said. "We all needed to know this, especially if you're sure Nepharyl is under Yolie's control."

"I do sense something abnormal in his brain," Silma said thoughtfully.

"I told you to leave him!" Phareth protested.

"I must live according to the code of my order," Silma answered. The Blood initiate still knelt beside Nepharyl, one hand poised in the air over his forehead. Anarinda smiled tightly and Telamar gave a cold chuckle. The Blood magus went on, "Who is this Yolie you speak of?"

"Yes, please explain," Anarinda added.

"And why did you bring Nepharyl here, where it's even easier for him to spy on us?" Telamar added.

Holding to his patience, Phareth explained to Silma, "Yolie is a sorceress of Costera, one of the elite. It seems like she's secretly been dominating Nepharyl's mind for at least five years."

"Such a torment must have placed him under great strain," Silma mused, her eyes were focused on Nepharyl. "This might be the injury I sense."

Turning to Telamar and Anarinda, Phareth continued. "I brought Nepharyl here because there's a chance I can make her mental link with him work both ways. Then I can spy on her, instead. We need to know what she's planning."

Anarinda raised her brows, interested, but Telamar sniffed, "And this had to happen in the middle of the night?"

"While she's asleep and vulnerable, yes," Phareth told him. "I want to do it here because—" he made another slight bow to Anarinda "—it is definitely going to be dangerous and I may need help if she detects me."

Telamar's lip curled slightly, but Marton interrupted before he could voice his doubts.

"How will this help me find Valdira?"

Now it was Anarinda who frowned, clearly suspicious of Marton's motives for locating his daughter.

"Valdira is Yolie's house guest, or she was," Phareth explained. "But I have to tell you that since we spoke earlier, I've tried to contact both Valdira and Ryamon and I can't do it."

"You can't find them?" Marton demanded, gripping his axe.

"Because they're sleeping?" Telamar suggested icily.

"No," Phareth replied curtly. "I mean I can't feel their minds at all, and I've been able to locate them whenever I wanted to.

Yolie may have done whatever she did to shield Nepharyl from probes, or it could be something else. This makes it all the more important that I scan Yolie's memory and find out what's going on. Remember, our last instructions were to bring Valdira and Ryamon back to Polvest."

"Yet now Valdira is blank to you," Anarinda repeated thoughtfully. Glancing at Silma and Telamar, she said, "I'm afraid Phareth is right. We need to deal with this."

"May I point out," the Shadow magus said, "the longer I have to argue with all of you about it—"

"Don't try to blame us," Anarinda flared back at him. "We're a team. No one should be sneaking off on their own."

She pinned Phareth with a stern look. He met her gaze firmly. Anarinda was prettier than Telamar, but he refused to back down to her, either.

"What if you can't spy on Yolie?" Silma asked.

"I'll have to sever her link with Nepharyl from his end," Phareth replied. "Theoretically, he'd be free, but if she's been dominating him as long as Mother thinks, his mind may be permanently damaged. Also, there could be a backlash."

"Which means?" Marton growled impatiently.

"Nepharyl will need Silma's help even more," Phareth said. "Or, we both will."

A slight twitch of brows implied that Telamar liked this idea.

"All right, then," Anarinda said crisply. "You'll try to probe Yolie's mind, but if that doesn't work, you'll break her control over Nepharyl."

Phareth shrugged. She made it sound as if she had decided all this. And as if it would be easy.

Telamar nodded grimly. "I guess you'd better get busy."

"If you insist," Phareth replied with sarcastic courtesy.

"Oh, stop!" Anarinda cried, covering a yawn with her hand. "Just do it, Phareth."

~ * ~

Phareth sat cross-legged at Nepharyl's head and shut out everything—the ache of night's cold, his cracked lips smarting, flickers of thought and emotion from the magi around him. He checked his mental shields once more. Then the world blurred as he released a long breath and slipped into Nepharyl's mind.

This time Phareth didn't skirt the nobleman's sleeping thoughts. He boldly plunged in. With his magic he experienced Nepharyl's psyche as a realm of dark waters. Bits of thought swirled like debris carried on a flood. Quickly Phareth reshaped himself to suit this place. In the guise of a fish, he darted between fragments of memory and dream.

All the currents led to one place, where a huge marble statue dammed the flow. It looked like Countess Guilberta, of course. Phareth drifted, staring up at the monumental image. How could he get past it?

He focused his mind, hoping to force the idol into its true shape, but he had never seen Yolie in person. He couldn't make the image change. He glided closer, seeking an opening. The statue was no longer pristine white. Veins of darkness ran through the marble. As Phareth looked more closely, they began to writhe and twist against each other. Before he got close enough to touch the statue, the veins came alive as a seething mass of vipers. They were white as chalk, gray-streaked along their sides, with eyes like lightless holes.

Here was the trap Phareth had expected—the first of many, perhaps. The vipers slithered and hissed, arched their spines and bared their fangs. He stopped beyond their reach and carefully reshaped himself again. As one more white serpent he slithered over to join the mass.

Slowly, cautiously, Phareth slipped between scaled bodies toward what felt like the center. Snakes pressed their corded bodies against him on all sides. Their weight forced the air from his lungs. He twisted harder, and then he was through.

The water and snakes were gone. A single white serpent slithered over dry, hard floor. Phareth stopped, flicking his tongue to taste the air of this new place. It felt like a tunnel shaped out of solid rock. There was no light, yet somehow he saw the smooth walls and arched ceiling. The air was still, but not stale. The passage saw use, then.

With a thrill of triumph, Phareth realized he must have penetrated into Yolie's link with Nepharyl. Revenge was that much closer. He didn't take too much time congratulating himself, though. The passage ran in both directions without so much as a crack to show where he had come in. Nor was there any indication which way he should go.

Here was another trap, he guessed. If he chose the wrong direction, he would be lost for a long time—maybe forever. Still in the form of a snake, he coiled himself and considered his predicament. There had to be some way to find the correct path, and it had to be quiet or Yolie might sense him.

To see himself as a snake or fish was all subjective, he knew. The conceit helped him make sense of this combination of magic and dreams. Yet it could be a tool, as well. Phareth reshaped himself again, this time choosing the form of an owl. The stealthy night birds were often used as examples in Shadow lore because of their exceptional hearing.

Resting on the floor felt awkward, but he ignored that and concentrated on his hearing. At first he heard nothing, not even the ringing of blood in his ears. Slowly, though, he recognized a slight tickle in his left ear. Was that a noise, almost too faint to hear?

He had to believe so. Phareth launched himself into the air and flew down the tunnel in that direction. Even the muffled sigh of feathers on the air sounded loud in the stillness, so he glided when he could. The tunnel seemed endless, with no changes in the architecture to mark his progress. Eventually, his great eyes detected a pale glow ahead. He dropped to the floor, reshaped himself into a mouse, and crept toward the light.

Now he came to a curtain that blocked the passage from wall to wall. Phareth nosed at the cloth and found an absurdly soft, dense velvet trimmed with heavy fringe. The thick fabric hung straight as a wall, but it didn't quite cut off the glow and sound of voices on the other side. A line of sallow light crossed the floor.

Cautiously, in case this was another trap, he pushed his mouse nose into the gap. The fabric was so heavy, his efforts didn't even make it move. At least it's weight also muffled the scratch of tiny claws as he wriggled his way under the curtain.

The light brightened. His beady eyes, so used to darkness, burned with it. When he seemed about to break through into the next chamber, Phareth stopped and blinked his vision clear.

Beyond the curtain, which he now saw was searingly red trimmed with gold braid, was a row of gigantic feet. At least, they looked huge when Phareth was the size of a mouse. There were gentlemen's boots, polished black, and ladies' slippers stitched with silvery thread, half-seen beneath skirts that seemed as stiff and heavy as the velvet drapery. The colors were intense: amethyst, sapphire, emerald and topaz that struck against each other as if the wearers were carrying on some kind of silent quarrel.

Phareth was too small to see faces, but he recognized the court styles of Costera. He also noticed these dream figures were as inert as the curtain he had forced his way through. They were only the backdrop for whatever Yolie was dreaming.

Beyond the line of enormous shoes were muted voices and some kind of music. The sounds were confused and disjointed, details unclear in the dream. The voices, by contrast, were sharply defined. Chief of them was a woman's voice—Yolie herself, Phareth guessed. He had succeeded in penetrating her mind.

What form could he take to remain undetected? Phareth cast about in his mind. He needed something small and stealthy, yet something that could climb. First because he wanted to see the whole room and second because he didn't like being tiny among so many giant feet.

Perhaps a spider? They were excellent climbers. But no, Yolie might be afraid of spiders. If she saw him, she might wake before he found out what he needed to know. For the same reason, he couldn't stay in the shape of a mouse.

Muted thunder shook the room. Yolie had finished speaking and the dream figures were applauding. Phareth needed to know exactly what Yolie was dreaming about. Then he realized the answer was all around him.

Still in his mouse guise, Phareth scurried along behind the throng. He stayed near the curtain, because he didn't want to lose track of the exit this time. Near the end of the row, he focused his will and changed again. Now he was a man, with olive skin and middling-dark hair like the folk he had seen in Logoll. His embroidered jacket was deep red velvet that should blend with the drapery. With so many watching, Yolie wouldn't notice one more.

Phareth straightened, moving only his eyes as he looked around. The chamber walls were white plaster with elegant golden traceries. Crystal lamps blazed there, their glow redoubled by a marble floor polished to glasslike slickness. The distorted music continued, though Phareth saw no sign of any musicians.

Those who stood around him were more like mannequins than people. They were pretty or handsome in a bland way, with eyes and mouths painted onto skin that had an odd, eggshell look.

The ladies had their hair up in tall, fantastic towers and wore the tight, revealing gowns of Costeran court dress. The gentlemen were clad in fine waistcoats. Strangely, none of these beings had hands. Sleeves, but no hands.

Phareth had no time to analyze why Yolie would imagine followers who were so incomplete. The dream people faced toward a platform at the end of the magnificent hall. There sat a lady on a golden throne. It, too, was polished to reflect light in a sparkling halo around her. This had to be Yolie herself. Her features were individual and her skin looked real.

Yolie was extremely beautiful, with fair skin and dark eyes. Her gown was bright pink brocaded with gold. The cut of the bodice made her almost ridiculously voluptuous. Her sleek, dark hair was done in another of those fanciful arrangements. Jewels blazed at her wrists and neck.

Another of the puppet men stood near her right hand. This figure looked slightly more like an actual person. Phareth's blood chilled as he recognized the commanding frown. It was Darmosh.

This was only a dream, Phareth reminded himself. A ghost of his enemy. It couldn't hurt him.

"See, my brother," Yolie proclaimed. "Our enemies are in my hands. They have no hope of escape."

Diamonds glittered as she waved toward the center of the hall. Something large wavered into being. Squinting, Phareth saw a huge ball of crystal or glass with dark shapes inside. It was suspended in the air without a pedestal.

"You have done well, dear sister." The image of Darmosh bowed obsequiously. "Never could I have imagined this triumph."

Phareth held back a sneer. Darmosh would never be such a flatterer. Well, this was Yolie's dream. She could congratulate herself as much as she pleased, here.

The shapes inside the glass orb were coming clearer. A blonde woman in a green gown, a red-haired man in a lavender suit. The two were frozen, suspended in the act of turning. The man had obviously been trying to protect his companion. Phareth's heart dropped again. Though they wore foreign clothing and faced away from him, he was sure he knew who they were.

On her throne, Yolie smirked and preened. "So much for the mighty Valdira. Can you believe she thought she was prettier than me?"

"That is like comparing an ornyx to a swan, dear sister."

"With these spies in our hands, there is no more excuse to delay. Domen Tirlith will have to act!"

"You are so clever," the shadow of Darmosh said.

"Let the fool reject me for his hussy," Yolie hissed with sudden hate. For the first time, Phareth noticed a lurid red mark on her upthrust bosom. It almost looked like a handprint. Even as he saw it, the mark faded.

"He will pay for hurting you," Darmosh assured her.

"Arkanost will be mine," Yolie gloated.

"My armies will make sure of it," Darmosh vowed.

"Show me, brother," Yolie commanded eagerly. "Show me my victory!"

The shadow of Darmosh bowed low, and the two captives vanished from the giant crystal orb. Phareth watched intently as new images formed. First were men in leather jerkins, bundles of arrows on their backs. Then came ornyx chariots, skimming over the ground. The drivers were armed with spears and long, thin swords. Their numbers seemed endless. Once again, he heard the muffled cheering of courtiers whose mouths were nothing but painted lines.

So this was their plan—an invasion using Valdira and Ryamon's presence as an excuse. Phareth had to reminded himself not to be afraid. It was still only a dream. Yolie could inflate the numbers of Darmosh's forces just as she did her own bosom.

"Stop!" Her sudden, sharp voice brought him back to his surroundings. "Who is that?"

The crystal and its images were gone. Yolie stood up from her throne to point dramatically across the throng. She was looking straight at Phareth.

In a thunderous voice, she accused, "You're not part of my dream!"

Chapter Twenty-Three

"He's an intruder," Yolie screamed. "Kill him!"

The character of the dream world changed in an instant. Distant music died; golden light took on a ruddy hue. The doll-like courtiers turned toward Phareth, their sleeves no longer empty. Instead of hands, sword blades, whip lashes and hissing serpents struck toward him with one will.

Phareth was already moving. He plunged backward, forcing his way through the drapery behind him. Even the fabric came alive. It wrapped around him to cling in smothering folds. Yolie's power tried to pin him under the curtain.

He willed himself into the form of a sword and spun in place, slicing the fabric into ribbons that curled through the air around him. Then he stumbled into utter blackness on the outside of the Yolie's mind.

Later, Phareth would wonder what he had done to give himself away. For now he welcomed his Element. He melted into the darkness and became one with it, hoping to escape.

~ * ~

"Did you feel that?"

Ryamon snapped to alertness. *"What?"*

He and Valdira still drifted in the void between past and future. There was no way to know how much time had passed outside their prison. All light had faded from the room. Only the time bubble glimmered faintly in tarry blackness.

Because they had been touching when Yolie imprisoned them, the lovers were able to communicate. Ryamon had hoped this would be an advantage but it had been a liability at first. Valdira's raw emotions tore at him: rage at Yolie's trick, anxiety over the fate of her future child, and most of all, hysterical fear at being trapped. Nothing Ryamon had said reassured her. He couldn't even retreat to let Valdira control herself.

At last exhaustion brought an end to her frantic struggles, and Ryamon could make her listen. They had been standing on a marble floor when Yolie caught them. He couldn't feel the tiles, but he knew they were there. Pooling their magic, he had sought to push his will into the polished stone. Again and again Ryamon tried, but Yolie's malicious words were true. Their magic couldn't help them.

The last effort had left him drained. They both fell into a kind of daze, unable to sleep but not truly awake. He thought it was just a dream when he felt a shudder through the solidified air around them.

Yet Valdira had sensed it, too. Her thought came back to him: *"I don't know what it was."*

"Keep watching," Ryamon urged. *"Maybe it will happen again."*

"It's so dark," Valdira said. *"Yolie must be asleep by now. Maybe her control is slipping."*

She sounded grim, not truly optimistic. Ryamon knew she was right not to expect too much. Still, they had to hope. What other choice was there?

Even as he thought so, he felt it again: a tremor through the solid stuff of the magical bubble. Ryamon he caught his breath. Incredibly, the air's rigid grip had relaxed enough for his chest to expand a tiny bit.

They both had the same thought in the same instant: *"Try to move!"*

He focused on his left hand, which had been pressed against Valdira's back as he tried to shield her from Yolie. The hard lines of her bodice laces were under his fingers. He twisted his wrist and managed to lift his fingertips. Only a little, however, and not enough to be helpful.

Meanwhile, he sensed Valdira's effort as she tried to turn her head. It wasn't working. Her thought came to him: *"Magic is holding us. We need magic to get out."*

"I'll try the floor again."

He reached for the stone, trying to push his mind through the sorcerous barrier. Without being asked, Valdira added her powers to his. It felt like the heavy mud of the bog in Selkest, trying to drink in his power and hold him back. Ryamon summoned all his will to persevere.

And the cool strength was there, silent and sturdy. Stone. Triumph blazed within him. *"I did it!"*

The surge of Valdira's relief was followed immediately by rising anxiety.

"Get me out of here!"

"I'm trying," he assured her, though a spark of anger flickered into life. Did she think he wanted to be stuck like this?

"I can't help it!" Valdira thought back with a tinge of renewed hysteria. *"I can't stand being in a cage."*

Argument would only delay their escape, so Ryamon tried to crush that spark out. He had to work the stone, but he could only sense a limited area and he had no idea what part of the manor house was beneath Valdira's chamber. Should he just open the floor and hope they would drop through?

"We would fall," Valdira warned.

"You can heal us if we're hurt," Ryamon said.

"Yes, but that will delay us," she argued. *"We could even be recaptured."*

"All right! Just let me think."

Ryamon sighed to himself, knowing there was nothing he could to keep Valdira from sensing his frustration. This was going to be complicated. Stairs were too difficult to shape, but maybe he could make a ramp. Without knowing what lay below them. Drawing in enough material without collapsing the floor. Hoping the ramp wouldn't be too thin to hold their weight. His head ached just thinking about it.

Slightly to his surprise, he felt a warm trickle of his lover's power within his body. The headache went away.

Chastened, Valdira said, *"Tell me how I can help."*

Ryamon thought a kiss back to her. *"Have patience."*

Since he couldn't see where he was going, there was no point planning. He started shifting stone as far in front of him as he could reach, trying to leave a surface he and Valdira could stand on. A misshapen gap opened in the floor as his tongue of stone flowed blindly under them. Ryamon's head throbbed again with the effort of fighting through Yolie's magic. There was no time for fine workmanship. He probed downward at an angle, hoping to connect with the floor rather than a wall of wood or plaster, which his power wouldn't affect.

Despite his best efforts, the hole in the floor swiftly ate its way toward them. When he had nothing else to work with, he thought to Valdira, *"I'm sorry, sweetheart."*

"Hurry, then, would you?"

Ryamon pushed harder as the floor flowed out from under

their feet. He felt a moment's panic as he lost contact with the stone. Inside the time bubble, nothing seemed to happen. They were still imprisoned, and now they had no hope at all! Valdira's panic began to echo Ryamon's, but then he realized he was starting to sink downward through the gelid air.

"It's working!"

"Are you sure?"

Slowly, so slowly, Ryamon's feet passed through the bottom of the sphere. *"Yes. I can wiggle my toes."* Joy blazed in his mind again. *"Sweetheart, we can get out!"*

"I'm not moving!" Valdira cried, panicking again.

"I'm sinking faster because I'm heavier," Ryamon assured her. *"Don't worry, I won't go anywhere without you."*

Inch by inch they dropped. He could feel Valdira restraining her impatience as they sank with agonizing slowness out of the time trap.

As soon as Ryamon's feet touched the ramp, he refocused his efforts. The stone felt fragile. The ramp would definitely break if it had to hold both of them. He pulled in more material from behind them. At last, the ramp touched floor down below.

"That's it!" Ryamon cried.

Finally he had enough to work with. Calling on Valdira's power as well as his own, he drew up more stone from the level below to strengthen the ramp. He was loose up to his knees now. He bent his knees to help his weight pull him down faster.

"I can feel it." Relief brightened Valdira's tone. Ryamon tried to hold more tightly to her waist as he waited for gravity to work.

"We'll be free soon," he promised.

The more of them that fell out of the sphere, the faster they came. Still, it seemed to take a very long time before they both dragged free. Balancing on the narrow ramp, the lovers shared a hug of triumph. It was a relief, after being trapped outside of time, to feel the thud of their hearts again. Only then did Ryamon realize how eerie it had been to not hear the ordinary sounds of a house at night.

"Come on, let's go," Valdira murmured.

"Lean on me." Ryamon, who sensed the ramp through his link with Stone, carefully helped his lover down the narrow path. They wobbled a little, but managed to descend safely onto a rough floor. The chamber they had entered was as dark as the one upstairs. Somewhere in the distance, he felt the rhythm of running feet.

"Where do you think we are?" Ryamon's whisper echoed around them. They must be in a very large room.

"I don't care," came Valdira's retort from the blackness, "as long as we find the door."

She was right, of course. Keeping his right hand on her waist, he raised his left hand, palm up. A single flame bloomed in the darkness. Blinking, he looked around.

They seemed to be in a ballroom or reception hall. Its floor was so polished that his small fire lit the whole space. The chamber was even bigger than he had suspected. At the base of the ramp, ripples in the tiles showed how he had twisted the stone. It made a stain like spilled tea on the brilliant gloss of the dance floor.

At one end was a dais, a golden chair centered upon it. Smaller chairs lined two walls and red velvet curtains along the third side probably covered windows to the outside.

"I'll bet there's a door," Valdira murmured, looking toward the draperies.

"Should we sneak out while she's busy?" Ryamon whispered back.

"It would make the most sense," Valdira said. "I can summon an animal to carry us away from here, but I want to be farther off before I try it. Yolie might sense my magic and come after us."

Even as she said it, Ryamon sensed Valdira's reluctance. Escaping would be sensible, but as long as they had the chance, maybe they could get a little revenge—and keep Yolie from following them right away.

"Let's give her something to keep her busy," he said.

In the flickering light of his flame, Valdira's lips curved in a wicked smile. "I like the way you're thinking."

~ * ~

Though his heart hammered with panic, Phareth quieted his mind and hid in the darkness. The curtains shredded and Yolie burst through. She, too, had to pause and orient herself.

Phareth guessed what she was going to do next. He acted fast, shrank to mouse form and dove beneath what was left of the red velvet drapes. An instant later her power lit the area, turning the dark tunnel to daylight. Still and small, Phareth waited while

Yolie looked around.

"Where is he?" Her frustrated voice rang in the tunnel.

What now? Phareth wondered. The exit at the other end of the tunnel had vanished when he entered it. He was trapped, unless he could get his enemy to lead him out.

"I will find you," Yolie growled to herself.

Still blazing with rage and power, the enemy sorceress set off down the passage. She glided on air, not truly walking. There was no sign of the doll people or throne room now, only darkness outside the area of Yolie's glow. The curtains, too, faded. Phareth was forced to take a chance. He darted after Yolie and leaped for the hem of her sweeping skirts. There he clung, not daring to move.

This was all psychic imagery, he reminded himself. He wasn't really using tiny claws to hold onto his enemy's brocade gown. Nor could he let himself think about the absurdity of this image. If he laughed, or emitted any other strong emotion, she would detect his presence.

Yolie knew where she was going, at least. Only moments later, she reached a blank end to the tunnel. At her commanding gesture, the wall shimmered away. Yolie stepped out onto a ledge above the churning torrent of Nepharyl's dreams. A glow faint as starlight outlined the looming marble statue of Countess Guilberta.

Through the sound of rushing water, Phareth heard Yolie's contemptuous laugh. She waved her hand and the image took its true form. A monumental statue of Yolie stood at the center of Nepharyl's mind. The stone looked sickly white in the dim light.

"Nepharyl, my pet," Yolie called. Her sugared voice held no affection.

Still clinging to the hem of Yolie's gown, Phareth felt the vibration of her summons. There was no change in Nepharyl's dreamscape. Nor would there be for some while, Phareth hoped. He had hit Nepharyl hard enough he should remain unconscious for several hours.

Yolie scowled at the lack of response. Her voice echoed over the waters.

"I do believe someone has been playing tricks with you, my pet. Now who could it be?"

Hearing her redoubled fury, Phareth decided now would be a good time to go. He was more familiar with Nepharyl's mind. He should be able to escape with news of Yolie's plan. His mouse-claws released their frantic grip on his enemy's dress. When he had crept a few feet away, he changed shape again. In the form of a fish, he slipped into the water.

He knew he hadn't been careful enough when the water burst into spray around him. Tentacles came out of nowhere, whipping around him. Phareth wiggled and thrashed, but the many suckers stuck even on his slippery scales.

"There you are," Yolie crowed.

~ * ~

Once she decided, Valdira wasted no time. On the left-hand wall, two sets of double doors were nearly hidden by the white-and-gold ornamentation. Valdira strode toward the nearest pair of doors. Muffled voices came from just beyond it. Ryamon hurried to catch up.

"Sweetheart," he protested. "Let me go first. You're..." He trailed off as she glanced over her shoulder, one hand on the door latch.

"Pregnant?" One eyebrow quirked upward in annoyance. "And now I'm helpless all of a sudden?"

"No," he faltered, dismayed by her directness.

Valdira gave an exasperated sigh. "You can't pamper me because of that. We don't have time."

Ryamon nodded, but he firmly shouldered his way in between Valdira and the door. Obstinate though she was, Valdira carried his child. He meant to protect her even if she didn't think she needed it.

"You just told me yourself, there are no animals here for you to call on," he said. "On the other hand, I have access to both my elements. I fully intend to pull this house down around Yolie's ears, but not until you're safely outside. So let me see who's out there, all right?"

She frowned, but stepped back. Ryamon brought his flame down to a flicker before he pushed the door open just wide enough to see through.

The wavering light of a candle revealed the mansion's foyer. The two curved stairways rose on either side of them and the exterior doors were straight ahead. Something had apparently roused the household servants, for half a dozen women stood at the base of the steps. They all wore nightgowns, and their loose hair straggled over their shoulders. One of them held the candle.

"We heard a noise," an older woman called up the stairs. She spoke with the irritated air of someone continuing an argument.

"Does Dama need us nor not?" added a younger, dark-haired girl. Ryamon recognized the two women who had helped him with his bath.

Someone else, another woman, answered from the landing above Ryamon and Valdira. "She cried out in her sleep, but now she lies quiet. In one of her workings, no doubt."

Workings? That could mean Yolie was casting some sort of spell. Maybe her attack on Arkanost had already begun.

"We shouldn't call the guards?" the first maid asked.

"I'd not risk disturbing her," the woman above them replied.

The dark-haired girl yawned. "I'm going back to bed."

Watching, Ryamon debated within himself. He had forgotten, when he spoke of burning Yolie's mansion down, that it was home to so many others. In good conscience, there was only one thing he could do.

Behind him, Valdira radiated irritation because she couldn't see what was happening. Ryamon had to make his move before she did. He met his lover's gaze over his shoulder.

"Give me a moment."

Without waiting for her agreement, Ryamon pushed the door the rest of the way open. As he strode through, he raised his hand and made his fire blaze until it engulfed his whole hand. The sudden light startled the maidservants, who jumped and cried out in alarm.

"Dom!" gasped the one with the candle.

They all started to bow, then stopped at various elevations. Obviously they were torn between the habit of fearful respect and the knowledge that Ryamon was an enemy, no longer someone to be obeyed.

The woman at the top of the steps called down, "What's going on?"

The maidservants shuffled back, clinging to each other in terror, as Ryamon stepped forward until he could look up at the landing.

"If there is anyone in this house you care about," he announced to the lot of them, "go find them and tell them to run."

Up on the landing, another maidservant shrieked, "He's loose! Call the guards!" Her voice echoed behind her as she ran along the hallway toward Yolie's chambers. "Dama! Dama!"

Ryamon glared at the other servants, who still gaped at him, paralyzed. Fire crackled as he let the flames spread farther up his arm to the shoulder. His own Element couldn't hurt him, but they didn't know that.

"I thought I told you to run!" he snapped.

They did run, nightgowns flapping and loose hair flying. They screamed like frightened birds. Valdira must have heard the noise because she burst out of the darkened ballroom, holding what looked like a broken leg from one of the chairs.

"What are you doing?"

"Getting them out of here," Ryamon answered. He hoped they would do as he'd said and warn the rest of the staff. "Come on, the door is clear."

He let his fire die again and beckoned his lover forward. They crossed to the huge, carved front doors and cautiously peered out. There was no noise outside, although the cries of the maids still filled the entryway with echoes. Ryamon urged Valdira through.

"Get away from the building," he said. "Then see if you can find us something to ride."

"I'll try for that montus we saw when we first got here." Hefting her club, Valdira slipped into the night.

~ * ~

Phareth felt himself hoisted into the air. Tentacles flowed out of Yolie's arm where her hand should have been, though the rest of her body retained its impossible beauty. She smirked down at him with no light in her eyes.

"Aren't you the clever one. I'm going to enjoy breaking you."

Recovering from his surprise, Phareth felt a surge of anger. There was no way he'd let Yolie beat him. He still had to pay her back for Kylethia, and he'd had enough of her endless bragging.

He changed again, growing too explosively for Yolie to hold him. She backed up a step, shaking her tentacles in a pained gesture. Phareth was himself again, equal in size with his enemy.

"Not if I break you first," he said, and he punched her in the face.

"Gyah!" Yolie staggered back another step.

His knuckles throbbed, but it was a pleasure to see the red mark blooming on her pale cheek. Phareth swung again. Yolie ducked aside and swung back at him. He dodged in turn. They separated and stood poised, two gigantic figures in black and white above the seething flood of Nepharyl's nightmares.

Phareth didn't want this fight. What he needed was to get away and return to his own mind so he could relay a warning of the coming attack.

Strangely, his enemy was smiling. "I know who you are. We almost had you in Logoll."

She was trying to upset him, put him off balance. Phareth knew it, yet he couldn't stop the crimson shame that flooded his face.

"After Nepharyl gave us false information," he spat back.

"It worked." She smiled with feigned modesty. "Still, there's something I wanted to ask you. Your father—is his name Phostan, by any chance?"

Phareth scowled, determined not to be drawn into her game. "What about him?"

"I thought so." Yolie spoke sweetly, as if confiding a delicious secret. "We're cousins, did you know? Phostan is my father's younger brother. He lacked power, alas. I suppose he must have turned traitor."

"Phostan would probably say you betrayed him," Phareth retorted.

He knew the fate of any child born to the nobility of Costera who wasn't gifted with magic. Now that Yolie mentioned it, Phareth could see the similarity in their dark hair and eyes. Yet he refused to accept any kinship with Darmosh, who had Kylethia's blood on his hands.

Yolie shrugged. "It doesn't matter. That's all I wanted to know."

She lashed out with her tentacles, almost too fast for Phareth to duck. He replied with a blast of force, using only his mind so she wouldn't have anything to grab onto.

"Oh, come now." Yolie laughed. Her tentacles whipped out again, stretching across the distance. This time Phareth was a heartbeat too slow. She caught him across the shoulders. He bent and twisted, but still those tentacles found his throat. They were slimy, cold, hard as steel.

Fighting, he braced his feet, dragging back as Yolie pulled. Although he wasn't truly breathing, he felt the tentacles' tightness on his throat. Despite his struggles, she pulled him toward her. She raised her left hand, where a sword blade flashed. His head pounded. If Yolie killed him here, the death would be all too real.

"My brother thought he had you cowed," she said, "but I see you have some spark left. I suppose it's up to me to finish this."

She drew back her sword-hand, preparing to strike. Spark, Phareth thought. Fire! And flames were everywhere, burning with the heat of his panic. Yolie paused to brush at them.

"Is this really the best you can do?"

Despite himself, Phareth's knees sagged. Darkness crept in at the edges of his vision. Then, from out of nowhere, a woman's shrill voice cried, "Dama, help us! He's here!"

"What?" Yolie gasped as echoes rebounded across the waters.

Phareth felt her grip loosen. He wrenched free, rubbing his throat. He didn't know what had distracted her, but he wouldn't waste the moment. He staggered back and changed himself.

"No!" Yolie howled with frustrated rage. In the shape of a black eel, Phareth plunged into the water and swam for freedom.

~ * ~

Yolie's manor house was built mostly of stone, but there was plenty inside it to burn. Ryamon tasted the heaviness of smoke as fire spread freely around him. Hungry flames chewed at the elaborately carved double doors and raced up the stairway rails. Smoke darkened the fire's glare enough that he barely saw the maidservant run back toward the landing.

"Have mercy, Dama!" she wailed, looking over her shoulder. Then she skidded to a halt, despair twisted her face as she saw the stairs burning.

"You fool! Do you know what you've done?" Yolie shrieked, striding onto the landing after her. The sorceress was fearsome despite being in her nightgown, with hair falling loose down her back.

Yolie stopped, taking in the smoke and flames that were turning her perfectly coifed home to ashes.

"You," she snarled, looking down at Ryamon.

"See?" begged the maidservant. "Please, Dama, spare me!"

Ryamon let go an angry sigh. Even though she insisted on betraying him, the maidservant was just a pawn, after all. He reached out with his other Element to jerk at the stuff of the upper floor. Mortar tore loose at once and the landing simply fell out from under them. Ryamon shaped the blocks and tiles into a rough chute. The screaming maid tumbled to the floor.

As she tottered to her feet, Ryamon pointed commandingly toward the side corridor, where he hoped there was an exit.

"Get out!" he called. "My business is not with you."

Yolie, meanwhile, stretched out her arms and hovered. There was no longer any beauty in her face as she descended toward Ryamon.

"Do you dare to attack me?" she snarled.

Ryamon experienced a moment of panic. He would never go back into that time bubble. Valdira needed him! Not bothering to reply, he extended his power to wrench more loose stones from the landing and stairs. Both walls shuddered.

Even through the fire's hungry roar, Yolie heard the over-stressed structure grinding and groaning. Her head snapped up. Ryamon glimpsed her startled expression as both walls collapsed toward her.

Chapter Twenty-Four

Heart pumping wildly, adrenaline burning in his veins, Ryamon kicked through the charred front door. He ran down the steps. He felt no joy in victory to leave Yolie beneath the burning rubble, only a grim determination that she not get the chance to come after them. When he was safely outside, he pushed the front wall down for good measure.

Flames leaped high on the hilltop, turning midnight to an amber haze. Sparks flew everywhere. Through heat and smoke and the fire's roar, he heard random bangs and crashes whose source he couldn't see. Servants in their nightclothes ran wailing down the slope. Some cried out for guards, for water to fight the fire, or simply for help.

In the village down below, lights must be coming on. Serfs would be rushing from their hovels to see the manor house alight. Ryamon hoped none of their relatives had still been inside when the building collapsed.

Thinking of loved ones reminded him of Valdira. Where was she? He looked around urgently. She knelt on the far side of the gravel circle, just at the edge of Yolie's flower garden. Her hand was pressed to the earth in a familiar gesture.

At his approach, she smiled with dark elation. "You are so incredible."

The familiar surge of desire rushed through him, but there was no time to take advantage of it.

"She might be able to get out of this," he warned.

"We'll be gone by then," Valdira assured him. "Here comes our ride."

As she spoke, Ryamon became aware of heavy steps thumping closer. A pair of great gray beasts crested the hill, grunting as they ran. This explained the banging noises. The twyerons must have kicked their way out of whatever stable they were kept in. Even with their horns filed down, they were a menacing sight.

"What happened to the montus?" Ryamon asked, daunted.

"These are faster," Valdira said as she brushed past him. "Besides, if Yolie does come after us, she won't be riding in her fine carriage."

"Nepharyl said they're pretty fierce."

"Nothing I can't manage," she tossed over her shoulder. "What, are you afraid?"

Smiling to egg him on, Valdira patted the larger of the two twyerons, then jumped lightly onto its back. Ryamon never could resist when she smiled that way.

"I suppose it's a little late for that," he admitted.

The second twyeron twitched its ears back to hear his footsteps. A sort of tufted crest ran down its back. He grabbed it and awkwardly swung his long legs over. Valdira's beast was already lumbering off, and Ryamon's followed. He knew he shouldn't complain, but it would have been easier to hang onto a montus' shaggy hide.

~ * ~

Gasping wildly, Phareth came back to himself. A wave of fear engulfed him as he opened his eyes to blackness. Heart jumping, he realized it was only normal darkness. The campfire had burned low and the mountain night was always dark.

"Phareth?" Anarinda's voice came thick and confused. "What's wrong?"

Rubbing her eyes, she sat up on the floor of her tent. Telamar rolled over in the tent next to hers. Even Marton dozed with his back against the rim of the rock ledge. Phareth's mental exploration must have taken longer than he expected.

"I'm all right," he answered softly. Muscles aching with inactivity, he crawled past Nepharyl's still form and added wood to the fire. Phareth was glad of the pain. It meant he was still alive.

As flames crackled and flared, Marton opened one eye. "What's all the noise?"

"Phareth is back," Anarinda replied.

"You were snoring," Telamar half-accused, as if he thought Phareth had really been sleeping.

"I fought the Costeran sorceress," Phareth replied. "She was choking me."

Anarinda settled on her blankets, blinking against the increasing light. With one hand she brushed loose curls from her face.

"Was it Yolie?"

"Yes," Phareth said. He carefully straightened his legs, easing the cramped muscles. "Mother was right. She was controlling Nepharyl."

"What else did you find out?" Telamar asked, sitting up.

"And where's my daughter?" Marton demanded.

"Valdira may have been captured," Phareth was forced to admit. "Yolie was asleep, at first. I only saw what she was dreaming. Dreams aren't always reliable, but the image of Valdira and Ryamon was pretty clear."

Marton didn't answer. He turned his head and scowled into the darkness. It didn't take a Shadow magus to see the concern beneath his rough exterior.

"We'll get her back," Phareth promised, and not only because doing so would thwart Yolie and Darmosh.

"That's right." Telamar's impersonal tone suggested imprisonment rather than the rescue Phareth had in mind.

"There's more," Phareth said. "They have an army and it's coming this way."

"An army?" Anarinda asked, alarmed.

Phareth nodded. Looking around, he compared Yolie's vision of archers and chariots to the ragtag band from Lornest. The three magi of his team were frazzled and way-worn; Marton was untrained; Silma had severe arthritis; and there were a handful of farmers. Even if the dream was overstated, they were in trouble.

"We're going to need help," Telamar said, echoing his thoughts.

A strangled cry interrupted them. The magi jumped as Nepharyl's body convulsed in a massive spasm. Eyes open but unfocused, he moaned, gurgled, kicked up dust. Phareth stumbled out of the way as Silma rolled to her feet and crawled around the fire. She slapped her hands to both sides of Nepharyl's head. Phareth felt her power flow through the stricken nobleman. With a strangled groan, he lay still.

"What happened?" Anarinda asked, appalled.

"Is he dead?" Marton was as uncaring as Telamar had been a moment before.

Phareth had to agree. Nepharyl sounded as if the life had left him. He didn't want that; Nepharyl might still have information they needed.

"He's had a terrible shock," Silma murmured. She settled cross-legged with Nepharyl's head on her lap and began to move her hands around his face in a series of complicated passes.

"He was asleep," Telamar argued. "What could shock him?"

"I have a thought." Phareth moved around to Nepharyl's other side and extended his own hand so Silma would know he was also working. He probed lightly, trying not to tangle the weave of Silma's energies. A moment later he looked toward Telamar and Anarinda.

"I think she's gone."

"Yolie?" Anarinda guessed.

Now it was Marton who glared as if Phareth would make up stories. "How?"

"Good question," Phareth replied.

He backed a few steps from Silma and settled cross-legged. In the camp around them, he sensed confused or worried thoughts from villagers awakened yet again by Nepharyl's scream. He brushed past them and reached southward with his mind.

To his surprise, he immediately found two personalities he hadn't expected: Valdira, concentrating fiercely, and Ryamon, his mind blazing with agitation. Phareth listened, trying to pinpoint where they were, then realized he was only delaying what he really had to do. The battle in Nepharyl's mind was vivid in his memory and part of him hesitated to risk another encounter. He couldn't let fear rule him. Phareth stretched his senses farther, but now it was Yolie he couldn't find. Instead he encountered a chorus of terrified mind-voices. Serfs. Something burning? Before he could figure out what they were experiencing, a fresh rush of power burned along his nerves like sparks from the fire.

"You did this?" Darmosh's grief and fury cut into Phareth's mind like the claws of a shorbak.

Before he could react, his enemy attacked. Phareth didn't bother protesting, just burrowed behind his shields like a ground squirrel escaping into its den.

"You minion, you nothing!" Darmosh raged, pounding at his shields. *"I'll make you bleed for this!"*

And what, Phareth wondered, would he be bleeding for? It didn't matter. He held his shields, timed his enemy's blows, and found a gap in the rhythm. At the right moment he twisted loose and, for the second time that night, escaped with his psyche intact.

He hovered for a moment, collecting himself in case Darmosh pursued him. When it felt safe, he returned his attention to the runaway magi. He was sure they had been Yolie's prisoners. Now they were free.

Weeks ago, Ryamon had stolen the element of Fire. That was why the Collegium magi were after him in the first place. Having fought the rogue magus himself, Phareth had an idea why Yolie's house was on fire.

Cautiously, fearing another clash with Darmosh, he probed until he found the two lovers. In Ryamon's memory he saw images that explained everything.

~ * ~

Phareth returned to himself amid a circle of anxious faces. Looking first to Marton, he said, "They got away again."

The brewer sighed, exasperated, and Phareth felt the rasp of his thoughts: *"Can't you make up your mind?"*

Phareth shrugged, smiling wryly. "I don't know what Yolie did to them, but they escaped. And—" he looked around, savoring the surprise "—I think they killed her."

"You said you couldn't find Nepharyl and he was still alive," Telamar pointed out.

"True," Phareth said, "but Darmosh is beside himself with grief. He sure believes she's dead."

"That's one less problem, isn't it?" Marton said.

"Maybe there's hope after all," Anarinda added.

Phareth nodded, but he smiled wearily. "We're still going to need help. Darmosh sensed me. He thinks *we* killed Yolie, and he's the one who actually has the army. They can't move in the middle of the night, but as soon as dawn breaks..." He trailed off suggestively.

"We'll have to come up with a plan," the Storm magus said.

"Not now," Silma interrupted. "We've been up half the night, and Phareth had to fight for his life."

"Twice," Phareth put in.

"Psychic combat," Telamar began dismissively.

Phareth glared at him. "Maybe you'd like to try it."

"Stop!" Anarinda warned them both.

"Psychic combat is just as difficult as a physical battle," Silma corrected. "As the senior Initiate, I insist we all sleep before we do anything else. I can monitor Lord Nepharyl. The rest of you get back to bed."

"You're right, sister magus," Anarinda said after a moment.

"We're all tired, and no one can make wise decisions after a sleepless night."

"I won't argue," Phareth said. Even with the mental disciplines instilled by the Tower of Shadow, he felt ill and shaky after too many emergencies in a row.

Telamar looked mutinous until Marton got to his feet.

"Better listen to your elders, boy," he growled. "Silma knows her business."

The brewer sketched a bow in Silma's direction. Phareth caught a flash of surprise on the Blood magus' face as Marton limped off toward the wood pile.

As if his departure gave them permission, the other magi also returned to their own tents. Despite his exhaustion, however, he feared sleep would not come easily.

~ * ~

Gray dawn found Valdira and Ryamon at the edge of the Valley of White Sand. The chalky plain, with its layers of drifting steam, looked ghostly in the wan light. The sulphurous odor carried on the wind was no more pleasant than it had been before. Ryamon's seat on the lumbering twyeron had gone from uncomfortable to actively painful. It felt like he would split up the middle if he didn't get off.

"Can we rest for a while?" he called.

"Fine," Valdira said.

As she spoke, the twyerons stopped. Only Valdira's will, it seemed, had kept them moving. Ryamon slid gratefully to the ground. The change of posture left him dizzy. He felt the great beast's sides heaving as he leaned on it for balance.

It felt like they had been galloping all night. That wasn't true, of course. Even these massive beasts couldn't keep such a pace indefinitely. Instead they had alternated walking with a bone-shaking canter. In addition to searing muscle cramps, Ryamon felt as if his skeleton had been pounded to jelly. Only now that he was off the brute did he feel the painful tingling of his numbed buttocks.

Nevertheless, he knew Valdira would expect him to show gratitude. Somewhat cautiously, he patted the twyeron's burly shoulder. "Thanks."

The creature twitched its ears and made a deep grumble,

almost as if it understood him. Then it ambled off to join its fellow. The animal also moved stiffly, its head swinging low. Ryamon felt a little bit better.

Valdira strode a short distance to a gap in the trees, where she would be hidden from sight if anyone else rode into the valley. She rested on the short grass at the edge of the white earth. Trying not to totter on his feet, Ryamon went to join her.

"Can I get you anything?" he asked. "Water?"

"Don't fuss," she answered, but her voice squeaked from a dry throat.

"You'd better get used to me fussing over you," Ryamon said, "because you deserve it."

Valdira smiled. She raised her head to kiss him. Ryamon longed to sink down beside her, but he knew there was more to do.

"I'll be right back." On aching legs, he headed toward the river.

Fortunately, walking did ease his cramped limbs. The bank was sandy and steep above the rippling stream. Using buried stones, he formed a set of crude steps. The bridge he had raised on their last visit was just a short distance downstream.

Even the slight effort was enough to make Ryamon feel how wrung out he was. He and Valdira had been captured in the early evening. They hadn't been tired when they escaped because, for them, no time had passed. But that had been hours ago and they had both used a lot of magic. Dawn felt like deep night, his powers drained and his will like mush.

Ryamon shook his head, telling himself he had no energy to waste being feeling sorry for himself. He had to take care of Valdira and their baby.

The air of the valley might smell strange, but the water was clear and cold. He knelt on the bank and drank deeply. Then he looked for something to take water back to Valdira. Of course, there was nothing. They had left it all in Laceto—Valdira's basket, Ryamon's waypack, their clothes, tools and supplies. It was all ashes by now.

For a moment, the cold hand of fear gripped his heart. They faced the wilderness with nothing. Ryamon shook his head again and picked up a large rock from the riverbank. Scraping together what was left of his willpower, he shaped it into a cup.

The result was lopsided, not worthy of a magus. Focusing, he tried again. The walls thinned and took on a graceful curve. A flat base formed beneath a slender stem.

"That's more like it," he said to the delicate goblet in his hand.

Grunting and heavy steps sounded nearby. Ryamon turned to see the twyerons raising a plume of pallid dust as they plodded down the bank. They were sure to churn up silt when they reached the river. Ryamon acted first, scooping water into the goblet and carrying it up the steps. Going up hurt a lot more than going down.

In her shady bower, Valdira leaned against a tree, eyes half closed. It was a birch tree, of course. Ryamon crouched beside her.

"Sweetheart," he called gently. She sat up fast, eyes bright with alarm. Ryamon offered the goblet. "Have a drink."

"Thanks." She relaxed and drank, then murmured sleepily, "You're so good to me."

Ryamon settled beside her. Pure joy warmed his bones as she snuggled against his side.

"You took care of me for a couple of months," he reminded her. A smile tugged at Valdira's lips as she rested her head on his shoulder.

"City boy." She must have been thinking some of the same things Ryamon had, because she sighed to herself. "We're in trouble, aren't we?"

"We got away," he said.

"With nothing."

"I know." Thanks to the Fire within him, Ryamon no longer felt the morning's chill, but Valdira wasn't so lucky. The green dress she was wearing might look pretty, but it was strictly indoor wear. He hugged her against him in case she was cold.

"We had to leave our luggage," he said, "but those are just things. I've already made this." He tapped the newly shaped goblet. "We'll figure out the rest as we go."

The lovers fell silent. Ryamon didn't pry into Valdira's thoughts. He'd had enough of that when they were stuck in the time trap. Yet if he hoped to rest and recover his strength, it was easier said than done. In his mind he kept seeing the flaming wreckage pour down on Yolie's head. He must have killed her, and it sickened him.

After trying to spare the servants—and he couldn't be sure he had succeeded—he had inflicted a painful death on their mistress. Who was he to decide someone deserved to live or die? Being in Laceto, even for such a short time, had changed him in ways he didn't like.

It was a relief when Valdira interrupted his thoughts.

"Where do you want to go?" she asked. "Back to Arkanost?"

"I don't know," he answered quietly. "We're pariahs there, but I'm not sure Costera would welcome us, either. We—I mean, I. I killed one of them."

"Maybe they don't know. Yolie never introduced us to anyone but her brother." Valdira's voice was dark with disgust. "I have a feeling they were keeping us a secret."

"Could be," Ryamon said, "but someone is sure to wonder where Yolie got to. It won't be too hard to figure out what happened, even if Darmosh doesn't rouse them all against us."

"We don't know how soon he plans to attack," Valdira pointed out. "It sounded like Yolie was his main ally. Maybe losing her will stop his plans."

Ryamon sipped from the goblet and thought about it. The feral intensity of Darmosh's eyes was vivid in his memory. Foreboding sat heavy as a stone in his stomach.

"No," he said, "a man like that won't give up. From what they said, the rest of the wizards are their rivals. They didn't trust anyone but each other. Darmosh will want revenge for taking that away from him."

He passed the goblet back to Valdira, then continued, "I don't think we have much choice, do you? There's only one road out of here…"

"That we know of," Valdira pointed out.

"We don't have time to search for other routes when Darmosh is bound to come after us," Ryamon said. "The road we've seen leads past both Laceto and Olalu. We'd have to sneak by Darmosh, make our way across Costera to one of their big ports, like Logoll, and then find passage to one of the other wizard kingdoms."

"And with what money?" she asked gloomily.

"Yeah." Ryamon reluctantly voiced an idea that had been growing in his mind. "I suppose we could stay in Laceto."

Valdira leaned away to gaze up at him under arched eyebrows.

His side felt strange and cold without her.

"Well, I killed Yolie," he said defensively. "By their laws, I have the right to claim her estate."

"It was a magical battle, too," she said with a sour chuckle. "Do you really want to live in a place where they saw the horns off animals and people aren't allowed to talk?"

"Not really," Ryamon admitted. "I'd be right where Darmosh could find me, and I'd constantly be fighting every other wizard who thought they'd be a better lord. I just thought we should think about it before we get too far away to turn around."

"Well, now we have. Anyway, you burned the place down. Nobody will be living there for a long time." Valdira snuggled up against Ryamon again, decisively ending the discussion.

They rested together in silence. Ryamon was surprised to feel a surge of pure joy at the pleasure of holding his lover in his arms. Despite everything that had happened, they were still together. They were free, in the wilderness where it would be easier to hide. They had magic, and they had each other. Fear for the future couldn't spoil that accomplishment.

~ * ~

After all too little sleep, Phareth sent his thoughts toward Polvest. Murcrys answered quickly, as if she had been expecting to hear from him.

"Where's Nepharyl now?" she asked when Phareth had reported the night's activities.

"Still unconscious," Phareth replied. *"Silma is monitoring him, so we know he isn't faking it. She's getting worried. I didn't hit him that hard. He should have come to by now."*

In his mind, he felt his mother shrug. *"If Yolie was dominating his mind as completely as we suspect, he may not be able to function without her."*

"You think her death destroyed his mind?"

"If she is dead," Murcrys answered darkly.

"Darmosh seemed to think she is."

Phareth tried not to let his mother feel him fretting. She hadn't commented yet on his personal foray to retrieve the missing nobleman. And there was something else, too, though he wasn't sure he wanted to hear the truth.

Shields firmly in place, he asked, *"Do you believe what Yolie said?"*

Murcrys immediately understood what he was asking. *"That you and she are cousins?"* Her mind was guarded now. *"It may be true. Your father never hid that he was from Costera. It's been more than twenty years. I couldn't honestly tell you who his family was."*

Phareth wasn't sure he believed her. Murcrys had always been a Shadow magus. He couldn't imagine her sleeping with a man whose mind she hadn't explored.

He realized his shields had a hole in them when she tartly inserted, *"I was younger then. He was exotic."*

Phareth refused to be chastised. *"Why didn't you tell me?"*

"Would it have helped?" Murcrys asked back. *"To know you were infiltrating an enemy kingdom and those enemies were tied to you by blood?"*

Despite himself, Phareth's mind shied away from remembering the harrowing experience he'd had in Logoll. His stomach churned to think his own kin, Darmosh, had struck his lover down.

Rebelliously, he said, *"You wouldn't have sent me if you didn't trust me to do my job."*

Almost gently, Murcrys told him, *"If your father's identity had been known, could I have sent you, son?"*

"You're a Mage Lord. They couldn't tell you not to." But Phareth knew it wasn't that simple. If Salovik or Akayel had known Murcrys once had a Costeran lover, no matter how long ago, they would never have accepted her as Shadow Lord. *"They would assume you were trying to trick them, wouldn't they."*

"Without a doubt."

Phareth sighed to himself and let the subject drop. Thinking again of Nepharyl, he asked, *"What does Guilberta have to say?"*

"She totally repudiates him," Murcrys said. *"It's sad, really. If he doesn't die on his own, Guilberta's likely to hang him for the stain upon her leadership."*

Murcrys' mental tone seemed a bit sharp. Phareth tried not to squirm. He didn't like Nepharyl, but he knew how the man would feel if he ever came back to himself. Phareth, too, had faced the consequences of a failed mission. He was sure his mother would never have sacrificed him, or any other Shadow magus, to salve her own ego.

"I'll be watching for Darmosh's army," he said. *"Aside from that, do you have any other orders?"*

"Not yet. The Collegium has been gathering every morning to discuss the

situation. *I'll have to invite Guilberta and inform her of Nepharyl's capture. That will slow us down.*" Phareth could feel her irritation even across the distance. "*The one thing most of us agree on is that we reach our own decision on Valdira and Ryamon without Guilberta's meddling.*"

"*What about them?*" Phareth asked.

"*We're still deadlocked. Salovik is that stubborn, the fool. However, I believe Klaive is making headway with Chrysen and Akayel.*"

"*If you still want us to bring them back, it would help if we had something to offer.*"

"*Yes, I've mentioned that,*" Murcrys said wryly. "*In your opinion, is that what's best? To bring them back home?*"

"*Well, we don't want them going over to Costera. Not if they're capable of defeating Yolie.*"

"*True.*"

Phareth sensed Murcrys observing him intently, assessing his reactions. Although he'd never met the rogue magi in person, he had been following them and listening to them for so long, he felt he knew them. They were almost like friends. It was different from the way he viewed Nepharyl. He wasn't sure why, but it was.

Finally, he said, "*You once told me their powers should be explored. I believe that's true, but more, I think they have something to teach all the Collegium. The question is whether they'll work with us or run again.*"

"*What choice do they have?*" Murcrys countered. "*If Darmosh catches them, they're dead.*"

Her cold logic chilled Phareth. In his mind, he scrambled for some alternative. What he came up with surprised even him.

"*Wait, Mother,*" Phareth said. "*I have an idea.*"

Chapter Twenty-Five

After Murcrys approved Phareth's plan, he sat on the hillside above the rock ledge. The sun crept upward between jagged peaks. Then the crisp morning air suddenly blew cold across his neck. Phareth's heart dropped slightly as he saw Telamar striding up the slope. Marton, Anarinda and Silma followed. The Blood magus struggled a bit with her staff but still made her way determinedly over the rocks.

Anarinda and Telamar carried steaming mugs. A faint, appealing aroma wafted up the hill. After so many days in the hills, the fragrance of tea provoked an overwhelming craving. But his mother would never forgive him if he gave their scheme away to satisfy some base urge.

"Yes?" Phareth asked.

"Have some." Telamar bent to offer Phareth a mug. He moved stiffly, as if unaccustomed to social graces.

"We have food," Marton added, hefting his leather wallet.

Trying not to let his eagerness show, Phareth accepted the drink. After all, it would be ice cold within minutes if he left it in Telamar's hands. He sipped, bracing himself for the confrontation that must be coming.

The other magi settled on the hilltop around him. Prim as a girl, Telamar brushed dust from his robe. Phareth wondered why he bothered, since it was almost more gray than white now. Habit, perhaps. Silma lowered herself into a sitting position and accepted Anarinda's extra mug of tea, while Marton brusquely passed out dry rolls and cheese. Phareth eyed them all over the rim of his mug.

"What's going on?" he asked.

"We wish to take council with you, Initiate," Silma intoned with a formal air.

Telamar spoiled the effect by adding, "Because we know you're up to something."

"I beg your pardon?"

"We can tell," Anarinda said. A spark of impatience flared in her blue eyes. "You're up here by yourself, not talking to anyone.

What else should we think?"

If they were trying to embarrass him, it wouldn't work.

"That I love nature and I'm finding peace in the sunrise," Phareth countered in a bland tone. Anarinda scowled prettily.

"And I'm a Sea magus," Telamar retorted. He sounded matter-of-fact, not angry.

"They've got you," Marton growled around a mouthful of cheese. Phareth shrugged and took another sip of his tea.

"We won't let you keep secrets from us," Anarinda went on firmly. "Now what did the Shadow Lord say?"

Phareth looked at her a moment longer, weighing how much to tell them. Anarinda was partly right. They had to act together before Darmosh's army made their rivalries irrelevant. But would they be willing to follow him if they knew everything? Marton's brows quirked upward in a wry question, and Anarinda's irritation sizzled in the air around her.

"She's concerned, of course, to learn of Darmosh's aggression," Phareth began, using the same type of language Silma had. "Unfortunately, it will be several days before the Collegium can respond."

"Days?" Marton burst out.

"The king must formally order the Collegium to act," Silma explained.

"Or some of his commanders may be visiting their home estates. They'll have to travel back to Polvest," Anarinda went on. "It will also take time to raise troops from the countryside."

"Quite true." Phareth nodded to her. "The various orders must also summon their battle magi, who may be stationed in remote locations, and then coordinate with the king's forces."

"But Darmosh is coming now," Telamar said.

"Since we're on scene," Phareth answered carefully, "the Collegium would like us to delay him while the defense gets organized. Or stop him altogether, if we can."

Worried glances passed among the magi. Phareth knew they were assessing their total abilities much as he had earlier. He would never have a better opening.

"Because there are so few of us, and because Marton's abilities are limited," he went on, glancing an apology to Valdira's father, "I've asked Mother's permission to invite Valdira and Ryamon to join us in our defense."

Anarinda brightened. "That makes sense."

"I knew it would be something like this," Telamar said coolly.

Marton shot him an irritated glance. Silma asked, "Do you think she will?"

"The last I checked, they were coming back toward Arkanost," Phareth said. He spoke slowly, as if thinking things through, while in reality he listened for reactions among his companions. "This suggests they're opting not to stay in Costera."

"That doesn't mean anything," Marton said broodingly.

"I hope it means they have an interest in protecting our borders," Phareth argued politely. "Darmosh isn't just invading, he's chasing them."

He sensed Silma's and Anarinda's acceptance, but nothing from Telamar. The Ice magus sat silent, gray eyes narrowed.

"If we have to do this without them, so be it," Phareth said. "First, it's important that we all agree. Can I count on you to work with them, not against them?"

He looked straight at Telamar, who deliberately chewed his mouthful of bread and swallowed a gulp of tea. Finally, the Ice magus replied.

"I thought you'd never ask."

None of the others looked surprised, but Phareth couldn't hide his reaction. "I thought all you wanted was to—"

"You thought," Telamar interrupted. "You assumed you knew what I felt and believed, what I would do. You never asked me."

His voice was level, unemotional, yet Phareth felt the reproach.

"I did ask for help," he replied. "When we were lost in the hills, I asked you to find Valdira."

"That was ages ago," Telamar replied. "We fought together and I thought we were going to work as a team, but nothing has changed." He glanced momentarily at Marton. "When you wanted to track Nepharyl down, you asked him for help, not Anarinda or me."

The brewer frowned at being singled out. Silma shifted restlessly, easing her arthritic knee. Then she repeated her question.

"Will Valdira and her young man agree? If you ask their help and then try to arrest them—"

"That won't happen," Anarinda interrupted now in a determined tone. "We'll see to it."

"Good," Marton growled.

"Well." Phareth's sigh of relief was only a little bit exaggerated. "I hope Valdira will be as cooperative."

"Contact her and ask," Anarinda ordered.

"We don't have much time," Marton added.

Phareth smiled. Inside himself, he said, *"Watch out, Darmosh. I'm coming for you at last."*

~ * ~

"Ryamon!"

Sudden shaking and Valdira's agitated voice jerked him out of slumber. Ryamon stumbled to his feet, dizzy and confused.

"What's wrong?" he asked, voice thick with sleep.

"We fell asleep!"

"Sorry," Ryamon mumbled automatically.

He looked around, struggling to comprehend. The barren white plain stretched before them, cut by the sunken riverbed. The twyerons stood nearby, browsing from low branches.

"We fell asleep," Valdira repeated tightly. "We should have been running!"

Ryamon's heart jumped as he gathered his senses. As he came more awake, he realized they hadn't lost much time. The sun was still low above the horizon.

"It's all right. We only slept a few hours, and we needed the rest." Valdira especially, he thought. Ryamon reached to hug her, but she stepped away. An angry hand pushed back loose wisps of hair as she shook her head.

"No. He's back."

"Who?"

"She means me." A stranger's voice inserted itself into his mind, clean as a knife through bread. The Shadow magus from the valley!

"Watch out!" Ryamon cried. He could never forget the feeling of that mind in his. Exhaustion forgotten, he turned wildly around. Fire surged through his veins, seeking a target.

"You see?" Valdira's green eyes blazed with anger. "Show yourself!"

With startled snorts, the twyerons lumbered to her side. Heads swinging, pawing up dust, they looked for something to fight.

"Calm down," the Shadow magus replied. *"If I wanted to hurt you, I already would have."*

It sounded like he was standing behind them, talking right

into Ryamon's ear. Unnerved, he looked around. Of course, there was no one there.

"What do you want?" Valdira rapped out. Though she spoke aloud, the intruder seemed to hear her perfectly.

"To negotiate," the Shadow magus replied. *"My name is Phareth, Initiate of Shadow. I give my word, as we are brother and sister magi, that I will not attack you at this time."*

The feeling now was definitely different than when he had used Ryamon to get at Valdira. The silent voice was almost apologetic. However, Ryamon hadn't forgotten the rumors he'd heard in his days as a novice of Stone.

"Or trick us?" He thought clumsily back to their old enemy. Phareth seemed to roll his eyes.

"I promise, I only want to talk."

Ryamon and Valdira shared another distrustful glance. However, Ryamon didn't see how they could stop the Shadow magus if he really wanted to impose on them.

He was getting a headache trying to speak telepathically, so he asked, aloud, "What about?"

"Darmosh. His army."

"How do you know about that?" Valdira asked.

"I've been watching you, naturally. Listening in. Since we were ordered not to follow you into Costera, it was about all I could do."

Ryamon squirmed uncomfortably, remembering his doubts about Valdira's love and the terrible scene with Yolie only yesterday. Had Phareth been watching all that? If he had, he didn't say so.

"I know you stayed at Laceto, home of Dama Yolie, and that she's been sending agents into Arkanost—"

"You mean Nepharyl?" Valdira interrupted. Her sharp expression told Ryamon she was eager to show that Phareth wasn't intimidating her.

"Nepharyl is our prisoner. Since Yolie is dead—"

"Dead! Are you sure?" Ryamon demanded.

"Darmosh certainly believes so. He's too dangerous for me to spy on, but he does appear to be grieving."

Phareth waited a moment, perhaps giving them a chance to ask questions. Ryamon's stomach turned over at the knowledge he had really killed someone. It made no difference that Yolie wouldn't have hesitated to strike him down.

The Shadow magus continued, *"She and Darmosh have been*

involved in several conspiracies to overthrow the throne of Arkanost."

"They claim to be descended of the last Wizard King," Ryamon said. "They want to reestablish the rule of a magical elite."

Something about this seemed to bother Phareth, but the Shadow magus only said, *"It's possible. Darmosh has sworn vengeance for Yolie's death, so we have to assume he's coming this way with his army."* He seemed to bow toward Valdira, acknowledging her discovery.

"We guessed," Valdira retorted.

"We were coming back to warn you," Ryamon said.

"A fact that will weigh in your favor," Phareth said. *"When I sensed you were returning, I asked permission to negotiate with you. We—myself, Anarinda of the Order of Storm, Telamar of the Order of Ice, and Silma of the Order of Blood—are the only magi in the area. We could use assistance to stop Darmosh."*

"Silma is there?" Valdira glanced a question at Ryamon.

"She always looked out for your interests," Ryamon pointed out.

"Yes, Silma is here. After you tossed us in that pit—" Ryamon sensed Phareth speaking to him particularly *"—Silma brought a group of villagers to help us. And I have to warn you, Marton is here, too."*

"My father!" Valdira all but yelled. "What did you bring him for?"

Ryamon's stomach lurched again. More than ever, he was afraid to face Valdira's father. Yet he staunchly declared, "I won't let him hurt her."

"Since he's not a trained magus, Marton can't be part of the defense," Phareth answered. *"Only Anarinda and Telamar will be joining you to face Darmosh."*

Something about that phrase, not a trained magus, stuck in Ryamon's mind. Before he could ask about it, Valdira cut in. "He would never agree to work with Silma."

"Marton understands himself a little better now," Phareth answered drily.

"What does that mean?" Valdira snapped.

"I'll let him explain," Phareth said. *"Marton will stay here with Silma and the villagers. They're going to look for a place to set up a defensive line if the four of you can't stop the Costerans."*

"What about you?" Ryamon asked.

"It would take too long for Anarinda and Telamar to walk where you are," Phareth said. *"I'll be using an advanced technique to send them to your*

location. It will leave me too drained to fight."

"That's convenient," Valdira said.

"Believe me, I wish I could be there," Phareth said. *"I have my own reasons for wanting to bring Darmosh down."*

The Shadow magus spoke with such grim feeling, Ryamon found himself believing it.

"Then do you want us to meet them somewhere?" he asked.

"Wait a minute," Valdira interrupted. "I haven't agreed to anything!"

Ryamon looked at her, uncertain. He understood why she was upset, but it didn't seem like they had many options. After facing Yolie, Ryamon wasn't eager to take on Darmosh by themselves.

"Can you give us time to talk?" he thought to Phareth.

"Of course."

The mental presence withdrew, leaving Ryamon strangely unbalanced. As if he had been wearing a hat and hadn't noticed its weight until the wind blew it away. Phareth hadn't said when he would contact them again, but that wasn't the most important thing.

He turned to embrace Valdira, moving carefully in case she objected. She stood tense in the circle of his arms, but didn't try to push him away.

"Are you all right?" Ryamon asked. He didn't know what he would do if she refused to work with the Collegium magi.

Valdira shrugged unhappily. "I didn't want to face my father so soon. He'll hate me. This is exactly what he said would happen."

"You're not alone this time. We got away from Yolie, didn't we? We'll figure this out, too."

Valdira looked up at him, almost hesitant. "You can't kill him."

"I don't want to," Ryamon assured her, heartened that she wasn't so bitter that she wanted her own father dead. "Your mother wouldn't like it."

Her lips twitched in a half-smile, but her eyes retained their brooding caste. Sometimes he wondered if he would ever really understand Valdira.

"What about Phareth?" he asked. "Do you think we can trust him?"

"No." Valdira was more herself now, her voice lively with scorn. "He's up to something. Can't you tell?"

"Yes, I sensed that, too. Still, this might be our best chance to return home with honor. They might make a deal with us if we help turn the invasion back."

"Hm." Valdira answered skeptically.

"The other thing is, Phareth might think he knows it all, but I don't think he does," Ryamon went on. "Remember what Yolie told us, that our being in Costera was the excuse they were waiting for?"

"Darmosh is coming no matter what," Valdira said heavily.

"We can't let him seize any territory," Ryamon said. "So if we have to fight him, I'd rather do it together."

"Hm," Valdira repeated. Ryamon knew she didn't want to agree, but she would have to come around in the end. Really, they had no choice.

"You think about it." Ryamon knew better than to push Valdira into something she didn't want to do. "I'll see if I can find something to eat."

He kissed her lightly and moved into the woods nearby. During his first days in Selkest, Valdira had shown him how to find wild lettuce. Ryamon was sure he had seen some on their first trip through, but he hadn't bothered to gather it since Nepharyl had such ample supplies. Now he slowly roved under the trees, looking for clumps of flat, round leaves with pale centers.

The leaves were tender, if slightly sour, but it was better than raw birds' eggs, which was the next most likely food he would find. They had to keep their strength up, especially if they were going to be fighting again.

~ * ~

"They'll do it," Phareth reported.

"Excellent." Anarinda smiled down the slope. After sighing that she had no clean robes left, she had spent the past few minutes brushing her hair and restoring its many curls to their usual order. Telamar, who was fitting his neatly rolled tent into its duffle, merely looked up and nodded.

"She trusts you?" asked Marton, who had been helping the two magi pack up. Phareth shrugged.

"I didn't say they like it," he answered.

Looking around critically, Anarinda asked, "Is there anything else we need?"

"The less weight, the better," Phareth warned.

"If we get stuck out in the woods again, we'll need basic

equipment," Telamar answered. For all his fine words, he seemed to relish making Phareth work harder.

"Take this, too." Silma hobbled down the slope with a bulging sack. Seeing Phareth's expression, she added, "It's food. You said they were on the move all night. They won't fight well if they're weak with hunger."

"Thank you for thinking of that," Anarinda said.

"Yes, I suppose they'll need something to eat," Phareth admitted.

In truth, the magi had done reasonably well in separating the necessities from the bulk of their gear. Anarinda and Telamar each had their tents, staves, the clothing on their backs, and now the food. Marton was wedging everything else under the rock ledge. Personally, Phareth thought if they didn't defeat Darmosh the luggage wasn't going to matter.

Anarinda accepted the parcel from Silma and said, "I think we're ready."

Phareth nodded and reached out to Ryamon's mind. The rogue magus was alert and waiting. Through Ryamon's eyes, he saw Valdira sitting on a log. The vision vanished in a burst of panic, and Phareth realized Ryamon had shut his eyes. The memory of how Phareth had leaped from his mind to Valdira's was too strong to ignore, it seemed.

Phareth waited a moment, letting Ryamon steady himself. Then he said, *"We're ready."*

"I'm not sure we are," Ryamon's anxiety whispered. Focusing with obvious effort, he thought back, *"What do you want me to do?"*

"Look for a clear spot near you," Phareth directed. *"Space for two people and a couple of bags. Not near the edge, please."*

"I guess they wouldn't be much help if we drowned them in the river," Ryamon admitted.

Phareth projected an ironic chuckle. He felt the razor edge of Valdira's suspicion, but Ryamon consciously did not look toward her.

Birch trees surrounded the clearing where they were sitting on three sides, but the fourth side was open to a wide plain with patches of short grass.

"That area seems fine," Phareth told him. *"You'll be anchoring me for the transit, but don't worry. You don't have to do anything. Just keep looking at the target point."*

"All right." Pushing his reluctance aside, Ryamon concentrated on the area Phareth had asked for. A true magus, his images were crisp and bright. Blinking his vision clear, Phareth looked up at Telamar and Anarinda.

"We're ready," he said, forgetting to speak aloud. *"You're going to fall a few inches. I don't want you to incorporate inside the ground, so I'm putting you slightly above the surface."*

Anarinda nodded, curiosity lighting her delicate features. She had never traveled this way before, and Phareth felt her keen interest. Telamar's hand tightened on his staff, the only sign he might be uneasy. Phareth stared at them, taking in as much detail as he could: outlines of their baggage, the fine hairs on Telamar's chin, the faint sheen of stitches down the front of Anarinda's robe.

Fixing this image in his mind, Phareth linked with Ryamon. In the picture he was sending, Phareth added a vision of his companions. He drew a breath, held it. The image was clear: the two magi suspended just above the surface of dirt and tufty grass.

He pushed with all his strength. There was an eerie noise, as if he had ripped the sky. An inward rush of air lifted dust from the hillside where he sat. In his mind, he felt a startled yip from Anarinda, and Ryamon's final burst of worry that he was doing the right thing by cooperating.

Then it was just as he had pictured it. At the rock shelter, Phareth, Silma and Marton. On the edge of the ghostly valley, Anarinda and Telamar faced Ryamon and Valdira.

To all of them, Phareth said, *"It's up to you now."*

~ * ~

"They're coming," Ryamon said.

Valdira shrugged, acknowledging his words. The pair of twyerons stood restless guard at her side.

Ryamon knew his lover was concentrating on some animal messenger, trying to find out where Darmosh and his forces were. Since they needed the information, he decided not to disturb her.

As Phareth had requested, he concentrated on the level ground before him. The chalky soil blazed with reflected sunlight and patches of grass swayed in a light breeze.

Phareth's power flowed through him without warning. He fought the feeling that he was choking and tried to stay calm. Like stone, the anchor Phareth needed. The twyerons snorted fretfully. Then was a strange noise, a tearing he felt as much as heard, and the Collegium magi were there.

The Ice magus stood tall in his white robe, a watchful stillness about him. The Storm magus was less what Ryamon had expected —a dainty girl only a little older than Valdira. Her hair was dressed as elaborately as Yolie's. However, in her case, the arrangement suited her.

"It's up to you now." Phareth's words held a hint of warning. Then his power dropped away, and he was gone.

Ryamon heard Valdira's light step as she came to stand beside him, and the heavier treads of the twyerons moving to flank them. Ryamon put his arm around Valdira's shoulders. They stood for a moment sizing each other up, the rogues in their foreign attire and the Collegium magi in their dusty uniforms.

"Good day." Valdira's voice was brittle and unfriendly. Ryamon sensed the implicit threat as she brushed her hand casually along the neck of the twyeron nearest her.

"Good day," the Ice magus said, not at all intimidated.

"Greetings, sister and brother," the Storm magus replied in a slightly breathy voice. She made a little bow. "I am Anarinda, Initiate of the Order of Storms. This is Telamar, Initiate of the Order of Ice."

"I'm Ryamon," Ryamon said, and hesitated. How should he introduce Valdira? She wasn't his wife, but calling her his companion made her sound like one of the twyerons.

"Valdira," she cut in, sparing him the decision.

"It's good to meet you at last," Anarinda said with what seemed to be a genuine smile. "By the way, Silma sent this."

She offered a cloth-wrapped parcel, which Valdira and Ryamon stared at warily.

"It's food," Telamar told them curtly.

At these words, Ryamon's hunger fairly exploded within him. He had given Valdira most of the wild lettuce, and water was a poor substitute.

"That's kind of her," he said, reaching for the parcel. Anarinda readily passed it over.

"It sounds like something Silma would do," Valdira admitted. "How is she?"

The casual question hid a sharp edge. She was testing them,

Ryamon sensed—making sure they knew Silma as she did. He stopped pulling at the knots to watch their reply.

Telamar shrugged. "It was a long walk from Lornest. Her arthritis is bothering her, but she's well otherwise."

Valdira seemed satisfied. "Hurry up with that," she ordered as Ryamon resumed trying to open the package. "I'm hungry."

"No more than I," he answered, resuming his efforts to get at the food.

"If you like," Anarinda offered prettily, "we can look around while you eat. If this is to be the battleground, we should get to know the terrain."

"Fine," Valdira said with a shrug, "but don't take too long. The invaders are closer than you think."

Chapter Twenty-Six

"What do you mean?" Telamar demanded.

And in the same breath, Anarinda asked, "How do you know?"

Valdira shrugged and sank her teeth into a hard roll. "I asked an elgus to go look."

Anarinda said, "Oh, yes, we heard about that. You can control animals. That's very interesting. Can you really communicate with trees, too?"

Valdira chewed the bread, eyeing her warily. Even Ryamon wondered whether the newcomer's friendly manner was genuine.

"Yeah." Valdira tossed her head in the direction of the nearby birch grove. Ryamon heard a familiar susurrus and saw a stir among the branches. Telamar watched the trees cautiously.

"How did you discover it?" Anarinda asked.

"How did you discover your element?" Valdira retorted. "I always could. It came naturally, so I used it."

A familiar edge of defiance was back in her tone. Ryamon ate his cheese and dried fruit as fast as he could without choking, and hoped she wouldn't start another fight. Telamar frowned, affronted, but Anarinda apologized with every appearance of sincerity.

"I meant no offense, sister magus."

Before Valdira could answer, a husky roar interrupted them. Telamar and Anarinda turned around fast. Just across the river, one of the geysers was erupting. The foul odor from the valley redoubled as sheets of steam shot over the water.

"What is that?" Telamar asked, as wary as Valdira has been a moment before.

"It's called a geyser." Ryamon gestured to usher everyone toward the fallen log where Valdira had been sitting before the magi arrived. "There's fire under the ground here. The springs you see are too hot for swimming, and water flowing in the ground has carved out channels beneath the surface."

"It's a dangerous place." Valdira resumed her place on the fallen log. "Nepharyl told us people come here to gather the minerals. Sometimes they die when they break through into hidden pools."

"And what are those stones?" Anarinda asked, pointing to the line of low rock plinths which snaked across the valley floor.

"I made markers to show a safe path," Ryamon said.

"You're not a Sea magus," Telamar said accusingly.

"The water is boiling. I can sense the heat even though it's deep below us." Ryamon was determined not to be led into any more quarrels. After all, they had promised to work with the Collegium magi.

"That sounds useful." Anarinda gave Telamar a scolding look. He blinked back at her, unrepentant. "Maybe we need to share information about ourselves as much as this landscape."

She, too, sank onto the fallen log. By unspoken accord, the two men remained standing, poised.

"Valdira," Ryamon said, "did you find out where Darmosh is now and how many people he's brought with him?"

Now it was Valdira who gave him a scolding look. Ryamon shrugged in reply. Much as she enjoyed deflating the pompous Collegium magus, this wasn't the time for childish games.

"It would be helpful to know," Anarinda agreed in an extremely polite and respectful tone.

Valdira tore a bite from a strip of jerky and reported, "They must have set out from Olalu before dawn, because they've just left Laceto."

"Where?" Telamar asked, still irritated.

"Laceto is Yolie's estate," Ryamon explained. "It's a six-hour walk from here, but I don't think they're walking."

Valdira nodded, chewing slowly. "They're in ornyx chariots, about fifty. Each one has a driver and an archer as a passenger."

"What were they doing?" Telamar asked.

"The elgus can't hear, only see." Valdira seemed to accept the truce, because she added, "The fire's out. It looks like Darmosh left some of his soldiers to recover Yolie's body from the wreckage and guard the area."

"Who would attack them out here?" Anarinda asked.

"According to their customs," Ryamon said, "since Yolie is dead, her property is free for the taking. Darmosh probably has a relative he'd like to inherit it, but another wizard lord could claim the estate before Darmosh comes back to it."

"Yes, Phareth said Darmosh's sister had died." Anarinda glanced approvingly at Ryamon.

"Unfortunately, we can't look for any help in Costera," he said, trying not to squirm.

"None we'd want, anyway," Valdira added grimly.

Anarinda nodded, accepting the back-handed apology. Another rustle went through the trees as Valdira spoke. Ryamon glanced at the tossing branches. Valdira must have asked the trees to shift over and block the road. Knowing how slowly they moved, he hoped they had enough time.

"How long will it take Darmosh to catch up with us?" Ryamon asked.

Valdira sucked on the frayed end of her jerky, thinking. "The ornyxes are faster than us. It could be as little as two hours."

"Then we have that long to figure out a strategy," Telamar said.

~ * ~

"I've been listening in on Ryamon," Phareth reported to the Shadow Lord. *"They're working on a plan."*

"So far so good," Murcrys said. *"Do you think they can do it?"*

"I should hope so. It's four to one. What of your task, Mother? Has the Collegium agreed?"

"They have," Murcrys answered. *"Half of them are curious to meet Valdira and the rest want to make sure Costera doesn't gain a foothold in Arkanost."*

"I hoped they would see it that way." But Phareth felt a hint of irritation behind his mother's shields, so he wasn't surprised when she continued.

"There's just one small change."

"How small?"

"Guilberta wants to come."

"What?" Even telepathically, Phareth squeaked with alarm. He could picture the elderly countess in her formal black dress with the fussy lace and ivory buttons, diving for cover as magic roared around her. The image would have been funny if it wasn't so horrifying. *"She'll be helpless if Darmosh gets close to our position!"*

"I've mentioned that, but she's adamant," Murcrys replied. *"There has to be a witness who's not a magus, one whose loyalty to the throne is beyond suspicion. Guilberta accepts the risk."*

"What does she plan to do, knock Darmosh on the head with her cane?" Phareth demanded sarcastically.

"If I thought it would be that simple, I'd let her try." Murcrys projected a wry smile. *"More likely, she wants to knock on Nepharyl's head. Has there been any change?"*

"None. Silma thinks it's still too early to know."

"I assume you've checked to be sure he isn't feigning unconsciousness."

"Of course." Phareth was mildly insulted that Murcrys would think otherwise. *"His body functions at a basic level, but his mind is empty. He must have died along with Yolie."*

"Too bad," Murcrys said. *"We could have learned from what she did to him."*

"Maybe that's why Yolie bound her to him so tightly. She didn't ever want him to free himself."

"Perhaps. Now, as to your straying off to capture Nepharyl…"

Phareth's heart raced. *"We couldn't leave him out there spying on us,"* he argued.

"I'm sure. And I'm equally sure you don't plan to take this much upon yourself in the future," Murcrys said with steely sweetness.

"Of course not," he answered with all the humility he could muster.

"That's good, because a few of my brother magi wondered about your motives." She meant Salovik, Phareth was certain. *"We don't need to give them any more reason for suspicion."*

"As you say."

Phareth sensed a break in his mother's concentration, as if someone else was speaking to her. Then she said, *"The Collegium is reconvening. Call on me again when the battle is near."*

"I will."

Phareth was relieved to break contact. He didn't think he had fooled Murcrys. She knew very well he had been on a personal vendetta. In truth, he hadn't expected to fool her. For all he knew, she had assigned him this mission in the hope he would undertake that very vendetta, confront his fears and put Logoll behind him.

If all went well, he wouldn't have to pursue his revenge any longer. After today, it would all be taken care of.

~ * ~

Dense fog hung over the Valley of White Sand. It was warm and sticky with a sulphurous sting. Ryamon understood why Anarinda had created it, but that didn't make it any easier to wait and sweat under the stifling shroud.

One by one, the marker stones vanished from sight. He couldn't help feeling that his freedom, too, was slipping away. Even after the accident of falling asleep, he and Valdira had been well ahead of Darmosh. They could easily have escaped. Once back in the hills of Selkest, they surely could have slipped past the Collegium magi. By now they would have been far away, safe and free.

Yet Ryamon knew running wasn't the answer. If he was any kind of man, he had to defend Valdira and their child. So instead of heading for safety, he waited and fretted, dreading the battle to come.

Beside him, Valdira asked, "What's wrong?"

"Just nerves." Ryamon felt isolated by the thick vapors. When he caught his lover's gaze, the danger and fear seemed to press on him as heavily as the fog. He blurted, "I won't let them hurt you."

"Which ones?" Valdira smiled crookedly.

"Any of them," Ryamon vowed. The lovers embraced, although it was uncomfortable inside the sticky fog. Valdira rested her head on his shoulder.

She said, "I can take care of myself."

"I know," he replied, "but Yolie got the drop on both of us."

"You got us out of that."

"I was lucky," Ryamon said. He held her, savoring the feel of her body. "I wish you'd keep going and let me do this."

Valdira rolled her eyes. "What would that solve? This whole thing is about me."

"And me," Ryamon protested. True, he was only in Selkest because of Valdira, but now that he knew her, he wouldn't have it any other way.

"Nothing would be settled if I scamper off," Valdira insisted. He felt the prickle of her irritation and released her before she started to wiggle out of his embrace.

Ryamon peered through the fog. The lovers were on the south side of the river, between the bridge and the gap where the road had been. He could just barely see the edge of the trees. The road to Laceto was still visible, though much narrowed. The trees had gone ominously quiet. Valdira wandered a few steps, kicking at tufts of grass.

"Stay close," Ryamon cautioned. "I can protect you from the geysers and hot springs."

Valdira rolled her eyes again. "I know. I remember the plan."

A chorus of eerie howls rang from the forest along the south side of the valley. Eridow. Ryamon glanced at his lover.

Valdira nodded. "They're coming."

They both heard a loud crackle from the area of the river. Anarinda's flare signaled that she understood the warning. The two Collegium magi were hidden somewhere in the mist. Ryamon didn't know exactly where. Like himself and Valdira, they would stay together and guard each other. They had all agreed on this precaution in case Darmosh tried to steal the information from their memories.

Just thinking of the wizard lord made Ryamon's heart pound in his throat. He was paralyzing himself, letting fear control him. He breathed deeply, forcing his chest to expand and break tension's grip. Beside him, Valdira stood still as a tree. Her face was rigid with concentration and her eyes gleamed in the murk. More howling sounded, but from slightly different places. The eridow pack was moving. The Costerans had to be close.

Adrenaline surged in his veins. His Fire wanted to explode outward, to sear and destroy. Ryamon held it close within his heart. It was too soon to strike and the light would give their position away.

Between howls, he heard noises in the forest: ornyxes squawking, the bump and rattle of chariot wheels. There was a distinct crash and a man's yelp of pain. Glancing at Valdira, he saw her wicked smile.

Having experienced the trees' ill-will for himself, Ryamon could imagine the difficulty of squeezing an armed column through the birch grove. Even if they didn't block the trail, they could lift up their roots or drop branches to make a bumpy road. Others, like the dark spruce trees, could hang their graceful boughs at just the height to bother the running ornyxes.

"Well done," Ryamon murmured. Valdira glanced at him, shrugging with malicious modesty, before her gaze turned inward to focus on her Element again.

So far, Valdira's tactics seemed effective. Yet, as Ryamon remembered all too well, they hadn't changed the outcome of the last battle. He picked out the first flicker of movement through the mist. One, then two, and then a fitful stream of chariots emerged from the trees. Some wobbled on damaged wheels.

Others fought to control spooked orynxes. From the jerking of their heads, the birds didn't like the blinding, stinking fog. Ryamon tried not to feel sorry for the charioteers and archers who clung to careening vehicles. These were just soldiers, not the real enemy. Darmosh was the one they had to reckon with.

Holding his position, he watched the confusion grow. Valdira had said there were about fifty chariots, but it was hard to count as they milled around.

"Can you see where Darmosh is?" Ryamon murmured. If they got rid of him, maybe they wouldn't have to hurt anyone else.

She frowned, eyes unfocused. "There's a group of them hanging back under the trees. I'll bet he's there."

"It doesn't sound like him to hide behind commoners," Ryamon observed. Her shoulders twitched in a shrug.

"He probably thinks that's all they're good for, shielding him while he figures out where we are."

"Maybe." Ryamon did recall Darmosh having that cautious manner. The pulse of Fire beat within him, demanding action. "I guess I'll have to lure him out."

He stepped away from Valdira, then slowly let his breath out. The fog around him turned from white to gold as he released his fire. Flames licked his hands and raced up his arms, melting the mist from the air. The charioteers didn't seem to notice at first. They were struggling to get their orynxes into formation. Ryamon decided on a bold attack, something that would be impossible to ignore.

With a sweeping motion, he threw a ball of fire skyward. Flames fluttered as it arced high and then streaked toward the enemy lines. He kept it small until it reached the first row of chariots, then released his power as a wheel of fire in the midst of the disordered army.

Inky smoke mixed with white dust in a cloud that obscured his vision, but he heard the screams of men and birds as fire took them. He searched the gloom, waiting for Darmosh to show himself. Chariots emerged from the smoke, some empty and others veering wildly with the passengers barely hanging on.

Even as he heard the cries of stricken creatures, Ryamon felt the velvet rush of Valdira's power. There was a different kind of explosion as her power swept the already-frightened orynxes into blind hysteria. The cacophony reached an even greater pitch as the terror birds bolted, swerving and kicking.

Drivers and archers were thrown to the ground, where other chariots ran over them.

Again and again Ryamon loosed his fire into the smoke and dust. Flames caressed his entire body, scorched the grass beneath his feet. Elation burned in his veins; it started to not matter that he was hurting people.

It seemed impossible for Darmosh to hear him through the melee. Then again, the man was supposed to be a wizard. Ryamon bellowed, "Darmosh! What kind of coward are you to hide behind serfs? Come out and face me like a wizard!"

A shudder came in the air, then a soft whoosh that somehow dominated the chaos. Dust, smoke and fog whipped aside like a curtain being drawn. Another chariot came out of the forest. A midnight blue pennant flapped on a pole at the front. This ornyx seemed completely under control. The driver rolled a bit farther and turned, stopping where his passenger could look straight across the ashen plain.

Even over the distance, Ryamon could see Darmosh's blood-less face under his dark curls. His voice was rough and terrible.

"Mongrel, I do not fear you. You shall suffer for what you did to my sister."

Without waiting for a reply, he raised both hands and whipped downward. Something massive surged toward Ryamon and Valdira. It was invisible, but the air churned as it came. Ryamon set his feet and sent a column of fire to meet the assault square on.

The two forces met with a throaty crash. Ryamon felt the force and staggered, but called on the Stone beneath him to stand firm. The blast rippled away.

With ringing ears, he realized Darmosh had summoned a cyclonic wind. He had at least partial command of Storm. That was how he projected his voice and moved Anarinda's fog. If Darmosh knew half the things a Storm magus knew, they were in more trouble than they thought.

"Sweetheart," Ryamon said, "can you make his ornyx run?"

"I'm trying, but it's protected."

"Then can you drop a tree on him?"

"No!" Valdira snarled, fierce as any eridow. "I can't tell them to commit suicide for me. I'd be just as bad as Yolie!"

"Sorry!" Ryamon answered, although he clearly remembered a tree falling on him when he was trapped in a bog. He wondered what made this situation different.

"You fools," Darmosh raged. "Bicker if you wish, but I'll suck the life from both of you."

Startled, Ryamon realized their enemy could also hear what they were saying. Darmosh was moving his hands again, bringing forth some new magic.

"Step back," Ryamon warned. Trying to strike first, he called on his fire again. Flames crackled as a wheel of fire roared toward his enemy.

In his chariot, Darmosh made a punching motion. A flare of dull-red energy met Ryamon's wheel of fire, shattering it into a shapeless cloud of cinders. Ryamon felt the impact. Staggering, he realized Darmosh's attack had pierced the fire. For one frozen moment he saw it coming on, crackling like lightning yet straight as a spear. He felt a burst of panic and ducked instinctively.

"Look out!" Valdira cried.

Whatever this magical energy was, Ryamon felt a harsh tingle as it passed over his head. A moment later, every ornyx on the plain dashed in front of Darmosh. Clawed feet and chariot wheels kicked up new layers of dust, hiding them from his sight. While Darmosh berated his army, Ryamon called his flames in and waved Valdira into the cover of the fog.

He felt slightly sick with relief that they were safe, but he also realized he was using too much power, too fast. He had to fight smarter than this.

Before he could plan a new strategy, Valdira ran in front of him. She reached for his shoulder, then jerked back from the flames that still flickered around him.

"Don't be an idiot," she cried. "Stick to the plan!"

"Oh. Right." Ryamon nodded, feeling jittery with adrenaline. He remembered now, they were supposed to be leading the Costerans further into the valley.

Valdira picked up her skirts and ran for the bridge. Ryamon followed, looking over his shoulder every few steps.

Darmosh's voice echoed from the turmoil of his army: "Leave the chariots. Form on foot and follow me. I will not accept failure!"

~ * ~

On the other side of Arkanost, Murcrys asked, *"Are you ready?"*
"Yes."

Phareth reached across the vastness of Arkanost, linking with Murcrys, Gallitaw and two other Initiates of Shadow. Their magics flowed through him, combining to transport the waiting team from the Grand Collegium to Selkest. This time Phareth was the anchor. He shut out weariness and pain to concentrate on the rocky lake shore, water sparkling and reeds whispering in the bright morning sun.

Even with so much help, the effort was like a chain wrapped around Phareth, pulled tight and squeezing him. Just as he thought he would be sliced in two, the tearing came loud as thunder. Ah, blessed relief when it was done! Phareth swayed on his feet. Someone he barely even sensed reached out to steady him.

The little camp on the lake shore was suddenly awash in noise and color. Seven Mage Lords stood among rustic tents and fire pits. Mystical runes glittered on their fine robes, and gemmed staves shone with the light of power. The villagers had been warned but still they crowded back, babbling alarm. Farther off, the ornyxes picked up the general nervousness. Their squawking added a note of urgency to the scene.

"Are we all here?" Murcrys' voice rose above the din. Various others responded, their voices muffled by the commotion.

Phareth leaned on his unknown benefactor. Gallitaw turned toward him, and he felt a quick probe. *"You felt shaky there. Are you all right?"*

"It's been a long week," Phareh replied. In truth, he felt gray and depleted. He'd used a lot of power in the past days and had little sleep. A familiar headache drummed inside his forehead. Even tired as he was, Phareth refused to show weakness in front of them.

"We have sibban *if you want it,"* Gallitaw offered.

"I just need to rest."

"If you're sure." Gallitaw withdrew.

"You weren't kidding that it took a lot out of you," Marton grumbled in his ear. Phareth glanced at him wearily. He was slightly surprised to see the brewer was the one helping him.

"Why would you think I was kidding?" Phareth asked.

Leaning heavily on Marton's shoulder, he felt a shrug. "I never know whether to believe you."

Phareth was too tired to block the man's emotions. Marton bristled with resentment because Phareth had tricked him last night. Used, he no longer trusted. In a way, that stung more than any play for guilt.

"I did what I had to." Phareth shielded himself as best he could while Marton helped him toward the rock shelter.

"Let me pass," a clipped voice demanded. In the corner of his eye, Phareth saw Countess Guilberta push her way through the assembled magi. Fire Lord Akayel and a few others frowned at her peremptory manner.

The royal counselor sported her usual severe black dress and lacquered cane. Gray hair was pinned into an immaculate bun beneath a black straw hat. Blearily, Phareth thought she had knife blades tucked into the satin hat band. A moment later he realized they weren't knives but white feathers.

"Where is the traitor?" Guilberta looked around imperiously.

"This way, I believe." Minaric, the Blood Lord, gestured up the slope toward the rock ledge, where Nepharyl still lay. Silma got up to greet them, leaning heavily on her staff.

Guilberta swept up the hillside, her cane tucked under her arm. To Phareth, it seemed she was preparing to draw the blade hidden inside it.

"If your grace will permit," the Blood Lord said, "I should examine Lord Nepharyl first. The Shadow magi kindly relayed my Initiate's conclusions, but I would like to see for myself."

As he spoke, they passed Marton and Phareth. Minaric caught Phareth's eye and nodded slightly, acknowledging his contribution.

"Very well." Unlike Minaric, Guilberta brushed past the two men as if they weren't there. Phareth felt a moment's indignation as Minaric scurried after, trying to match her pace. He also sensed Marton's scowl at being cut off on the narrow trail.

"Hold on," Phareth murmured. It was obvious there would be no room for them to rest under the ledge with Silma, Minaric and Guilberta all crowding around Nepharyl. Fortunately, the worst of his dizziness had already passed. "I'm all right now. Thanks for your help."

Marton grunted and stood away, watching until he was sure Phareth could stand on his own. Satisfied, the brewer asked, "Who are all these people?"

He jerked a thumb at the assembled magi. For their part, the Mage Lords, who seldom left their comfortable Towers, regarded their rustic surroundings with surprise and a slightly condescending humor.

"The Lords of the Seven Exalted Orders," Phareth explained. "That's the Sea Lord, Chrysen, in blue, and the Ice Lord, Salovik, in white. Blood Lord Minaric just went by us…"

"Never mind," Marton cut in. "I won't remember and they don't look to be chatting with likes of me." He shot a nasty look after Guilberta. "Who's the old lady?"

Phareth chuckled at Marton's blunt designation. "That's the royal liaison. Don't cross her. She can make your life miserable."

"Ha!" Marton actually laughed. "She's years too late for that."

"I suppose so." Phareth turned as he felt a light mental touch. Murcrys separated herself from the other Mage Lords and came toward them. Phareth bowed at her approach.

"Good day, Mother."

"Son." Murcrys seemed completely at ease, although he saw her eyes flick up and down him, taking in the bruises on his face and the dust on his robe. Truthfully, he had been in the hills so long that he hardly noticed any more.

Surprised in turn, Marton drawled, "Mother?"

"Everybody has one," Phareth replied coolly. "This is Shadow Lord Murcrys, my mother."

"And you must be Marton," Murcrys went on, eyeing him now.

"That's right." Marton tried to meet the Shadow Lord's eyes with bluff pride. Murcrys considered him. After a moment, he hastily and awkwardly tried to copy Phareth's bow. Mollified, Murcrys bowed in return.

"Quite a day," she said. Her dark eyes now focused on the rock ledge, where Minaric was telling Guilberta exactly the same things Silma had already told Phareth.

"Is there no chance he will recover his wits?" The countess's hard voice carried down the hill. Phareth wondered if Guilberta expected a different prognosis just because she had come in person.

"Alas, your grace," Minaric replied. "The longer he remains comatose, the smaller his chances. In the Tower of Blood we have masters who specialize in brain healing. He will have the best of care we can give him."

"See to it," Guilberta replied, "but make sure he has no chance to escape. Advise me at once if he comes to his senses."

Minaric bowed, then turned to speak with Silma. Phareth wondered if it would occur to them that a Shadow magus might be able to help. He was about to suggest it when he realized they had other problems. Even without trying, he sensed alarm in Ryamon's mind. That could only mean one thing.

"Mother." Murcrys' gaze flicked to him. "The battle has begun. If the Collegium is to bear witness, you'll need to hurry."

Chapter Twenty-Seven

"Ah, no waiting. I like that." Murcrys gave one of her droll smiles. "We'll go, then. But we really must talk later."

This last was addressed to Marton, who frowned in surprise at being recognized. Before he could reply, Murcrys walked toward the lake shore. Phareth heard her calling the Collegium together.

As Minaric and Guilberta hurried to join them, Murcrys glanced back at Phareth. *"Rest, son. You've done well."*

Phareth bowed, acknowledging her private message.

The Shadow magi spaced themselves around the Mage Lords. Strands of power wove around them, creating cords as tough as leather. Another rending of the sky, and they vanished.

The watching villagers shook themselves as if emerging from a dream. Phareth heard someone mutter, "Ain't that a thing."

To them, he supposed it was—an amazing achievement, yet also frightening. Phareth knew Guilberta was of the same mind. For Valdira and Ryamon's sake, he hoped she would finally decide to trust the Mage Lords.

~ * ~

Milky soil gave way to rock as Ryamon followed Valdira's fleeing form through the dense mist. The river's rushing was barely audible as they crossed the stone span. A distinct brightening of the mist on his left hinted at something white behind it. From the chill blowing down the stream bed, it had to be ice.

The Collegium magi must be nearby. Ryamon wondered what they had planned, but he mostly concentrated on keeping up with Valdira. After feeling a few of Darmosh's blows, he was more than willing to let someone else have a turn.

"Sweetheart?" he called in a low voice.

"Over here."

Valdira waited near one of the marker stones. Ryamon leaned on it, drawing on the strength of Stone to ease his aching lungs. Knowing his fire would make him easier to find, he pulled the flames back into himself. Only his hands glowed with the dull blaze of banked coals. He glanced at Valdira. Her face was tense with concentration.

Nervously, he watched the fog grow thicker. A nearby hot spring bubbled and hissed. Sporadic thuds hinted at the presence of animals nearby. It should have been comforting, except that Ryamon knew Darmosh and his army also lurked in the mist.

"Where are they?" he murmured to himself.

"Can't tell," Valdira whispered back. "The ornyxes are still running and the eridow can't see them."

"Wait, I feel something." Slowly at first, Ryamon sensed the beat of running feet through the earth. "They're coming."

"Just like we planned."

Somewhere in the murk Darmosh cried, "Archers ready!"

Ryamon felt the vibrations more strongly as they started over the bridge. It gave him an idea. He touched Valdira's shoulder lightly, hoping it wouldn't be the last time, and slowly backed into the mist. Ryamon worked his way back to the left so that when he released his fire it could draw eyes away from her.

Working quickly, he raised the stones of the plain, shaping half a dozen pillars much like the markers but roughly human-shaped. He didn't know whether Darmosh would be able to sense his magic, but he had to take the chance. Vibrations of running feet told him they were almost across the bridge.

A static charge snapped in the gloom. Anarinda's signal—but for what? A faint quiver came through the air. Darmosh must have heard it, too.

"Mark!" the wizard lord shouted. There was a kind of ripple in the mist. It split cleanly, exposing everything beneath it to stark daylight.

Ryamon ducked behind one of his pillars, blinking at the sudden change in light. The Costerans stood on the bridge in neat lines. Charioteers, robbed of their vehicles, stood with swords bared and flashing in the sun. Archers were behind them, arrows ready on their bows. Darmosh's chariot was at the back, its pennant waving in the breeze.

To Ryamon's right, behind the troops, something sheer and white blocked the whole riverbed. It looked like a wall of solid ice. More urgently, Valdira stood in plain sight before the army.

"Loose!" Darmosh commanded.

"No!" Ryamon breathed.

As one man, the archers drew and fired He heard the snaps

of bows and hiss of arrows in flight. In the same instant, lightning lanced downward from above the bridge. There was a powerful report and a flash so bright it turned the sunlight pale. Darmosh's chariot exploded. The driver and ornyx spasmed and burned. Suddenly realizing that they were also vulnerable, soldiers started to scream and curse and run.

Terror surged through Ryamon as the gleaming missiles arced toward Valdira. Desperately, he sent a wave of fire to sear them as they flew. He hoped he'd got them all, but an arrow glanced off the pillar he was hiding behind. He ducked for cover.

After a moment, he dared to look out. His heart rose when he saw that the barrage had been scattered. There were too many targets. Some had aimed at Valdira, some at Ryamon, and many had mistakenly targeted the statues Ryamon had made to confuse them.

Meanwhile, lightning struck again and again. Someone—it had to be Anarinda—was walking on air high above the bridge. The proud army dissolved into chaos as some men tried to run back across while others bolted for the open ground ahead of them.

Ryamon couldn't see Darmosh. Had he been killed by the first bolt of lightning? No, they couldn't be that lucky—and they weren't. As Anarinda aimed another blast at the bridge, it suddenly twisted in the air. Supple as a snake, it curled around and roared back at her.

He had no time to watch them battle. Some of the Costerans had escaped the bridge and Valdira was right in front of them. She hesitated, maybe waiting to be sure they saw her. As soon as they stopped to aim their bows, she dashed into the fog, weaving from side to side.

Ryamon let his flames sweep free as he raced to stop the Costerans. Fire blasts struck the soil in front of them, igniting bow strings and tufts of dry grass. The archers yelled and threw their weapons away, but now the charioteers surged to the fore.

A loud pop was almost lost in the tumult. It sounded like something huge breaking. Behind the invaders, shards of ice spun glittering through the air. Then came a foaming roar many times greater than the voice of a geyser. Ryamon glimpsed a figure in white on the near bank. Telamar had split his ice dam to release the water behind it.

Lightning flared between bridge and sky as Darmosh and Anarinda continued their duel, but now a raging flood of ice and water surged toward Darmosh's position. The main Costeran force was still trapped, trying to get off the narrow bridge. Then the freed river swamped it, taking hapless men before the tide.

Though it sickened him, Ryamon knew what he had to do. Calling upon the power of Stone, he wrenched at the central support. A gap opened and the water tore at it. The span crumbled under the onslaught. Anyone left on the bridge was swept into the flood and gone. Ryamon hoped that would include Darmosh.

Then he heard a faint whistling and ducked instinctively. He had been standing still too long. Some of the archers still had their bows, and he was the most obvious target. More arrows whistled behind him as he sprinted into the fog.

"Valdira!" he called. The mist was thinning, since Anarinda was too busy to keep it there. Even so, it was disorienting. He barely felt the heat of a hot spring in time to swerve past it. Then he saw a flicker of movement through the shifting layers of vapor.

"Ryamon!" Valdira ran to meet him. Her face was flushed and shining with sweat, and her eyes blazed with adrenaline.

"The bridge is down," he reported, breathing hard from his sprint. He laughed wryly. "We've got them trapped. Now what do we do with them?"

"What about Darmosh?" Valdira asked, ignoring the jest.

"I couldn't tell."

"Then he's still out there," she said. Ryamon felt a familiar vibration getting closer.

"The rest of them are chasing me," he warned.

"Stay close. I'll make my next move."

Ryamon moved back, keeping enough distance that his fire wouldn't hurt her. Deeper in the mist, animals grumbled and snorted. It took no magic to feel the new tremors that shook the ground. Ryamon saw movement and a group of swordsmen burst from the fog on the other side.

"They're here!" one of the men called.

More soldiers were coming now, swords gleaming in the filtered light. Ryamon let flames wreathe his body, hoping to intimidate them.

Through the roiling wall of fire, he commanded, "Lay down your arms or I'll melt them in your hands!"

The men hesitated, torn between their orders to attack and the knowledge that commoners must never defy a wizard. The first man, who had a large rosette on his hat, gathered his wits.

"Remember what the master said," he cried. "Have at them!"

They started forward, but the rumble of hooves had become a thunder. Bawling animals stampeded from the last wisps of the fog. The two twyerons were in front, huge and gray as boulders running. A herd of sobi followed with horns low, threatening.

The startled soldiers had no chance to escape. Dust rose again, obscuring the sun, as they fell screaming beneath the rush. A few were smart enough to run along with the beasts, but Ryamon knew a man could never keep pace with a running sobus. Sooner or later, they were doomed.

Valdira must have seen the dismay on his face. "What?" she snapped, pale but defiant.

"I didn't say anything."

"Come on. Let's find Darmosh and settle this."

Ryamon followed Valdira, trying not to look at the crushed remains and hear the moans of stricken men. As the last of the sobi thundered past they headed toward the river. A wind keened low over the plains, making Valdira's skirt flap vigorously. It sucked the dust away. Once again they had a clear view.

Anarinda was still aloft, fighting hard. Using streaks of lightning like strangely deformed arms, she lashed at Darmosh on the ground. Somehow the wizard lord had made it to the near shore, where heaps of broken ice remained from Telamar's ice dam. He had to be calling that eerie wind, for the air distorted around him, deflecting Anarinda's strikes.

It seemed like they were winning. Darmosh's army was dead or fleeing, and they would be coming at him three-to-one. Yet something nagged at Ryamon as they ran toward the river.

"Where's Telamar?" he asked.

"I don't see him," Valdira said.

Darmosh must have heard. He turned with a jerk to stare hate across the steaming pools. Anarinda seized the moment to unleash a massive bolt.

The wizard lord seemed to vanish in the flare, but he wasn't gone. The air ripped open behind Ryamon.

"Look out!" he cried.

He spun, but too late. Something hit him between the shoulders. Ryamon screamed as a terrible chill collided with the fire in his veins. Numbness poured down his spine like the icy flood on the river. His cry broke off. His fire puffed out. All feeling gone, he collapsed in an ungainly sprawl.

"Ryamon!" Valdira wailed.

It should have hurt, yet he felt nothing as he landed on trampled ground. There was dirt in his eyes and mouth but he couldn't blink or cough. Ryamon could see and hear, panic and confusion roared in his ears, but he couldn't move his paralyzed limbs or summon his magic.

"Stand where you are!" Darmosh commanded. "Make no move, or your lover pays the price."

Limp arms dangling, Ryamon was hauled up by his hair and yanked around to face Valdira. Her incandescent rage turn to ashen fear.

"That's better," Darmosh said. His voice was thick with triumph. "You know, I'm disappointed. Even for Arkanostian worms, you're fools. Did you think those tricks could stop me?"

"Put him down," Valdira hissed. Her shoulders were tight, hands outstretched as she summoned a power Ryamon could no longer sense. "People aren't toys you can play with."

"I disagree," Darmosh replied. "In my country, we're not afraid to use our power. Magic gives me the right to do as I choose. To rule is my heritage and my destiny. I shall raise up a new generation of wizards who deserve to be feared and obeyed. Only fools would stand in my way."

Ryamon dangled helplessly, forced to listen to Darmosh's hateful creed. Valdira's face showed her contempt.

"You're disgusting." Her voice shook. "I never thought anything could be worse than all the rules in Arkanost. Until I met you."

"Are you any better? Look what you've done." Darmosh laughed, taunting her. From the corner of his eye, Ryamon saw him gesture to the dying and wounded soldiers. "Go ahead and summon your herd. Try to trample me. But know that whatever you do to me will fall first upon your lover."

Unable to blink, Ryamon was forced to watch Valdira's face as Darmosh mocked her. In his mind, he yelled at her not to stand there talking. She should leave him and escape. Call a twyeron. Ride to safety, for her sake and the child's.

When Valdira hesitated, Darmosh laughed again. "You see? You're weak. Don't think I'll make my sister's mistake of trying to keep you alive. I already have an heir."

Everything tipped again as Darmosh stepped forward, dragging Ryamon's legs behind him. There was a snick and something flashed steely bright near his face. A sword! Darmosh advanced slowly, Valdira stepping back before him.

"Stand where you are and I'll make this quick." The calm of Darmosh's voice made the menace all the more deadly.

Valdira drew herself up, straight and proud. In a trembling voice, she said, "Fine."

Ryamon screamed denials in his mind as Darmosh stalked closer. She couldn't just stand there and let herself be stabbed. She had to fight for her life!

Darmosh raised his sword, but a new cry intruded: DON'T TURN YOUR BACK ON ME!"

It was Anarinda, her voice magnified by her Element. She sounded high above them. A wind was shouting, too. She must have brought a tornado with her.

"From what Nepharyl told us, you're the softest one of all," Darmosh retorted, goading her. There was no way Ryamon could warn her not to play into his hands.

"I'LL SHOW YOU HOW SOFT I AM!" Anarinda cried. Ryamon heard the ozone crack of lightning.

Helpless, he spun, lifted high, to glimpse a yellow-clad figure framed by sun and sky. Her lightning caught him full in the chest. Still he felt nothing, but the world went white and black and fiery crimson. Through the roar he heard Anarinda's cry of dismay and Valdira's anguished scream.

Everything faded. Ryamon wondered if he was dying. Faintly, he heard Darmosh's scornful remark, "Oh dear. Be careful what you aim at."

Then a jerk. Ryamon was tumbling, falling. He landed on something lumpy and bloody. Through singing ears he heard more yelling, but now it sounded like Darmosh.

Ryamon's slack body rolled to a stop facing backward, so he saw Valdira grappling with the wizard lord. She clung to his back, both arms wrapped around his shoulders. A reddish mist stained the air around them.

Blood! Ryamon recognized it when Darmosh spun around,

trying to knock her loose. Blood seeped through his fine jacket. The skin on his hands split under Valdira's touch, vessels ruptured, bones shattered. Blood magic tore at her enemy like a wild beast intent on killing instead of healing. In the silence of his mind, Ryamon urged her on.

She groped for Darmosh's neck, but he finally shook her off. Valdira stumbled backward and gathered herself to spring again, but Darmosh was faster. He stepped forward, thrusting with his sword. Valdira side-stepped, too slow. The blade bit deep into her side. With a raw shriek she staggered back. Trapped in his useless body, Ryamon howled his despair.

Darmosh reeled, too, his face a mask of blood. Lightning rained around him as Anarinda rejoined the fray. Half crouched, the wizard lord seemed to summon all his strength. The sky tore and he was gone.

"NO!" Anarinda shrieked with cheated rage. The wind died suddenly and she landed at a run, heading for Valdira.

Ryamon watched, unable to turn away, as his lover stumbled to her knees. Crimson sheeted down her dress, adding to Darmosh's blood which coated her arms to the elbow. Coughing and moaning, she bent over her injury like any wounded beast.

"Don't try to move," Anarinda said, shrill with fear.

Darmosh's hateful voice rang from somewhere across the river. "YOU HAVEN'T WON. I'LL BE BACK TO KILL YOU ALL FOR WHAT YOU'VE DONE!"

Anarinda's pretty face was truly terrible to see. Sparks crackled in her golden hair.

"He's transported across the river," she said. "Don't worry, I can catch him."

The wind keened again as she gathered herself, but Valdira spoke first. "No." Anarinda looked back, hesitating. Valdira smiled with ghastly humor. "He's covered with blood and surrounded by predators. I hardly have to tell them what to do."

Even as she spoke, Ryamon heard the screech of ornyxes and snarling of eridow. He was facing the wrong way to see, but it didn't sound like Darmosh got the chance to teleport again.

"Oh." Anarinda looked disappointed. The sparks cracked away from her hair.

Valdira sagged, curling around her pain. No, no, no, Ryamon begged in his mind. It couldn't end this way. They had won.

Valdira couldn't die!

~ * ~

"I thought I told you to rest," Silma said severely.

"I'm only listening," Phareth murmured, half in trance.

With a doubtful frown, Silma leaned across the campfire and offered Phareth a steaming cup.

Marton batted her away. "Let him be. I want to know what's happening."

Silma flinched and jerked back. It was clear in her mind that she didn't trust Marton after so many years of fearing his violence. Emerging fully from his trance, Phareth reached for the cup.

"Don't, I want that," he said. Marton sat back, grumbling.

They were the only magi in camp again, at least until the Collegium returned, so they had a bit of privacy by the rock ledge. The villagers clustered around their own main fire, muttering nervously about what was going on. Phareth had been monitoring the distant battle. Even tired as he was, he refused to miss out on the action. Especially since Darmosh was involved.

Marton watched irritably as Phareth savored the warmth of tea mixed with *sibban*. "Well?" he finally demanded.

"It's all right," Phareth replied, though he could hardly believe it himself. "They're alive."

"Are they winning?" Marton pressed.

"Yes, but it wasn't easy." Phareth was too tired to mince words. "Telamar and Ryamon are both paralyzed and Valdira's been stabbed. Calm down," he said as worry flooded Marton's mind.

"She's a Blood magus," Silma reminded them. "If she wasn't killed outright, she can heal herself and the others."

"Maybe." But Marton still projected a stinging blend of anger, alarm, even guilt.

Phareth tried to shield himself but he was still so tired, and another reality was sinking in. He gulped his tea, but it couldn't dissolve the lump growing in his throat.

"Darmosh," he whispered.

"He got away?" Marton looked around as if he wanted to grab his axe and confront Darmosh himself.

"No, he's dead." Phareth's hand trembled. He barely felt the sting as hot tea slopped onto his hand.

Silma quickly took the mug. Phareth's eyes prickled, and

everything blurred. He was weeping and couldn't stop. He drew his knees up and pressed his forehead to black fabric, trying to compose himself.

Gently Silma asked, "Isn't that good news?"

"It's very good news," he mumbled through a stuffy nose.

"Then what's the matter?" Marton demanded.

Phareth didn't even try to answer. How could he explain what it meant that Darmosh was gone? For so many months, he had lived with shame, grief, guilt. Fear always in the back of his mind, chaining his spirit and hobbling his power.

He knew the strike Darmosh had used on Ryamon and Telamar. It was the same he had done to Kylethia. Paralyzed her and then dumped her in Logoll harbor to drown. Grief welled up once more, but it would pass. Even though Phareth hadn't struck the blow, he had done his part to bring Kylethia's killer down.

Finally, Darmosh was dead and Phareth was free.

~ * ~

Seeing Valdira swoon, Anarinda whipped around.

"Is it bad? What can I do?" Her voice went high with fear and Ryamon saw her swallow convulsively at the sight of so much blood.

"Don't worry about me," Valdira said, her voice thin with pain. "I was a Blood magus. I can heal this." Her shoulders shook with a sob, giving the lie to her bold words. "But oh, does it hurt."

Once again Ryamon saw the reddish glow where her hands pressed to her side. Relief trickled through him. Yes, she was healing herself.

"All right," Anarinda said, doubtful. She bent over Ryamon. "Can you hear me?"

Paralyzed, Ryamon was unable to respond. She turned him on his back, waved her hand in front of his eyes, and finally pressed a finger under his chin.

"How is he?" Valdira asked.

"He's breathing and his heart is beating, but I can't tell if he's aware," Anarinda called to Valdira. "It's the same with Telamar. What did he do to them?"

"It's nerve damage." Valdira still sounded strained. "Give me a minute, will you?"

"I'm sorry," Anarinda replied, abashed.

Of course, Ryamon had no choice but to wait. It was as bad as being in Yolie's time trap. Frustration at being paralyzed warred with his concern for Valdira. Since Anarinda had moved him, he couldn't see her.

"I'll go get Telamar," Anarinda decided. "He's helpless right now, and—"

Valdira interrupted, "Men are always helpless."

Ryamon added indignation to his feelings of frustration and worry. Bad enough to be humiliated by their enemy, stripped of his magic and dragged around by his hair, but now his lover insulted him!

Anarinda gave a ragged laugh. "I'll be back soon. We should stay together until we're sure the rest of them are gone."

She stepped back. With a whisper of wind, gentler this time, she lifted off. Ryamon lay silently fretting, but he soon heard the shuffle of feet over coarse dirt. They sounded unsteady. Concern leapt to the fore once again.

It got even stronger as Valdira crossed in front of him. The wound was worse than he had thought. The front of her green dress was all but black with blood, and half-dried gore streaked her arms.

"I've stopped the bleeding. That'll do for now," Valdira remarked conversationally. She settled behind Ryamon, lifted his head and scooted forward until his head rested between her crossed knees. "Just promise you won't burn me when your Element returns."

As if he ever would!

Valdira bent over. Her hair hung around them like a screen. Ryamon guessed she was trying to prevent Anarinda from using her air element to eavesdrop.

"I know you can hear me," Valdira murmured stealthily. "I can sense your emotions, but you probably can't feel mine."

Ryamon was ridiculously relieved to know their mental bond, troublesome as it sometimes was, still held.

"That was a nasty attack he used," Valdira went on. "I can mend it, and Telamar, too, but I'm not sure what happens after that. I'd love to think this is over, that we've won and we can just rest and congratulate each other. Problem is, I don't think it is over."

She meant the Collegium. They were far away in Polvest, but

their pride and rigid traditions threatened everything he and Valdira had fought for. Ryamon wished he could move so he could face them instead of lying here like a broken toy.

As if to punish his impatience, a streak of pain sliced down his back. It hurt like madness, and Ryamon was helpless to avoid it.

"Sorry," Valdira murmured. "Healing your knee was simple compared to this. Just be patient."

Ryamon tried to focus his thoughts, distracting himself from the burning sensation. If the battle was truly over, the next step would be a hearing before the Collegium. A fair one, this time. Phareth had promised them.

Although, looking back over the confusion of the day, Ryamon found he could no longer recall what deal he actually had made with the Shadow magus.

"You and Telamar are both paralyzed and I've been stabbed, all to keep Arkanost free," Valdira said quietly. "They'd better be good to us."

Ryamon hoped the Mage Lords would appreciate their sacrifices. All he could remember from his last visit to the Collegium was a row of sallow faces in the dark. It was hard to feel much hope. Valdira might have sensed his thoughts, for she leaned forward, embracing him upside-down.

"No matter what happens, I want you to know—" she paused, voice trembling, then blurted, "I love you. I'm glad for everything we did together. If you still want to marry me, I will. Our baby should have a father. A better one than I had," she finished bitterly.

Hearing these words brought a kind of healing sweeter than any physical remedy. Marshalling his will, Ryamon tried to think how happy he was, how much he wanted her and always would. The Collegium would have to kill him before he let anyone separate them. Valdira kissed his forehead. He wished he could feel it.

He heard a faint whistle of wind. Anarinda must be back with Telamar. But why had Valdira gone tense? A stranger spoke. It was a woman's voice, warm and sly.

"There's no need for all the drama," she said.

Chapter Twenty-Eight

"Who are you?" Valdira cried, startled into fierceness. Ryamon's head bobbed as she tried to jump up. She stopped with a groan, her hand clasped to her injured side.

"My child, don't do that," came a low, gentle voice. A man. "You are wounded. Stay as you are."

"We're here to help," another man said in a reassuring tone.

"Actually, he wouldn't leave until he was sure Anarinda's all right." It was the woman again, drolly humorous.

"I thought I was being helpful by bringing you down here," the second man answered.

"Don't come any closer!" Valdira warned.

Apparently the newcomers weren't listening. Ryamon lay helpless, listening frantically as clothing rustled and footsteps scuffed the ground. Those voices sounded familiar. If only he could see! But his view remained unchanged—chalky soil, trampled bodies, the ruined bridge farther back. Anarinda gliding toward the rubble of the ice dam. Across the river, a moil of eridow, ornyxes and broken chariots.

"Who are you?" Valdira repeated, but she suddenly sounded unsure of herself.

"Take a wild guess," the woman answered.

Finally, two men and a woman walked in front of Valdira. They all wore magus' robes, heavily decorated on the front. The men wore scarlet and yellow respectively. The woman's was black as night. Each carried a staff lacquered in matching colors, with crystal knobs shining in the sun. If he'd been able to feel his heartbeat, he would have felt it stop cold.

"Lord Minaric." Valdira spoke tightly.

"Oh, good. You do know your own mage lord," the woman said with a mocking sting.

"Murcrys, stop." The yellow-robed man with broad shoulders had to be the Storm Lord. Ryamon groped for names. Klaive, that was it, and Murcrys was the Shadow Lord.

Ignoring the banter of the other magi, Blood Lord Minaric knelt beside Valdira and Ryamon. Above his crimson robe, a copper circlet held back waves of silver hair. He was older than Ryamon remembered, but his voice and expression were gentle.

"We really have come to help. Heal yourself, my child, and I shall tend to the young man."

Ryamon couldn't see Valdira's face, but he could imagine her defiant expression.

"How did you get here so fast?" she demanded.

"Oh, we were watching the whole thing." Murcrys waved casually to some point behind them which, of course, Ryamon couldn't see. "There's an overlook on the valley rim. Anarinda found it for us."

"I thought she was scouting the terrain," Valdira said through her teeth.

"She did that, too," Klaive replied amiably. "However, some of the Collegium feared that four magi wouldn't be able to hold off an army, particularly as two lack formal training. It seemed prudent to be here just in case."

If that was all they wanted, any group of initiates could have done the job, Ryamon thought. Valdira retorted, "You just wanted to be sure we don't escape."

"Well, look at your record," Murcrys answered.

"We do need you to come with us," Klaive added, "but we're asking very nicely."

"Hmph." Valdira snorted.

"If I may suggest." Minaric spoke to his fellow mage lords with an unexpected note of command. "We have two injured and another coming. Can this discussion wait?"

"You're right, of course." Murcrys awarded him a small bow.

Minaric reached over to pat Valdira's shoulder. "Healing first, my child. Your questions will be answered soon enough."

Ryamon, lying paralyzed and helpless, couldn't help agreeing with him. Whatever lay ahead, he wanted to face it on his own two feet.

~ * ~

The villagers jumped, startled by the noise as the sky ripped and the Collegium was back. Phareth swayed with weariness after anchoring their return. Silma rested her hands on his back and he felt his fatigue lift.

"Thank you," Phareth murmured. He had already relayed the

results of the battle, but he still sensed concern in her touch. "Valdira's fine," he assured her.

"I have to see for myself," Silma replied.

A babble broke out as the party of magi came up from the lake shore. The villagers hastily got out of their way. Countess Guilberta's voice cut through the noise.

"My lords with me, if you please."

This announcement was met with a rumble of complaint. Phareth picked out Chrysen's voice saying, "I wouldn't mind having something to eat first" and Salovik's cool question, "Will we have no time to consider what we've seen?"

"Can we eat and talk at the same time?" Senorith reasoned.

"If you must," Guilberta sighed.

The villagers backed away and the magi took over their seats without a word. For a moment, Phareth wondered if they were really so different from the despised Costerans. When the villagers offered to share their food, the mighty mage lords looked upon the simple fare with surprise and confusion. It might do them good to eat like serfs, Phareth thought.

"I think we're going to need more tea," he remarked. Then he smiled when he realized he stood alone. Silma was working her way down to the lake shore as quickly as she could over the rough ground. Ahead of her were four figures Phareth knew well.

They were a tattered band. Anarinda supported Telamar, whose face was almost as white as his robe. Ryamon, too, looked ill in his lavender suit. Valdira's pale green dress was coated with blood from the chest down. Even though Silma had been warned of the injury, her mind radiated shock at the sight.

"My child!" She rushed to embrace her runaway novice. "Thank goodness you're safe."

Valdira returned the embrace with one arm. The other arm was tucked through Ryamon's.

"I'm sorry." From her shaky tone, she knew how inadequate the words were.

"It can't be helped." Silma neither approved nor condemned. To Ryamon she added, "I see you found her."

"Yes." Despite his weakness, Ryamon regarded his lover with a lingering gaze like an embrace on its own.

"I found him," Valdira retorted.

"You don't always have to be right, child." But Silma chucked as she said it.

Watching, Phareth felt a pang of self-pity. He and Kylethia had shared such closeness, once upon a time. He was distracted when Marton came limping through the press. The brewer halted suddenly, hands closing into fists. He might have been wondering who Ryamon was, or maybe the sight of Valdira's injury shocked him. Phareth shielded his mind so he wouldn't have to know.

Silma didn't see Marton. "Come," she told Valdira, "we must get you something clean to wear. That blood's going to dry stiff, and no one will like the smell."

"I don't have anything else," Valdira said. "We left it behind when we ran from Yolie."

"Maybe something of mine will do," Silma replied.

Voices faded as Silma led them up toward the rock ledge. Marton watched them a little farther. Phareth wondered if he was going to leave it at that. After a moment, the man shook himself. Slowly, uncertainly, he hobbled away.

That left two others at the lake shore. Phareth went to join them. Anarinda was trying to help Telamar toward camp, but they had come to a halt.

"It isn't my neck, it's my ankle," Telamar said, terse with pain.

"If it still hurts, you should have told Lord Minaric," Anarinda said.

"Can I help?" Phareth asked, moving to Telamar's other side.

"Yes, please," Anarinda said, exasperated. Telamar's cool eyes flicked over him, searching for some sign of mockery. Seeing none, he nodded.

Phareth took his place on the opposite side from Anarinda. They started up toward the ledge, Telamar shuffling slowly with his right foot bent up behind him.

"He fell on it when Darmosh paralyzed him," Anarinda explained.

"Quite a battle," Phareth remarked.

"He was tough," Anarinda said, agitated by the memory. "He knew everything I did and a few more tricks."

The Ice magus shuddered. "That was horrible! I never understood why you were so afraid of him."

A few days ago, Phareth would have issued some retort and denied the slight to his courage. Now he simply nodded.

"It was his signature attack. I escaped before he used it on me, but he killed my partner in Logoll."

"We remember," Anarinda said softly.

"I can believe it," Telamar added.

Phareth nodded, accepting the implicit apology. He offered one of his own. "This time the whole team came back alive. I'm grateful for everything."

"We did what we came for," Anarinda demurred.

"Our assignment was to bring Valdira and Ryamon to the Collegium," Telamar objected.

"We brought the Collegium to them," Phareth quipped. "Doesn't that count?"

To his surprise, Telamar chuckled softly. Through their touch, Phareth sensed the three of them were actually in agreement. That was possibly the biggest victory of all.

~ * ~

Ryamon watched absently as Silma rummaged in her tent. He had never appreciated the simple acts of standing on his own and moving when he wanted to. Yet part of his mind was still jumpy, ready for battle. He couldn't believe they were surrounded by magi and no one was attacking them. He glanced around warily when Valdira touched his hand. She silently pointed to the rock ledge.

A familiar figure lay on pine branches where their bed used to be. Nepharyl's face had a waxy pallor under a haze of unshaven whiskers. He breathed only fitfully.

"So that's where he got to," Valdira said.

"What's wrong with him?" Ryamon spoke softly, lest he disturb the sleeping man.

Valdira shrugged. He felt her thought: *"We have our own problems."*

At that moment, Silma emerged from her tent. "I have a clean shift, but I'm afraid I only have my own robes."

"It will have to do," Valdira said. He sensed her reluctance to take on the colors of an order she had no intention of rejoining.

"Lord Minaric will understand," Silma said. "That dress is simply unfit to wear."

"I'll be glad to get rid of the dress," Valdira said, "but I don't want to wear a robe, either. Everything is just a way to label me."

"As if that would work." Both women jumped at this new voice. Ryamon whipped around, fire leaping to his left hand.

"What do you want?" Valdira demanded in a hard tone.

The man looked like one of the villagers. He wore a simple suit of brown wool, a faded plaid shirt and worn work boots. His crudely trimmed hair was the same color as Valdira's and they both had the same tense expression. Guessing who this must be, Ryamon let his flame die.

"Your mother sent a package along," Marton answered. "I'm not sure how she knew you were going to get stabbed."

He grinned at the weak joke. Ryamon could tell he wasn't used to laughing or smiling. However, he did have a small canvas bag tucked under his arm.

"Rhella is smarter than people think," Silma said tartly.

"I can admit that." Marton seemed a bit relieved to talk to the Blood Magus instead of his daughter. "We've had some troubles…" Valdira bristled and he quickly added, "…Troubles that were my fault. When I get home we'll have some things to talk through."

Valdira folded her arms, glaring at him. "If Mam sent it, I guess I'll take it. Only because I need it."

Flushing a little, Marton offered the package. She snatched it away from him. He jerked back, and it occurred to Ryamon that he might actually be afraid of her. Then Marton's face darkened and his legs bent in a crouch. He, too, was ready for battle.

Valdira faced him defiantly. At the edge of camp, the ornyxes started screeching and pulling at their picket line. All the tales Ryamon had heard of Marton's brutality flashed through his mind. Without thinking, he stepped up to Valdira's side.

"Let me handle this," she said, a feral gleam in her eyes.

"Nobody threatens you while I'm around," Ryamon replied. He laid an arm over her shoulder.

Marton jumped again. His savage regard was focused on Ryamon. They locked eyes, no word spoken. Ryamon flushed, the fire in his heart poised to bring his enemy down. He'd already fought a wizard lord and survived. He could face his future father-in-law, too.

But Marton caved suddenly, the light of anger dying from his face. Perhaps he realized how his own actions had cut him out of her daughter's life. Shoulders slumped, he turned away.

"I have a lot to set right," he repeated in a strangled tone. And he limped away.

"Don't talk to me until you've said sorry to Mam!" Valdira yelled after him.

Marton didn't respond. Farther down the slope, the villagers scattered out of his way. Ryamon felt faintly embarrassed that everyone had seen the confrontation.

"Thank goodness," Silma murmured. Looking to Ryamon, she added, "That was brave of you."

But Valdira whirled, shaking loose of Ryamon's arm. "What did you think you were doing?"

"Backing you up," Ryamon said. "I know there's a history to this, but do we want another war right now?"

He jerked his chin toward the campfire, where the Mage Lords had been eating and talking loudly. Until a moment ago, when they all stopped to stare at the tantrum going on among the ornyxes. Villagers hurried toward the agitated birds, while Shadow Lord Murcrys stared at Valdira.

"History?" she snapped. "You don't know anything about it."

"Maybe not," Ryamon said, "but I know I love you and I don't want the past to poison our future."

Valdira's set face trembled. "Don't you make me cry," she warned.

"I hope I never will," he answered softly. "Now can you do something about those ornyxes? We don't want the Collegium to think you can't control your powers."

~ * ~

The council meeting dragged on into the afternoon. Valdira and Ryamon both tried to eat, but food sat sour in their stomachs. In the end, they waited near the rock ledge. The other initiates had been called down to testify, so they sat alone. Ryamon had no doubt they were being watched all the same. He stared at the shallow hearth, feeling the drowsy murmur of the glittering coals there. To have this bond with Fire was a prize he had sought all his life. He hoped he wouldn't have to pay too dearly for the privilege.

Valdira touched his arm. Ryamon turned with a jerk. Silma approached from the direction of the main hearth.

"Are they ready?" Valdira asked. Her mentor nodded.

They both stood up. Valdira was back in peasant attire, a brown dress with wooden buttons up the front and a plaid scarf over her hair. She wasn't pretty, not the way Anarinda was, yet Ryamon swallowed a lump in his throat at her fierce beauty. No matter what else happened, this was the Valdira he always wanted to remember.

Ryamon brushed dust from his trousers and glanced at Silma, trying to read their future in her face. The Blood magus was serene. As they followed her down the hill, Ryamon reached for Valdira's hand.

"We'll face this together," he murmured.

"If they let us," her thought came back bristling with anxiety. He squeezed her hand and then let go.

The Collegium was seated in a rough half-circle around the fire ring. Junior magi stood behind their Mage Lords, since there weren't enough rocks and stumps for all of them. At the center, Guilberta sat still as a heron waiting for a frog to jump. The villagers from Lornest clustered to one side.

In many ways, the situation was precisely the opposite of Ryamon's previous encounter with the Collegium. It had been dark then. This day was sunny, the afternoon heat making everyone sweat. No cushions and lecterns here; the mage lords sat on makeshift chairs, no two the same size or height. An audience of peasants in work clothes replaced the well-dressed nobles of Polvest. A few bird calls broke the silence. Most of all, the stuffy atmosphere gave way to crackling interest as Ryamon and Valdira stood facing the assembly.

"Who shall begin?" Guilberta's commanding voice turned thin in the open air.

"Easiest first, I'd say," Chrysen replied. Murmurs of agreement swept the circle.

Ryamon felt Valdira tense beside him. "Just a minute!" she called out. The startled Mage Lords looked at her.

"Sweetheart?" Ryamon asked.

"We're getting married," Valdira announced. "Anything else has to account for that."

She threaded her arm though Ryamon's and glared at them, daring anyone to argue. He quickly put his arm around her waist. Despite the circumstances, joy flooded him. Deep in his heart, he had feared Valdira would change her mind.

The villagers rumbled among themselves, apparently most interested in Marton's reaction. The brewer stared at his boots.

Fortunately, most of the Mage Lords seemed amused.

"Was that supposed to surprise us?" Murcrys asked with mock sweetness.

"Granted," Guilberta snapped, retaking control of the situation. "Senorith should have the floor, I believe."

The Stone Lord rose, the sleeves of his gray robe flapping as the wind gusted. Nearby, Klaive raised a hand. The breeze fell away.

"Several months ago," Senorith began, "Ryamon requested to be released from the Order of Stone. I agreed to his request then and do so still. Is my brother the Fire Lord now willing to accept this novice?"

Akayel stood, thin and angular in his orange robe. "What I saw today has convinced me Ryamon's calling is true. He will be welcome into the Order of Fire."

Ryamon's heart leaped. This was what he had always wanted —at least, until he met Valdira. It was hard to believe he might get them both. He bowed.

"Thank you, my lord."

Akayel turned pale blue eyes on him. "You have good instincts, but you need a lot of training. Under the circumstances, I'm willing to be flexible about the timing."

"Yes, my lord." Ryamon couldn't help grinning.

Akayel sat back down and Senorith continued.

"I understand you have learned to command Stone after all. It is against our traditions for any magus to bring the Mysteries of one order into another. Before you can enter the Order of Fire, your connection to Stone must be severed. My sister?"

Murcrys now rose. "I or one of my initiates will place a block on Ryamon's connection with Stone. Also," she favored him and Valdira with a stern gaze, "it's natural for lovers to have a close bond, but please don't expand your Shadow skills any farther."

Ryamon's joy deflated at her words. An image seared his mind, Valdira falling as if dead after Phareth blocked her magic. Everything in his being rebelled against this demand, but looking around the circle, he saw no mercy.

"Why do you have to do that?" Valdira protested. "What he's done isn't good enough? You can't trust him?"

"This is written in the strictures of every order," Guilberta replied severely. "The law must be upheld."

"But we've seen that a magus can command more than one Element," Valdira argued. "It does us no harm. Look at Darmosh. He had Storm, Blood, Shadow, and who knows what else!"

"Exactly," Salovik answered coldly. "Look at Darmosh and the evil he did."

"That is the reason we have only one Element," Minaric said. "We are human, fallible. No one can be trusted with so much power."

Valdira opened her mouth to argue, but Sea Lord Chrysen cut her off. "Listen to me. Of course it's possible to blend Elements. Ice and Sea, for example, work very well together. It isn't that we can't combine elements. We choose not to. We accept these restrictions voluntarily."

"Why—to make other people feel better?" Valdira swept a scathing glance at the onlookers. The villagers shifted nervously and Guilberta's face took on stern lines.

"That puts it rather crudely," Senorith murmured.

"It's the truth." Valdira pulled away from Ryamon and stepped forward. Her voice rose passionately. "Magic is huge and wild. It isn't something we can cut up and put in little boxes, fire over here and stone over here. It's wrong to make magic smaller than it is."

"Much of what you say is true," Klaive answered, "but I would not say we reduce ourselves to make people feel better. Rather, we accept these limits out of respect for their feelings, because everyone deserves to live without fear."

"After seeing Costeran life, you must admit that those who cannot defend themselves have reason to worry," Minaric said.

"Enough!" Guilberta called out. For a moment, even the singing birds went quiet. She turned a steely gaze on Valdira. "You will hear our verdict in your turn." To Ryamon, she said, "Those are the terms. Do you accept?"

"It won't hurt," Murcrys added with a touch of compassion.

Valdira snorted, but Ryamon laid a hand on her shoulder.

"It's all right." Fear tasted like ashes in his mouth, yet he couldn't deny the Collegium's logic. "Yes, I accept."

"Good," Guilberta bit out.

"Then I am satisfied," Senorith said. "We can make specific arrangements after we've finished."

He sat, the only person who appeared truly comfortable seated on a rock.

"Blood Lord?" Guilberta called, and the old man in crimson stood up.

"As to Valdira," he began, but a harsh voice interrupted.

"Just a minute," Marton limped toward the center of the circle. "I have something to say."

"This isn't a public hearing," Guilberta scolded.

"He's her father," one of the villagers said, a man Ryamon didn't know. "He should speak for his own."

"Beh," Valdira grumbled at the suggestion Marton had power over her.

"What can it hurt?" Klaive reasoned.

"Oh, very well," Guilberta said, clearly exasperated.

Marton hobbled to the fireside. Nervousness was etched on his face.

"All of you sitting there—" he waved a hand to take in the Collegium—" in your fine robes and living in your fine towers, don't forget that your rules aren't just in those little books. They shape our lives. Twist them, sometimes.

"I followed those rules all my life." Marton's hands clenched into fists he probably wasn't even aware of. "Even though it meant hiding who I was from my kin and friends. Hating myself for a curse that shouldn't exist. It about killed me, living like that.

"Now this is my girl." He pointed at Valdira, who skipped back a step. Ryamon saw some of the Mage Lords raise their brows at this reflex. "She has the same curse, but she took what she got instead of running from it. She's braver than me, way braver."

Marton shook his head, perhaps reliving some terrible memory. After a deep breath he choked on, the words torn from deep in his soul.

"Well, you're not to punish her for that. You've got to learn, the way I should have. Make her a place where she can be herself and be safe."

A pause followed as everyone waited to see if he was through talking. Ryamon saw sympathy on the faces of the Collegium, but Valdira wouldn't look at her father.

"That's all I wanted to say," Marton mumbled.

"Thank you," Guilberta said briskly, but another of the villagers was already stepping forward.

"Your grace, I want to speak." He removed a battered straw

hat from a nearly bald head and clutched it nervously before him.

Guilberta sighed, but waved him to continue.

"This Marton, he was my friend upon a time. Until that darkness ate him from the inside and he kicked away everyone close to him. You must do right by them."

He bobbed a nervous bow and stepped back, clearly relieved to be finished, but another man was hard on his heals. The Mage Lords stirred, restless.

"Really!" Guilberta exclaimed. "This must be the last testimonial."

"Your grace, our mayor ain't here, but I know what he would say. The family's brought trouble to the village, I have to say."

Ryamon felt Valdira go rigid beside him. If her eyes had been knives, the fellow's skin would have been peeling away from his bones.

"But these are our own. If this can settled in a way that brings peace, we'll be content." He glanced around at the villagers, who nodded and murmured support. "And may I also say, your grace, that having those raiders come so close, we wouldn't mind a bit of protection. So if you please, tell the king he shouldn't forget about us because we're far away."

Ryamon watched Valdira's face as her neighbors stood up for her and Marton—even the ones who didn't like him. Old anger battled new understanding of the burden her father labored under. It wasn't much, but it was a start.

"Thank you, good people of Lornest." Guilberta spoke in a softer tone now. "His majesty King Sedlin values every subject. His charge to me is to guard you against magical dangers. I shall do so. Now, if you will kindly allow the Blood Lord to speak."

"Your grace," Blood Lord Minaric stood. "The Collegium also hears the words of our people, and now it is we who must call upon the crown and populace to respect our needs. This crisis reminds us that we must be flexible when we face challenges from outside our realm. That knowledge has guided our decisions."

Minaric waited a moment, but no one interrupted. Turning to Valdira, he said, "Although you swore to my order, it is clear your talents lie elsewhere. However, it is the decision of the Collegium that I shall not release you from your oath to Blood."

Valdira glared at him. Ryamon slipped his arm around her shoulder.

"Instead," Minaric went on, "you will have special status with the following conditions…"

"Are you going to block my power?" Valdira burst out.

"On the contrary," the Blood Lord replied. "We wish to learn from you. The Collegium directs you to continue exploring your unique abilities. Your ties to Blood will not be altered lest it interfere with this process."

Relief washed over Ryamon. He tightened his grip, hugging Valdira lightly. Valdira wouldn't be imprisoned or robbed of her powers! She smiled up at him, but only briefly.

"These are the conditions," Minaric said. "First, you will cooperate with the existing orders to test your gift and find its limits. Second, you will develop a program of training for others like you."

Valdira frowned, as if she thought she hadn't heard right. Ryamon noticed that not all of the Mage Lords looked happy, either.

"Shadow Lord Murcrys has offered the services of her order to search the kingdom for those with similar abilities," Minaric said. "If there are but a few, you will be classified as a specialty within one of the existing orders. If there are many, a new order will be created so that you and yours can serve the kingdom within the limits of the law."

Ryamon felt shock run down his spine. Valdira might be a Mage Lord herself one day!

"In all cases, your must act within the Strictures," Minaric stressed. "To assure this, your efforts will be supervised by myself and Shadow Lord Murcrys. Your progress must be reported to the Collegium and to Lady Guilberta."

It sounded fantastic. Too good to be true, really. But something else damped down Ryamon's relief and joy. He cleared his throat. Minaric looked to him expectantly.

"Will we have to go to Polvest?" Remembering life in the crowded capital, Ryamon doubted Valdira would like it there. The old man seemed to consider.

"It might be better to remain here. Initiate Phareth reports Valdira's power is based at least in part on her connection with this land. Moving might disrupt it. Also, as I understand, the village of Lornest is quiet and private. You would be able to pursue your studies without interruption."

In other words, Costera and other enemies would have a hard time figuring out what Valdira was working on.

"If you stay out here," Murcrys inserted, "you can keep an eye on the southern border, as your neighbors have so reasonably requested."

Smiling widely, Ryamon clasped Valdira against his side. *"This is wonderful,"* he thought to her. *"A lot of responsibility, to be sure, but…"*

"It can't be this easy," her suspicious thought came back to him.

Another thought intruded, quick as a moth in the dark. *"I thought I asked you not to use Shadow magic."*

They both started, eyes flashing across the fire circle where Murcrys sat among the Collegium.

"It's true that you've been bold, Valdira. You had to be. But you've also been childish, and that must end. Some of us have extended ourselves on your behalf. Work with us, please."

Her presence withdrew, and Ryamon was aware of Lord Minaric asking, "Do you have any other questions?"

Valdira stared at him, gathering her thoughts. She blurted, "Is this some kind of trick?"

"No," Klaive answered patiently.

"After everything that's happened," Valdira said. "Hiding myself and living with guilt and being chased all over the countryside…"

"Don't insult them," Ryamon silently pleaded.

"Oh, take their side!"

"The Collegium does not play games," Akayel replied.

Even Guilberta smiled with wintry humor. "Dear girl, we came a long way to see you. What would be the point of trickery? Arkanost benefits far more from your cooperation."

"We've offered a generous compromise," Salovik added, and it clearly irked him. "Are you going to refuse?"

Valdira looked around at the mage lords and her neighbors. Ryamon felt a tug-of-war between her habitual defiance and the relief of acceptance. He tried to quiet his thoughts. Valdira had to make this decision on her own.

"I guess not," she finally said.

"Excellent," Guilberta said. "I look forward to hearing of your progress. And now, some of us must return to Polvest."

Already she was rising from her seat on a tree stump. The

mage lords also stood and a general murmur of conversation filled the camp site. Ryamon felt many curious eyes as he and Valdira embraced.

"It's over. You won!"

"I still can't believe it," she murmured.

"It's more than I dared to hope for," he exulted. She shrugged, resigned.

"They're putting me in a box."

"You get to build the box," he offered.

"It's still a cage."

The Shadow Lord approached them, dark eyes agleam with triumph. "I'm going to enjoy working with you, Valdira."

"Don't think you can push me around," Valdira snapped at once.

"I wouldn't dream of it." Murcrys smiled, but just as quickly turned serious. "I do want to clarify one thing. There's a story we heard. Some sort of fighting ring?"

Ryamon had no idea what she was talking about, but Valdira's face was flushed.

"That only happened once," she hissed with sudden fury. "And it wasn't my idea. Those stupid boys…"

"I believe you." The Shadow Lord raised her hands in surrender. "As long as you understand how your activities reflect on the Collegium, no more need be said."

"Then why did you even mention it?" Valdira stared at Murcrys, hands on hips. Ryamon could only assume this was about something that had happened before he came to Lornest. Something he was much too smart to ever ask her about.

"Relax," Murcrys said. "I know you don't trust me yet, but you fought hard for this. You've earned it, both of you. Congratulations."

~ * ~

Guilberta and the Mage Lords milled about on the lake shore, preparing to depart. Ryamon felt a bit giddy with relief, but he still had one nagging question. A few of the villagers were edging up, obviously wanting to talk to Valdira. He slipped away and went in search of the person who could answer them.

Phareth seemed to sense Ryamon wanted him. He separated himself from the small cluster of Shadow magi and beckoned for

Ryamon to join him at the water's edge. With dark patches under his eyes and stubble on his chin, the Shadow magus looked almost as tired as Ryamon felt.

"Well done," Phareth began.

"Thanks."

They started walking, stones crunching under foot. The reeds made a thin whistle as wind brushed their tips.

Ryamon gathered his nerve to say, "You lied to us."

"Pardon?" Phareth asked politely.

"Before the battle," Ryamon prompted. "You said it would only be Telamar and Anarinda helping us, but afterward the whole Collegium was there."

"Ah." Phareth smoothed his dark hair, a chagrined smile tugging at his lips. "I guess I did lie, a little, but only to help."

"Why the charade?"

"Because the Collegium had to make a decision about you and Valdira, and it had to be something Guilberta could support. Since she agrees, the king will accept their conclusions," Phareth explained. "Also, if things didn't go well, then our most powerful magi would be there to stop Darmosh."

"Thanks for your confidence," Ryamon said with some irony.

"It was just a precaution," Phareth assured him. "After fighting you and Valdira, and seeing Anarinda in action, I didn't think you needed help. But I wasn't going to take chances with Darmosh, either."

Ryamon glanced at him, startled by these grim words. After a moment, he said, "So the Mage Lords were watching and they saw what Valdira had to offer. You didn't trick us—you tricked the Collegium!"

"Not so loud," Phareth murmured, but his smile was a little wider. "It was the best way to make them give you a fair chance. If it worked, everyone would be grateful. If it didn't, I'd be the only one who was disappointed."

"Huh." Ryamon blew out a sigh. "Why didn't you just say that?"

"No one trusts a Shadow magus." Phareth answered blandly.

"Can't see why," Ryamon muttered, but it was hard to be angry. As Phareth had said, everyone was happy.

Ryamon walked a few steps farther before he realized his companion had stopped. He turned to see the Shadow magus facing back toward the camp.

"They need me," Phareth said before he could ask. "I'll be staying on here to monitor the border, at least for a while. We can talk later."

He would probably also be the one to sever Ryamon's link to Stone, but there was nothing he could say about that.

"Fine."

The Shadow magus strode off to join his fellows. Ryamon stayed where he was. The weight of the day seemed to press on his shoulders. And what a day it had been: escaping from Yolie, battling Darmosh, confronting the Collegium. Now a host of challenges lay ahead of him.

Planning a wedding. Preparing a home for his wife and child. He thought of the little house he had made where Valdira's original rock shelter had been. The project had seemed like a disaster at the time, but actually it might be perfect. It was far enough from Lornest to please Valdira, yet close enough to satisfy the Collegium.

Somehow he must do all this while training in the Order of Fire. It seemed impossible. Yet, as he turned toward their camp, Ryamon saw something that drove all his worries away.

Valdira stood waiting for him. Silma and a few of the villagers lingered behind her. They might be only farmers, but these were Valdira's people. They probably wanted to look him over, not as a passing stranger but as a new neighbor.

But the most important thing of all was Valdira. Peace came over him. Everything they had done had seemed impossible, until they did it. Surely the rest was possible, too.

He strode up the hillside to meet his future.

Meet the Author

Deby Fredericks has been a writer all her life, but thought of it as just a fun hobby until the late 1990s. She made her first sale, a children's poem, in 2000.

Fredericks has had short work published in *Andromeda Spaceways*, selected anthologies, and small magazines. Most recently, she self-publishes her fantasy novellas and novelettes, bringing her to 15 books in all. Her latest project is The Minstrels of Skaythe series.

Learn more from her web site: www.debyfredericks.com.

More Books from WolfSinger Publications

Tails from the Front Lines 2: The Thin Blue Line
   – edited by Carol Hightshoe

Come meet some of the four-legged members of Law Enforcement who also serve and protect.

Here our authors will introduce you to the brave K9 officers who serve alongside their human partners. They are their eyes, ears, noses and sometimes when necessary they are their shield, protecting others.

Proceeds from this anthology will be donated to the El Paso County (Colorado) Sheriff's Office K9 program in memory of K9 Jinx who was killed in the line of duty on April 11, 2022.

Ring of Fire – edited by Dana Bell

Enter the Ring of Fire, as unpredictable as the land masses shaking a city and volcanoes erupting covering the landscape. Could there be other reasons for these events? Or could these rings be more than a geological location.

They may be dragons playing tricks
or magic portals opened to mysterious realms
or sacrificing the best work of a lifetime.
Perhaps a rescue during a forest fire
or an attempt to raise the dead
or even while attending a high school reunion.

Journeys are taken to far off lands, another world, and through caves, each with their own unique twist.

Each tale presents a new idea on what the Ring of Fire could be. It is more than what many have been led to believe. Pull up a chair and warm yourself by our fires—just don't let yourself get burned.

Coyote – Charles Combee

While camping in a remote canyon in Utah Jim accidently

sees an ancient rite taking place with a coyote like creature presiding over it. Now this creature wants Jim dead.

Audrey and her family go hiking in Utah and are attacked by this creature. Audrey is the only survivor, but she is pulled into a strange world of darkness and glass. She is 'rescued' by Jim, but is still linked to the creature, whose hold on her will end in her death unless Jim can find a way to break that link.

In his dreams, or are they ancient memories, Jim begins to learn more about Coyote as well as the magics that previously bound him. But those dreams end without teaching him the full magics. Can he find a way to free Audrey and stop Coyote from once again terrorizing humankind?

Believing is Seeing – Joanna Michal Hoyt

What we believe shapes what we see. Sometimes the stories we tell free us. Sometimes they trap us.

Some people see things their neighbors can't or won't see. Are they inspired? Delusional? Who decides?

As the faithful people of her village cry out for their god's help in disaster, a young peasant woman faces the terrifying possibility that she may be that god.

A time-traveling Jewish refugee visits 21st-century churches and confronts almost unrecognizable versions of himself.

Three troubled people make the dangerous visit to The Library where the maddening stories lodged inside them can be removed—on certain demanding conditions.

Having been warned away from the vacant lot which is said to house a portal to Hell, the new girl in town naturally goes to investigate.

Early in the grid collapse—or apocalypse?—a Christian lesbian farm couple paint "WELCOME" on their barn and await visitors.

An old man in the Terran diaspora enlists in a crusade to save humanity and belatedly wonders if he's on the wrong side.

Step inside these stories and see what you believe—but don't believe everything you see.

Out of the Darkness – edited by Carol Hightshoe

Mental Health issues have long been stigmatized, with those facing them pushed into the shadows, often unable to deal with the darkness they find themselves trapped in.

In this collection, stories explore many types of darkness—Suicidal Ideation, Death from Suicide, Survivor's Guilt, PTSD, Chronic Pain, Chronic Illness, Depression, Death of a Loved One, Secrets, Bullying, and other forms of darkness are explored. Some related to mental health issues and some not, but all of them offer very human perspectives. As in real life, some stories have happy endings and sadly others don't.

We offer these stories of darkness without judgement, but with hope and compassion. Some roads should never have to be traveled—but we understand that for many they are being traveled alone.

Proceeds from sales of Out of the Darkness will be donated to the American Foundation for Suicide Prevention—or more information on AFSP please visit their website at: afsp.org

Never Cheat a Witch – edited by Carol Hightshoe

Magical curses. Arcane revenge. Being transformed into a frog. Things evil witches do to mere mortals who cross their path. But, what if there is more to the story…

Deals made with a witch are magically binding and can bring dire consequences to those who even think about breaking them.

Whether they are seeking revenge for wrongs done to them, helping others or simply trying to live their lives—it is NEVER wise to try and cheat a witch.

Open your spell book and join our authors as they relate tales of witches and mortals. From classic fantasy witches to modern day witches and even the legendary Baba Yaga. Good and Evil as well as every shade of gray in between. And, yes—there is a prince who is turned into a frog.

Blood Bride – Belle Blukat

Dr. Bertram Hoel had ignored all women he'd met until being introduced to Cira Landon at his first Science Fiction convention.

Knowing he should ignore the attraction, he still takes the dangerous step to begin a relationship, aware that by doing so he is placing her life in peril.

Cira Landon wrote tales of vampire lovers unaware the handsome scientist she'd just met actually was one. Drawn to him, she finds her life threatened by an old enemy who would do anything to exact his revenge, including kidnapping her and selling her on the black market for rare blood types.

With no other options, Dr. Hoel is forced to appeal to the Elders for assistance, hoping rescue does not come too late for Cira and knowing if she is found, there is but one ancient tradition that may save her life.

Return of the Black Witch – M.R. Williamson

One should not expect to slap the hand of an old crone and expect to walk away without at least a limp. The old witch Ethrel Ibenus is up to her tricks again and this time they've turned deadly. But where did her spirit go after Professor Martin shot her with his wee pistol?

Now, all are looking for the crone's familiar, Seleene. But the big timber wolf cannot be found. The search for the spirit of Ibenus now begins in earnest. Will Entwhistle and her Dwarves be able to help? Perhaps the Green Witch Pereen will be able to use a crystal derived from one of the Witch's own spells will do the trick. Fearing failure, Entwhistle improvises a plan 'C', the use of a mythical creature once thought to be long dead.

Time Capsules – edited by Carol Hightshoe

Time Capsules—history and mystery—a gift or a message from the past to the future.

Messages that can easily be misunderstood.

What were the reasons for passing along a pair of pink, fuzzy handcuffs?

A glass vial containing a perfect dandelion puff?

A Japanese Katana?

A red and blue scarf?

A wooden spoon?

What magic do these items contain? What stories do they tell?

From the past to the future. Mysteries and meanings abound within these pages, as well as reminders of the things people find precious. What will you find?

US/THEM – edited by Carol Hightshoe

US/THEM – THEM/US

Fear of the Other breeds hatred of the Other

They aren't like us—so they must be bad...inferior... dangerous...

Humans are by nature social animals, but we tend to bond with other humans with whom we have something in common: beliefs, experiences, likes and dislikes, etc.

With the expansion of humans across the planet, it seems that, even as our numbers grow, we find ways to whittle our groups into ever narrower, specialized, and exclusive blocks. We target the Other for the most minor differences and interpret everything from THEM as an insult or an attack.

Within these pages you will witness hatred, intolerance and fanaticism as well as love, understanding and acceptance. Most of all, I, and the authors, hope you discover stories that will cause you to pause and think before condemning someone as being THEM and not US.

Crunchy with Ketchup – edited by Carol Hightshoe

It has been said that one should never meddle in the affairs of dragons—for you are crunchy and taste good with ketchup.

Come enter the dragon's lair.

Take your chances with other would-be heroes and heroines who decide to face off against one of the biggest, baddest predators ever.

Witness a dragon civil war.

Hear the true story of the Battle of New Orleans.

Find out what it's like in the belly of a dragon.

Discover why cats can spell disaster when stealing a dragon's egg.

Meet a group of dragon riders who protect us from nuclear

devastation.

Follow legends of modern dragons, only to find something very unexpected.

And more...

So enter in **BUT** tread carefully—remember you are crunchy and taste good with ketchup.

Crunchy with Chocolate - edited by Carol Hightshoe

It has been said that one should never meddle in the affairs of dragons—for you are crunchy and taste good with chocolate.

Come enter the dragon's lair and roll the dice. Within these pages you will still meet some of the biggest, baddest predators ever—but if you are lucky, you will also discover some that have a sweeter side.

Meet a dragon with a soft spot for hard luck cases and another who is a hopeless romantic.

Enjoy a musical battle between a dragon and the specter of one of the greatest guitarists to ever play.

Meet a dragon in trouble with other magical creatures because he enjoys hanging out with human children.

Join a mother and daughter and their teams of dragons on a dangerous cross-country race.

Reconnect with an imaginary friend—who is not so imaginary and escape the isolation of the pandemic.

And more...

So enter in **BUT** tread carefully—remember you are crunchy and taste good with chocolate.

Time Out – Jamie Mason

After the war, Chris's family fled to Earth. Chris grew up believing he was human. But his parents' unique cruelties soon awaken him to the truth: he and his family are Chronox, alien beings capable of time travel, now hidden among humans.

Dissatisfied with refugee life, Chris's father decides to break the Chronox pact and use time travel to gain dominion over their human hosts. Chris resists, sabotaging his father's efforts to create a working time machine for the military. In punishment, Chris is placed in the ultimate "time out" by being flung back and imprisoned within the pre-digital past of the 1960s. There he experiences a glimmer of acceptance among Laura, Theodore and Yogi Joe, whose friendship inspires him to awaken his repressed Chronox powers and return to the future to set things right.

The battle-lines are drawn. On one side, Chris. On the other, an implacable alliance between time-traveling aliens and the U.S. military. A frightened, shattered boy who has never known love must begin a desperate race through time to stop a global genocide.

Bast's Chosen Ones and Other Stories – Dana Bell

Long ago in the land of the flooding Nile and sweeping sands, Bast created warriors called the Chosen Ones. They are her warriors. To them has been given the responsibility of protecting cats, whether on Earth or other worlds. Not always an easy task since often an ancient evil lurks, ready to pounce.

Not all felines walk in the goddess's domain. Some live in the far reaches of space, battling beside their humans or walk in lands long thought legend. Others tell their own version of human stories, walk as envoys of the creator, or appear as ghosts.

These cats walk where others dare not and do not prefer the comfort of cuddly lap warmers. Rather, they wish adventure, in present day, the past, or the far future.

Beyond Big-G City – S.D. Matley

The year is 2025 and Hermes is on the Olympus, Inc., hot seat. He has two short years to halt climate change before the irretrievable tipping point is reached, an existential threat to mortals and immortals alike.

David Bernstein embarks on a quest to learn about his unnamed mortal father. Assisted by would-be girlfriend, Cleo Petra, David scours the Middle East for clues that lead him to Rome, Italy, and points beyond.

Jim Smith observes unsettling changes in Stella, his mental health client, and fears an evil force, The Power, has secretly escaped its prison to terrorize the City of Mount Olympus once more.

And what of Seattle? Clifford Essex leads a desperate race to solve the riddle of an unstable seawall, poised to crumble and take a major transit tunnel with it.

From Mount Olympus to the Underworld, from Petra, Jordan, to Seattle, Washington-much is afoot Beyond Big-G City!

And more – check out our books at www.wolfsingerpubs.com

www.ingramcontent.com/pod-product-compliance
Lightning Source LLC
Chambersburg PA
CBHW061522050726
47503CB00015B/2382